**Praise for the House-Flipper Mystery series**

"A cat, a can-do heroine, and a corpse in a flower bed. You're going to laugh." —Christie Craig, *New York Times* bestselling author of the Texas Justice series

"With *Dead as a Door Knocker*, Diane Kelly introduces a heroine who is as good with a hammer as she is with a one-liner. Whitney and her adorable scaredy-cat Sawdust are a welcome addition to your home and bookshelf." —Kellye Garrett, Anthony, Agatha, and Lefty award–winning author of the Hollywood Homicide series

**Diane Kelly's Paw Enforcement series**

"Funny and acerbic, the perfect read for lovers of Janet Evanovich." —*Librarian and Reviewer*

"Humor, romance, and surprising LOL moments. What more can you ask for?" —*Romance and Beyond*

"Fabulously fun and funny!" —*Book Babe*

"An engaging read that I could not put down. I look forward to the next adventure of Megan and Brigit!" —*SOS Aloha* on *Paw Enforcement*

"Sparkling with surprises. Just like a tequila sunrise. You never know which way is up or out!" —*Romance Junkies* on *Paw and Order*

# DEAD IN THE DOORWAY

## DIANE KELLY

St. Martin's Paperbacks

This is a work of fiction. All of the characters, organizations, and events portrayed in this novel are either products of the author's imagination or are used fictitiously.

First published in the United States by St. Martin's Paperbacks, an imprint of St. Martin's Publishing Group.

DEAD IN THE DOORWAY

Copyright © 2020 by Diane Kelly.
Excerpt from *Murder with a View* copyright © 2020 by Diane Kelly.

For information, address St. Martin's Publishing Group, 120 Broadway, New York, NY 10271.

www.stmartins.com

ISBN: 978-1-250-19745-0

Our books may be purchased in bulk for promotional, educational, or business use. Please contact your local bookseller or the Macmillan Corporate and Premium Sales Department at 1-800-221-7945, ext. 5442, or by email at MacmillanSpecialMarkets@macmillan.com.

Printed in the United States of America

St. Martin's Paperbacks edition / April 2020

10  9  8  7  6  5  4  3  2

*To Rudolph, a sweet little runt and survivor of the streets. It's not the same without you.*

# ACKNOWLEDGMENTS

I am so grateful for the hardworking team at St. Martin's Press who take my work from the first draft to finished product. Thanks to my editor, Hannah Braaten, and her editorial assistant, Nettie Finn, as well as Allison Ziegler, Kayla Janas, Sara Beth Haring, Holly Rice, Talia Sherer, and the rest of the St. Martin's crew for all you do to get our books into the hands of readers, reviewers, and librarians. Y'all are great to work with!

Thanks to designer Danielle Fiorella and artist Mary Ann Lasher for creating such a cute and perfect cover for this book!

Thanks to my agent, Helen Breitwieser, for all you do to advance my writing career.

An enormous thanks to my good friend Paula Highfill, who helped me brainstorm ideas for this new series, mentioned that there was a lot of renovation going on in Nashville, and said, "Maybe you should write a house flipper series." Great idea, Paula!

Thanks to Liz Bemis and April Reed of Spark Creative for your prompt and professional work on my Web site and newsletters.

Thanks to all my writer friends who have encouraged me along the way and offered your invaluable input on my work. I wouldn't be here without you!

And finally, thanks to you readers who chose this book! Enjoy your time with Whitney, Sawdust, and the gang.

# CHAPTER I

# PEANUT BUTTER AND JEALOUSY

## WHITNEY WHITAKER

*Knock-knock.*

My fluffy cat Sawdust raised his head from the sofa and eyed the door. Curious to see who had come by, he hopped down from the furniture and followed me as I walked to the door and pulled it open.

Nashville might sit in the South, but winters here could nonetheless be quite frigid. My cousin Buck stood on the porch, blowing into his cupped hands to warm them, his shoulders hunched inside his heavy winter coat. Given that our fathers were brothers, Buck and I shared the last name Whitaker. We also shared a tall physique, blue eyes, and hair the color of unfinished pine. But while Buck sported a full beard, a monthly waxing at the beauty salon kept any would-be whiskers away from my face.

As half owner of the stone cottage I called home, Buck could have let himself in with his key. But he was polite enough to respect the privacy of me and my two roommates, Colette and Emmalee. I waved him in. "You're just in time for lunch."

"Looks like I timed my arrival perfectly."

After stepping inside, he removed his coat and hung it on a hook near the door. He reached down and gave my cat a pat on the head. "Hey, boy."

Sawdust offered a *mew* in return.

The cat trotted along with us as Buck followed me to the kitchen. My best friend, Colette Chevalier, stood at the counter preparing warm sandwiches on her panini press. Colette had adorable dark curls and a bright smile, and she somehow managed to remain thin despite working in the restaurant at the Hermitage Hotel in downtown Nashville. I was jealous. Thanks to her irresistible cooking, I'd gained five pounds since we'd moved in together.

The two of us had been best friends since we'd gone potluck for roommates in the freshman dormitory at Middle Tennessee State University and been assigned to live together. We'd hit it off right away. While some of the other girls spent their weekends at parties or nightclubs, loud crowds weren't our style. Not that we weren't fun-loving. Colette and I often hosted small gatherings in our room at the dorm and watched movies, made crafts, or played board games with friends. We'd even started a monthly book club. We'd pool our spare change for snacks, and Colette would prepare simple yet delicious appetizers for the group.

After we'd graduated, Colette had followed me up the road to my hometown of Nashville. While she'd gone on to complete a culinary-arts program, I'd continued to help out at Whitaker Woodworking, my uncle Roger's carpentry business. I'd also landed a part-time job as a property manager for Home & Hearth, a mom-and-pop real-estate firm. Colette liked to feed people, and I liked to house them. We were both domestic goddesses, in our own right.

Colette cut a glance at my cousin. "Here to mooch a meal, Buck?"

"It's only fair." He plunked himself down on one of the stools at the breakfast bar. "After all, I installed all those lights under the cabinets, like you asked me to. Never asked for nothing in return, neither."

"You got me there." She slid the sandwich she'd made for me onto a plate, cut it diagonally, and set it down in front of me. She used the knife to point to the variety of breads, cheeses, and meats next to the press. "What'll it be, Buck?"

"How about a peanut butter and jelly?"

She brandished the knife and gave him a look that was as pointed as her kitchen tool. "I am a professional chef. Would you ask Harry Connick Jr. to sing 'Yankee Doodle'?"

A mischievous grin played about Buck's mouth. "Surprise me."

As Colette set about making Buck's sandwich, I inquired about her late return home the night before. The restaurant closed at ten, and she normally arrived home around midnight after working a late shift. But it had been after two when she came through our front door last night. I knew because I'd stayed up late in my bedroom binge-watching home renovation shows. What can I say? I'm addicted to them. "You were late getting home last night. Problems at the restaurant?"

She seemed to stiffen, and hesitated before replying. "No, no problems." She added another slice of cheese to Buck's sandwich and closed the press.

I picked up one of the halves of my warm panini.

"Let me guess. You finally had that glass of wine the sommelier has been begging you to drink with him."

Buck straightened in his seat next to me. "The sommelier's been hitting on you? That's harassment. You should turn him in."

"He's not in my chain of command," Colette said. "He's just a coworker. Besides, I'd hardly call his behavior harassment. All he did was ask if I'd like to sample a rare vintage he'd bought."

Buck's eyes narrowed. "You and who else?"

"Only me. He knew I'd appreciate it. It was a two-hundred-dollar bottle of burgundy. A 2008 Domaine Leflaive Puligny-Montrachet Les Folatières Premier Cru."

Having been born and raised in New Orleans, Colette spoke French impeccably. Buck's attempt to speak the language, on the other hand, was downright embarrassing.

"La-di-da," he said. "Mercy boo-coos."

"How was the wine?" I asked.

Colette kissed her fingertips. *"Magnifique."*

Buck scowled. I wondered if he could be jealous. My cousin and my best friend got along well, even ribbed each other on a regular basis, but I'd never considered that either of them might be interested in something more than friendship. His reaction told me that maybe I'd been naïve. Then again, Buck was old-fashioned, a southern gentleman. He could be simply looking out for Colette.

"I thought I smelled something cooking." Our third roommate, Emmalee, entered the kitchen, still in her pajamas despite the fact that it was half past one in the afternoon. Her coppery hair was pulled up in wild pile on top of her head. She rubbed her eyes with her freckled hands, looking only half-awake.

Buck lifted his chin in greeting. "Hey there, Raggedy Ann."

"Hey, Buck." She turned her attention to Colette. "What're you making?"

"Paninis," Colette said as she lifted the top of the device. "Want one?"

Emmalee slid onto a stool next to my cousin. "Do you even have to ask?"

Emmalee was a nursing student in her early twenties, seven years younger than Colette and me. She worked as a waitress at the same fancy restaurant where Colette served as a chef. That's where they'd met. The three of us had become roommates only a few short weeks ago. Colette had broken up with her long-term boyfriend and needed a new place to live. Emmalee's previous roommate got a job transfer and left her looking for a new living arrangement. I'd been living like a hobbit in the converted pool house behind my parents' house, and it had been high time for me to get a place of my own.

Although Buck and I had originally planned to flip this place, we'd decided it made more sense for me to move in rather than put it on the market. I'd invited Colette and Emmalee to share the house with me. The three of us got along great. Colette did the grocery shopping and cooking, Emmalee did most of the indoor cleaning, and I made repairs and maintained the lawn. From each according to her ability, as well as one-third of the utilities.

Colette set Buck's plate in front of him. "Eat up, big boy."

He picked up the sandwich, took a bite, and moaned in bliss.

Colette smiled. "I take it you like the surprise?"

He nodded and rubbed his tummy as he chewed. She

sauntered over to the fridge, retrieved a pitcher of sweet tea, and poured him a glass to go along with the sandwich. With Buck all set, she proceeded to prepare one for Emmalee.

Emmalee turned toward me and Buck, running her gaze over our work boots and coveralls. "Y'all got a carpentry job today?"

I'd spent the morning at one of the properties Home & Hearth managed, replacing a couple of rotten boards on the back deck. Buck had been helping his father and his younger brother, Owen, build a custom entertainment center at a house in Nolensville. But after lunch, we planned to head over to a property I'd just purchased with the help of Marv and Wanda Hartley, the owners of Home & Hearth. The Hartleys were a kind, down-to-earth couple nearing retirement age. They'd known Buck and I were looking for a property to flip, and they realized the fixer-upper on a quiet, established cul-de-sac could be the perfect project for us. They'd not only brought the listing to my attention but also had made me a loan at a ridiculously low interest rate so I could afford to buy the place. I couldn't ask for better bosses.

"I'm going to show Buck the place I bought," I explained to Emmalee. "In just a few weeks, when we put it up for sale, we'll net a nice profit." I rubbed my hands together greedily.

Buck was more cautious. "Best not count our chickens before they're hatched."

He was being a party pooper, but he had a point. Flipping houses was a risky business. Sometimes what started as a minor renovation could turn into a major overhaul, depending on what troubles a house might have hidden. What's more, the real-estate market was subject to wide fluctuations. Properties could go up or down in value virtually overnight. But Buck and I knew good and well what we were getting ourselves into. Both of us were willing to take a chance. We might not be able to count on much in this business, but we could always count on each other.

When we finished our lunch, we thanked Colette and offered to clean up the kitchen before we left.

"I got it," she said. "No worries. But before you go, I've got something for you, Whitney."

"What is it?"

Colette went to a shopping bag on the counter, dipped her hand into the bag, and dug around. When she pulled her hand out, it was clutching a small pink canister with a metal ring on the end. "Pepper spray." She pressed the device into my hand. "You never know when a crazy tenant might come after you again."

People tended to get angry when they were evicted. One such irate tenant had come after me recently. It couldn't hurt to have a means of defense at the ready. "Thanks, Colette. I'll attach it to my key chain."

Buck and I headed for the door. Before we left, I grabbed Sawdust's carrier and harness so he could come take a look at the house, too. Between the carpentry work, the property management gig, and working on flip houses, I wasn't home much. I felt guilty leaving my cat alone for long stretches of time. I missed him, and I assumed he missed me. Besides, cats were instinctual explorers, furry and four-footed Davy Crocketts or Daniel Boones, Lewis and Clark with mews and claws. He'd have some fun exploring the flip house.

# CHAPTER 2

# GRAND TOUR

WHITNEY

*Click. Click-click.*

My breath fogged in the frigid air as I stood on the cracked concrete driveway and snapped cell-phone pics of the dilapidated white colonial on Songbird Circle. Later, I'd look the pictures over and make a list of the repairs to be done and the materials needed.

From off to our right came the muted rumble of an airplane engine as a flight took off from the Nashville airport, aiming for the heavens. Plane traffic was to be expected in the Donelson neighborhood, which bordered the BNA property. Fortunately, this house was far enough away that the sound amounted to nothing more than white noise, hardly noticeable. In fact, the home's easy access to the airport, Percy Priest Lake, and the Gaylord Opryland Resort and Opry Mills shopping mall would be selling points when we put it on the market. The fact that the house sat atop a small slope, offering a view of the downtown skyline, was another plus. The outer suburbs might have newer homes, but they didn't offer the Donelson neighborhood's convenience.

Sawdust performed figure eights between my legs, wrapping his leash tightly around my ankles as if he were a cowboy at the rodeo and I were a calf he'd roped. I slid my phone into the pocket of my coveralls, leaned down to extricate my legs from the tangled leash, and picked up my cat before turning to my cousin. "What do you think?"

Buck's narrowed gaze roamed over the structure, taking in the peeling paint, the weathered boards, and the missing balusters on the front-porch railing. Several shutters had gone AWOL, too. A wooden trellis stretched up the side of the house, looking like an oversized skeleton trying to scale the roof. Several of its slats hung askew, like broken ribs. The climbing roses that graced the trellis had withered in the winter weather, awaiting their annual spring rejuvenation.

Buck cocked his head as he continued his visual inspection. "We've got our work cut out for us. But I don't see anything we can't handle."

The home's former owner, a widow named Lillian Walsh, had lived a long and happy life here before passing from natural causes. Her fixed income hadn't allowed for much upkeep, though, and her two sons had put the place on the market as is rather than deal with the cost and hassle of repairs. That's where flippers like me and my cousin come in.

House flippers maximize their profits by investing both their money and sweat equity in their properties, fixing up the homes themselves rather than hiring the work out at a markup. As a professional carpenter, Buck had the know-how to spruce the place up. Having regularly helped out at Whitaker Woodworking over the years, I'd grown adept at carpentry, too. What's more, thanks to my property-management work and YouTube tutorials, I'd learned how to handle all sorts of minor repairs. If you need drywall patched or a sticky door rehung, I'm your gal.

Looking back at the house, I felt hopeful. *A new year means a new beginning, doesn't it?* There was no better way to start a new year than by renovating a house. I motioned for Buck to follow me. "C'mon. I'll show you the inside."

We ascended the crumbling brick steps to the porch. A bristly doormat that read WELCOME lay in front of the door, greeting us directly and, more subtly, inviting us to wipe our feet. A yellow door-hanger advertisement for an income-tax-preparation service hung from the door-knob, the business proprietor attempting to get an early jump on the competition. A two-foot-tall ceramic frog with a fly on his unfurled tongue stood next to the door, his bulbous eyes seeming to stare at us. I could understand why the frog was smiling—he was about to enjoy a snack. But why the tiny fly was smiling was beyond me. He seemed clueless about his fate.

"Fancy door," Buck said as he stopped before it.

Indeed, it was. The door was made of heavy, solid wood with an ornate oval of frosted glass to let in light yet provide some measure of privacy. Once it was sanded and treated to a new coat of glossy paint, it would really add to the curb appeal. "Maybe we should consider painting it red. Add a splash of color to the place."

"Not a bad idea."

Setting Sawdust down on the porch, I unlocked the door and the three of us stepped inside, stopping on the landing of the split-level house. The landing's mock-tile linoleum featured small squares in a lovely shade of lima-bean green that had been popular back when disco was the rage and a loaf of bread cost thirty-six cents. But at least the steps were real hardwood.

To the right of the landing was a coat closet with a rickety folding door that was either half-closed or half-open, depending on how you looked at it. But optimist or pessimist, you couldn't miss the smell of mothballs coming from inside. So many dusty jackets and coats were squeezed into the closet that the rod bent under the weight, threatening to break. The outerwear shared the lower space with a mangled umbrella and a hefty Kirby vacuum cleaner circa 1965, complete with attachments. The shelf above sagged under the weight of a reel-to-reel home-movie projector, around which mismatched mittens, scarves, and knit caps had been stuffed. Lillian's family had cleared the house of everything of value, leaving the worthless junk behind for the buyer—yours truly—to deal with. *Sigh.*

After closing the front door behind us, I unclipped the leash from Sawdust's harness, setting him free to explore. Noting that the house felt warmer than expected, I checked the thermostat mounted next to the closet. It read seventy-two. *That's odd. Didn't I turn it down to sixty the last time I was here?* I hoped I'd merely forgotten to adjust it when I'd left. I'd hate to think the HVAC system might be on the fritz.

I reached out and gave the lever a downward nudge. The three of us wouldn't be here long. No sense paying for heat nobody would be needing.

The thermostat adjusted, I swept my arm, inviting Buck to precede me upstairs. "After you, partner."

We ascended the steps with Sawdust trotting ahead of us. On the way, Buck grasped both the wall-mounted railing and the wrought-iron banister and gave each of them a hearty yank, testing them for safety. While the banister checked out, the wooden rail mounted to the wall jiggled precariously. One glance at the support brackets told us why.

"It's got some loose screws," Buck said. "Just like you."

I rolled my eyes. "Ha-ha."

"Put it on the list."

"Will do." I pulled my phone from my pocket and snapped a photo of the loose bracket as a reminder to myself.

As we topped the stairs, Buck came to a screeching halt, one work boot hovering over the carpet as he refused to step on it. "Yuck."

Couldn't say that I blamed him. The carpet was hideous, worn shag in the same greenish-brown hue as the hairballs Sawdust occasionally coughed up. Ripping out the carpet would give us no small pleasure. But I wasn't about to let some ugly, balding carpet spoil my enthusiasm. I gave my cousin a push, forcing him forward. "Go on, you wimp. It's not going to reach up and grab you."

"You sure about that?"

To our left, the living and dining areas formed a rectangle that ran from the front to the back of the house. The master bedroom and bath mirrored the layout to the right. In the center sprawled the wide kitchen.

"Wait 'til you see this!" I circled around Buck and pushed open the swinging saloon doors that led into the space.

Buck proceeded through them and stopped in the center of the kitchen to gape. "What is this place? A portal back to 1970?"

Between the harvest-gold appliances, the rust-orange

countertops, and the globe pendant light hanging from a loopy chain, it appeared as if we'd time traveled back to a much groovier era. But while the kitchen was hopelessly out of date, it was also wonderfully spacious. Plus, the cabinets would be salvageable if the outdated scalloped valances over the sink and stove were removed.

"Replacing the appliances and countertops is a nobrainer," I said. "But look at all this space! And the cabinets just need refacing. They're solid wood. That'll save us time and money."

Buck stepped over and rapped his knuckles on the door of a cabinet. *Rap-rap.* Satisfied by the feel and sound, he nodded in agreement.

The counters bore an array of Lillian's cooking implements, including a ceramic pitcher repurposed to hold utensils. Cutting boards in a variety of shapes and sizes leaned against the backsplash. A recipe box stood between an ancient toaster and a blender. A quaint collection of antique food tins graced the top of a wooden bread box. Hershey's cocoa. Barnum's animal crackers. Arm & Hammer baking soda.

As Buck and Sawdust took a peek at the plumbing under the sink, I walked over to the end of the cabinets and spread my arms. "Let's add an L-shaped extension here." An extension would increase the counter space and storage, and after all, kitchen renovations were the most profitable rehab investment.

Without bothering to look up, Buck agreed. "Okeydoke."

My cousin and I had an implicit understanding. He left the design details up to me, while I gave him control over the structural aspects of the renovations.

While he continued his inspection, I meandered around the kitchen, snapping several more pictures before stopping at the fridge. A dozen blue ribbons were affixed with magnets to the refrigerator door, proudly proclaiming Lillian Walsh the baker of the "Best Peach Pie" and "Best Peach Cobbler" at various fairs and festivals throughout the state. With my cooking skills, I'd be lucky to earn a participation ribbon.

A hutch on the adjacent wall was loaded with more cookbooks than I could count. I eased over to take a closer look. One book was devoted entirely to potato recipes, another to casseroles. A quick glimpse inside a few of the books told me the recipes were as likely to clog the arteries as fill the tummy. Some of them sounded darn delicious, though. I returned the books to the shelf and turned to find Sawdust traipsing along the countertop while Buck peered into the drawers.

My cousin pulled out what appeared to be a caulking gun, along with a heavy metal lever-like tool with a rubber-coated handle. The latter resembled an airplane throttle. He held them up for me to see. "What the heck are these gadgets for?"

"You're asking the wrong person." While I loved working *on* kitchens, I didn't particularly like working *in* them once they were complete. Boxed mac and cheese marked the pinnacle of my culinary skills.

"Let's have Colette take a look," he suggested. "She might could use some of these things."

While Colette already had an extensive complement of kitchen equipment, this room contained items that probably hadn't been produced in half a century or more. If nothing else, she'd find these artifacts intriguing.

Having fully explored the kitchen, Buck and I moved on to the master bedroom. Like the kitchen, the room was dated but spacious. The walls bore peeling wallpaper in a flocked fleur-de-lis pattern. Only the bed and a night table remained. A stack of books towered on the night table, some hardcover, some paperback. Sawdust hopped up onto the bed to inspect the random items that had been placed there. Several pairs of ladies' shoes. A stack of Sunday dresses still on the hangers. A small jewelry box. A quick peek inside told me it contained only a few pieces of what I assumed to be cheap costume jewelry. I let Sawdust take a quick and curious sniff before closing the lid.

We continued into the master bath, which featured a once-fashionable pink porcelain tub, toilet, and sink. Wallpaper in a gaudy yet charming rose pattern adorned the walls. Fresh, if faded, towels filled the under-sink cabinet, along with an assortment of medications and beauty products. A tin box sat next to the sink. The top was open, revealing a trio of pink soaps in the shape and scent of roses. As we looked around, Sawdust leapt up onto the edge of the tub and circumnavigated it with the ease and agility of a tightrope walker.

I snapped a pic before turning to Buck. "Let's replace that old bathtub with a walk-in shower, and add a jetted garden tub over there." I pointed to an open space under the window.

He pulled out a measuring tape to size up the space and, satisfied the tub would fit, issued an *mm-hmm* of agreement.

Having completed the tour of the master suite, we made a quick pass through the living and dining rooms, which contained a slouchy velveteen sofa, a framed still-life painting depicting a bowl of assorted fruit, and a glass-top coffee table that bore the sticky telltale fingerprints of spoiled grandchildren. A small wooden box sat atop the table. The box was intricately engraved with hearts, diamonds, spades, and clubs along the sides, and a fancy letter *W* on the lid. The lid was open, revealing two yellowed decks of playing cards nestled inside. The cards rested face up, the two jokers at the top of the decks grinning wickedly up at me as if they shared a sinister secret. Sawdust seized the opportunity to sharpen his claws on the couch before following us downstairs.

*Creak. Creak.* The bottom step complained under my weight, then Buck's. *Looks like we've got a loose tread.* Sawdust stepped soundlessly down, too light to elicit a response.

Other than a rusty washer-and-dryer set and a couple of wire hangers on a rod, the laundry room was empty. The guest bedroom contained a full-size bed covered in a crocheted afghan and a basic bureau with three empty cans of Budweiser sitting atop it. They appeared to be only the latest in a long series of beers enjoyed in the bed, as evidenced by a pattern of ring stains roughly resembling the Olympic symbol. I wondered who Lillian's beer-guzzling guest had been.

The other bedroom had been converted to a sewing room and appeared untouched. A white Singer sewing machine sat on a table, while a bookshelf to the right sported a selection of thread and rickrack, as well as a pincushion in the quintessential tomato shape. A plastic box filled with spare, shiny buttons sat open on one of the shelves like a miniature treasure chest filled with gold. Swatches of fabric were draped over a quilt rack.

After a quick trip to the garage, the tour was complete. The bottom step creaked again as we made our way back up to the front doorway. There, I shared my overall vision for the house. "Classic black-and-white tile in the baths and kitchen. Paint in robin's-egg blue for the walls." The look would be neutral and timeless, and would tie in well with the exterior colors. "Black hardwood floors would be a nice complement, too."

"Works for me," Buck said.

After noting that the thermostat reading was on its way down, I patted my leg and called for my cat to meet us on the landing. "Sawdust! Here, boy!" When Sawdust trotted up the steps, I reattached his leash to his harness and we headed out the door into the gathering winter dusk. With my hands full of keys and the cat's leash, I left the tax-preparation ad hanging from the knob to be dealt with later. Buck and I agreed to meet at the house at noon the following day to take measurements and start on the demolition. House flippers don't take weekends off.

Buck raised a hand out of the window of his van as he backed out of the driveway and drove off. I looked up at the house one more time, feeling heartened and hopeful. *Yep. A fresh start.*

# CHAPTER 3

# HARD LANDING

## WHITNEY

Having spent a dateless Friday night at home and too excited to wait until noon, I arrived at the flip house at nine Saturday morning. I'd need Buck's muscles for the heavy lifting later, but for now I could get started cleaning out closets and cabinets. I set my toolbox down on the porch, noting that the advertisement that had been hanging from the doorknob was now gone. A glance around the porch and yard showed no sign of it. Looked like the ad had blown away.

Cradling Sawdust against my chest, I unlocked the front door and went to push it open. It barely budged. *What the heck?*

I pushed harder, putting my shoulder into it this time. The door opened an inch more but that was it. Something inside was blocking the doorway.

Unable to see anything through the small gap, I cupped my hand around my eyes and put my face to the frosted glass, doing my best not to squash my cat. Though I could see something lying on the landing inside, I couldn't make out exactly what it was. My eyes could only distinguish several blurred colors. Had the coat closet's overburdened rod or shelf given way? It seemed so. It also seemed any effort to get through the front door would be futile, so I pulled the door closed and relocked it.

Sawdust seemed to realize something was amiss and looked up at me. *Meow?*

"Something's blocking the door," I explained. The fact that he couldn't understand me was no excuse for ignoring his question. "Let's try the garage."

Returning to my SUV, I retrieved the remote and jabbed the button to raise the bay door. I ducked under it as it squealed and rattled its way up. Once inside the garage, I strode to the interior door and pressed the doorbell-style button mounted beside it to send the garage door squealing and rattling back down again. *A squirt of WD-40 should do the trick.* I had a can in my toolbox, which I'd left on the porch. I'd grab it once I got the front door open.

I set Sawdust down, unclipped his leash, and unlocked the interior door, opening it for him. "There you go, boy." I ruffled his head, tucked his leash in my pocket, and headed after him into the house.

From the bottom of the staircase I could see a pile of mixed fabrics on the landing. Looked like I'd been right. Either the coat-closet rod had broken or the shelf had collapsed. Maybe both. *Ugh. The list of repairs keeps growing.*

The bottom step creaked as I stepped onto it. Above me, Sawdust hopped up onto the clothing heap, climbing down the other side. As I ascended the stairs, my eyes spotted something white and fluffy among the fabric. *Did the stuffing come out of a torn coat?* As I drew closer, my foot involuntarily stopped and hovered over the final step, much as Buck's had done the day before.

*That's not stuffing. That's hair!*

What's more, the hair was still attached to a head— an elderly woman's head. Her head was bent at an un- natural angle. The rest of the woman was bent at odd angles, too, as if she were playing a solo game of Twister and giving it her all. She lay on her stomach, her right cheek pressed to the green linoleum, her right arm crooked out of sight under her belly. Her eye was closed. I was grateful for that.

*There's no way the woman can still be alive, is there?*

The odds seemed infinitesimally small. Still, what kind of person would I be if I didn't make sure she was truly beyond hope? Taking a deep breath, I bent over her and pressed my hand to her neck to feel for a heartbeat. "Ma'am? Are you okay?"

The lack of response along with the cold, stiff skin and absence of a pulse told me the woman was anything *but* okay. My mind went woozy, my vision tunneled, and my heart and stomach fought to see which could oc- cupy my throat first. *Who is she? What happened? How did she end up dead in the doorway of an unoccupied, locked house?*

Sawdust, on the other hand, was unfazed. With feline curiosity, he poked the woman's cheek with his paw.

I gasped. "No, boy! No!" As I reached out to grab my cat, an unmistakable and terrifying sound met my ears.

*Creak.*

Someone was coming up the stairs behind me.

# CHAPTER 4

# CAT'S CURIOSITY

**SAWDUST**

Sawdust wasn't sure why Whitney had scolded him. He'd only poked the woman to see if she was alive. Sawdust couldn't help himself. Just like he couldn't help himself now when he peeked around the wall to see who had caused the stair to creak on the lower flight.

A guy in rumpled clothes was coming up the stairs. *Who is he? What's he doing here? Should I run, or might he have a tuna treat hidden in the pocket of his pajamas?* There was a time, not so long ago, when Sawdust would have dashed away immediately like the fraidy-cat he'd been. But he'd become braver since successfully scaring off an intruder who'd tried to break into his and Whitney's home.

Unsure, Sawdust looked up at Whitney to gauge her reaction. When Whitney shrieked in terror, Sawdust joined in, arching his back and hissing. Though instinct told him to run, he wasn't about to leave Whitney in danger and unprotected. He whipped out his claws and readied his paw. *I'll shred this man if I have to!*

# CHAPTER 5

# MISSTEP OR MURDER?

WHITNEY

The shriek seared my tonsils. There was no time to dig through my purse for the pepper spray. I grabbed the mangled umbrella from the coat closet and brandished it at the skinny, ginger-haired young man coming up the stairs in a rumpled T-shirt, stretchy lounge pants, and bare feet. "Stop right there, kid!"

Sawdust joined in, hissing and spitting in warning, his claws raised at the ready.

The young man stopped his ascent and held up his hands. "It's okay! I'm Lillian Walsh's grandson. Dakota. And I'm not a kid. I turned twenty-one last month."

I lowered the umbrella a little to get a better look at him. While he definitely had a baby face, on a closer look I could see it bore some light peach fuzz along the jawline. "What are you doing here?"

He kept his hands up. Smart guy. One wrong move and I'd poke him in a far more violent manner than Sawdust had been poking the body lying behind me. *Did Dakota have something to do with this woman's death?*

"I slept here the last few nights," he said. "I'd been crashing on a buddy's couch, but he kicked me out. Guess I overstayed my welcome. Granny always let me stay here when I was between places."

His presence explained why the thermostat had been cranked up. While I was relieved to know the heating system wasn't malfunctioning, I had much bigger problems at the moment. "How'd you get here?" I hadn't seen a vehicle outside, and there'd been none in the garage, either.

"Hitch-a-Ride," Dakota said, referencing a new ride-sharing service that touted itself as a discount Uber and advertised with a tongue-in-cheek slogan: RIDERS ALWAYS GIVE US A THUMBS UP! He continued, "The bank repossessed my car three months ago. I got a little behind on my payments again, and they wouldn't work with me this time." He leaned slightly to the side and spotted the body behind me. His eyes went wide and his mouth gaped. "What happened to Mrs. Dolan?"

"I was going to ask you the same thing. You don't know how she got here?"

He shook his head. "Is she . . ."

Though he didn't finish his sentence, it was clear what he was getting at. "I'm afraid so."

The woman now had a name, Mrs. Dolan, though I still had no clue what she was doing in my house or exactly how she'd perished. Dakota had startled me, and my mind had jumped to murder. But statistically, it was far more likely she'd died of a health condition or as the result of an accident.

*Uh-oh.*

A horrible thought entered my mind and a sick feeling flooded my stomach. *Had the banister come free and caused her to fall down the stairs?* I chanced taking

my eyes off the guy for a split second and forced myself
to take a look. The railing on the upper flight of stairs
was still attached to the wall. *Thank goodness!* Still,
seeing as she appeared to have fallen down the stairs,
it seemed strange she hadn't grabbed the loose banister.
Maybe she'd suffered a massive heart attack at the top of
the stairs and been dead before she'd begun to fall. Or
maybe arthritis prevented her from successfully clutching the rail. *Who knows?*

I transferred the umbrella to my left hand, dug my
cell phone out of my purse, and placed a 911 call, not
taking my eyes off Dakota Walsh again. He might be
short and scrawny, but that didn't mean he wasn't a
threat. Call me overly cautious, but I wasn't about to
take a chance with my life or Sawdust's. "I just found a
body," I told the male dispatcher. "In the front doorway
of my house."

"Is the person deceased?" he asked.

"I believe so. I couldn't find a pulse and her skin is
cold and stiff."

"Victim's age?"

"Her age?" I repeated, glancing at Dakota and arching my brows in question. He shrugged. "I'm not sure,"
I told the dispatcher. "She's elderly."

"You don't know her?"

"No. There's a young man here who called her
Mrs. Dolan, but I don't know him, either. He's slept in
the house the past few nights without my knowledge or
permission."

The dispatcher asked for the address and said he'd
get an ambulance en route right away. "We'll send police, too."

"Thanks." The call concluded, I slid my phone back

into my pocket and returned my attention to Dakota. "How do you know Mrs. Dolan?"

"She lives in the house next door."

When he began to lower his arms, I jerked the umbrella in a *keep-'em-up* motion. "Any idea why she was here?"

"Granny'd sometimes have the neighbor ladies over to sew or play cards or talk about books. My dad called them her hen parties. But now?" He lifted his skinny shoulders again to indicate he didn't know why Mrs. Dolan would have been in the house given that his grandmother was no longer alive. Dakota's eyes narrowed as he apparently decided it was *his* turn to ask questions. "Who are *you*? And what are *you* doing here?"

"I bought the place. You didn't know?"

"No," he said. "I knew Granny's house had been put up for sale, but my dad and uncle thought it would be hard to find a buyer since the place needs a lot of work. I didn't know they'd sold it yet. I haven't talked to my parents in a few days."

The fact that the FOR SALE sign had been taken out of the yard might have clued him in that the house had sold, but then again, maybe he hadn't seen the sign in the first place. The FOR SALE sign had been up only a matter of days while I took care of the paperwork. Because I'd paid for the place with cash, no appraisal had been necessary and the process had moved at warp speed.

"How'd you get inside?" I asked.

"Granny gave me a key. I keep it in the frog's mouth so I can come and go whenever I want to."

"The frog's mouth?" I repeated. "You mean the ceramic frog on the front porch?"

"Yeah."

"Why didn't you keep the key with you?"

He had the sense to look sheepish, ducking his head and blushing slightly as he averted his eyes. "I tend to misplace things."

Though the guy's explanation of his presence here made sense, there was still the matter of the dead woman in the doorway behind me. I wasn't ready to put down the umbrella just yet.

Dakota leaned slightly to the side again to take another look at Mrs. Dolan. He grimaced, closed his eyes, and shook his head, as if his mind were an Etch A Sketch screen and he was trying to clear away the image. "What do you think happened to her?" he squeaked. "Did she fall down the stairs and break her neck?"

"Looks that way to me. The police and paramedics will figure it out."

A siren sounded off in the distance, drawing closer. Within the next minute, both an ambulance crew and the police arrived. Through the frosted glass, I could see the blurry images of the medical crew at the curb and a single police officer in a dark uniform coming up onto the porch. Another officer waited in the yard. A rap sounded on the door. *Rap-rap-rap.*

"Metro police," came the no-nonsense woman's voice. "Officer Hogarty here."

"The body is blocking the door!" I called through the glass. "You'll have to come in through the garage." Fortunately, I still had the remote on me and hadn't locked the door that led from the garage into the house. I aimed the remote down the lower staircase and pressed the button to raise the garage door. The house vibrated as the door rolled up.

"That's what woke me up earlier," Dakota said. "The shaking from the garage door."

"You didn't hear me come in? Talking to my cat?"

He shook his head. "No. I sleep with earbuds in. I guess that's why I didn't hear Mrs. Dolan fall, either." His face clouded and he swallowed hard. "Do you think I might have been able to save her if I'd heard?"

I was no medical specialist, but judging from the odd angle of her head, I assumed she'd died immediately from a broken neck. "I doubt it."

Officer Hogarty's voice came from out of sight downstairs. "Hands up, everyone! We were told there's an intruder and a body. If you're holding a weapon, put it down."

Sawdust cocked his head, as if trying to comprehend what the disembodied voice from downstairs was saying. But when I bent down and laid the umbrella on the floor at my feet, he decided the umbrella was more interesting and promptly set about sniffing it. Looked like he'd forgiven me for scolding him. I supposed he couldn't be blamed for poking the body. Cats were naturally curious creatures, after all.

I raised my arms over my head and called out, "My cat's in here! He runs when he's scared! Please don't hurt him!" The last thing I wanted was my precious baby startling the officer and taking a reactionary whack from the business end of her police baton.

"Thanks for the warning." A head of brown hair worn in a pixie cut appeared as Officer Hogarty peeked around the corner downstairs. Her gaze took in Dakota before it ventured up the staircase and met mine. She stepped into the open in the ground-floor hallway, her gun held at the ready at her side. "Both of you turn around. We need to frisk you. No sudden moves."

The "we" was Officer Hogarty and her younger female partner, who stepped into sight now, too. Sawdust darted up the upper staircase as I turned to face the front door, raising my head so I wouldn't see Mrs. Dolan's body in my peripheral vision. Another creak sounded as Officer Hogarty began her ascent up the stairs. Her firm hands made their way up and down my body, patting me down. Satisfied I had no weapons hidden on my person, she stepped back and motioned for me to come downstairs.

"May I get my cat?" I asked.

"Make it quick."

I walked up the steps to where Sawdust stood at the top of the staircase. I scooped him up in my arms, attached his leash to his collar, and carried him down to the bottom floor, where the officers stood watch over Dakota.

Hogarty stepped to the open door that led into the garage and motioned to a trio of paramedics waiting on the driveway. "Come on in," Hogarty told them. "But watch your step. We don't know yet whether we're dealing with a crime scene."

After they came inside, she led me out to the garage, leaving her partner in charge of Dakota. She closed the door behind us, probably so Dakota wouldn't be able to hear our conversation.

Her intent gaze locked on my face. "What happened here?"

Following her lead, I kept my voice low, giving her a quick rundown. I recently bought the house to fix up for resale. I'd arrived a few minutes earlier to start working on the house. I'd been unable to get in the front door because something was blocking it. I used my remote control to access the garage and my key to enter the house from the garage. I was on my way upstairs when I found the body on the landing. I checked the woman's neck for a pulse but found none. Dakota suddenly appeared downstairs. I didn't know him, and I'd had no idea he'd been squatting in the house, which used to belong to his grandmother. I'd grabbed an umbrella to improvise a weapon but, fortunately, hadn't had to use it. I called 911 and, I concluded, "Here we are."

"So the front door was locked when you arrived?"

"Yes."

She gestured to the door that led from the garage into the house. "That one, too?"

I nodded.

"What about the other doors and windows?"

I raised my shoulders. "I haven't checked."

"We'll have the team take a look." She narrowed her eyes. "Any idea how the kid got into the house? Did he jimmy a door? Break a window?"

"His grandmother gave him a key that he kept in the frog's mouth on the front porch."

"So you haven't changed the locks since you bought the place?" Her lips pursed in judgment.

"No." *Next time I buy a property, it'll be the first thing I do.* "Dakota said the woman on the stairs is the next-door neighbor. He called her Mrs. Dolan."

"You don't know her?"

"No. I haven't met the neighbors." As cold as it had been lately, few people wanted to venture outside unless it was absolutely necessary. I couldn't blame them for not coming by to introduce themselves. Besides, my visits to the house had not been lengthy.

Hogarty nodded, her head bobbing as she seemed to be mentally sorting through the details I'd provided. "Did Mrs. Dolan have a key to the house?"

"I don't know." It was certainly possible. Neighbors often exchanged keys in case of emergency, or so they could tend to each other's plants, pets, and packages while one or another of them was away on vacation. "Dakota said he didn't hear me come in because he sleeps with headphones in his ears. He told me the vibration from the garage door woke him. He said he didn't hear the woman fall, either."

Hogarty issued a noncommittal grunt and angled her head to indicate the door. "Let's get you back inside and the kid out here."

Dakota and I swapped places, with me now waiting inside while he talked with Officer Hogarty in the garage. As the two of them reentered the house a few minutes later, the paramedics came down the stairs. The one in the lead exchanged a glance with Officer Hogarty and shook his head. In other words, there was no hope for the woman in the doorway.

Hogarty turned to address Dakota and me. "Remain in the laundry room for the time being. This situation looks like an accident to me, but it's not my call. The medical examiner's office has to investigate all deaths that aren't from natural causes. The pathologist might have some questions for you. I'm going to call homicide, too, see if they want to send someone out to take a look." She turned to her partner. "Cordon off the yard. We don't need a bunch of lookie-loos getting in the way."

The younger officer nodded and headed out through the garage.

Officer Hogarty turned back to Dakota. "Is there a *Mr.* Dolan?"

"Yes ma'am," he said. "His name's Carl."

*Odd. Why isn't Carl Dolan over here looking for his missing wife?* A dark cloud seemed to cross Hogarty's face as she apparently had the same thought. The dead woman had been here long enough to grow stiff, but her husband hadn't yet realized she was missing? Then again, I supposed he could be sleeping in.

Over the next hour, as Dakota lounged against the wall and I sat atop the washing machine with Sawdust curled up in my lap, a number of people arrived on the scene. A two-person crime-scene team. An assistant medical examiner. And Detective Collin Flynn, the investigator who'd handled a murder investigation I'd been unwittingly sucked into. Flynn was green-eyed and dark-haired. While he was by no means tall or brawny, the detective nonetheless appeared formidable, with a wiry, athletic build and an intelligent intensity. He wore navy-blue pants and a starched button-down shirt under a police-issue windbreaker.

His eyes met mine as he stepped into the small room. "You again?" When Sawdust raised his head, the detective's gaze shifted to my cat. "Hey, kitty."

I let out a long sigh. "Me again. I had nothing to do with this death, either."

A wry grin played about his mouth. "That's what you always say." He looked down at Sawdust and gave him a pat on the head.

Sawdust replied with a polite *mew*.

Flynn went up the stairs and engaged in a brief pow-wow with the others before returning to the laundry room where Dakota and I waited. While the forensics team took photographs on the stairs and the ME examined the body on the landing above us, the detective performed a repeat interrogation, taking me into the garage alone and questioning me. I told Flynn everything I'd told Officer Hogarty, but added the fact that the dead woman on the stairs was married.

His brows formed a V. "Has the husband come by looking for her?"

"Not that I know of."

He glanced at his watch. "Quarter past ten," he mused aloud. "Hmm."

The door opened and the medical examiner joined us in the garage. He was a fiftyish Asian American man with salt-and-pepper hair and plastic-rimmed glasses. While Flynn's questions were broader, the medical examiner's questions specifically addressed the corpse. "Where did you touch the body?" As his glasses began to slide downward, he quirked his nose to force them back into place.

"On the side of her neck." I put a hand on my own neck to indicate the spot. "I felt for a pulse."

"Did you move the body in any way?"

The mere thought of touching the dead woman made me shudder involuntarily. "Not intentionally. The front door bumped against her when I tried to push it open, but it barely budged. I left her exactly as I found her after I came inside."

When the two were done questioning me, Dakota and I again traded places. The men took much longer interrogating Dakota than they had taken with me. *I wonder what that means.*

As the medical examiner went up the lower staircase a second time, the detective slid paper booties over his loafers and handed another pair to Dakota, instructing him to slide them over his bare feet. "Show me where you slept last night," he told the young man. "But keep your hands at your sides. Don't touch anything."

Was Flynn having trouble believing that Dakota hadn't heard the woman fall? I had to admit I had trouble believing it myself. There would have been several thumps as she rolled down the steps, and a loud *thud* when she came to rest on the landing. If she'd been alive as she'd fallen, she probably would have screamed, too. Who wouldn't cry out when losing their footing and finding themselves plummeting tail over teakettle down a staircase?

As I continued to wait, my mind pondered what the dead woman could have been doing here in the house. Why would a person enter a deceased neighbor's residence several weeks after the neighbor had passed away? Had she left something here and come to reclaim it? Had she come to borrow something?

The detective summoned one of the crime-scene techs and the two looked about the room Dakota had slept in. The tech snapped several photos before closely examining Dakota's shoes and the clothing strewn about. The tech also shined a flashlight around the room, photographed the remaining contents of the dresser drawers and closet, and bent down to look under the bed and other furniture. A few minutes later, Flynn emerged and returned to the laundry room with Dakota in tow.

The detective looked from me to Dakota. "Both of you are free to go for now. If I have follow-up questions once the autopsy is complete, I'll get in touch with you."

Dakota glanced down at his feet, which sported only the thin booties. "Can I get my shoes and my jacket?"

"Sorry," Flynn said. "We need to keep the house as is until the forensics team completes their inspection."

I gestured to the front of the house. "You can wait in my SUV until your ride gets here." While I'd initially thought the kid might have something to do with Mrs. Dolan's demise, the fact that the detective had released him told me my suspicions had likely been unjustified.

The three of us made our way out onto the driveway. Yellow cordon tape stretched from the fence, to a tree, to the mailbox, and on, delineating the perimeter of the lawn. Officer Hogarty's police cruiser was parked at the curb, Flynn's unmarked sedan behind it. At the end of the drive sat the medical examiner's vehicle, a white, windowless van long enough to transport human cargo. It wouldn't take a genius to figure out there'd been a death here.

While it was only a few degrees above freezing outside, several neighbors had nevertheless come outside to gawk, no doubt wondering what was happening at the house. They were so bundled up I could tell little about them. Their breath left steamy conversation bubbles in the air as they spoke to each other, probably speculating on what had taken place. Other residents opted to avoid the cold, and instead had pulled back their curtains to watch the goings-on from their windows. One of those residents was a silver-haired woman in the house on the immediate right. She hadn't yet ventured out to pick up her newspaper, which lay under the holly bushes next to her front walk. Couldn't say that I blamed her. With Jack Frost nipping at noses and earlobes, today would be a good day to stay inside and get your news from the television or gossip mill instead.

Flynn turned to Dakota. "Which house belongs to the Dolans?"

"That one." Dakota had wrapped his arms around himself in an attempt to stay warm, and merely lifted an index finger to point to the house that sat to the left.

Like the others on the cul-de-sac, the Dolan home was a two-story colonial. But while the others sported traditional, cheerful shades of paint in yellows, blues, and greens with nicely contrasting shutters, the Dolan home was a monochromatic and unattractive orangey pink, like undercooked salmon. The color might work on a Mediterranean-style stucco home or a beachside snow-cone stand, but on a colonial? Not so much.

No one stood outside the Dolan home, and the curtains were closed on every visible window. While these signs might indicate nobody was home, the two cars in the driveway seemed to say otherwise. One of the vehicles was a white Chevrolet Impala that was neither new nor old, neither fancy nor plain. The other was a turquoise-blue Mercury Tracer station wagon that had rolled off the assembly line in the last century. One of the neighbor moms had driven one like it in my elementary school carpool years ago. *Not many of those still on the road.* The back right fender bore a sizable dent, and the front right wheel was missing its hubcap.

Flynn returned his attention to Dakota. "Do you know who those cars belong to?"

"Mr. and Mrs. Dolan drive the Chevy," Dakota replied. "The old blue car belongs to their daughter. She moved in with them a while back. Granny said something about a messy divorce."

Judging from the fact that Mrs. Dolan was elderly, her daughter was likely middle-aged. The old, damaged vehicle the daughter drove said she wasn't wealthy. *Not likely she and her ex-husband had fought over money.* Perhaps they'd fought over the lack of it. They wouldn't be the first couple to split up over financial woes.

While Dakota used his cell phone to summon a ride, I asked the detective what the neighbors had been told.

"Only that there appears to have been an accident in the house," he said. "We said nothing about potential victims. We need to notify the next of kin first."

I didn't envy him. It couldn't be easy having to break

bad news to the loved ones of a person who'd met a tragic end. I gestured to the porch. "Can I get my toolbox? I'm pretty useless without it."

When I wasn't collecting rent and showing properties to prospective tenants, my job as a property manager for Home & Hearth often required tools. Ditto for the moonlighting I performed for my uncle Roger. During my childhood, while my parents were gallivanting around Europe, I'd spent many a summer at Uncle Roger and Aunt Nancy's cabin up near the Kentucky border, having fun with my two cousins. Though I adored Owen, who was a year younger than I was, I'd always looked up to Buck, who was born a year before me. My uncle had started off by showing us kids how to build birdhouses. We'd earned some spending money selling the finished houses to bird-watchers in the area. Not a bad summer job for an adolescent girl. It beat babysitting. No bottles, no diapers, and I got to spend the days outside in the sunshine.

"I'll get the toolbox for you," Flynn said.

As the detective rounded up my toolbox, I ducked under the cordon tape at the end of the driveway and loaded Sawdust into his carrier in the backseat of my SUV. He issued a small growl of protest, probably tired of having been restrained most of the morning. I couldn't blame him. Being stuck in the laundry room while a dead woman lay only feet away hadn't exactly been an uplifting experience for me, either. I ran a soothing hand down his back. "Sorry, boy. It's been a bad morning for all of us. When we get home, I'll give you a tuna treat."

His eyes brightened on hearing his favorite words and he issued a chirp of excitement.

Flynn retrieved my heavy toolbox from the porch and carried it over to me, the metal implements inside clinking against each other. I circled around the back of my SUV to open the cargo bay, and Flynn slid the toolbox inside.

He took a step back so I could shut the bay door. "I'll call you when we're done so you can come back and lock up."

As Flynn headed out to the Dolans' house next door, I climbed into the driver's seat and cranked the engine, willing the motor to warm up quickly. Dakota completed his call, ducked under the yellow tape, and rushed over to climb into my front passenger seat. I handed him a spare pair of paint-splattered coveralls to use as a blanket until the heater kicked in.

"Thanks!" He wrapped the arms around his neck like a scarf. "My teeth were starting to chatter."

My gaze went to the clock on my dash. 10:53. *Buck will be awake by now.* As I retrieved my cell phone from my purse, Flynn climbed up to the porch of the Dolans' home next door and rang the bell. A few seconds later, a stout man with dark gray hair answered. His still-broad shoulders bore a slight stoop. He wore a pair of flannel pajamas and house slippers. A fiftyish blond woman with a similar sturdy build stepped up beside him. Like the man, she was still dressed in her nightclothes, though she'd covered her pajamas with a fluffy pink robe. Looked like the two had been enjoying a lazy morning. Both looked past the detective, spotted the law enforcement vehicles, and gaped. Flynn said something to them and they stepped back to allow him inside, closing the door behind him.

After shutting my eyes and sending up a short, silent prayer for the family, I placed a call to my cousin. "No need to come to the house," I told Buck. "We've got a body on our hands."

# CHAPTER 6

# I WANT MY MOMMY

## WHITNEY

Buck groaned. "You've got to be kidding me!"

"Wish I were." After giving him the details, I said, "It looks like Mrs. Dolan's death was nothing more than an unfortunate accident."

"Thank heaven for small favors."

While a murder on site could negatively impact a property's value, an accidental death was unlikely to affect its worth. Given that the house was an investment for me and Buck, as well as the fact that our finances were already stretched thin, we couldn't afford to take a hit.

We ended the call and I tried the heater. The air blowing from the vents was nice and toasty. I turned it up full blast and the windows fogged, obscuring the view outside. If only the heater could fog up the window in my mind and cloud the image of a dead Mrs. Dolan.

A few minutes later, blurry images moved outside my window and a rap sounded on the glass. I used my sleeve to wipe the condensation away. A face filled the space. It belonged to a man who looked the way Dakota would if you added twenty-five years and twenty-five pounds to the boy. *He must be Dakota's father.* He shared the same ginger hair as his son, though a few lighter strands had crept in around his temples.

I pushed the button to unroll my window. As soon as it was down, the man stuck his head inside in my car, forcing me to press myself back against my seat lest we bump noses.

The man looked past me to his son. "Are you okay, Dakota?"

"I'm fine, Dad." Dakota extricated himself from the straightjacket he'd concocted from my spare coveralls and tossed them into the backseat. "Just a little shook up is all."

As Dakota opened his door and slid out of my car, his father turned to me and stuck an arm in, too, offering me his hand. "Wayne Walsh."

*Seems everyone is intent on invading my space today.* I shook his hand awkwardly in the tight space. "Whitney Whitaker." I raised my left elbow to rest it on the window ledge, hoping the guy would take a hint and back away.

He retreated only an inch or two, hovering over me like a fly over a dung pile. Of course that would make *me* the dung pile. *Ew.* My metaphors could use some work.

"I understand you've got big plans for mom's house," he said.

The house no longer belonged to the man's mother, but there was nothing to be gained by pointing it out. "My cousin and I plan to make some updates."

"Uh-huh, uh-huh." He stood up straight, reached into the inside pocket of his blazer, and retrieved a brochure.

"You'll require cleaning products, that's for sure. Luckily for you, I can supply everything you need."

He leaned back in and shoved the brochure in my face. The cover featured the logo of RAGS-2-RICHE$, a multilevel marketing platform, as well as photos of the company's merchandise and its grinning founder. *Sheesh. Peddling products when a woman has just been found dead here? Does the man have no shame?*

"Thanks," I said, "but we're all set."

Not taking no for an answer, he tried a different tack. "You're no doubt a smart woman who knows a good deal when she sees it. You could join my sales team, give yourself another income stream."

I already worked as a property manager, carpenter, and house flipper. The last thing I needed was another gig. "I'm too busy to take on another job," I told him. "But you take care now." I jabbed the button to roll up the window, giving the man no choice but to back off or risk decapitation. Not exactly a polite gesture on my part, but my nerves were frayed and all I wanted was to get away from there.

I slid the car into gear and drove off, leaving the detective, the crime-scene technicians, and the medical examiner to tend to their business and Mrs. Dolan.

Half an hour later, I pulled into the driveway of my parents' house in the Green Hills neighborhood of Nashville and parked next to my mother's pearly white Cadillac. Mom helped out with billing and other administrative tasks at my father's otolaryngology practice a few days a week, but rarely on Fridays. Or Mondays. Or any day that Nordstrom was having a sale.

A red cardinal perched on the picket fence that surrounded the backyard. He stared at me, tilting his head to one side, then the other. I'd heard that cardinals were spirit messengers, a sign from those who'd passed on to the hereafter. I could only wonder if this cardinal had been sent by Mrs. Dolan to tell me something and, if so, what that message might be. Of course, the more likely scenario was that the bird had come to feed in the back-yard. My mother kept her bird feeders well stocked with various seed mixes, including one specifically formu-lated for the pretty red birds. My parents' backyard was constantly atwitter with flocks of finches, chickadees, wrens, and doves. When I'd lived in the guesthouse out back, Sawdust used to love to watch the birds from the top perch of his cat tree at the window. Sometimes he'd even crouch and make a chirping sound back at them, though I suspected it wasn't so much an imitation of their calls as a sign of how badly he wanted to pounce on them. For such a sweet little guy, he could have quite the killer instinct on occasion.

I carried Sawdust inside. We found my mother stand-ing at the kitchen counter, cutting roast beef into tiny little bites for her black-and-white Boston terrier. Yin-Yang waited at my mother's feet, her tongue lolling out the side of her mouth, eagerly looking up at her lunch with her bulbous bug eyes. Yep, the dog was just as spoiled as Sawdust. Like her pampered pet, my mother was pe-tite. I'd gotten my height from my father. My blond hair came from both of my parents, though my father's had mostly faded to a soft beige over the years. Mom's styl-ist kept her hair trimmed, colored, and coiffed, not a single gray to be found.

My mother looked over with a bright smile that fiz-zled like a wet firework the instant she saw my face. "What's wrong?"

I set Sawdust's carrier down on the floor and released

him before stepping toward her, my lip quivering as emotion took hold of me. At nearly thirty, I was probably too old to need my mommy. But having experienced first the shock of finding a corpse in my flip house and then the terror of discovering a squatter sneaking up the stairs behind me, my nerves were beyond frayed. All I wanted was for her to wrap me in her arms and tell me everything would be okay, just like she did when I was a kid and scraped my knee or stubbed my toe.

Instinctively, she spread her arms and encircled me in them, patting my back softly.

I closed my eyes and leaned my head on her shoulder. "I found a body."

She stiffened and reflexively pushed me back, gripping my shoulders in her hands, her eyes bugging out nearly as much as Yin-Yang's. "You found a what?!"

"Body," I squeaked through the tiny airway remaining open in my throat. "An elderly woman. She'd fallen down the stairs. She was lying in the front doorway of our flip house."

"Oh, honey!" My mother pulled me to her again. "That must have been terrible for you!"

It had indeed been terrible. It had been much worse for Mrs. Dolan, of course, but naturally my mother was more concerned about her daughter than a stranger at the moment. She ushered me over to the table and pulled out a chair for me. I melted onto it. She sat next to me and held my hands tightly as I gave her the details. I told her about Dakota, the medical examiner, and Detective Flynn. "They think it was an accident, that she lost her footing and fell."

"So there was no evidence of foul play?"

"No."

"Thank goodness!"

Yin-Yang, who'd been very patient waiting for her lunch, could wait no longer. Her nails clicked across the tile floor as she walked over and raised a paw to tap my mother's leg, as if to say, *Aren't you forgetting something?* But while her paw was on my mother's leg, her gaze remained on the roast.

With my emotions now under control, my mother released my hands, stood, and returned to the counter to finish preparing her dog's lunch. "What was the woman doing in your flip house?"

"I have no idea," I said. "Dakota didn't seem to know, either. I suppose the detective will figure it out when he talks to her family."

"Could you and Buck have some liability? I've heard of folks suing for injuries, even when they were trespassing. I wonder if the woman's family will try to pin the blame on you."

*Great. Something else to worry about.* "I hope not. I'm not aware of anything that would have made her trip." Then again, that hideous shag carpet wasn't tacked down well. Several small nails protruded from the tack strip at the top of the stairs. Because we'd planned to rip the carpet out, Buck and I hadn't bothered to fix them. Even so, it seemed a stretch to think the tiny tacks could have tripped her. *Should I call our insurance company?* I supposed it made sense to wait until the medical examiner issued his official report. We'd learn more of the details then, know whether he ruled it an accident or negligence.

My mother filled Yin-Yang's bowl with the meaty tidbits and placed it on the floor in front of her pup. The dog promptly set about gobbling the bites down. Curious, Sawdust sauntered over, his tail forming a question mark as he ignored Yin-Yang's growl and sniffed at the bowl.

Mom looked down at her pet. "Hush, Yin-Yang. You're being rude to your buddy. Let Sawdust try a bite if he wants to." She turned her attention back to me. "Have you had lunch?"

"Are you offering me a bite of Yin-Yang's roast, too?"

"No. I'm offering you a pimento-cheese sandwich."

"I'd love one."

Mom fixed us each a sandwich and cut mine into four triangles, just as she'd done since I was a kid. It wasn't nearly as fancy as the gourmet panini my roommate had prepared for me the day before, but I'd take it. As my mother placed the plate in front of me, she said, "Maybe you ought to give some more thought to getting your real-estate license."

*Here we go again.* As much as I loved my mother, she and I had very different aptitudes and attitudes. She couldn't understand why I'd want to dress in unflattering, stained coveralls and strain my muscles repairing and remodeling houses. I, on the other hand, couldn't understand how she could be happy performing routine tasks over and over while stuck behind a desk day after day.

To appease my mother and attempt a compromise, I'd signed up to take the real-estate agent's examination weeks ago. Unfortunately, due to an untimely interrogation by Detective Flynn, I missed the exam. But maybe missing the test was a blessing in disguise. I'd only signed up to take it because my mother had relentlessly pestered me into doing it, much as she was doing now. While I loved working in real estate, I preferred physically working on properties to dealing with clients and processing paperwork. Besides, being a natural homebody, I didn't have the extroverted personality and extensive social network needed to ensure a steady supply of clients. Seemed my destiny was to remain a part-time property manager and carpenter until I could focus full-time on flipping houses.

I didn't bother arguing with my mother, opting instead to stuff my face with white bread and pimento cheese. Luckily for me, she moved on to other topics. "Dad and I are considering a summertime cruise. I've heard wonderful things about the Amalfi Coast."

While I was content with weekend trips to the Smoky Mountains, Memphis, or Mammoth Cave up the road in Kentucky, my mother wanted to see the far-flung corners of the world. Travel was yet another area where we differed. It's not so much that I didn't want to visit places and learn more about other countries and cultures, but when it would mean being away from my own bed and my sweet little cat, I knew I'd feel too homesick to really enjoy myself. I was happy to babysit Yin-Yang while my parents wandered the world, and to enjoy their vacation photos when they returned home.

"You should go," I told her. "Yin-Yang is more than welcome to come stay with me and Sawdust." After all, despite the dog's earlier growl, the two were best friends. In fact, they were currently chasing each other around the sofa in the living room.

"I'll let you know once we decide on dates."

After we finished our lunch, my mother suggested I lie down in my former bedroom. "You've been through a lot today. You look exhausted. Some rest will do you good."

I wasn't sure I'd be able to nap after the horrors of the morning, but then again, the adrenaline spike I'd suffered that morning had long since receded, leaving me feeling drained and depleted. I took my mother's advice and lay down on my bed, snuggling up with a plush possum that had served in lieu of a security blanket to comfort me in my much younger days. Not to be left out, Sawdust snuggled up with us, too.

I closed my eyes but dozed only fitfully, awaking to a vibration in the pocket of my coveralls and the folksy strains of Peter, Paul and Mary singing "If I Had a Hammer." The ringtone seemed fitting for a carpenter.

I pulled the device from my pocket. The screen indicated it was Detective Flynn calling. I tapped the button to accept the call.

"We're all done here," he said. "You can come back now. And Whitney?"

"Yes?"

"Change the locks to the house ASAP. You don't know who else might have a key."

# CHAPTER 7

# WAKE AND BAKE

**WHITNEY**

Early Tuesday evening, I drove back to the flip house. I'd returned to install new locks late Saturday afternoon after the police and medical examiner had finished their work and taken Mrs. Dolan's body away, but I hadn't been back since. Buck and I had agreed it would seem callous to start the demo work on the house directly on the heels of the woman's death there. But an hour from now there'd be a memorial service, a symbol of closure, and we figured we could start the renovations tomorrow without causing offense.

Buck and Colette had already arrived, his van parked nose to nose with her Chevy Cruze at the curb, as if their front bumpers were kissing. The two of them were waiting for me in Buck's van, where they could keep warm. They climbed out as I pulled into the driveway, and the three of us met up on the porch, greeting each other with informal "Hey"s.

Colette would be off to work at the Hermitage Hotel restaurant soon, so she was dressed in black pants and her white chef's coat. She'd pulled her curls up in a tight bun atop her head so they'd fit under her chef's hat once she donned it later at the restaurant. Her tote bag hung from her shoulder. Out of the top peeked a rolled-up spare chef's coat. She always took one with her to work, in case of a kitchen mishap. A chef could easily end up splattered in grease or gravy.

After unlocking the front door, I subconsciously eased around the edge of the landing, not wanting to walk where the body had lain. Colette followed my lead and Buck closed the door behind us.

Colette pointed down and whispered, "Is this where you found her?"

Buck whispered back, "Why are you whispering?"

Colette cringed and continued to speak softly. "I don't know. It just seems right."

Invisible hands seemed to have wrapped around my throat, and all I could do was nod in response. I waved my cousin and friend forward, and headed up the stairs. I turned to warn Colette about the loose railing only to find that Buck had already taken her arm.

"Careful," he told her. "That railing's not secure."

She looked up at him. "Thanks, Buck."

He escorted her all the way up, like a groomsman escorting a bridesmaid. She posed no objection. I found myself wondering again whether something could be happening between the two of them and, if it was, when they might acknowledge it.

As Colette entered the kitchen, her head turned to the outdated gold refrigerator. She stepped over to the appliance to admire Lillian's blue ribbons, murmuring aloud as she read them. "Best peach pie. Best peach cobbler. Best peach crumble. Blackberry-peach coffee cake. Raspberry-peach tart. Spicy peach puffs. Peach preserves." She glanced back over her shoulder to address me. "The lady you bought the house from sure did know her way around a peach." She pulled the handle to open the fridge and peered inside. "She must've really liked beer, too."

"The beer belongs to her grandson Dakota," I explained.

"Not anymore." Buck reached in and grabbed a can. "Finders keepers. It's only fair. He's been squatting here for free and ran up our heating bill, treated the place like an Airbnb."

Colette glanced up at my cousin. "Do you really think you should be drinking beer before a funeral?"

Buck shrugged. "Seems as good a time as any."

"Miss Manners would disagree." Colette took the beer out of his hand and stuck it back in the fridge.

Buck grunted. "Party pooper."

Colette turned to the counter, flipping open the lid on Lillian's recipe box and riffling through the index cards. "None of her blue-ribbon recipes seem to be in here. Too bad. I'd be curious to try them." She pulled a few of the cards out for a closer look. "There's one for celery-stuffed tomatoes and another for wild-rice casserole that sound good." She glanced over at me. "Is this box up for grabs?"

"Take anything you'd like," I told her. "Lillian's sons have already gone through the house and removed the stuff they wanted to keep." Including, presumably, the prize-winning recipes.

"In that case, this box is mine now." She tucked the recipe box into her tote bag.

Moving over to the counter, I pulled a drawer open,

removed the odd devices Buck and I had found, and held them up for Colette to see. "These are those weird tools I told you about."

Buck grabbed the one that looked like an airplane throttle, placed it on the countertop, and pulled back on the lever. Putting a hand over his mouth to mimic a microphone, he said, "Ladies and gentlemen, we have reached our cruising altitude of twenty-two thousand feet. I'm turning off the seatbelt sign. Feel free to move about the cabin and annoy those around you."

Colette rolled her eyes and took the device from him. "It's a French-fry cutter, you doofus." She lifted the handle to demonstrate. "See? You put the potato in the bottom part, push the lever down to cut through the potato, and *voilà*! French fries."

I held up the long tube. "So I'm guessing this isn't a caulking gun?"

"Not even close," she said. "It's a cookie press, for making shaped cookies. It's a quicker alternative to cookie cutters. There should be some discs with cutouts that fit on the end."

I dug through the drawer and found a plastic bag full of metal discs that resembled stencils. One had a heart cut out of it, another a flower shape. A third bore a crisscross pattern. "Is this what we're looking for?"

"Yep." She took the bag from me. "These devices will really come in handy. Lots of the kitchen tools they make these days are plastic and they break easily. But these metal relics?" She held up the heavy tools, one in each hand. "These were made to last."

We spent the next few minutes rummaging through the cabinets and drawers to see what else might be of use.

Buck pulled out what appeared to be a silver comb with extra-long teeth. "What's this? Is it for spaghetti?"

"That's called a cake breaker." Colette took it from him and added it to her pile. "It's for cutting delicate cakes like angel food."

I found some small round dishes with shapes in the bottom. "And these are . . . ?"

"Butter molds," Colette said, solving yet another mystery. "I'll take those, too."

When all was said and done, Colette had collected quite the cache of kitchen gadgets. A strainer sieve. An egg-poacher pan. A rolling meat tenderizer that resembled a medieval torture device. She gestured to the antique tins. "Some of those old tins could be collectibles."

Buck picked one up, his expression incredulous. "You're saying these ancient artifacts might be worth something?"

"They're nostalgic," she said. "People are into that these days. You could probably get ten or twenty dollars apiece selling them online."

I turned to Buck. "Maybe we should take them to Lillian's family tonight."

He scoffed. "They left a bunch of worthless junk behind that we'll have to sort through, box up, and cart off. If we make a little money off the stuff, I'd call that a fair trade."

He had a valid point. They'd had their chance to remove anything from the home they cared about. If they'd overlooked a few things, they had no one to blame but themselves. Still, if we came across anything that had more than nominal value, we'd turn it over to them.

Colette paged through several of Lillian's cookbooks and selected three of them to take with her. When we wrapped up in the kitchen, we locked the house and made our way outside to our cars, where we bade goodbye to my roommate.

An hour later, Buck and I walked into the funeral home. Though we hadn't known the deceased, we felt a moral duty to attend her memorial service given that she'd perished on our property. I'd found the information about her service online, on the funeral home's website.

A photograph of a middle-aged Nelda Dolan sat on a small table outside the sanctuary, along with a guest book. The woman in the photo had dishwater-blond hair giving way to white, and dark, dull eyes, no hint of merriment in them at all. She also had a stern set to her jaw and no smile on her face, making the picture an odd choice. Usually families chose a flattering photo of their deceased loved one to display. *Is this the best they could come up with?*

After putting our cell phones in silent mode, Buck and I signed the guest book, took one of the printed programs to share, and slipped into the room. We were greeted by the mellifluous sounds of harp music and the cloying scent of stargazer lilies from the standing spray next to the podium. There was no casket at the front of the space. Looked like the family had decided on cremation. Was it wrong of me to be glad about that? Though I hoped Mrs. Dolan would rest in peace, I had no desire to see her face again. My mind couldn't let go of the image of her lying bent and broken on the landing.

After silencing our cell phones, Buck and I took seats on the back row to leave space for those who knew Nelda better, sitting quietly as they filed in. As the minutes ticked by and the time of her service drew near, we realized we needn't have bothered. Only a handful of people had come to pay their last respects. A couple of white-haired men with military pins affixed to the lapels of their suit jackets. An African American couple of advanced age. The elderly lady who lived to the right of our flip house and had observed Saturday's events through her front window, along with another Caucasian woman with a champagne-colored coif. Dakota and Wayne Walsh. Usually a suit made a man look older and more dignified, but Dakota, who teetered on the precipice between boy and man, only looked more childish in the one he wore. He'd probably borrowed it from his father. The lapels gaped, the sleeves hung down to his knuckles, and the pants puddled around his shoes. He must not have any dress clothes in his current wardrobe, but at least he'd tried to look nice. With Dakota and his father was another man who shared the same ginger-colored hair, though this man was balding and arrived alone. *A bachelor uncle, perhaps?*

In the front row reserved for immediate family sat the man and woman I'd seen in their pajamas in the Dolans' doorway Saturday. Flanking Mr. Dolan and his daughter were curvy twin twenty-somethings, also blond, though their shade was golden. An officiant stood to the side, awaiting his signal to begin.

The somber funeral director who'd been tending the double entrance doors used his shiny shoe to lift the doorstop on one of the doors. Just as he went to shut the other, Detective Flynn slipped through. He took a seat in the back row, across the aisle from me and Buck, and greeted us with a nod. Rather than his police jacket, he wore a dark blue suit with a green tie that brought out the emerald color of his eyes. *Hmm. Did the detective come simply as a courtesy, or is more going on here?*

The officiant stepped up to the podium to start the service, opening with a simple prayer. He spent several minutes reciting words and verses he seemed to know from rote memory. The prepackaged program was respectful yet impersonal. The eulogy, if it could even be called that, was very short, more a recitation of the facts of Nelda Dolan's life rather than a sharing of loving memories. The officiant looked down at the index card before him. "Nelda Pitts was born and raised in Hopkinsville, Kentucky. There, she met Carl Dolan, an army recruit attending basic training at Fort Campbell in preparation for deployment to Vietnam. The two married upon his return stateside and settled here, in Carl's hometown of Nashville, where they raised their daughter, Becky. Nelda was just shy of her seventy-fifth birthday when she was called home by the Lord last Friday evening."

As soon as the man wrapped up, one of the twins stepped to the front of the room, a mandolin in her hands. Her dress bore so much colorful fringe she resembled a piñata. She looked up at the ceiling. "This is for you, grandmother."

After taking a seat on a tall stool, she treated the mourners to a beautiful rendition of The Beatles' classic "Let It Be," her voice husky and soulful as she filled the room with song. Dakota stared, rapt, his jaw slack. *Someone's got a crush.* When she finished, Dakota burst into hearty applause. The girl gave him a coy smile in return.

The officiant took the podium again and concluded the service with a somber recitation of the Lord's Prayer. Strangely, I'd heard not a single sniffle during the short ceremony, seen no one dab an eye. It had been only four days since Mrs. Dolan's unfortunate and unexpected death. Her family and friends wouldn't have been prepared for her passing. *Hmm.*

Just as surreptitiously as he'd slid into the room, Detective Flynn made his escape, slipping silently out the door on the final "Amen." *What's that all about?*

Buck and I filed into the hallway after the others, stopping along with them to don our winter coats. The two white-haired men shook hands with Carl Dolan, each of them putting a consoling hand on his shoulder as they did so. As Carl's friends headed for the door, Buck and I eased through the crowd to introduce ourselves and express our condolences.

Carl spotted us approaching and offered a smile. "You're the two who bought Lillian's house, aren't you?"

"That's us," Buck replied. "Buck and Whitney Whitaker. Cousins."

"Nice to meet you." Carl introduced his remaining family. The middle-aged blonde was Becky, Nelda and Carl's daughter. The twins were Becky's girls, Dahlia and Daisy. Carl turned his focus back to me. "They say you're the one who found Nelda. That must have been hard for you."

*Harder than losing a spouse you'd been married to for over fifty years?* "It was a shock," I admitted, not telling him it was my cat who'd first discovered the body. "I'm so sorry you've lost your wife."

"Could be worse," he said matter-of-factly. "The coroner said it was quick. She didn't suffer."

Becky exhaled sharply, muttering under her breath. "She caused plenty of suffering, though."

Buck and I exchanged a glance. Carl sure was taking things well, and there didn't appear to be much love lost between Becky and her mother. I supposed I was lucky my parents had a healthy relationship, and that we all got along well.

As the Dolans headed for the door, the elderly couple who'd been in the service stepped up to me and Buck.

"Excuse me," the woman said, "but I hear we're going to be neighbors."

"You have a lovely neighborhood," I said, "but my cousin and I aren't actually planning to move in. We both own homes already. We're going to fix the house up and put it back on the market."

"Flippers, huh? Well, until you sell it, you'll be an honorary neighbor." She gave us a wink. "I'm Gayle Garner," she said before putting a hand on her husband's shoulder. "This is my better half, Bertram."

I shook their hands and introduced myself. Buck also exchanged handshakes and names.

"We're hosting a wake at our house now," Gayle said. "You two should come, get to know the people on the block. We're all friendly folks—at least now, anyways."

*What did she mean by that?*

Before I could give Gayle's odd comment much thought, she went on. "We'll have lots of good food. If there's anything the ladies of Songbird Circle know how to do, it's cook."

Buck's stomach growled, as if replying for us.

Bertram chuckled. "We'll take that as a yes. We're the green house that sits catty-corner from yours. See you there."

We followed the couple out the door to the parking lot. They climbed into a shiny silver coupe with a Fisk University Alumni sticker on the back bumper. The historically black university was located in the northeast part of the city, and had a proud history of socially active students who advocated for civil rights and societal progress. The campus was home to Jubilee Hall, a beautiful Gothic Revival–style building. In dark days, a bell had been rung atop the hall to alert students to invasions of the campus by the Night Riders, who were precursors to the KKK. The worst thing I'd had to worry about in college was whether the dorm cafeteria would run out of pizza before I could get there.

Buck and I climbed back into my SUV. As I drove out of the lot, I spotted Detective Flynn sitting in his unmarked police car, watching the people depart. *Why hadn't he spoken to the family? Extended his condolences?*

Evidently, Buck noticed Flynn, too. "That detective seems to be keeping a close eye on things out here."

"He sure does."

Was Flynn simply being courteous, giving the mourners a chance to depart before he took off? Or could he be watching them for another reason?

# CHAPTER 8

# DISHING IT OUT

**WHITNEY**

I reached out and jabbed the button to turn on the radio. One of my favorite female singers crooned over the airwaves, lamenting her lost love's cheating heart and vowing to crush said organ under her boot. *You go, girl!* Buck and I sang along, my cousin improvising a shrill falsetto that threatened to shatter both my eardrums and the windshield. Fortunately, it was only a short drive back to Songbird Circle. I parked in the driveway of our flip house and we strode across the cul-de-sac to Gayle and Bertram's place.

Bertram greeted us at the door, loosening his tie as he did so. "Come on in and make yourselves at home. Gayle's setting up in the kitchen. In the meantime, what can I get you to drink? Sweet tea? Coffee? Soda? Wine? We've got a fully stocked bar. I make a mean mint julep."

*Wine and cocktails?* Looked like this would be an Irish wake. Not unusual, I supposed. The surname Dolan was of Gaelic origin, after all. Besides, the customs for grieving seemed to be evolving, with "celebrations of life" now often replacing the more somber traditional observances. Even so, I figured it might be best to see if the other guests chose to imbibe before taking a glass of the hard stuff. "I'll start with tea, please."

"Same for me," Buck said, following my lead.

While Bertram rounded up our drinks, Buck and I stepped into the living room. There we found the two older women we'd seen sitting side by side at the service. They were seated in wingback chairs on either side of the roaring fireplace. Between them, on a colorful braided rug, lay a dozing black dog with a white blaze on his chest, one white paw, and some white hairs on his snout telling me he'd entered if not his golden dog years, at least his silver dog years. He was a big dog, too, some type of Labrador-retriever mix. His side rose and fell as he slept peacefully, basking in the warmth of the fire.

Up close like this, I could tell much more about the women. The one who lived to the right of our flip house was petite, with round, silver-rimmed glasses and shiny, silvery hair cut in a traditional yet stylish bob. Her eyes, too, held a soft, silver-gray hue, reminiscent of pussy willows. She wore sensible flat shoes along with a dark blue dress that, despite being plain, nicely complemented her natural coloring. The other woman was tall and thin, her champagne-blond tresses teased into a soft, spongy pouf atop her head. She wore a black suit with a fitted, feminine cut and high-heeled pumps. She'd applied copious quantities of makeup, though she looked classy rather than tacky, like a movie star who'd aged well, a Glenn Close or Helen Mirren type. Each of the women had a stem glass of white wine in her hand.

When they both made a move to stand, I raised a hand to stop them. "No need to get up on our account."

"Thank goodness. Getting up gets harder every day."

The movie star stretched out her hand from her seat, the gemstones in her various rings glinting in the firelight. Her fingernails were long and tapered, nearly talon-like, and coated in a glossy plum-colored polish. "Hi, you two. I'm Roxanne. I heard you've bought Lillian's house?"

"That's right," I replied, taking her hand. "I'm Whitney and this is my cousin Buck." I released her hand and raised mine to indicate my cousin.

The silvery woman offered her name and hand, as well, though her hand was unadorned, her fingernails unpainted and trimmed short. "My name's Mary Sue Mecklenberg. I own the house to the right of yours. Pleased to meet you folks."

Roxanne reached down to the dog lying between her and her neighbor and gave him a nice scratch behind the ear with her long nails. "This big lump of fur down here? He's Mosey."

On hearing his name, the dog opened his eyelids halfway. He raised his head an inch or two to take a look at Buck and me before settling his cheek back on the rug and closing his eyes again. Apparently, he didn't perceive us two strangers as a threat. He didn't seem to find Buck and me interesting enough to warrant getting off his warm, comfortable rug, either. Couldn't say I blamed him. He had the best spot in the house.

Introductions complete, Buck and I took seats on the sofa.

Whether this gathering was intended to be upbeat or mournful, I figured it couldn't hurt to offer my condolences. "I'm sorry about your friend."

Roxanne snorted. "Nelda wasn't our friend."

My mind whirled in confusion. "Dakota told me you ladies met up to play cards and sew, talk about books?"

"That's true," Roxanne said. "But we only included Nelda because it would have been rude to invite all the gals on the circle but her. Besides, she'd have pitched a hissy fit and made our lives miserable if we'd left her out."

Buck and I exchanged a glance. *This woman sure is blunt.*

Mary Sue frowned slightly. "Now, now, Roxanne. It's not nice to speak ill of the dead."

Undeterred, Roxanne snorted. "Why not? Nelda spoke ill about the rest of us all her life."

Mary Sue cringed. "You knew about that?"

"Of course! I know what she called me behind my back."

When Mary Sue merely pursed her lips, Buck cocked his head and eyed Roxanne. "What did she call you?"

I elbowed my cousin in the ribs. We had no business stirring things up. Still, I had to admit I was curious, too.

"She called me a hussy! Can you believe it?" Roxanne shook her head.

Mary Sue tried to smooth things over. "Nelda only said that because she envied you, Roxanne. You were always the beauty of the bunch."

"And you were always the peacemaker." Roxanne turned back to me and Buck. "Mary Sue never has a harsh word against anyone. There's not a mean bone in her body."

Mary Sue groaned. "There's not a bone that osteoporosis hasn't got hold of, either."

Roxanne waved a dismissive hand and issued a *pshaw*. "We old gray mares ain't what we used to be, but we've got a few good years left in us." She raised a glass in salute before taking a generous sip.

"'Hussy' isn't so bad, really," Mary Sue said. "You could've been called worse."

"True," Roxanne said. "Gayle and Lillian got the worst of it. 'Hussy' is much better than 'cheat' or 'thief.'"

Buck chimed in again. "Mrs. Dolan called the other ladies a cheat and a thief?"

"Sure did!" Roxanne said. "Nelda had some gall accusing Gayle of cheating. We always played with the cards Gayle had given Lillian as a housewarming gift decades ago. Nelda seemed to think they were marked somehow, and that's why Gayle won so often. 'Course there was no truth to that. Gayle is just good at cards, is all. Wins nearly every game we play."

My mind went to the box of playing cards I'd seen on Lillian's coffee table. "Are you talking about the cards in the wooden box? The one with the W engraved on top?"

"That's them." Roxanne cocked her head. "They're still in the house?"

"They are," I said. "On the coffee table."

"I'm surprised Wayne or Andy didn't take them." Roxanne took another sip of her wine before continuing her tirade. "Anyhoo, why Nelda got her granny panties in such a bunch was beyond me. We play penny-ante poker. The winner gets peanuts. Talk about a sore loser." She tsked. "Nelda accused Lillian of pocketing her sapphire pendant, too. It was in the shape of a peacock. Carl bought it for her years ago when he was off in the war. Nelda realized the thing was missing after one of our quilting sessions and insisted it had fallen off in Lillian's house. None of us remembered her wearing it that night. It probably fell off in her own house or on her walk over."

Mary Sue bit her lip, looking uncomfortable at the

direction the conversation had taken. "Nelda could be helpful, though, too. She always made sure the kids got to school on time when it was her day to drive carpool."

Roxanne scoffed. "You mean when she'd pull into the center of the cul-de-sac and blast her horn? The kids hurried so their eardrums wouldn't burst. That busybody grilled the kids about our personal business when they were in her car, too. She once asked my daughter whether I'd had a tummy tuck. The nerve of that woman!"

Nelda might have been a busybody, but Roxanne was certainly a gossip. Maybe she shouldn't be pointing fingers.

*Ding-dong!* The doorbell interrupted our exchange. Mosey opened his eyes halfway again, but didn't bother lifting his head this time.

Bertram handed us our tea, strode to the door, and opened it. Carl, Becky, Dahlia, and Daisy filed in, bringing a savory aroma with them. All of the women carried dishes covered in aluminum foil. Bertram handed Carl a glass of whiskey he had at the ready and took the ladies' drinks orders as they made their way to the kitchen with the food.

Bertram had just headed off to gather drinks for the Dolan women when three quick knocks sounded at the door. *Rap-rap-rap.*

"I got it, Bert!" Carl called to his friend.

Carl opened the door to reveal Dakota and Wayne. Wayne carried a slow cooker from which a spicy scent emanated. I was guessing chili. The man with the receding ginger hair eased through the door after them.

Roxanne raised her hand and waved. "Hey, Andy! Come meet the folks that bought your mother's house."

He stepped over, and during the next couple minutes

of conversation, we learned that he was Lillian Walsh's
younger son, in his early forties, and single.

"Don't you worry, Andy," Roxanne said. "The right
woman's out there somewhere, just waiting for you to
find her."

"I don't see how I will," he replied, "unless she falls
into my lap. I'm putting in sixty hours a week or more
at the office."

Wayne, who'd just wandered into the room, waggled
his brows. "I've heard of places where women will fall
into your lap. It'll cost you twenty dollars, though."
He cackled when Andy blushed and frowned. Turning
his back on his brother, Wayne headed over to me and
Buck. He fished two sales brochures out of his jacket
and forced them on my cousin. "Take a look at these.
Whitney said you're set for cleaning products, but I dab-
ble in other merchandise, too. You're in the fixer-upper
business, so you'll be interested in our water and air pu-
rifiers. Vitamins, too. All that hard labor takes a toll. It's
important to stay on top of your health."

Buck's stiff stance told me he found the man's untimely sales pitch as inappropriate as I had, but my
cousin managed to keep his tone cordial. "We'll keep
that in mind."

"Uh-huh, uh-huh." Wayne gave Buck a too-familiar
shoulder squeeze before turning his head to address
Bertram and issuing a hoot. "Sure smells good in here.
When can we put on the feedbag?"

Gayle called out from the kitchen. "It's ready!"

Bertram waved for the crowd to follow him. Seeming
to realize food was in the offing, Mosey pushed himself
up off the rug and, true to his name, moseyed after us.
We entered the kitchen to find every square inch of table

and counter space filled with potluck dishes in charmingly mismatched serving pieces.

Gayle stood next to a stack of plates and brandished a wooden spoon. "Y'all know the rules. No pushing, no shoving, no cutting in line. I catch anyone mixing up the utensils and you will be banned from dessert." She pointed her spoon at her dog. "That goes for you, too, Mosey."

Murmurs of "yes, ma'am" sounded all around us. Buck and I added our own. Clearly, this group had gathered often, felt at ease with each other, treated each other like family. Not many neighborhoods like that these days.

Gayle directed that, as the bereaved family, Carl and his progeny should start. "Dolans first." She waved her spoon as if directing an orchestra. "Dig in."

Once the Dolans were done, the rest of us shuffled forward, filling plates and bowls with the variety of offerings. Lasagna. Squash casserole. Wayne's three-alarm chili that made both your taste buds and eyes water. Cornbread baked and served in a heavy-duty cast-iron skillet.

Gayle and Bertram had put the leaf in their dining room table and added extra folding chairs. We crammed in, shoulder to shoulder. Bertram filled Mosey's bowl and set it down in a corner, where the dog could be part of the event but not underfoot.

Dakota eased in between Becky's twins, grinning like he'd won the jackpot. Becky cut a glance in his direction. Was it just my imagination, or had a scowl crossed her face as she raised her glass to her mouth?

Andy held a forkful of potatoes au gratin aloft and eyed me and Buck. "You two are professional carpenters?"

Buck dipped his head in confirmation. "My father

owns a carpentry business, operates a small sawmill in his barn. Whitney and I both work for him. He's taught us all the ins and outs of woodworking."

Andy sipped his tea and returned his glass to the table. "We're glad you'll be sprucing the house up. Mom was embarrassed about the condition of the place these last few years, but there wasn't much she could do on her fixed income."

Gayle and Roxanne exchanged a discreet glance across the table. *What's that about?*

Andy went on to ask about our plans. "I'd love to hear what you've got in mind for the house."

Buck deferred to me. "I'm just the muscle. Whitney's the designer."

The group turned their attention to me, eager to hear the details for the renovation.

I gave them a basic list. Replace the carpet with wood floors. Install new appliances and countertops, and add an extension to expand the counter space in the kitchen. Pull out the old tub in the master bath and replace it with a separate garden tub and walk-in shower. "We plan to repaint inside and out, too. We're going to maintain the black-and-white color scheme on the exterior, but we'll paint the front door red. It'll be a nice accent color."

"Soon as it warms up," Carl said, "I'm going to get rid of that ugly-as-sin paint Nelda insisted on. I told her the color reminded me of pork rinds, but she wouldn't listen." He frowned at the memory before raising hopeful eyebrows. "You got any color suggestions? You're the expert."

Though I binge-watched HGTV any chance I could and pored over home and garden magazines, I had no formal training. Still, I seemed to have a natural knack for design. If nothing else, I was good at emulating things

I'd seen elsewhere. "What about burgundy?" I suggested. The color would tie in nicely with the other homes in the cul-de-sac while offering its own unique look. "White trim would look nice. Maybe navy blue for the shutters and front door?"

Becky's face brightened and she leaned forward to address first her father, then me. "That's a great idea! Can you recommend a painting company?"

"I'd be happy to," I told her. "I work in property management part-time, so I've got lots of contacts."

Mary Sue leaned forward to get a better view down the table. "How's college going, girls?"

"It's going well," Dahlia replied.

Becky beamed. "Dahlia made the dean's list last semester."

After congratulations were offered all around, everyone's eyes shifted to Daisy, who had yet to reply to Mary Sue's inquiry. She responded with a shrug. "I didn't make the dean's list, obviously. Dahlia's the smart one. I'm the fun one." She cut a sideways glance at her sister, a grin playing about her lips. "I'm also the pretty one."

Dahlia rolled her eyes. "We look exactly the same."

"Do we?" Daisy gestured to her flashy fringed outfit before holding out a hand to indicate her twin's demure black dress.

"Okay," Dahlia acquiesced. "We look the same *in the face*." Despite Daisy's teasing, Dahlia seemed to sense that her sister might feel slighted or embarrassed, and she came to her twin's defense. "Daisy performed at an open-mic night at a coffee shop near campus. The crowd loved her. The owner asked her to come back next week."

While praise rained down on her other daughter this time, Becky's face seemed to tighten. "Will the owner be paying you?"

"No," Daisy said, "but she's going to let me put out a tip jar."

Becky chewed her lip, apparently conflicted. "Just make sure you don't neglect your schoolwork. Your tuition is costing me an arm and a leg."

Daisy groaned. "I know, Mom. You've told me a million times."

"Sorry, hon," Becky said, "but until I get that divorce settlement . . ." She shook her head, leaving her sentence unfinished and the rest of us to fill in the blank. *Until she gets the divorce settlement, she'll be spread thin financially.*

Carl sighed and cut a sharp look at his daughter. "You wouldn't be having such a hard time if you'd taken my advice all those years ago and held out for a nicer man."

Becky cut her father a scathing look right back. "You're really not in a position to lecture anyone on marriage, are you, Dad?"

*Whoa.* What did she mean by that? Had Carl and Nelda Dolan's marriage been rocky?

"I suppose not," Carl conceded, reaching out to give his daughter's hand a conciliatory pat.

Gayle intervened and expertly steered the conversation in a more positive direction. "Bertram and I are planning a vacation to Gatlinburg this spring. It's been a long time since we visited the Smoky Mountains."

"We took the boys there a few years ago," Wayne said. "Spent most of our time at Dollywood. They loved the Barnstormer ride. Well, all of 'em but Dakota. He was too scared to go on it."

Dakota's face flamed bright red. "I wasn't scared," he insisted. "Those kinds of rides just make me sick." His gaze darted to Daisy as if to gauge her response.

She chuckled. "Don't be embarrassed. I don't like amusement park rides, either."

He gave her a soft, grateful smile.

The group continued to make small talk throughout the meal, though surprisingly little of it involved Nelda. Even so, it didn't seem the neighbors were purposely ignoring the proverbial elephant in the room. Instead, it just seemed the woman's passing had little impact on those gathered. How sad would it be to pass away so uneventfully, to fail to leave even a temporary void? I hoped there would be lots of people missing me once I was gone.

Bertram uncorked a fresh bottle of white wine and held it up. "Any takers?"

Roxanne was the first to hold up her glass. "Fill me up, Bertram."

Several others followed suit.

As everyone finished up, I helped Gayle gather the dirty plates and transport them to the kitchen sink. Meanwhile, Becky and Mary Sue carried the desserts and dessert plates into the dining room.

Carl's gaze moved among the cakes and cobblers, and for the first time, he appeared genuinely sad, his eyes and mouth drooping. "I hate to say it, but these get-togethers just aren't the same without Lillian's peach pie."

Murmurs of agreement went up around the table. I could relate. My aunt Nancy made the best sweet potato pie on the planet. The holidays wouldn't be the same without it.

"Lillian had quite a collection of blue ribbons on her fridge," I said. "That pie must've been really good if it won awards."

Carl moaned, as if the thought of the pie brought him

pure bliss. "I'd kill for that pie. Best-tasting thing I ever ate in my life."

"We know, Granddad." One of the twins rolled her eyes as she teased her grandfather. "You've told us ten thousand times."

Becky's lip curled up in what was as much a smirk as it was a smile. "It used to make Mom so mad when Dad would fawn over Lillian, tell her how good that pie was. Mom begged Lillian for the recipe, but Lillian wouldn't give it to her." Becky turned to Mary Sue. "You were Lillian's best friend. She never gave you the recipe?"

"Nah." Mary Sue waved a dismissive hand. "Lillian knew as well as y'all do that I'm better on the stovetop than in the oven. My mashed potatoes and fried okra can't be beat, but I can't bake to save my life."

"That's not true," Gayle insisted. "Your cornbread is the delicious."

"I agree." Buck put a hand on his belly. "I went back for seconds. Twice."

Mary Sue sent a soft smile his way. "That's called thirds, hon."

Buck shrugged. "I never was much good at math."

My cousin was being much too humble. He'd actually excelled in math in high school. Ditto for his class in computer-aided design. He could've gone on to be an engineer if he'd wanted to. But, like me, he preferred hands-on work.

Wayne turned the conversation back to dessert. "Mom never gave me her peach pie recipe, either. She said that pie was the only thing that brought her boys home. Of course she said she'd pass the recipe along on her deathbed so it wouldn't die with her."

Given that there was no peach pie on the table, I

asked the obvious question. "I take it that didn't happen?"

Wayne shook his head. "Mom didn't keep her peach pie recipe in her recipe box in the kitchen. She had a stroke before she could tell us where she'd hidden it. She spent several days in the hospital before she passed, but she wasn't able to speak during that time. We looked all over the house when we were cleaning things out, but it never turned up."

Carl cut a look to me and Buck. "Maybe you'll come across the recipe during the renovations."

"I'd be surprised if they do." Mary Sue tapped her forehead. "Lillian kept that recipe up here. She could bake that pie in her sleep."

Could be. Colette had her favorite recipes memorized and could prepare them without consulting her notes. Nonetheless, she'd immortalized them in writing in her personal cookbook. After all, she'd had to keep detailed notes as she'd developed and taste-tested the various versions of the recipes, tracking the measurements of the respective ingredients, temperatures, and cook times until she'd perfected the particular palate pleaser. The painstaking process consumed quite a bit of time and effort. She wouldn't risk her work being lost in her busy brain. While I'd never met Lillian and didn't want to discredit Mary Sue, I had a sneaky suspicion the pie recipe might still be in the house somewhere. I'd keep an eye out for it. While Nelda seemed to have been a thorn in their sides, Lillian and her peach pie had clearly meant a lot to those gathered here. I couldn't bring Lillian back, of course, but maybe I could resurrect her beloved, award-winning dessert.

Andy caught Carl's eye across the table. "No rush,

Carl. But I've got the necessary forms at my office for you to sign whenever you're ready."

*Forms? What forms is he talking about?*

Carl lifted his chin in acknowledgement. "I'll stop by tomorrow."

I supposed it was none of my business. Even so, I was curious. I told myself I wasn't nosy, that I was only trying to get to know my new neighbors. But, really, it was pure nosiness. I addressed my question to Andy, hoping to appear more interested in his work than in Carl's forms. "What line of business are you in, Andy?"

"Insurance."

That explained things. Probably Carl had some sort of life insurance or burial policy to cash in, or maybe a supplemental Medicare policy that covered his healthcare expenses.

Dakota turned to Daisy. "Why don't you sing some more? Give us a show while everyone has dessert?"

Encouraging murmurs came from all corners of the table.

"You don't have to ask me twice," Daisy said with a grin before retrieving her instrument. She spent the next quarter hour strumming her mandolin and treating the group to a variety of tunes, ranging from country classics to bluegrass to female pop ballads. I was stunned by how beautiful her voice was. *Adele's got nothing on this girl.*

After enjoying generous slices of Gayle's butter-pecan cake and Daisy's melodic voice, Buck and I stood to go, saying good night to the group. Gayle and Bertram walked us to the door.

I followed Buck out onto the porch and turned back to address the couple. "Thanks for including us."

"Of course, hon." Gayle took both of my hands in

hers and gave them a gentle squeeze. "You're one of us now. The ladies of Songbird Circle. At least until you sell the house." She pointed a finger at me. "That means you're on the hook for a side dish for Friday night's poker game. Lillian always used to host, but Mary Sue has offered to take over. Be there at seven." With that and a coy grin, she closed the door on us.

# CHAPTER 9

# CREATURES OF
# THE NIGHT

### SAWDUST

Sawdust had the house to himself tonight. It had been fun for a while. Whitney's roommate Emmalee had left her door ajar, and he'd pushed it open to explore her room. He'd found a balled-up sock under her bed and batted that around for a while. He'd kneaded her pillows and taken a catnap in her clean laundry in the basket on the floor. He'd also taken advantage of the alone time to sharpen his claws on the wood trim around the bathroom door. Whitney always scolded him when she caught him doing that, but she always forgave him, too. *Being adorable has its benefits.*

Eventually, Sawdust had done all the exploring he cared to. He was in the mood to have his ears rubbed and chest scratched before settling down for the night.

*Where did Whitney go?* He liked the evenings when she stayed home with him. It was their special time to play and cuddle. *When will she come home?*

He hopped up onto his cat tree by the front window

and climbed to the tallest perch to watch for her. He waited, and waited, and waited, for what felt like forever. As he watched for Whitney, a raccoon sauntered across the front yard. The creature stood on his hind legs and stretched his nose up to sniff a garbage can hidden in the bushes next door. He must not have smelled anything appetizing, so he fell back to all fours and ambled off.

A moment later, a car pulled to a stop at the curb across the street. With his superior feline night vision, Sawdust could see a man sitting in the driver's seat. The man turned off the car's lights and motor. He didn't climb out of the car, though. He seemed to be waiting and watching, too. But for what? Or who?

Finally, Whitney's SUV turned in to the driveway, her headlights sweeping across the window. *Hooray!* Sawdust stood and arched his back, giving it a good stretch to get his blood flowing and his muscles moving. Whitney slid out of her car, bleeped the locks closed, and headed to the porch.

Sawdust leapt down from his cat tree and ran to the front door. He expected to hear Whitney's keys in the lock, for Whitney to open the door and come through at any second. What he didn't expect was to hear her scream.

# CHAPTER 10

# A BLOODY MESS

## WHITNEY

My scream rang in my ears as I rounded on my pursuer, my key-chain pepper spray at the ready.

"Sorry!" Detective Flynn raised his hands to protect his face. "I didn't mean to scare you."

*Sheesh. What is it with men sneaking up behind me the last few days?* "You nearly got a face full, mister."

"Wouldn't be the first time," he said. "Got showered in the stuff once at the mall when I was still a beat cop and tried to arrest a shoplifter."

"My gosh!" I said. "What did you do?"

"Sprayed the woman right back," he said. "Then neither of us could see the other. We got into a blind slapping match. Took me a minute or two, but I finally caught her arms and managed to get her cuffed. Had to dunk my head in the outdoor fountain to wash off the spray."

I fought a grin, imagining the straitlaced detective engaged in such antics. *Maybe he's not as straitlaced as I think.* "What are you doing here?"

"I've been trying to call you all night but you didn't answer."

I reached into my purse again, this time to retrieve my phone. Sure enough, the screen noted three missed calls from Detective Flynn. I'd forgotten to turn the ringer back on after the memorial service. *Oops.* "What were you calling about?"

"I heard from the medical examiner. He found something interesting when he was performing Nelda Dolan's autopsy."

"Uh-oh." Collin would have tried to contact me only if the "something interesting" meant Nelda's death hadn't been an accident, right? Otherwise, the information could have waited until tomorrow. A sick feeling spread through my gut.

"I should've known it wouldn't be a cut-and-dried case," he added. "There was a full moon Friday night. Full moons bring out the crazy in people."

I waved for him to follow me into the house. It was too frigid to stand outside and chitchat. I shut the door behind him and tucked the canister of pepper spray into my purse. Emmalee and Colette were both at work, so the house was quiet. Sawdust mewed and weaved around my ankles in greeting. I picked up the cat, giving my little boy a big kiss on the head before putting him down again. I pulled off my coat and scarf and hung them on the hooks by the front door. The detective eased a large manila envelope from inside his coat, then hung his coat on the hook next to mine.

I crossed my arms over my chest and skewered the detective with a pointed look. "If you're going to tell me Nelda Dolan was murdered on my property, I'm going to need a hot toddy."

"Round up a mug, then. In fact, make it two."

"You're joining me? Aren't you on duty?"

"Only until I fill you in. Then it's bottom's up."

We made our way to the kitchen, Sawdust skittering ahead of us. The detective took a seat on a barstool at the narrow island while I quickly whipped up a batch of spiked spiced cider and poured the steaming amber liquid into two mugs. I took a generous gulp from one of them to steel myself and set the other on the countertop in front of him. Plunking myself down on the adjacent stool, I turned to face him. "I'm ready now. Shoot."

He loosened the metal brad on the envelope as he spoke. "When we left the house Saturday, the assistant ME, Officer Hogarty, and I all thought Nelda Dolan's death looked accidental. At first it seemed odd that Nelda was found in your house, but her husband told me Nelda had spotted Dakota entering the place when she went to close their bedroom curtains Friday night. She said she was going to run over to let Dakota know that the house had sold and that he was trespassing. It appeared she'd gone upstairs to look for Dakota, didn't find him there, and was on her way downstairs when she tripped and fell. Dakota told me he had earbuds in his ears and music playing, so it would explain why he didn't hear her knock or ring the bell, or fall down the stairs."

I wrapped my hands around my mug to savor its warmth. "The story makes sense so far, but why did it take Carl Dolan so long to realize his wife was missing? She'd been gone more than twelve hours before you went over to tell him what happened."

"Carl said he climbed into bed and fell asleep while Nelda was next door. He claimed he's a heavy sleeper and didn't realize Nelda hadn't come to bed all night. When he and Becky woke in the morning and Nelda wasn't around, they figured she'd gotten up early to make her weekly run to the grocery store."

I raised my mug for another sip. "They didn't check to see if the car was gone from the driveway?"

"They hadn't looked outside, and they didn't know anything was wrong until I showed up. Or so they say."

"You have reason to believe they might be lying?"

"Possibly." He pulled some pictures from the envelope before gesturing to my mug. "You might want to drink up. I need you to take a look at these autopsy photos."

*Autopsy photos? Yikes.*

I took a huge gulp to prepare myself as he spread three photos on the countertop. Sawdust jumped up onto the counter and sniffed the photos, flopping down on his side when they failed to interest him. Sucking in a deep breath, I forced myself to look down. All three photos showed Nelda Dolan's exposed torso. To respect her privacy, sheets had been draped over her chest and hips, leaving only her belly exposed. Most of her skin had turned a dark red, as if she were sunburned from a long day at the beach. However, there was an odd, light-colored band that started on the right side of her body and made its way across her rib cage to the other side, where it ended in what appeared to be a triangle shape, though only two edges were visible.

Fortunately, my curiosity replaced my aversion. "What am I looking it?" The odd shape couldn't be a birthmark or the colors would be reversed, with the mark being darker than the surrounding skin.

"The coloring? That's what happens when livor mortis sets in."

"*Livor* mortis?" I'd heard of rigor mortis, when a body stiffens after death. But livor mortis was new to me.

Collin gave me a quick lesson in livor mortis, which he said was also known as lividity or hypostasis. "Ever sat on a slatted lawn chair or bench and noticed the stripes on the back of your legs when you stood up?"

"Yes."

"That's gravity pulling blood to the lower points in your body. The same thing happens after a person passes away, but because the heart has stopped circulating the blood and the body doesn't move, the blood remains pooled and turns the skin permanently red or bluish-purple. The stain on the skin tells us how the body was lying."

I wasn't exactly a science wiz, but gravity was a concept I could easily comprehend. "I'm with you so far."

He pointed at the narrow part of the image that ran from the edge of her torso across her ribs. "That's Nelda's forearm."

I recalled the woman's right arm being tucked under her when she lay in the doorway. I pointed to the triangle. "Is that her hand? Was it lying flat under her?" Even as I asked the question, something told me the triangle couldn't be her hand. The ninety-degree angle was too perfectly shaped, with well-defined edges that in no way resembled fingers.

"No," the detective said.

"What was it, then?"

"I was hoping you could tell me. She appears to have been holding something. Whatever it was remained in place under her body for several hours after she died. If it had been removed right away, it wouldn't have left the pattern on her skin. But the object was gone when the medical examiner arrived."

"Somebody removed it between the time she died and the time I called 911?"

"Yes. We believe that person also pushed her down the stairs. There are some scratch marks on the back of her hands and neck. We initially thought they'd resulted from the fall. You may have noticed that the carpet wasn't tacked down well at the top of the stairs and some of the small nails stuck out."

I had indeed noticed this fact. Like the banister over the stairs, the carpet, too, seemed intent on pulling free. Maybe the railing and the carpet planned to run off together, like the dish that ran away with the spoon in the old nursery rhyme.

"We're thinking the scratches on her hands were incurred in a struggle over the unknown thing she was carrying. The ones on the back of her neck could be the result of someone reaching out from behind to shove her down the stairs."

I cut the guy some serious side eye. "You're not accusing *me*, are you?"

"If I thought you had anything to do with Nelda's death," Collin replied, "I wouldn't have shared this information with you. But I thought you might know if there was something of value left in the home that a burglar, or Nelda herself, would have been tempted to take. Something someone else would have wanted bad enough to come back for."

"And it would have been triangle shaped?" Knowing the shape would certainly help us narrow things down.

"Possibly," he said. "But it's also possible that the right angle that's visible on her skin is the corner of something square or rectangular."

"Oh." *So much for narrowing down the list of potential items.*

"It's also possible the item of value was inside something with a right angle."

"Some type of box or container, you mean?"

"Right. There's no way to tell from the pattern on Nelda's skin whether the shape was solid or hollow."

My mind went back to the many items Lillian Walsh and her sons had left behind in the house. A cake server I'd found in a kitchen drawer was triangular, but it had no right angles. Same for the plastic hangers hanging in the closets. Besides, the hangers weren't solid. Did Lillian own a speed square? The triangular tool, also known as a Swanson tool, was commonly used by carpenters like me for framing and as a saw guide for cutting wood. But even if there had been a speed square in the house, it seemed highly unlikely Nelda would take it and that someone else would then steal it out from under her. That left me with squares and rectangles to consider. The list of such items was endless. The collectors' tins Colette had pointed out in the kitchen. The playing cards. The small jewelry box full of costume jewelry. The rose-shaped soaps in the box in the bathroom. There'd been several rectangular boxes of buttons and other items in the sewing room. Still, none of these seemed especially important or valuable. *Then again . . .*

"When I was at the wake at the Garners' house tonight, one of the neighbors mentioned that Nelda had accused Lillian of stealing a pendant from her. It was in the shape of a peacock and made of sapphires. Carl bought it for Nelda years ago, when he was a soldier in Vietnam."

Flynn's brows rose. "The angle could have been the corner of a jewelry box."

"There was a small one on top of Lillian's bed last Friday. I took a quick peek inside. It was filled with jewelry, but I didn't pay much attention to the contents. Her sons had left it behind so I assumed everything inside was costume pieces that weren't worth much." *Could Nelda's peacock pendant have been inside? Had Nelda's accusation against Lillian been valid?* "I used my phone to take photos at the house last Friday, but I didn't take any pictures of the inside of the jewelry box. I was taking the photos to document the work we needed to do."

"They could prove helpful, though. They might show what's missing." The detective jotted a note in his notebook. "Anything else you can think of? Anything at all?"

As I looked up in thought, my eyes spotted the recipe box and cookbooks Colette had taken from the flip house and stashed in our glass-front cabinet. *Could a cookbook have left the imprint on Nelda's belly?* I turned to the detective. "Carl Dolan mentioned Lillian's prize-winning peach pie at the wake tonight. Lillian used to make it for their get-togethers, and from the way everyone talked, they all loved it. She'd told her sons she'd give them the recipe before she died, but she didn't get around to it. The recipe wasn't in her recipe box. I know because my roommate looked through the box." I pointed at the cabinet. "That's the box right there. Colette saw some other recipes in the box she was interested in, so she brought it home, along with those cookbooks. Do you think the recipe card could have been hidden between the pages of a cookbook? Maybe that's what was under Nelda."

Hiding the recipe in a cookbook would keep it within easy reach. Of course, the possibility presupposed that the recipe was written down. Maybe Mary Sue was right. Maybe Lillian Walsh had committed the recipe to memory and kept it only in her head. Clearly, Lillian had wanted to safeguard the recipe, and memorizing it would be a sure way to prevent it from being discovered.

Flynn stood and walked over to the cabinet, noting the titles of the cookbooks Colette had brought home with her. After donning a pair of latex gloves, he removed the recipe box and cookbooks, flipping carefully through them. There were no recipe cards stashed between the pages of the cookbooks. "Nothing here." He returned everything to the cabinet and pulled off the gloves, dropping them into our garbage can before turning back around. "Can you meet me at the house at nine o'clock tomorrow morning? I'd like to see if we can identify what's missing."

"Of course. Anything to help with the case." The sooner the matter was resolved, the better.

"By the way," he said, "the only fingerprints on the front doorknob were yours."

The import of his words struck me. "So before I arrived Saturday morning, someone had wiped the knob clean?"

He nodded. "Ditto for the key in the frog. There wasn't a print on it." In other words, the killer had used the key from the frog to access the house, lock it back up, or both.

I pointed out the obvious. "Someone covered their tracks."

"And covered them well," Flynn said. "I need to determine who that someone was."

My body buzzed and my mind whirled a mile a minute, like a well-oiled chainsaw. "Lillian hasn't been gone long. Is it possible someone targeted her house because they saw her obituary in the paper? Obituaries normally list the deceased's survivors. The fact that no husband was listed could have clued a potential burglar in to the fact that her house would be unoccupied. Or at least presumably so."

"That type of thing has happened before," Collin acknowledged. "Sometimes the survivors' homes are targeted during the service, when the thieves know they'll be out for a few hours." He exhaled sharply. "It takes an especially horrible person to prey on people who are grieving."

It also crossed my mind that if Nelda was killed by a random burglar, the burglar might have chosen the house because it had belonged to an elderly woman, who would be an easy target. The burglar might not have even known Lillian had passed away. He could have been someone who'd provided some type of service in her house—a plumber, an exterminator, the cable guy. He might have thought that if he waited a few months before returning to the house, he'd be less likely to be suspected of burglarizing it. I raised the possibility with Collin. "What do you think?"

"Wouldn't be the first time that type of thing has happened, either," he acknowledged. "Statistics show that most burglaries are committed by someone who lives within a two-mile radius of the home that was hit. Nelda could have walked in on a burglary in progress, have tried to save whatever she was holding when she fell. Or maybe the burglar dropped a weapon or tool, and Nelda inadvertently landed on it when she fell. The burglar might have later realized the weapon or tool was left behind, and returned to retrieve it. There are a couple of convicted burglars who live in the area near your house. I'm planning to pay them each a visit, see if they have an alibi for the night Nelda died."

Maybe one of them had been the culprit, up to old tricks. Maybe this case would be solved quickly. I could hope, right?

The detective dashed my hopes almost immediately.

"Of course, I've got other theories besides a botched burglary."

"You do? What are they?"

His mouth formed a tight line as he nodded. "Often, when a person is killed, the guilty party is someone who was close to them."

"Like a family member or friend?"

"Exactly."

*Yikes.* Nelda's family and friends were the very same people I'd just spent the evening with. They also lived on the circle where I'd be working for the next few weeks. The thought that I might unknowingly rub elbows with a killer caused an icy chill to creep up my spine.

"If the killer was someone who knew Nelda," Collin added, "it stands to reason that there would have been an incident recently, something that finally pushed the killer over the brink. Otherwise, why wouldn't the person have done away with her already?"

"What kind of incident are you talking about?"

"An argument. An insult. Some other type of slight, or maybe even a physical altercation. Anything that might have been a final straw." Collin raised his hand, his small finger crooked. "Hold up your pinky."

"Why?"

"Everything I've told you tonight is confidential. I don't want anyone to be tipped off that Nelda's death is now being investigated as a homicide. If they realize I'm running a murder investigation, they'll clam up, lawyer up, or both. I need you to pinky swear that you won't tell anyone the department considers the case a homicide."

"Is a pinky swear official police protocol?"

A grin tugged at his lips. "Yes. Violations are punishable by fifty years' hard labor."

"Hard labor doesn't scare me." I flexed my arm muscles. "Heck, every job I have involves hard labor."

"You wouldn't be able to bring Sawdust to prison with you." Detective Flynn sure was learning how to push my buttons.

"That would be a cruel and unusual punishment!" I cried. "Can I at least tell Buck? It wouldn't be right to keep this information from him. He'll be working at the house and will need to be extra cautious."

"Can he keep a secret?"

"He never told my aunt Nancy about the time he caught me raiding her cookie jar in the middle of the night." Of course he'd made me share the cookies with him, but that was a different matter.

"All right," Collin acquiesced. "If you vouch for him that's good enough for me."

I held up a crooked pinky. "I swear."

He curled his warm pinky around mine and gave it a little tug. "There. You are now bound to secrecy."

The ritual was simply his goofy way of letting me know the importance of discretion in this case. It would be wrong to read more into the gesture, right? Still, sitting here alone with him in my kitchen, the touch felt oddly intimate. It also felt oddly nice. Like Andy Walsh, I worked long hours, leaving me with little time for perusing the dating apps or hitting the singles bars. Maybe this investigation would provide me the opportunity to get to know Detective Collin Flynn better.

He released my finger and raised his steaming mug as if in salute. "Now I'm off the clock." He took a big sip. "*Mmm*. That hits the spot. You're quite the bartender."

"I can't take any credit," I said. "It's my roommate's recipe. She's a professional chef."

"It must be nice to have a roommate with skills," he

said. "The only thing Copernicus and Galileo are good at is shedding on my couch."

Copernicus and Galileo were Detective Flynn's cats. I'd seen photos of them tacked to the bulletin board in his office when he'd questioned me in another case. His pets weren't as cute as Sawdust—no cat ever would be—but they were darlings nonetheless.

My mind returned to the events earlier that evening: the short memorial service, the jovial wake. "You came to the memorial service to spy, didn't you?"

"Guilty as charged. Nobody seemed very upset. With Nelda's death being a surprise, you'd think it would have hit everyone harder."

"That thought crossed my mind, too. Nelda Dolan seems to be have been tolerated, but not liked." I told Collin about Carl's nonchalant demeanor in the hallway after the service, and repeated Becky's comment about the suffering her mother had caused. I'd heard there were five stages of grief—denial, anger, bargaining, depression, and acceptance. Carl seemed to have reached stage five, acceptance, in record time. Becky still seemed angry, though her anger was directed at her mother, not fate. I pointed this out to the detective.

"That's not unusual," he said. "People feel abandoned when someone they're close to dies. They often become angry at the deceased."

He could be right, but Becky's anger seemed to have originated prior to Nelda passing. Becky wasn't the only one who appeared angry at Nelda, either. "That neighbor I mentioned? She also said Nelda called her a hussy behind her back and accused Gayle of cheating at cards."

He arched a curious brow. "What's this neighbor's name?"

"Roxanne. I don't know her last name, but she lives in the circle." I bit my lip. "She has long fingernails." I left it at that, letting him draw his own conclusions.

His eyes narrowed ever so slightly. "What else did Roxanne tell you?"

"That the other ladies put up with Nelda to keep the peace, but they didn't consider her a real friend." I repeated what Gayle had said, too. *We're all friendly folks—at least now, anyways.*

He was quiet a moment as he appeared to absorb the information. After a moment pondering, he looked me in the eye. "Be careful when you're working at the house. Keep all the doors locked and your phone within reach at all times. Whoever killed Nelda Dolan seems to have gotten away with whatever they were after, or to have at least made a clean getaway, but if the killer thinks you might stumble upon a clue, they might decide to do away with you, too."

*There's a happy thought.*

"Better yet," he added, "install a security system."

"Good idea." Buck and I hadn't budgeted for a house alarm, but under the circumstances we'd bite the bullet. Luckily, prices had come down and many of the systems were easy to install. Some would even send alerts to your cell phone, and send photos or video if someone rang the bell or a door or window was breached.

"Speaking of spying," Flynn said, "I could use your help. This isn't my only case and I can't be everywhere all the time. If you could keep an eye on things in the neighborhood for me, let me know if you see anything suspicious or unusual, I'd appreciate it."

"You're deputizing me?"

"No, I'm asking you to be a mole."

Despite the fact that moles were cute little creatures,

being referred to as a rodent wasn't exactly flattering. "Let's call me a 'confidential informant.' That has a more exciting ring to it."

"Tomato, to-mah-to," he said. "But I'll call you whatever you want if you'll feed me information."

"You got it."

Flynn tossed back the rest of his cider and stood. "I better get going."

I walked him to the door. Sawdust trotted along with us. *Polite little pussycat.* "Goodnight, Detective."

"Goodnight, Whitney." He looked down. "Goodnight, Sawdust."

I locked the door behind him and wondered what the morning would have in store for us. *Will we figure out what Nelda had been lying on and who had—literally—stolen it out from under her?*

# CHAPTER 11
# I SPY

### WHITNEY

Wednesday morning, I pulled my SUV into the driveway of the flip house and pushed the button on the remote to raise the garage door. As before, it squeaked and squealed on its way up, loud enough to wake the dead. Rounding up the can of WD-40 from my toolbox, I slid out of my seat and walked into the garage, aiming the spray at the track. After slicking it down well, I returned to my car and pushed the button again. The door descended with hardly a sound. *At least I can cross one thing off my to-do list.*

Not wanting to venture inside alone, I waited in my car and sipped warm coffee from my extra-large thermos as I kept an eye on the neighborhood like a good mole would. There was nothing to see except the ceramic frog who watched me from the porch, unblinking, his extended tongue seeming to taunt me. *You thought you'd get rich flipping houses, but that's not gonna happen. Neener-neener!*

I was contemplating smashing the insolent frog with

a hammer when Detective Flynn's unmarked cruiser rolled into the cul-de-sac and pulled to the curb behind me. We exited our vehicles and met on the walkway.

"'Mornin'," he said.

"'Mornin'."

He followed me up to the porch. I unlocked the door and led him into the house, where I nudged the thermostat up a few degrees and pointed up the staircase. "The master bedroom is on the upper floor."

We climbed the steps, both of us treading lightly on the landing as if not wanting to disturb Nelda Dolan's ghost in case it was lurking about. At the top of the staircase, I turned right and led the detective into the bedroom.

I stopped next to the bed. The jewelry box remained where I'd last seen it, next to Lillian Walsh's shoes and dresses. I pointed. "The jewelry box is still there."

"Has it been moved?"

I tried to visualize how it had looked the last time I'd been in the room. "I can't say one way or the other. I didn't pay much attention. But the pictures can tell us."

I retrieved my cell phone from my purse and pulled up the photos I'd taken in the bedroom on Friday, holding the phone up so the detective and I could compare the items in the pictures to the current contents of the room. We leaned in to take a good look, our heads nearly touching. Up close like this, I could smell the crisp, clean scent of the soap and shaving cream he'd used earlier that morning. That meant he could probably smell the WD-40 I'd sprayed on the squeaky garage door. *Lovely.*

"Looks like the jewelry box is in the same position." Collin whipped a latex glove from a package in his jacket pocket and slid his hand into it. He carefully used the tip of one finger to open the box. "You said you didn't take a good look inside the other day, but give it a try anyway. Can you tell if anything is missing?"

I peeked inside. As expected, I was uncertain about this, too. Like before, the box seemed to contain a random assortment of colorful beads and baubles in a style that was now vintage but had been popular decades ago. My own grandmother had a similar collection of brooches, bracelets, and necklaces, most of which contained fake gemstones made of colored glass. "I'm sorry, Detective. I can't say whether anything is gone."

He took my words in stride. "That's okay. If the shape on Nelda's body was the corner of a box or some other sort of container, the killer would have probably taken the box or container with them even if what they were after was inside it. Criminals generally try to be quick. It would've taken time to open a box, remove an item, and put the box back under her." He pulled a penlight from his pocket and shined it on the box, leaning in to take a closer look. "I can tell this jewelry box hasn't been wiped clean. There's light smudges on the wood."

Given that the doorknob and key had been wiped clean, it seemed the killer would have wiped clean any other potentially incriminating item left behind, too.

Collin stood up straight and shrugged. "Still, it can't hurt to take it in and have the lab see if there's any questionable prints on it." With that, he carefully picked the box up in his gloved hand and slipped it into a plastic evidence bag. Turning his attention back to me, he said, "Let's take another look at your photos."

We scrolled slowly through the pics, our gazes moving between the screen and the room. It was like playing a modified game of I Spy.

"Everything seems to still be here," I said.

He dropped to his knees and used his flashlight to look under the bed. "Any chance you and Buck looked under here on Friday?"

"No," I replied. "Our focus was on the renovations."

He stretched his hand under the bed and pulled out a flat plastic storage box. He removed the top to reveal a spare set of sheets for the bed. He pushed the box back under the bed, put a hand on the spread, and levered himself to a stand. "What about the closet?"

"I didn't take any photos inside."

"But you did take a look?"

"Yes."

He stepped over and pulled the door open. "Anything noticeably different today?"

I stood in the doorway and stared into the space, willing myself to remember exactly what the closet had looked like on Friday. There were some books stacked haphazardly on an upper shelf, but were all the books that had been there on Friday still there? I couldn't say. "I don't know if anything is missing from this closet," I admitted, "but do you think Lillian could have had a valuable first edition? Dakota told me that Lillian and the other ladies had an informal book club. They've all lived on the circle for years, so I assume they've been meeting since way back when."

"It's something to consider," Collin acknowledged. "With all the books on her nightstand and in here, it looks like she was a bookworm." He stepped closer and ran his eyes over the titles, taking several down to consult their copyright pages. "Some of these are old and probably out of print. I have no idea if they're worth anything, though."

He returned the books to the shelf and we continued

on, going through the master bath. Nothing there had changed.

We moved on to the kitchen. He, too, noticed Lillian's blue ribbons on the fridge. Hard not to notice when there were so many of them. "Wow. Looks like Lillian Walsh knew her way around a baking pan."

"The neighbors miss Lillian's pie more than they miss Nelda."

"Makes sense. From what you've told me, Nelda was crustier." He gestured to my phone. "Got a photo that shows the cookbooks?"

I pulled one up and handed him the phone. He flicked his fingers against the screen to enlarge the image, and stepped over to the hutch to compare the titles on the books in the picture to the ones that remained. After running his gaze over the shelves, he said, "The only cookbooks missing are the ones your roommate took to your house."

Looked like we could dismiss the theory that the intruder had been after a recipe card hidden among the pages of a cookbook.

Collin swiped through several photos as his gaze traveled the countertop, starting at the fridge and making his way to the other end. "Nothing else seems to be missing."

I hadn't photographed the insides of cabinets or drawers, so we had nothing to compare the contents to. It was possible whatever Nelda had been holding as she lay on the landing had been kept in a cabinet or drawer.

The instant we stepped into the living room, my gaze landed on the glass-top coffee table. "Aha!" While the smudges and fingerprints remained, the wooden box containing the two decks of yellowed playing cards was gone. I pointed. "The playing cards. They were on that table before, but now they're not."

Collin looked down again at my phone and pulled up the photo showing the cards on the table. "They're face up in the box," he noted. "There's no way of telling if the backs were marked."

An uneasy feeling slithered into my stomach as I read between the lines. "Do you think Gayle might have actually cheated at poker, like Nelda claimed?"

"It's possible. Maybe Nelda came to get the cards, to give them a thorough once-over. Maybe Gayle came with her, and Nelda accused her of cheating again. Maybe the two got into an argument about it."

"That's the type of thing that might push someone over the edge."

"It could. Maybe Gayle took the cards to hide her guilt. Or maybe there was something valuable hidden under the playing cards. Maybe Lillian Walsh hid her prize-winning recipe cards among them. Or maybe she'd found Nelda's pendant and put it in the box to give to her the next time the ladies got together for poker."

"That's an awful lot of maybes." I supposed Gayle could have killed Nelda, but I had a hard time seeing Gayle as a cold-blooded killer. She'd seemed warm, down-to-earth, and composed. Then again, I was basing my impression on one evening's interactions. I hardly knew the woman.

"I deal in maybes," Collin said. "Sometimes I trade them for certainties. Sometimes maybe is the best I can get."

"It must be frustrating when you can't find solid answers."

"It is. That's when I go for a long run around Radnor Lake. Pounding the trail helps."

"I pound nails when I'm frustrated." Nothing relieved stress like repeatedly whacking a hammer, and you might even end up with a nice new bookcase or shoe rack when you were done.

"Which house does Gayle live in?" he asked.

"The green one."

"I'm going to send these photos to myself." Collin tapped my screen to share the photos with his device. "They might be needed later as evidence."

*My pics could become exhibits in a murder trial? Eek.*

We made our way downstairs, the bottom step creaking as we put our weight on it. Based on both my camera pics and the photos taken by the police-department crime-scene tech, nothing downstairs appeared changed. The stair creaked again on our way back up, as if to remind me it needed fixing. The squeaky wheel might get the grease, but for now, the creaky stair was getting nothing but on my nerves.

After looking through the main house, we went up to the attic. Unlike the rest of the house, which was heated, the attic had no vents and the air was cold. It felt as if we'd stepped into a refrigerator. The attic smelled musty and dusty, too, causing my nose to crinkle of its own accord.

Several cardboard boxes of varying sizes were scattered around the space. I had no way of helping the detective determine if something had been removed from one of them. Fingerprints in the dust indicated that each of them had been opened recently, most likely when Wayne and Andy were going through their mother's things and rounding up the valuables.

A photo album had been left open atop one of the boxes. The album was open to a page of faded photographs

with white borders around the edges. Though the ladies
of Songbird Circle no longer wore beehive and bouffant
hairstyles, there was no doubt the smiling faces in the
snapshots belonged to Lillian, Gayle, Mary Sue, and
Roxanne. Nelda Dolan appeared in many of the photos,
too, though she was almost always off to the side, the
odd woman out, and unsmiling.

I flipped a few pages and traveled forward in time
to the 1970s. While Mary Sue and Lillian wore their
hair long and straight then, Nelda had opted for a layered Peter Pan–style and Gayle had gone for a cute,
curly Afro. Roxanne's feathered blond hair rivaled that
of the famous Farrah Fawcett. A couple of pages later,
we entered the eighties, and the women's hair expanded
upward and outward once again, held in place, no doubt,
by cans of extra-hold hairspray. By the nineties, all of
the ladies but Roxanne had adopted the more conserva-
tive, less time-consuming hairstyles sported by women
who had shifted their focus from themselves to their
children and grandchildren. Not Roxanne, however. On
trend, she'd adopted the shaggy tresses à la Rachel and
Monica from the TV show *Friends*. In her next incarna-
tion, she'd ditched her bangs and flat-ironed her hair into
straight, shiny sheets. Finally, the photo album took us
into the current era, where Roxanne had opted for her
shorter, sophisticated style.

Several of the photos from more recent years de-
picted Lillian being awarded her blue ribbons at various
county fairs and events. In several of them, while Lillian held up her prize-winning pie, puffs, or tart, Mary
Sue stood by her side, smiling in support of her best
friend's success. My heart became soft and gooey, like
pie filling. Colette and I had shared many moments like
this, and we'd surely share more in the years to come.

It was nice to have a close friend to take life's wild ride with you. Lillian and Mary Sue had already discovered where life would take them. I could only wonder where life might take me and Colette, and where it might take Buck, too.

Given that Lillian seemed to have dedicated this particular album to photos of her friends rather than family, it was understandable why her sons had left it behind. Even so, Lillian must have valued her friendships to have taken so many photos and maintained the album through the years. It would be a shame to toss it out, wouldn't it? I decided I'd share the album with the others, see if the ladies might want the photos themselves. After getting the go-ahead from the detective, I picked it up and carried it downstairs with me, leaving it on the couch for now.

Our tour of the house complete, Collin and I returned to the garage, where I posed a possibility that had crossed my mind. "Could whatever had been under Nelda be something she brought with her from her own house? Or something Dakota had brought in with him after I snapped the pictures?"

"Possibly," Flynn said. "At this point, all theories remain viable."

"What are you going to do now?" I asked.

"I'll speak with Gayle Garner, see if she knows anything about the missing cards. I'll pay a visit to Roxanne, too."

"Roxanne? Why?"

"She's the one who mentioned to you that Nelda called Gayle a cheat. She might have brought the matter up to intentionally implicate Gayle, to throw everyone off and provide herself a cover. I'll speak to Mary Sue, too, to cover my bases. I need to find out if any of them spotted unusual activity in the neighborhood in the days prior to Nelda's death. If Nelda Dolan was killed by a random burglar, chances are the guy cased the neighborhood beforehand. Maybe he realized the house was unoccupied but still contained some property. Burglars often go door-to-door pretending to be salesmen so they can figure out who lives in a house, or they'll keep an eye out for advertising flyers in the doors. Flyers that stack up tell them nobody's home. Sometimes the burglars leave flyers themselves. Other times, they sit in their cars and watch everyone coming and going, or they cruise up and down the street multiple times throughout the day, trying to figure out everyone's schedules."

An involuntary shiver shook my body. The thought of some creep lurking about, spying on innocent people and planning to invade their homes, turned my blood to slush. "There was a flyer on the front door of the house Friday," I told him. "A door-hanger type made of heavy yellow card stock. My hands were full when I left, so I didn't remove it. It was gone when I arrived Saturday morning." The thought that my failure to remove the ad could have attracted a burglar to the house made me feel sick. Then again, the ad was gone when I arrived Saturday morning. If Dakota had removed it when he came in, an intruder would have been put on notice that the house was occupied.

"I'm going to have another talk with Dakota Walsh," Collin said. "He seemed like a harmless kid, and I was willing to believe he hadn't heard Nelda fall, despite being in the house. But knowing what I know now, that someone would have had to come into the house a second time to remove something from under Nelda's body, I'm less convinced. I'm also going to speak with Hitch-a-Ride, see if the driver who brought Dakota here noticed anything suspicious about him or the house. But first, I'll check in with Carl and Becky Dolan, see if they're aware of anything Nelda might have been carrying."

Like sawdust off a whirring blade, this investigation seemed to be going all over the place. *Ugh.* I realized Collin had a murder to investigate, but I had a house to renovate. I couldn't do it if the remaining furniture, boxes, and junk weren't removed. "What about the stuff in the house? Do Buck and I need to leave everything as is, or can we get rid of it?"

Much to my relied, he said, "You can clear out the house. Whatever was under Nelda is likely elsewhere, maybe even disposed of or destroyed. We don't have space in the department's evidence room to store a bunch of household items that are most likely irrelevant. It would be unreasonable to ask you to store it all. That said, if you come across anything suspicious while you're moving things out, let me know." A small smile played about his lips. "Let me know if you smell a peach pie baking, too."

"Will do."

Buck arrived as Flynn was leaving. He looked from Collin to me and his face fell into a frown. "Uh-oh. Something's up, isn't it?"

I motioned for Buck to follow me to my SUV. "We need to buy a security system for the house. I'll fill you in on the way."

"We didn't budget for a security system."

"I know, I know."

He sighed. "I'm beginning to regret going into business with you."

"Really?" I replied. "If I were you, my regret would have started way before now."

# CHAPTER 12

# BACKGROUND CHECK

### WHITNEY

While the detective headed next door to speak to Carl and Becky, Buck and I climbed into my car and set out for the home improvement store. By the time we'd selected a security system, paid for it, and driven back to the flip house, Collin was gone, leaving me to wonder what, if anything, he had learned from his visits to Carl, Becky, Roxanne, Gayle, and Mary Sue.

Buck and I spent the better part of Wednesday installing the security system at the house. He installed devices upstairs, while I did the same downstairs. If anyone opened a window or door, a sensor would activate and not only sound an audible alarm, but also send an alert to our phones. The motion detectors would let us know if any movement occurred inside the house, and the cameras mounted over the front door and in the main hallways upstairs and downstairs would record any activity inside. Although the system was both extensive and expensive, we could tout the high-tech feature when we put the house on the market. A potential buyer would appreciate the fact that the house came with a security system already in place.

After I installed the last of the devices on the laundry room window, I headed up the stairs, the bottom one giving off its usual creak. *Quit your complaining, stair. I'll get to you as soon as I can.*

Buck had finished, too, and met me on the landing. Using my phone, I set up online access, establishing a user ID and a password, *Sawdust123.* Now that access was established, we'd be able to view the camera feeds from our computers and phones. I texted the login information to Detective Flynn so that he could access the video stream on his devices, too.

Buck tucked his phone into his tool belt. "I'll rent a truck tomorrow so we can clear out the house. I'll check with Owen, too, and see if he can help us move all the junk out."

We were already several days behind schedule. I'd have been much happier if Wayne and Andy Walsh had emptied the house before putting it on the market. But at least Buck and I could deduct the cost of the rental truck as a business expense, and we'd get a tax deduction for donating the furniture and other belongings to the charity thrift store. After all, we'd bought them along with the house. They belonged to us now.

My cousin and I called it a day, activated the security system, and went our separate ways. With any luck, Detective Flynn would call me soon and tell me he'd found prints on the jewelry box and solved the case.

Temperatures dove into the teens Wednesday night, and Sawdust curled up under the bedspread with me, burrowing his way down to my belly. Since my roommates and I were trying to keep our bills manageable, we'd set the thermostat to only sixty-two degrees. The extra warmth my cat provided was more than welcome.

At half past six Thursday morning, my phone yanked me from my sleep when it played Dolly Parton's classic "9 to 5" at what sounded like ten thousand decibels in the quiet room. The song choice was intentionally ironic, because my job as a property manager meant I was on duty not just nine to five on weekdays, but twenty-four hours a day, seven days a week. Proving my point, the call was an emergency plea from a Home & Hearth tenant whose pipes had frozen and burst overnight. *Not exactly a fun way to start the day.*

Foregoing a shower and slipping into my coveralls and work boots, I raced over to the rental house and turned off the water. While I could handle minor plumbing repairs on my own, the size of the impromptu ice rink on the lawn told me this job was well above my pay grade. I called a plumber first and the property owner second. Not surprisingly, the owner was none too happy about the unexpected emergency plumbing bill.

Before the plumber left, he admonished the tenants to keep a faucet dripping anytime the temperatures dipped near freezing. "That'll prevent the pipes from freezing again."

The ice crisis dealt with, I climbed back into my car and dialed Detective Flynn. I might be a buttinski, but Nelda Dolan's death had taken place on my property. Besides, he'd dragged me into this case by asking me to serve as a mole. I had a right to know what he'd found out, right?

He answered on the fourth ring.

"Any luck?" I asked without preamble.

"There were no matches for any of the fingerprints

on the jewelry box," he said, "but I've got some new leads."

"You do? What are they?"

"The pinky swear applies to what I'm about to tell you. Got it?"

Though he couldn't see me, I instinctively raised my little finger in accord. "Got it."

He went on to tell me that Becky and Carl indicated they knew of nothing missing from their home. Neither had an inkling whether Nelda had taken something with her to the flip house, or what in the house she might have attempted to remove.

"Did they wonder why you were asking?"

"Yes," Collin said. "Everyone I spoke to was curious. I told them the medical examiner assumed Nelda must have been holding something since it appeared she made no attempt to grab the handrail. I fibbed and said that whatever it was must have been set aside by the first responders, that I was only following up in order to finalize my report and make sure any property was returned to its rightful owner."

"Did they buy it?"

"Hard to tell," the detective replied. "Carl, Becky, and Dakota seemed to accept my explanation, but there's no telling what was going on in their heads. Roxanne wasn't home when I went by. I left my card with a note asking her to call me, but I haven't heard from her yet. Bertram asked a lot of questions. He seemed to realize my explanation was flimsy. I asked all of them whether they'd been in the house recently. Gayle admitted she'd gone into the house on Friday and taken the box of playing cards. She said she'd given the cards to Lillian Walsh and her husband as a housewarming gift when they'd moved in decades ago, and that Lillian's son Andy had told her awhile back that she was welcome to them. She said with all the holiday hubbub, she'd forgotten about the cards until she and the other ladies talked about getting their poker games going again. She said Lillian had given her a key to the house many years back, and she used that to get in and retrieve the cards."

"Why wouldn't Gayle wait until I was at the house and ask me for the cards then?" After all, she'd trespassed on my property. Trespassing was a crime. A small one, maybe, but a crime nonetheless.

"She kept referring to the place as 'Lillian's house.' Seems to me she felt comfortable going inside because she's spent a lot of time there over the years and still thinks of the house as her friend's place."

While I could understand that old habits might be hard to break, I didn't much appreciate Dakota and Gayle traipsing all over my property without permission. Nelda, either, for that matter. I wondered if she might still be alive now if she'd stayed out of my house. Had the killer come for her? Or had the killer come for whatever had been in Nelda's hands?

"The interesting part," the detective continued, "is that Gayle claimed she went into the house for the cards on Friday morning."

"That can't be true," I said. "The cards were still there when Buck and I went through the place Friday afternoon. My photos prove it."

"Exactly," Flynn agreed. "Her timing was off. I noticed Bertram cut a glance her way when she said she'd gone to the house in the morning."

"So she lied. I wonder why."

"I wonder why, too."

"You didn't point out to her that she couldn't have taken the cards in the morning?"

"No," Flynn said. "I decided not to play my hand, to see if her lie might lead somewhere."

Seemed like a good strategy. If Gayle knew she'd been caught in a falsehood, she'd put up her guard, be more careful. On the other hand, if she'd thought she got away with the misrepresentation, she might build on it, dig herself in deeper, create a house of cards that could be easily brought down.

"She showed me the box of cards," he added. "The top was carved with a *W* for the last name Walsh. A small gift card was tacked inside the lid. It read 'Welcome to Songbird Circle' and was signed by both Gayle and Bertram. There were two decks of cards in the box, but they were facedown."

The cards had been face up in the box when I'd snapped my photo. "So you can't be sure they're the same cards, then, can you?"

"Unfortunately, no. They're old cards, but whether they're the same decks, who knows? I told Gayle I'd have to take the box and cards and return them to you because you were the legal owner of all property remaining in the house on the date you bought it. Of course that explanation was only a ruse so that I could check the box for Nelda's prints and look the cards over more carefully. The prints aren't back from the lab yet, but the decks don't appear to be marked."

Gayle could have exchanged the original decks for others, so the fact that the cards now in the box weren't marked didn't exonerate her. She could, in fact, be a cheat, as Nelda had claimed. Or she could have taken the box because she knew it contained something besides the playing cards, too. Given that Gayle had misled the detective about the time of her visit to the house, I was inclined to believe there might be some truth to Nelda's accusation. I'd be sure to keep a close eye on her at Friday night's poker game.

"What about Mary Sue?" I asked. "Had she noticed anything unusual going on the neighborhood? Anyone casing the houses?"

"She said she'd seen some solicitors coming around, but that it was typical for their area. She hadn't noticed anything that seemed out of the ordinary. I posed the same questions to the others. Nobody saw anything unusual. I told them there'd been an attempted break-in nearby, and that I was asking to see what I might find out for that separate case. I didn't let them know I was really asking because it pertained to the Dolan investigation."

"What about Dakota?" I asked.

"Dakota had nothing new to say. He stuck to his story that he didn't see Mrs. Dolan in the house until he found you hovering over her."

I finished for him. "And by then, whatever she'd been lying on was gone."

"For what it's worth, Dakota said he removed the advertisement from the doorknob when he arrived at the house."

I exhaled in relief, glad to know my failure to remove the ad had little, if anything, to do with Nelda's death. If Dakota was the killer, the fact that the ad had remained until he arrived had nothing to do with it. If the killer was a stranger seeking out vacant houses with an accumulation of advertisements, the fact that the ad had been removed on Dakota's arrival should have told the killer that someone could be in the house. Either way, my conscience could be clear. "Good to know."

"After I spoke with everyone, I ran criminal background checks on all of them. Everyone came back clean except one."

"Dakota?" I asked.

"No. Bertram Garner."

"Bertram? A criminal?" While I'd have been willing to believe the man-child had done something to get himself in trouble with the law, I found a hard time believing that the well-mannered man who'd hosted Nelda Dolan's wake had a criminal record.

"He was arrested for assault and battery."

"Really?" My mind spun in surprise. Like his wife, Bertram had seemed like a laid-back, affable guy. But I could be wrong. I could identify a dozen different wood varieties, but maybe I wasn't as good at reading people.

"The arrest took place decades ago, in the late sixties. Mr. Garner was just twenty-two at the time. Nothing was computerized back then, and there's only a minimum of information in the database on old crimes. I've had to request the file from archives. I won't have the details for a few more days."

"You only said he was arrested. Was he later convicted?"

"No. There's no conviction listed, but that doesn't necessarily mean he's innocent. Any number of things could have happened. He could have been acquitted, or let go on a technicality. Or the district attorney might have decided there wasn't enough evidence to pursue the case. I won't know until I have the records."

"So that's the lead you mentioned?"

"One of them. I called Hitch-a-Ride to get the name and address for the driver who dropped Dakota at the house Friday night. His name's Luis Bautista. He's a college kid who drives in the evenings for extra cash.

I swung by the guy's apartment last night and spoke to him in person. I didn't call first, wanted to catch him off guard."

In other words, the detective didn't want to give him time to concoct an alibi if he didn't already have one.

"How'd it go?" I asked.

"He seemed nervous and evasive. He couldn't give me any details about Dakota, couldn't even remotely describe him. He only had three riders Friday night, so you'd think he'd remember, but he claimed he doesn't pay much attention to his customers, that they climb into his backseat and off they go. He said he didn't notice anything unusual at the house where he'd dropped Dakota, but that he didn't really take a good look. He couldn't describe the house, either. Of course, he could be pretending not to remember anything because he thinks it'll make him look less guilty. He might think if he acknowledges that he noticed anything about Dakota or the house, it might show that he was scoping things out."

"How soon was his next ride after he dropped Dakota off? Did he have enough time to get in and out of the house before he picked up his next fare?"

"According to Hitch-a-Ride's records, he accepted another ride seven minutes after dropping Dakota off. But during those seven minutes, his car was parked right around the corner from your flip house."

"Meaning he had time to go into the house, run into Nelda, shove her down the stairs, and scurry off into the night."

"Right. He claims he'd parked nearby to save gas until another job came in. From the records Hitch-a-Ride gave me, it was clear that tends to be his typical method. Drop a rider off, then wait nearby until another ride request pops up in the area."

"Did their records show whether he'd returned to the house later?" If so, it could indicate he'd come back to snatch whatever had been trapped under Nelda's body.

"No such luck," Collin said. "He drove a couple more hours, then went off duty. The app doesn't track the driver's location when they aren't in service."

*Darn.* "Too bad you don't have a mind-reading device."

He sighed. "No kidding. I could use a dozen more hours in the day, too."

I knew the feeling. Seemed nearly every job I worked on took twice as long as expected, especially when it came to the work on my own flip houses. There were always unanticipated issues, unavoidable delays. "Does Bautista have a record?"

"No," Collin said. "Hitch-a-Ride won't hire anyone with a criminal history. They don't want the liability. But my gut tells me something about the driver isn't on the up and up. I'm going to follow up with other people who've ridden with him recently, see if any of them have been burglarized. It's possible the driver saw Dakota put the key back in the frog's mouth after he unlocked the door, and used it to enter the house himself to see what he could steal. Nelda might have caught him in the act and grabbed whatever he was trying to steal out of his hands before he shoved her down the stairs, or the item she was lying on could have been a weapon he'd brought inside with him."

The scenario was plausible, if coincidental. I was beginning to think I should not only change the locks immediately every time I bought a property, but that I should install security cameras immediately as well. "What about the two convicted burglars that live in the area? Anything pan out there?"

"One has a solid alibi. He was in jail Friday night. An officer caught him sneaking around another neighborhood, trying car doors."

"Up to his old tricks, huh? What about the other one?"

"He claims he was home alone from seven o'clock Friday night through noon on Saturday. I asked him if anyone could substantiate his claim, but he couldn't offer me any names."

In other words, burglar number two was still a potential person of interest.

We wrapped up the call, and I headed to the flip house. I was disappointed the detective hadn't solved the murder already, but I supposed it was unrealistic for me to expect an instant resolution. After all, there weren't a lot of clear-cut clues, and nobody had stepped forward to confess. Crime solving, like home renovation, takes time and patience. Alas, both seemed to be in short supply for us right now.

# CHAPTER 13

# MISSION: DEMOLITION

### WHITNEY

It was half past ten when I turned into Songbird Circle. Buck's van was at the curb of our flip house, while Owen's van sat in the driveway, a flatbed trailer hooked up to it. A large rental truck sat in the other side of the driveway. The back of the rental truck was open, the metal ramp in place, the bay ready to be filled. *Good. The guys are already here.* We had a long day of clearing and demolition ahead of us.

I noticed Bertram carrying his plastic recycling bin down his driveway. The morning was frosty, and he'd donned a heavy coat over his pajamas, his feet clad in fleece-lined slippers. Mosey moseyed along with him, rocking back and forth on his old, stiff legs. A glance around the circle told me everyone but Roxanne had put their bins out, too. Mary Sue's bin next door was so full of newspapers she'd had to put a red brick on top of them to keep them from blowing away. The brick matched the ones outlining her flower bed. It must be an extra one she hadn't used. I supposed I should check to see if the bin parked in the garage at the flip house contained any recyclables.

Forcing a smile, I raised a hand in greeting to Bertram as I drove past. He waved back with both hands and danced a little jig. *What a ham.* I wondered if he'd feel like dancing if Gayle was arrested, or if she'd want to dance if he was hauled off to the pokey. While some husbands or wives might be thrilled if their spouse was taken away indefinitely, Bertram and Gayle seemed to have a happy relationship, as far as I could tell from the limited time I'd spent with them. *Why had Gayle lied to the detective? What happened during the incident that led to Bertram's arrest for assault?* I wish I knew.

Another possibility crossed my mind at that point. Maybe Bertram had been the one to retrieve the cards. Maybe he'd run into Nelda in the house and pushed her down the stairs. Maybe the odd look he'd cut his wife was because she'd covered for him, provided him with an alibi. After all, he'd been arrested once for assault and she might have feared he'd be the first person the police would look to. But what reason would he have to murder Nelda? Would the fact that Nelda had called Gayle a cheat be enough cause to kill?

I looked over at Roxanne's house. A small white business card was stuck in the front doorjamb. It must be the one the detective had left. Had Roxanne missed it? Could be. After all, lots of people entered and exited their homes through the garage and rarely used their front doors. Then again, maybe she'd murdered Nelda, seen the detective's card, and realized he could be onto her. She might have hopped on a plane and fled to Canada or Mexico. If I were her, I'd have opted for Mexico this time of year. With temperatures in the twenties in Nashville, a warm beach sounded darn good at the moment.

Ironically, the detective's card remaining in Roxanne's door was just the type of clue burglars looked for when trying to determine if residents were away from their home.

After parking at the curb behind Buck's van, I used the remote to open the garage door and climbed out of my SUV, surreptitiously keeping an eye on Bertram. One could never be too careful, right? The recycling bin sat in the back corner of the garage alongside the garbage can. Just like the house, it was full of discarded items left for me to deal with. Magazines. Junk mail. Beer cans. I supposed I shouldn't be surprised.

The yellow advertisement for the tax-preparation service lay on top of the bin. As I picked it up, a small slip of paper sticking out from under a grocery store circular caught my eye. The top of the paper read FAST FUNDS PAWN SHOP. I finagled the pawn ticket out from under the circular. The ticket was dated one week prior and made out to Dakota Walsh, indicating he'd been advanced $150 for a "bird necklace." *Holy hammers!* My head went light, as if my skull had filled with helium. Had Dakota pawned Nelda Dolan's missing pendant? Had I discovered another lead?

In the words of Detective Flynn, *Maybe, maybe not.* As busy as the detective was, I didn't want to send him down a rabbit trail if there was no rabbit to be found. I decided that after Buck, Owen, and I finished cleaning out the house, I'd swing by the pawnshop, see what I could find out. I tucked the pawn ticket into the breast pocket of my coveralls and carried the recycling bin out to the curb.

Bertram waited on his front walk while Mosey sniffed around the front yard, seeking the perfect spot in which to relieve himself. As I looked their way, a thought entered my mind. *I can't be a confidential informant if I don't learn anything, can I?* Before I could think things through, my feet carried me across the cul-de-sac. "You've got some great moves, Bertram."

He chuckled and danced an encore performance of his jig. "Gotta stay warm out here somehow. Mosey's in no hurry to do his business."

His comment gave me an idea. "Evidently, I was in too much of a hurry this morning. I got pulled over for speeding on my drive over here."

He gave me an empathetic shake of the head. "That's a lousy way to start the day."

"For sure. But I suppose a ticket's better than getting arrested and going to jail." I eyed him closely as I prodded him with my next question. "I wonder what that's like."

A cloud seemed to pass over his face. Before he could answer, the recycling truck rumbled past the end of the circle on its way down the main street, its contents clinking and clanking, the brakes hissing. Mosey raised his snout and barked, a furry, four-footed David trying to scare off the enormous metal Goliath.

Bertram turned away. "I better round up Mosey before he goes after that truck and tries to sink his teeth into a tire."

*Darn.* I'd hoped the question would be a natural segue into Bertram's arrest. Looked like I'd remain in the dark for now. "Have a good day, Bertram!" I called as he shooed Mosey back up the porch.

He raised a hand. "Do the same."

I returned to the flip house, entering through the garage. I found my cousins in the laundry room, wrangling the rusty washing machine onto a dolly. Owen, who was a couple years younger than Buck, resembled his brother in nearly every way. He, too, was tall, blond, and blue-eyed. But rather than a full beard, Owen sported no facial hair, opting to forego current trends and remain clean-shaven. His daughters had complained that his beard was too tickly. He might not be the most stylish man, but he was a darn good daddy.

Buck glanced my way. "About time you got done, dimwit."

I ignored the epithet, realizing the purported insult was actually an odd term of endearment. *Men and their emotional immaturity. Sheesh.* "Pipes froze at a rental property."

When Nashville had its first freeze forecast weeks ago, I'd sent an e-mail reminding all the tenants to take precautions, such as detaching all garden hoses, opening cabinet doors so that heat could reach the pipes under the sinks, and leaving the faucets dripping. Evidently, the couple with the busted pipes had ignored my advice. But that was water under the bridge now—or should I say ice under the bridge?

Putting one hand on top of the washing machine to hold it in place, Owen tipped the dolly backward. "I'll roll this out to the truck."

As soon as he was out of earshot, I turned to Buck. "I just spoke to Detective Flynn. He's following up on some new leads."

"Let me guess," Buck said. "He thinks Carl Dolan killed his wife."

"That's still a possibility." Carl could indeed have killed Nelda. Often the police didn't have to look far for the culprit when a spouse ended up dead. Some people considered *'til death do us part* as a suggestion for how to quickly and efficiently end a marriage. It was cost-effective, too. A funeral was cheaper than a divorce.

Even so, Carl hadn't yet emerged as the prime suspect. "The detective's focus right now is on the driver from Hitch-a-Ride and the Garners."

Incredulity caused Buck's voice to raise an octave. "The Garners? Never would've guessed that. They seem like nice, normal folks."

"I thought so, too. Until I found out Gayle lied to Detective Flynn."

His mouth gaped. "Say what?"

I told him how Gayle had misrepresented when she'd come into the house to take the playing cards. "That's not all. Bertram has an arrest on his record for assault and battery."

"Boy howdy!" Buck said. "Guess I'm not a good judge of character."

"Collin doesn't have all the details," I explained. "He's waiting on the paperwork from archives. The assault took place back in the sixties."

"The sixties? Shoot. That's a long time ago. Bertram wouldn't've been much more than a kid back then."

"He was twenty-two."

"Like I said. Not much more than a kid. Kids do stupid things sometimes. I know I did. Remember those jeans I bought with the shiny silver studs on the back pockets? Paid over a hundred bucks for 'em. Thought I'd look like Keith Urban. Instead, I looked ridiculous."

Buck had a point, both about the jeans and Bertram Garner. Even if Bertram had assaulted someone, did a violent act committed by a young man mean that same man would commit murder decades later? Bertram had no arrests in the interim, nothing to indicate he was habitually violent. "Dakota might have some explaining to do, too. I just found a pawnshop ticket in the recycle bin. He pawned a necklace for a hundred and fifty dollars. It might have been one Nelda Dolan claimed to have lost here in the house. I'm going to swing by the pawnshop later to take a look."

"Shouldn't you just turn the ticket over to Flynn? Let him handle it?"

Again, Buck had a point. But besides the fact that the detective was busy, I had to admit that I enjoyed chasing down clues myself. It was like a game, or a treasure hunt. Besides, Collin had mentioned how busy he was. He could use the help. "I'll let Collin know if anything pans out. I don't want to waste his time if it's nothing." Glancing about, I turned my attention to the matter at hand. "Where should I start?"

Buck gestured to a stack of collapsed boxes and a heavy-duty tape dispenser leaning against the wall in the hallway. "Grab some boxes and tape, and pack up the kitchen."

I rounded up several boxes and the strapping tape, tucked them under my arm, and carried them upstairs. My cousins had removed Dakota's beer from the refrigerator and unplugged the appliance, packing the beer cans into a portable cooler and leaving the doors open on the fridge and freezer compartments while they defrosted. A *drip-drip-drip* sounded as drops of condensation formed and fell inside the freezer. I made a mental note to set aside a couple of Lillian's old bath towels so I could wipe out the appliance later. Mildew would grow inside if it was closed up with moisture remaining.

After expanding a box and taping the bottom, I opened a cabinet. *Uh-oh.* Many of the items in the cabinet were fragile and could break in transit if not wrapped properly. I stepped to the top of the stairs, trying not to think about the fact that this was the exact spot where Nelda Dolan had stood when her killer shoved her to her death. *Eek!* I called down to my cousin. "Hey, Buck! Did you get packing paper?"

"Dadgummit!" he hollered back. "I knew I was forgetting something."

Rounding up the photo album from the couch, I headed down the stairs. "No problem. Mary Sue's recycling bin next door is full of newspapers. If they haven't been picked up yet, I'll ask her if we can use them. Can't imagine she'd say no."

I walked outside, glad to see the recycling truck hadn't yet made it to Songbird Circle. I strode next door and knocked on Mary Sue's front door. She answered a moment later, dressed in a pink velour tracksuit and matching pink sneakers.

"Brr." She pulled the hood up over her head to keep warm. But for a lack of pointy ears, she looked like a human-sized bunny rabbit.

"Sorry to bother you," I said, "but could I take some newspaper from your recycling bin? We're packing up Lillian's things to donate to charity, and some of the items are breakable. My cousin remembered to get boxes when he rented the truck, but he forgot the packing paper."

"Getting rid of everything, are you?" A somber shadow darkened her face. "I suppose there's nothing left but junk. Wayne already took Lillian's silver and china and the nicer pieces of furniture."

"He left one important thing behind," I said.

She tilted her head, her gray eyes sparkling with anticipation. "He did?"

"I thought you and the other ladies should have it." I held out the album.

She glanced down the book, a slightly confused look on her face as she took it from me. But when she opened it up to the first page, she cried out in delight, a wide smile lighting up her face. "Oh, my goodness!" She turned a page, then another. "Look at us! We were so young then. Groovy, too, wouldn't you say?"

I returned her smile. "Super groovy."

"Thank you, Whitney." She closed the book and hugged it to her chest as if it were a valuable treasure. "Help yourself to all the newspaper you'd like."

"Thanks." I took a single step before turning back. "By the way, do you know if Roxanne's around?"

"Far as I know," Mary Sue said. "Why?"

No way could I tell her the detective had Roxanne in his sights and that she'd failed to respond to his request that she call him. Instead, I said, "I noticed her recycling bin wasn't at the curb. I thought maybe she'd gone on a trip or something."

"Not that I know of," Mary Sue said. "She usually tells us when she's going somewhere so we can keep an eye on her house. She might have just forgotten to put her bin out. Or maybe it's not full and she decided it could wait until next week."

Could be. After all, Roxanne lived alone and probably didn't fill her bin quickly. I was probably feeling distrustful for no reason. "Have a good day!" I called as I turned away again.

"You too!" Mary Sue called after me.

I went to her recycle bin, lifted the red brick, and rounded up several days' worth of newspapers. Just in time, too. The recycling truck turned into the circle, clinking and clanking and hissing some more. After placing the brick back in the bin, I carried the newspapers to the flip house. The frog smiled at me as I climbed the steps up to the porch. I decided to leave him where he was for now. He added a whimsical touch to the place. Besides, he might have some sentimental value for Dakota. I'd offer the frog to him, see if he wanted it as a memento of his grandmother.

I went back inside to tackle the packing. After placing the collectible food tins in a box and taking it out to my SUV, I wrapped up and boxed the remaining smaller items in the house, while my cousins continued to wrangle with the furniture and appliances. We took a late lunch break at one thirty, and by two o'clock the main part of the house was empty. All that was left was the stuff in the attic.

I climbed up the pull-down ladder, a rag in hand to wipe the dust off the boxes. A layer of dirt filtered the meager light coming through the octagonal window, and I yanked the chain to turn on the bare bulb hanging from the rafters. After taking a quick peek into each of the boxes to make sure there was nothing of value inside, I handed them to Owen, who stood at the top of the ladder, visible only from the chest up like some type of jack-in-the-box. He, in turn, handed the cartons down to Buck, who stacked them in the hallway for us to carry out to the truck once we'd emptied the attic.

At the back of the dusty space I found a box bearing the RAGS-2-RICHE$ logo. The box was taped closed. The label affixed to the outside indicated it contained forty-eight jars of the company's Starlight Silver Polish. Wayne Walsh must have stored the stuff up here at some point and forgotten about it. Or Lillian Walsh could have bought it to support her son. While I could lay claim to it, I had no use for that much of the stuff. Might as well return it to him. But first, I'd take a look inside, verify that the box indeed contained silver polish and wasn't instead a spare box repurposed to hold Lillian's housewares.

I pulled a box cutter from my pocket and used my thumb to extend the blade. After slicing through the tape holding the top closed, I pulled the flaps open. One peek inside told me that the box held only forty-seven bottles of silver polish, one of them apparently having been put to use. I retracted the blade, slid the cutter back into my pocket, and taped the box shut once again.

I passed the box to Owen. "Hang on to that one. It's inventory for Lillian's son's direct sales business."

"Okeydoke," he said. "I'll stick it in the pantry."

He disappeared from sight. With the attic now empty, I turned around and headed down the ladder, too, joining Buck in the upstairs hallway. When Owen returned from the kitchen, the three of us tackled the stack of boxes, carrying them out to the rental truck. After I activated the alarm system and locked the house up, I hopped into my SUV and followed the rental truck to a local charity thrift store.

The woman overseeing the donation drop-off dock directed us where to place the items in their warehouse and wrote me a receipt. I handed it to Buck, whose income exceeded mine. "You can claim the tax deduction, cuz."

He noted the blank space where the donor was to fill in the items' value and glanced back into the storage bay at the stuff we'd brought in. "I'd say that junk was worth about fifty grand, wouldn't you?"

"At least," I said, playing along. "But if you get audited by the IRS, I never knew you."

He folded the receipt in half and tucked it into his wallet.

I followed my cousins to the truck rental facility and, after Buck turned in the vehicle, drove him and Owen back to our flip house so they could round up their vans and head home.

"Thanks, Owen." I gave my younger cousin an affectionate pat on the back as he slid out of my car. "We owe you one."

He arched a hopeful brow. "Babysit Saturday night and we'll call it even."

"It's a deal." I loved Owen's three adorable daughters with all my heart and then some. Spending time with them was never a chore.

# CHAPTER 14

# HOT PROPERTY

## WHITNEY

Alone in my SUV now, I finagled the pawn ticket out of the pocket of my coveralls and typed the address of the shop into my GPS. The store was only two miles away, and I arrived at the pawnshop in a matter of minutes.

While I'd purchased an occasional used tool at a pawnshop, I'd never pawned any item myself. I wasn't sure whether the staff would provide me with any information given that the loan had not yet come due, but it was worth a shot. I headed up to the counter. A hulking man with a shaved head, a barbed-wire tattoo encircling his neck, and five silver hoops through his left ear sat on a stool behind the register. *He's not someone I'd want to come across in a dark alley.*

The man looked up and gave me a smile, the overhead fluorescent light glinting off a capped incisor that resembled a bullet casing. "Hello there. Can I help you with something?" His cordial, professional tone told me that perhaps I'd been too quick to judge this book by its cover.

"I hope so." I lay the ticket on the counter in front of him. "I'd like to take a look at this piece of jewelry."

He picked up the ticket and perused it before his gaze returned to my face. "Are you Dakota Walsh?"

"No," I admitted. I briefly toyed with the idea of inventing some type of ruse, but decided to go with the truth. I'd never been a good liar. "I recently bought Dakota's grandmother's house and I found this ticket in the recycle bin. A neighbor is missing a pendant and might have lost it in the house. I'm trying to figure out if Dakota pawned it."

The guy cocked his bald head, the light reflecting off his shiny forehead now. "Why don't you just ask him?"

"I'd rather get my ducks in a row first. I'd hate to wrongfully accuse him of stealing if he didn't do it. For all I know, this could be an entirely different piece of jewelry."

He rubbed his chin for a moment in thought. "All righty. Give me a sec." He stood and walked to a Dutch door behind him. The bottom half of the door was closed, but the top half was open. He held out the ticket and spoke to someone out of sight. "Can you pull this piece for me?"

The ticket disappeared, snatched by an unseen hand. The sounds of someone rummaging around in drawers came from the back room before whoever was working there handed a small manila envelope to the clerk. The clerk returned to the counter, spread a white velvet cloth atop it, and opened the clasp on the envelope, tipping the contents out onto the fabric. Using his index finger, he spread the gold chain. The clasp was broken. The pendant lay upside down, an amorphous blob when viewed from the backside. *Is it a peacock?* I couldn't tell. The man gingerly turned the pendant over. *Yep.*

It was in the shape of a peacock and embellished with small sapphires. I gasped. *It's Nelda's necklace. It has to be.*

"You okay?" the clerk asked.

"Yes," I managed. "I'm just . . ." *Surprised? Confused? Freaking out that this find means Dakota might have had a reason to kill Nelda Dolan? All of the above?* I went with, "I'm not sure where to go from here."

He reached under the counter and handed me a form. "If this necklace was stolen, the neighbor will need to file a written claim along with a copy of the police report. The owner of the shop will review the claim and respond within ten days. Either he'll return the property, or your neighbor will have to go to court for a judge's order if she wants it back."

I didn't bother telling him the neighbor who'd owned the necklace was no longer living, and could have died in an argument over this very piece of jewelry. Instead, I asked if I could take a photo of the necklace. "I assume this is the pendant that was missing, but I never actually saw it myself. Okay if I snap a picture to show the neighbor?"

The guy shrugged. "Suit yourself."

I pulled out my phone and snapped a photo of the pendant. Returning my phone to my purse, I thanked the man for his time. He, in turn, returned the necklace to the envelope.

"Can I interest you in something for yourself?" he asked. "A guitar, maybe? Television? Or how about a gun?" He raised a palm to indicate the case of handguns to his left. "We got a pretty little pearl-handled model that would be perfect for a lady such as yourself. You never know when you might need protection."

His words sounded like an eerie premonition. But

probably I was just feeling upset and anxious over finding Nelda's necklace. "Thanks," I said. "But I'm good."

"All righty." He resumed his seat on the stool. "You
change your mind, you know where to find us."

I returned to my car and promptly texted Detective
Flynn a photo of both the pawn ticket and the necklace.
*Found this pawn ticket in the recycle bin today. Went
by pawnshop. The necklace is a peacock pendant. Possibly Nelda's?* I added a photo of the tax-service advertisement, too. *This was also in the bin.* With a telltale
*whoosh*, the text and pictures set out through cyber-
space.

As long as I had my phone out, I figured I might as
well take care of another piece of business—my side
dish for tomorrow night's poker game at Mary Sue's
house. My usual frozen pizza rolls weren't likely to
be well received by the ladies of Songbird Circle, so
I texted Colette for ideas and ingredients. She replied
with a list that included various fruits, fresh spinach,
portabella mushrooms, and phyllo dough. I thanked her
with a kissy-face emoji.

I drove half a mile down the road and turned into the
parking lot of a small neighborhood grocery store. After
grabbing a buggy and plunking a case of Sawdust's favorite wet cat food into it, I rolled to the frozen-foods
section. Fortunately, Colette had not only put phyllo
dough on the list but also indicated where to find it in
the store, near the frozen pie crusts. I'd have been lost
otherwise. Squeezing past a woman with three young
children squabbling over which type of frozen waffles
to buy—*Blueberry, no question!*—I headed for the produce section.

As I wound my way through the displays searching
for clementines, a man standing at the bakery counter

caught my eye. His back was to me, so I couldn't see his face, but his dark gray hair, stout build, and broad but slightly stooped shoulders seemed familiar. *Is that Carl Dolan?* He spoke to the bakery attendant, an attractive sixty-something woman with dark hair and a friendly face as round as the cinnamon buns gracing the top shelf of the glass case separating her from the man. Her tightly tied white apron emphasized rather than hid her voluptuous figure. She threw her head back and laughed at something the man said, her audible amusement traveling over the croissants, muffins, and loaves of French bread, all the way to the lemons where I now stood. As I eased closer to determine whether the man was, in fact, Carl Dolan, the baker bent over to retrieve a dozen glazed donuts from the case and place them in a large pink box. She stood and set the box on top of the case. Her name tag was visible now. It read *Dulce*. The man reached for the box with both hands. No wedding ring encircled his left ring finger.

"See you soon, *Sugar*," the man said, causing the woman to erupt in fresh giggles.

She corrected him with a girlish grin, her voice tinged with a Spanish accent. "How many times do I have to tell you? Dulce means sweet, not sugar."

"Okay. Sweetie it is."

"Enjoy your *dulces*, Carl," she said with a seductive smile and an exotic roll of the *r. Carrrl*. It sounded as if she were purring his name.

The man put the box in his cart and turned to head to the front registers, providing me with a full-on view of his face now. If the name the woman had purred hadn't been enough to convince me, the face did. It was Carl Dolan, all right, looking cocky, confident, and carefree. Nothing about his countenance would even hint at the fact that his wife had died unexpectedly a mere five days earlier. The fact that he'd already removed his wedding ring spoke volumes, too. He appeared to have adjusted to his single status swiftly, smoothly, and seamlessly. He failed to notice me watching him, the satisfied smile on his face telling me his thoughts were elsewhere, possibly on the baker's cinnamon buns.

I glanced back at the bakery counter. Though the woman pretended to be cleaning the top of the glass case with a cloth, she surreptitiously watched Carl depart. The blush on her cheeks and the gleam in her eyes told me her interest in Carl went beyond the usual baker-customer relationship. For all I knew, the two had something going on.

Could Carl have been having an affair with this woman? Had he taken advantage of Nelda's visit to my flip house to put an end to his wife and make it look like an accident? Or had Carl and this woman simply engaged in some harmless flirtation, and my imagination was running away with me?

# CHAPTER 15

# *PURRPETRATOR*

## SAWDUST

Sawdust wasn't sure what Whitney was saying to him. He didn't recognize the words *Carl* or *Dakota* or *peacock* or *bakery*. He only knew that when Whitney was upset or worried, she often took him upon her lap, talked to him, and ran her hand repeatedly over his back in an effort to calm herself. He supposed he should feel used, but he wasn't about to complain when he was the beneficiary of her anxious moods. Besides, he loved Whitney. If he could help her in any way, he would, even if it was simply by lying in her lap and letting her stroke him.

He rolled over onto his back and mewed, requesting she scratch his chest now. She obliged and he thanked her with a quick swipe of his tongue. Closing his eyes, he cranked his motor. *Purrrrrrrrrr.*

# CHAPTER 16

# CATCHING UP

## WHITNEY

As I entered the Home & Hearth office Friday morning, Marvin and Wanda Hartley looked up from their side-by-side desks. Both were plump, gray-haired, and nearing retirement age, but with no definitive plans to call the real-estate game quits just yet. The two offered me identical greetings. "'Mornin', Whitney."

"Right back at ya," I replied cheerily as I plunked myself down in the chair at my desk. I filled them in on my pending tasks. "A tree service is scheduled to remove the dead oak at the Mossdale Drive property tomorrow, the roofer patched the leak on Bellshire Terrace yesterday, and three potential tenants are taking a look at the duplex in Five Points this afternoon. All have good credit."

Mr. Hartley gave me a thumbs-up. "Great job, as always, Whitney. Our clients will be pleased."

Mrs. Hartley stood and eased over to the coffee maker, refilling her mug and pouring another for me. She placed the steaming mug on the desk in front of me and I thanked her with a grateful smile. She cocked her head. "How are the renovations coming on your flip house?"

"Slowly but surely." I supposed the same could be said for the murder investigation. Then again, it had been a mere two and a half days since Detective Flynn informed me that Nelda's death had been reclassified from accident to homicide. But two and a half days feels like an eternity when there's a killer on the loose and you can't relax because you're surrounded by suspects. "Buck and I have the place cleared. We're planning to work on the demolition this weekend. The materials will be delivered tomorrow."

"I can't wait to see it when you're done."

"Me neither," Mr. Hartley concurred. "You and Buck have a knack for rehab."

"You two will be the first to get the grand tour once it's finished," I said. "After all, we couldn't have done this without your generous loan."

Mrs. Hartley issued a *pshaw*. "You bust your behind working for us. It's the least we could do."

Unfortunately, that behind I busted seemed to be growing exponentially. Colette and I had lived together only a matter of weeks, but having a professional chef for a roommate meant the refrigerator was always full of tempting treats. I could usually count on the physical labor of my carpentry and renovation work to keep me in shape, but it might not be enough any longer. I might have to start going for runs around Radnor Lake, like Detective Flynn. Then again, if I was being honest with myself, maybe I was just looking for excuses to run into him. He was easy on the eyes, after all, and his work was intriguing. He liked cats, too, which was a big plus. He didn't seem to be emasculated by my height or my

job, like some men were. I didn't know much else about
him, but I might be open to learning more, seeing where
things would go. But could there really be a future for
two people who'd met over a dead body? It wasn't exactly a meet-cute story. Besides, even if I might be interested in Detective Flynn on a personal level, I wasn't
sure whether he looked at me that way. I supposed time
would tell.

I spent the early part of the day on routine tasks,
leaving midafternoon to install a FOR SALE sign in the
yard of a new listing the Hartleys had landed. I showed
the duplex to the prospective tenants, two of which were
interested in the place. I told them I'd pass their applica-
tions on to the property owner and let them know the
decision as soon as possible.

As I headed back to my SUV, my phone chirped with
an incoming call from Collin. I tapped the screen to accept the call and put the phone to my ear. "Hello, Detective. Any developments?"

"A few. Why don't you come by my office and we'll
talk about them? I can return the playing cards to you."

I pulled my phone away to check the time. I had an
hour before I'd need to run home to grab the potluck
dishes for tonight's poker game. I returned the phone to
my ear. "I'll be there in fifteen minutes."

I jumped into my car and, shortly thereafter, pulled
into the parking lot of the police station. After checking
in at the front desk, I aimed for Collin's office. The door
was open. I rapped on the frame and he looked up from
behind his desk, waving me into the small, windowless
space and gesturing for me to take a seat in the blue vi-
nyl chair that faced him. Just like the last time I'd been
here, innumerable stacks of files threatened to cause
his desk to collapse. *Guess I shouldn't complain about*

*my workload, huh?* A half-eaten container of takeout Chinese food had been pushed aside, giving the room a savory aroma. His gray cat, Copernicus, and his black-and-white tuxedo, Galileo, seemed to eye me over his shoulder from their photos tacked on his bulletin board.

As soon as my ever-expanding bottom hit the chair, he caught me up. "Carl Dolan confirmed the peacock necklace you saw at the pawnshop was the one he'd given Nelda. I visited the shop and learned it wasn't the only piece of jewelry Dakota had pawned, either. He's got a long history with the store. He's pawned several items of women's jewelry over the last three years."

"Do you know where he got the jewelry?"

"No. I've been trying to get in touch with Dakota, but he's not answering his phone. I keep getting voice mail. I stopped by his parents' place, but they aren't sure where he is at the moment. They said he stayed with them from Saturday through Tuesday night, but the last couple of days he's been purportedly searching for a job and hanging with friends. They said it's not unusual for him to be out of touch for a few days at a time. They have no idea who his friends are, though. Never met most of them. All they could give me were vague nicknames. Skeeter. Banjo. Tubbers. He's lost touch with most of his high-school friends, and I'm not sure where he knows these guys from. I've checked with Dakota's last few employers to see if these guys might have been former coworkers, but the nicknames meant nothing to them. He's not on social media, so that was a dead end. Our tech guys tried to ping his phone but they couldn't get a reading. Either the battery is dead or he removed it so the phone couldn't be used to track him."

"So he could be making a run for it?"

The detective scrubbed a hand over his head and let

out a loud, frustrated breath. "Looks that way. I've sent out an alert. If any law enforcement happens to come across him, they'll keep him in custody until I've had a chance to interrogate him."

"What about the ad for the tax service? Did you look into that?"

"I did. The service is legit. The owner paid his own fifteen-year-old son to hang the ads on doors."

"Any chance the kid has a juvenile record?"

"Nope. He's squeaky clean. Plays trombone in his high-school band. He's on the chess team and honor roll, too."

In other words, the ad wasn't put in place by a would-be burglar. Still, it was possible a burglar had noted that the ad remained earlier in the day last Friday, and later ventured onto the porch when night fell, spotted the key in the frog's mouth, and decided to take a chance even though Dakota had since removed the ad.

"What about Roxanne?" I asked. "I noticed your business card was still wedged in her door the last time I looked. Any luck there?"

"None. Roxanne hasn't called, either. She's not answering either of her phones. I left a message on the answering machine for her landline. I couldn't leave a voice mail on her cell phone because her voice-mail box isn't set up. I don't know if she's avoiding my calls, or just missing them."

*Moving on, then.* "What about the driver from Hitch-a-Ride? Luis Bautista?"

"I've been in touch with a dozen of his recent fares. None of them have been burglarized or robbed, and none had anything suspicious happen after riding with him. The strange thing, though, is that several of them mentioned their driver wore his hair in a man bun. The driver I talked to had short hair."

"Could he have cut it recently?"

"Again, maybe. There's also the possibility he was wearing a beanie with a pom-pom on top and the riders mistook it for a man bun. It gets dark early this time of year, and there wouldn't be much light in the car. He picked up nearly all of his fares from nightclubs and bars, including Dakota. Some of the riders were with friends and they told me they were too busy having a good time to give the driver much attention. They all admitted they'd been drinking heavily, so they're not exactly the most reliable eyewitnesses."

None of what he'd said surprised me. In many cases, people treated ride-share services as their designated drivers. A smart choice. Much better than getting on the road and risking arrest or causing an accident, though I suspected the drivers had their patience tested by their inebriated riders. "What about social media?" I asked. "Does Bautista have any photos of himself on any of the sites?"

"Nothing on Facebook or Twitter that I could find. He only seems to be on Instagram. His profile pic is his bulldog sitting next to that Elvis statue in front of that souvenir shop on Broadway."

I knew the statute he was talking about. Tourists often stopped to have their photo taken with it. Heck, I had snapped a picture or two with the hunka burnin' love over the years myself. "What about his posts?"

"They're useless," Collin said. "He doesn't post often, and when he does it's usually a photo of his dog."

*He owns a dog and posts photos of him?* Sure didn't sound like a cold-blooded killer to me. Then again, maybe Bautista hadn't intended to kill Nelda and had only done it out of necessity when she caught him in the house. Maybe she'd threatened to turn him in to the police and he'd panicked, shoved her down the steps so he could get past her and escape. Maybe he hadn't even realized he'd killed her. After all, the fact that her death was a homicide hadn't been publicized. "Are you going to talk to him again?"

"My gut says something's up with him," Collin acknowledged, "but my brain says there's no pattern of criminal activity and my time would be better spent chasing other leads."

"Which organ are you going to listen to? Your gut or your brain?"

"It's still up for debate." He opened a drawer, reached in, and pulled out the box of playing cards with the *W* carved in the top. "Here's the box of cards." He slid it over the desktop to me. "The lab results came back. There were several sets of prints on the box, including Nelda's."

My spine went straight. "So she could have been holding the box when she fell?"

"Yes, or she could have simply touched the box the last time the ladies played poker. There's no way to tell for certain how old the fingerprints are."

*If only the kings, queens, jacks, and jokers could talk* . . . "Were Dakota's prints on the box?"

"No."

"So he didn't touch it."

"If he did, he wore gloves or used some other type of protection to avoid leaving prints. At any rate, it wasn't wiped clean like the key and the front doorknob."

"That means it might not have been the object that was removed from under Nelda Dolan's body."

"*Might* is the operative word there."

I didn't like *might*. It was as wishy-washy as *maybe*. I was more than ready for some definitive answers. While the detective had managed to keep the murder investigation under wraps for now, it seemed inevitable that it would come out at some point if he didn't solve it soon. It would be difficult enough to sell a house where a homicide had happened, but harder still to sell one when the killer was on the loose and could return to claim another victim. Plus, my mother would have a fit when she learned the death at my new flip house had been a murder. I hadn't mentioned it to her yet. She worried enough about me already. I didn't need to put her through more anxiety.

As I slipped the box of cards into my purse, Collin stood to escort me out. "Continue to keep an eye on things in the neighborhood. Ask the ladies at the poker party tonight if they've noticed anything unusual. If you see or hear anything of interest, let me know."

I stood, too. "I will. By the way, I ran into Carl Dolan at the grocery store today. He and the woman working the bakery counter seemed awfully friendly."

"Friendly?" He stopped in his steps. "How so?"

I told him how Carl made Dulce giggle, how he had called her "sugar" and "sweetie," and how he had removed his wedding band already, so soon after his wife's death.

"If Carl has been involved with another woman," the detective said, "it could explain why Nelda's death had so little effect on him. He might have already checked out of the marriage, been planning to leave his wife. It could also give him a reason for doing away with her." He closed his eyes for a brief moment, as if mentally filing the information. When he opened them, he gave me a pointed look. "It could also give this Dulce a reason for wanting Nelda out of the picture."

"But what would Dulce have taken out from under Nelda?"

"Could be lots of things," he said, raising a shoulder. "Maybe a secret cell phone that Nelda had come across in Carl's things that had Dulce's number on it. Or a framed photo of Carl and Dulce. A pink bakery box full of cookies with a love note in the bottom."

Viable suspects seemed to keep popping up, like rodents in a game of whack-a-mole. Unfortunately, they all seemed to be yanking their heads back before we could land any solid whacks and eliminate them. If only we could figure out what had been under Nelda, we'd be able to whittle down the list of suspects, maybe even down to a single person.

Collin walked me to the front doors of the station. "You're surrounded by persons of interest. Stay in touch and stay aware."

He didn't have to tell me twice.

# CHAPTER 17

# FULL HOUSE

## WHITNEY

I ran home to round up the side dishes Colette had so generously offered to prepare for me. She'd arranged a beautiful fresh fruit salad in a glass trifle bowl. The orange slices, strawberries, blackberries, kiwi, grapes, blueberries, and raspberries were layered like a delicious, colorful rainbow. She'd also prepared phyllo triangles stuffed with sautéed spinach and mushrooms and baked to a golden brown.

She covered the cookie tray containing the latter with foil. "Just two or three minutes in the oven at three fifty will warm them right up."

"Perfect. The ladies will love these." I gave my best friend a hug. "What would I do without you?"

"Starve," she teased. She also handed me a small ceramic crock. "Red beans and rice. You can take the girl out of New Orleans, but you can't take the New Orleans out of the girl."

Colette loved Cajun and creole foods. It just so happened that cooking these regional dishes was one of her specialties. I enjoyed them, too, though I could tolerate far less spice than she could. She often had to make a wimpy portion for me, leaving out all but a dash of hot sauce.

As I left, I gave Sawdust a peck on the head and a scratch under the chin. He mewed up at me, a lonely look in his eyes. "Sorry, little guy. I know I haven't been around much lately. I'll make it up to you tomorrow morning. We'll cuddle on the couch together and watch TV." Sawdust's favorite shows were *Deadliest Catch* and *Wicked Tuna*. Given that he ate his fair share of tuna, I think the programs gave him an unrealistic view of where cats fell on the food chain. Those fish were huge! But we all engage in some sort of self-delusion on occasion. For instance, I was currently deluding myself that I wasn't going to take a bath on the Walsh house. Instead, I was determined to remain optimistic that Buck and I would actually earn a profit, despite the house being the scene of a murder.

After loading the food into the back of my SUV, I retrieved an adjustable wrench from my toolbox and slid it into the outer pocket of my purse, where it would be within quick reach if needed. After all, as Collin had pointed out, the women I'd be playing poker with to-night were persons of interest in a murder investigation. One could never be too careful. Of course, the pepper spray was in my purse, too, but I figured we'd all be in close proximity at Mary Sue's house tonight and a noxious spray could backfire and disable me, too, if I used it.

Properly armed now, I headed for Songbird Circle. The night was already dark as I drove into the cul-de-sac, but the streetlights and coach lights mounted on either side of the Dolans' garage door provided enough illumination for me to see two shiny, brand-new cars parked on the right side of driveway. At the front was a metallic red Mazda Miata convertible with a black top. *Nice.* Behind it sat a Ford Mustang in bright orange, the signature color of the University of Tennessee Volunteers. *Fun!* While the price stickers remained affixed to the windows of both cars, the Mustang was the only vehicle of the two that sported a huge bow on top. The left side of the driveway sat empty, Carl evidently having ventured out in his white Chevy Impala.

I had little time to ponder the new vehicles before a "Yoo-hoo!" pulled my attention to Roxanne's front door, where she emerged wearing a stylish peacoat and carrying a covered pot, thick quilted oven mitts serving as gloves. I raised a hand in greeting and waited as she set the pot down on the park bench on her front porch, removed the oven mitts from her hands, and tucked them under her arm as she turned to lock her door. Before she inserted the key, she bent down and picked up Detective Flynn's business card, which had fallen to the floor in her front hallway. She quickly looked it over, shoved it into her coat pocket, and locked up. After slipping her hands back into the oven mitts, she grabbed her pot again and headed my way.

"Hi, Roxanne!" I called in greeting as she approached. "What's in the pot?"

"Italian white-bean soup," she said. "The perfect thing for a cold night like this."

"Sounds delicious." I angled my head to indicate the new cars in the Dolans' driveway. "Someone's done some car shopping."

She turned her head and took a gander. "My goodness! It looks like an auto showroom over there. Becky must've finally got her divorce settlement." Her smile faltered. "I hope she didn't go crazy and blow all the money at once. After all these months of being forced to scrimp, it would certainly be tempting."

Another voice rang out in the cold night as Gayle ventured out of her house, too. "Hey, girls!"

Roxanne and I waited for her to catch up. She ambled toward us with a lilting gait. *Funny, I didn't notice her limping the night of Nelda's memorial service.*

When she reached us, she held up her hands. In one she held a glass jar of garlic-stuffed olives. In the other she held a jar of sweet pickles. "I asked Bertram to pick up something ready-made at the grocery store for me to bring to the poker game, and this is what he came home with. I suppose I should've been more specific. Men, huh? You can't live with 'em, you can't trust 'em to run your errands for you." She shook her head but smiled at the same time, letting us know she forgave her husband's ignorance.

Her hands full with the soup pot, Roxanne dipped her head to indicate Gayle's leg. "Your knee acting up again?"

"Something fierce!" Gayle grimaced. "That's why I couldn't cook. I couldn't bear to stand up long enough to make anything. My doctor gave me some new pain meds. Problem is, they throw me for a loop. I can't tell up from down or left from right. I took a pill a few minutes ago. Y'all might have to roll me home later in Mary Sue's wheelbarrow."

We joined forces and headed up the walk to Mary Sue's porch. With everyone's arms full of food, I turned and used my elbow to press the doorbell. *Ding-dong* rang out inside. Mary Sue opened the door and offered us a big smile and some help. "Welcome, ladies! Goodness, you're loaded down. Let me take something off your hands."

Gayle shoved the jars in Mary Sue's direction. "Take these. I've got to get off this knee before I accidentally say a word or two I shouldn't."

Mary Sue took the jars of olives and pickles and gave her friend a sympathetic look. "Your bad knee giving you trouble again?"

"Sure is," Gayle said. "Woke up Wednesday morning feeling like someone had taken a sledgehammer to it."

The very thought made me cringe. I'd hit my thumb with a hammer before, and it was pure agony. I could hardly imagine that pain multiplied several times over.

Roxanne jerked her head to indicate the Dolans' driveway. "Take a look at the new cars over there."

While Gayle ambled into the house, Mary Sue stepped out onto the porch, shielding her eyes from the porch light to get a better look. "Wow! Those cars are beauts. I'm glad to see Becky treating herself and her girls. She certainly deserves it after all she's been through."

Roxanne was less approving. "I just hope she hasn't been hasty."

We entered the house, greeted a second time by the enticing aroma of cornbread baking. We made our way to the kitchen, where Gayle had already taken a seat on one of the six padded chairs and propped a leg up on another. Roxanne set her large pot down on top of the stove and removed the oven mitts. Her long, pointy nails were freshly manicured, the plum polish she'd worn to the memorial replaced by a dark red, high-gloss variety.

While Roxanne arranged the food and Mary Sue poured glasses of punch for everyone, I stepped over to the oven to reheat the hors d'oeuvres Colette had made.

"My cornbread needs just a minute or two," Mary Sue said. "Feel free to pop your tray in there alongside it."

I did just that, noticing that the top of the cornbread in her cast-iron skillet had just begun to brown.

The doorbell rang again and Mary Sue hurried to the front door, opening it to reveal Becky on the stoop with a platter of brownies covered in cellophane in her hands. Mary Sue took one look and said, "My, don't those look delicious!"

I had to agree. I also had to admit I was relieved. If one of the ladies had produced a peach pie for tonight's poker party, I'd have been concerned. But it seemed clear now that whatever had been trapped under Nelda's body as she lay on the landing had nothing to do with the peach-pie recipe.

Becky raised her platter. "These brownies aren't as good as Lillian's peach pie," she conceded, "but I did include my own special ingredient."

"Love?" Mary Sue asked.

"Liquor." Becky grinned. "Amaretto, to be precise. It makes them fudgy and gives them a nice hint of almond."

"Yum!" I said. "I can't wait to try one."

Before closing the door, Mary Sue took another glance across the street. "We couldn't help but notice the new cars in your driveway."

Becky beamed. "Sporty, aren't they? The convertible's mine. After driving that ugly old station wagon for twenty-five years, I figured I deserved to treat myself. I'm surprising the twins with the Mustang next time they come home from college."

"They'll be thrilled." Mary Sue relieved her guest of the dessert and gave her a soft smile. "We assume your divorce finally got settled?"

Becky grunted. "I wish. My spiteful soon-to-be ex-husband is still dragging things out. It's ridiculous. The two of us hardly had two nickels to rub together in the first place. Guess he'd rather give the money to the attorneys than to me."

"I'm sorry," Mary Sue said. "But we're happy for you, no matter where you got the money for the cars."

Becky removed her coat and cleared up the mystery. "It came from the life insurance on Mom."

Mary Sue cocked her head in question. "Those fixed-rate policies we bought from Andy Walsh all those years ago? When he first went into the insurance business?"

"That's right," Becky said. "Dad had bought a two-hundred-thousand-dollar policy on Mom and took out another on himself. He made me an equal beneficiary under both policies. Andy took care of the claim for us, made sure we got our check right away."

I'd almost forgotten about the forms Carl and Andy had discussed at the wake. They must have been referencing the claim forms for Nelda's life-insurance policy.

"I'm glad they didn't keep you waiting," Mary Sue said. "You hear horror stories about big insurance companies delaying payments for weeks, if not months." She lowered her voice to just above a whisper. "I hate that Nelda had to go, especially in an unexpected accident, but it's also awful to think that if she'd fallen just a few weeks later, you and your father wouldn't have received a single dime."

Becky's brow furrowed. "Why not?"

"You didn't know?" Mary Sue said. "Those policies

expire automatically once the insured turns seventy-five. Mine lapsed a couple of years ago."

"Mine, too," Gayle chimed in.

"Ditto," Roxanne said. "Nelda was the baby of our bunch."

An odd look flickered across Becky's face. Was she bewildered by the coincidence? Or could her strange expression be a combination of anxiety and guilt? Had she already known that the policy was about to expire? I took an involuntary step backward as a terrifying thought struck me. *Becky might have killed her mother for the insurance proceeds.* She might have thought nobody would put two and two together, and she could be worried now that she'd become a suspect given the fortuitous timing of her mother's death. Heck, for all I knew Becky and Carl conspired to kill Nelda. They both stood to benefit from her death. Due to her pending divorce, Becky had been having money troubles. Maybe doing away with her mother had seemed like an easy solution to her financial woes. Carl might have done away with his wife so he could pursue a relationship with Dulce. Maybe Becky and Carl had followed Nelda over to the flip house and one of them had stuck out a foot at the top of the stairs to trip Nelda while the other gave her a push.

*Bzzzzzzz.* Before I could give the theory any more thought, the oven timer went off, letting us know Mary Sue's cornbread was done. *The phyllo squares should be nice and warm, too.*

As I pulled the oven open, Mary Sue turned our attention to more enjoyable matters. "Those appetizers smell absolutely delicious!"

I placed the cookie tray atop the stove. "I can't take

any credit. My roommate made them. The red beans and rice and the fruit salad, too. I'm handy with a hammer, but kitchen tools confound me."

Mary Sue gestured into the oven. "Would you mind grabbing the cornbread while you've got the oven open? That pan weighs nearly ten pounds. I just about break my wrist every time I lift it, but it bakes the cornbread perfectly."

I pulled the cast-iron skillet from the oven, too, setting it atop a trivet. The motion gave my wrist and forearm a real workout. A kettle bell had nothing on this pan.

We piled our plates with food. Mary Sue fixed a plate for Gayle so she wouldn't have to stand on her hurt knee. We took seats around the kitchen table and dug in. For the second time that week, I found myself feasting with friendly folks. While their delicious food went down easily, the fact that one of them might be a murderer was becoming much harder to swallow.

Roxanne reached down, retrieved a small bottle of Jack Daniel's whiskey from her purse, and spiked her punch with a generous dash of the brown liquid. She held up the bottle and tilted it playfully side to side. "I brought my friend Jack along. Any takers?"

Gayle declined. "Wish I could, but I'm not supposed to drink on these painkillers."

The rest of the ladies lifted their glasses and held them out so Roxanne could add a shot or two to their drinks. I declined. With a murderer potentially in our midst, I wanted to keep my wits about me. Besides, while these ladies only had to walk across a circle later to get home, I'd have to drive across town. I wasn't about to take a chance on safety.

When Roxanne pulled the bottle back, Becky wagged

her finger for a triple shot. "Keep it coming, Roxy. It's been a heck of a week."

We spent the next few minutes chatting amiably as we polished off our food and sipped our punch.

I managed to slip in the question Collin had told me to ask, performing my job as a mole to the best of my abilities. "Any of y'all notice anything unusual around the neighborhood lately?"

"Like what?" Mary Sue asked.

I raised my shoulders. "I don't know. Strangers coming around, maybe an odd car cruising by."

"Not me," Gayle said. "Why?"

*Why, indeed?* Fortunately, my mind coughed up a quick response. "Construction sites sometimes attract thieves," I said. "People looking for tools or materials to steal. I want to make sure our flip house doesn't become a target for criminals."

"The only thing I've noticed," Roxanne said, lifting her glass, "is that my drink is empty."

*Hmm.* Was she trying to change the subject away from crime?

She rose from the table and headed to the glass pitcher of fruit punch on the counter. After filling her glass, she said, "Might as well put on some party music while I'm up." She eased past us into the living room, where she rifled through record albums lined up on a shelf next to a record player. She pulled one of the albums out and removed it from its sleeve. "Johnny Cash's greatest hits. Now we're talking." She loaded the album onto the record player, set the needle, and raised her glass over her head, performing a sassy sashay back to the kitchen.

Mary Sue turned to me. "Roxanne's husband was

a session musician. He played with a bunch of the top country-western stars back in the day."

"Sure did," Roxanne said. "That man played a mean bass guitar. Played the dulcimer and the mandolin, too. Instead of bringing me flowers after we'd bicker, he'd serenade me."

Mary Sue cut her friend a knowing grin before turning to me. "In other words, he played Roxanne, too."

Roxanne hooted and lifted a glass in her late husband's honor. "Did he ever!"

Hoping the liquor might have loosened their lips, I decided to see if they might be willing to spill the beans about Bertram's long-ago arrest. Roxanne had provided the perfect segue. "I heard Johnny Cash got arrested a couple of times, spent some time in prison."

"Prison? No," Roxanne said. "He played music in prisons, even recorded an album in Folsom Prison out in California. But he never did any time. He got arrested twice back in the midsixties, though. Once was in El Paso, something to do with drugs he'd brought up from Mexico. The pills were prescription medicine rather than illegal drugs, so his sentence was suspended. He got arrested another time in Starkville, Mississippi, for public intoxication and trespassing, some silly business about him wandering onto private property to pick flowers."

I sipped my drink and did my best to sound nonchalant. "The sixties sound like a wild time. What about y'all? Any of you ever get arrested? Your husbands, maybe?"

Gayle eyed me, her gaze narrowed. *Uh-oh. Had I been too obvious?*

Roxanne hooted again. "I had a run-in or two with

the law. Some bar owners don't take too kindly to women dancing on the tables. But I always managed to sweet-talk my way out of trouble."

Gayle offered nothing, but rather than push the issue further and risk raising suspicion, I let the matter drop. Detective Flynn should find out soon enough why Bertram Garner had been arrested all those years ago. I stood. "Can I take anyone's plate?"

Becky and I cleared the table together, rinsing the dishes and putting them into Mary Sue's dishwasher. A quarter of the cornbread remained, so I covered the cast-iron skillet with aluminum foil. Becky removed the plastic wrap from the platter of brownies and placed it on the table along with a stack of fresh napkins. Everyone grabbed a treat and retrieved bags of spare change from their purses, stacking the coins in front of them like poker chips.

Mary Sue stood. "Guess I better round up some cards. Can't very well play poker without them, can we?"

"No need." I reached into my purse, pulled out the box of playing cards Collin had given me, and placed it in the center of the table.

Gayle looked down at the *W* engraved on the lid of the box before turning her gaze on me. Her face was tight, her eyes narrowed even more than before. "Detective Flynn gave those cards to you?"

"Yes," I replied. "He returned them today. He told me you retrieved them from the house. If I'd realized he'd planned to confiscate them from you, I would've told him it was unnecessary. They've got sentimental value for you ladies. You should have them, Gayle. Take them home with you tonight after we play."

Gayle's features relaxed. "That's mighty kind of you,

Whitney. We girls have had a lot of good times with these cards over the years."

Curious whether Gayle had a key to Lillian's house and who else might have one, I asked, "I didn't accidentally leave the house unlocked last Friday, did I? Please tell me that I wasn't so careless."

"No," Gayle said. "You weren't careless. All the ladies on the block exchanged keys decades ago, for emergencies and whatnot."

"Not all the ladies," Becky clarified. "Nobody exchanged keys with my mother. It was a sore spot with her. She felt like nobody trusted her. Of course she had nobody to blame for that but herself. She could be awfully nosy."

Gayle, Mary Sue, and Roxanne exchanged glances, their looks saying Becky had hit the nail on the head, though none of them wanted to say it out loud.

Turning everyone's attention to our pending game, Gayle became all business as she selected a deck of cards from the box and glanced around the table. "Jokers wild."

Gayle expertly shuffled the cards four times, the deck giving off a *rat-a-tat-tat* sound before she formed a perfectly arched bridge and let the cards fall into place. Despite being good with my hands, I'd never learned to properly shuffle a deck like that. After holding the deck out so Becky could cut it, Gayle dealt us each a hand.

I had a pair of threes, but that was it. I glanced around the table, trying to read the other ladies' expressions, guess what they might be holding. A soft scowl pursed Mary Sue's lips. Roxanne had sucked in an anxious lip. Becky's lips were curled up in a smile, but her eyes were dull. *She's faking.* Gayle scratched at her cheek, as if trying to hide a grin. *She's got a good hand, doesn't she?*

We played our first hand. Gayle won, bluffing until everyone else had folded, sacrificing their antes. She held up her cards. A two of clubs. A six of spades. A seven of hearts. A queen of diamonds. And a king of hearts. "Fooled you, girls! I got squat!"

"Wow," I mused. "You've got the best poker face I've ever seen."

Gayle scooped the coins toward herself. "That's why I win so often. I'm good at fooling people."

*Good at fooling people.* Was she fooling the detective about her involvement in Nelda Dolan's murder, pretending to be innocent when she was actually the one who'd sent her former neighbor tumbling down a flight of stairs?

Gayle handed the deck to Mary Sue, who dealt the next hand. Mine included two nines, the three of hearts, the eight of spades, and a joker. With the joker as a wild card, I had three of a kind. *What a great hand!* As my mouth tried to spread in a smile, I pressed my lips together to hold them in place.

Mary Sue arranged the cards in her hand and exchanged three of them for new cards. "I'm confused. How did the detective end up with Lillian's playing cards?"

"He came to see us," Gayle said. "He wanted to know if Bertram or I had taken anything from Lillian's house."

*My* house, I thought, but said nothing. Gayle didn't mean anything by the reference. *Lillian's house* was how she'd referred to the place for decades. Old habits were hard to break.

"Why?" Mary Sue asked Gayle. "Has something gone missing?"

*Yes! Something went missing right from under Nelda's dead body!* My face flamed, hot and red, threatening to betray me and the secret I held. I ducked my chin and stared at my cards with forced focus. The joker stared back at me with an evil grin that said, *You really need to work on your poker face. You make a lousy confidential informant.*

Gayle dealt Roxanne two new cards before taking three for herself. "He didn't specify anything in particular that might be missing. He just said it seemed strange that Nelda hadn't reached for the handrail when she fell. He thought she might have had something in her hands, and that's why she didn't grab it."

Becky took only one card. She must have a good hand, too. "The detective came to talk to me and Dad again, too. He asked if Mom had taken anything with her to the house when she went to tell Dakota the house had sold."

Roxanne frowned, her fingernails sticking up like bloody daggers as she held her hand. "He left his business card at my house. He'd written a note on it, telling me to call him. I haven't had a chance yet. I had to run down to Shelbyville Wednesday afternoon and help my daughter with the grandkids. All three of them came down with some type of twenty-four-hour stomach bug, one after the other. I only found the card when I was heading over here."

Mary Sue peered over her cards, both her silvery hair and eyeglasses glinting in the overhead light as she sought additional illumination. "He talked to me, too, but I didn't have anything to tell him. If Nelda was carrying something, shouldn't it have been obvious? Seems it would've fallen onto the stairs or landing, or rolled down the lower steps to the downstairs hallway."

She turned to me. "Did you see anything lying about when you found her?"

When all other heads turned my way, too, my already flaming face threatened to explode. I shook my head. "No, but I was totally freaked out. I'd just found Nelda, and then Dakota popped up downstairs. I had no idea who he was or why he was in the house. I didn't even think to look around on the floor. I called nine-one-one, and next thing I knew, paramedics and police officers were swarming everywhere."

Gayle issued an affirmative *mm-hmm*. "That's what the detective told us, too. He said that if Nelda had been carrying something, one of the first responders could have set it aside or kicked it away on accident."

Becky reached for her glass of spiked punch. "What would it matter if Mom had been carrying something? Either way, she tripped and fell."

All heads turned my way again. Some cocked in question. Brows rose on others.

Before I could bite back my words, I blurted, "Why are you all looking at me?"

Roxanne pointed an accusing finger at me. "Because you're red as a beet. You know something, don't you? You know why that detective is still poking around."

The joker was right. *Darn my lousy poker face!* "No!" I insisted. "It's just that I have a really good hand."

They stared at me for a few more seconds as if trying to assess my response.

Finally, Gayle harrumphed and turned to her friends. "Think she's bluffing?"

"About her hand?" Roxanne asked. "Or about whether she has the inside scoop on the investigation?"

"Either," Gayle said.

Mary Sue raised her shoulders. "Who knows?"

Gayle eyed me closely and let out a long, slow breath before her lips curled up in a cheeky smirk. "I think she's bluffing about her hand. I bet I've got her beat."

I gave her my best cheeky smirk right back. "Don't be so sure, lady."

"Woo-hoo!" Roxanne crowed. "This game is getting interesting. Someone's finally giving Gayle a run for her money."

Mary Sue folded right away. Becky bet fifty cents. I raised a quarter. Roxanne raised another ten cents. Gayle raised another nickel. The time came for us to lay our cards on the table.

"Three nines." I placed the cards face up in front of me and reached for the pot. Surely nobody could beat that hand.

Gayle wagged her finger at me. "Not so quick, hon." She laid her cards on the table. *Four tens.*

"Well, darn." I slumped in my seat. "I was sure I'd won."

She chuckled. "Don't fret. There'll be lots of time for you to win your money back."

Roxanne snorted jovially. "Or to lose more of it."

As Gayle scooped up the coins, I noticed her movements had become clumsy, her eyes glassy.

Mary Sue dealt the next hand and, between us exchanging our cards and placing bets, steered us back to our earlier topic of conversation, looking my way. "Speaking of that handrail, we all knew it was loose. That's probably why Nelda didn't bother grabbing it. At any rate, I'm glad you'll be able to fix the place up, Whitney, get it back in shipshape. Lillian had always taken pride in her house. Shame that she couldn't afford to keep it up these last few years."

Roxanne scoffed. "We all know why that was. That sorry son of hers bled her dry."

Given that Andy Walsh appeared to be gainfully employed selling insurance while Wayne was fixated on get-rich-quick schemes, I assumed Roxanne was referring to the latter. "Wayne, you mean?"

"That's the one," Roxanne confirmed. "He borrowed thousands of dollars from Lillian over the years. Never paid a single cent of it back, far as I know."

Mary Sue's words affirmed her reputation as the group's pacifist. "We can't blame Lillian for wanting to help Wayne out. After all, a mother's love knows no bounds."

Roxanne tsked. "It wasn't good for either of them, her always bailing him out and enabling him to jump into one risky business venture after another. Dakota's turning out just like his father. Another deadbeat who can't hold a job." Roxanne's gossip seemed particularly mean-spirited and relentless tonight, probably spurred on by the whiskey.

"I hate to say it," Becky said, saying it anyway, "but I don't like that boy spending time with my girls. Dahlia's got a good head on her shoulders, but Dakota keeps telling Daisy she'll be the next Taylor Swift. If he fills her head with such notions, she might do something stupid like drop out of school." She fished another brownie off the platter. "Mom never liked Dakota, either. He was the only thing she and I ever agreed on. Of course I'd be tickled to death if Daisy's dreams come true. I just think it's smart to have a backup plan, you know?"

We murmured in agreement.

Roxanne won the next hand, raking in a whopping dollar and thirty cents. As she scooped the coins up, the nail on her right index finger popped off and landed on the table. "I'm falling apart here." She picked up the artificial nail and turned to Mary Sue. "Got any heavy-duty glue?"

Mary Sue pushed back from the table and ventured over to her junk drawer. She rummaged around and returned with a tiny tube of super-hold adhesive. She handed it to Roxanne. "When did you start wearing artificial nails?"

"I don't normally," Roxanne said, "but this one broke a few days ago. It was either cut all the others short or have my nail girl put a fake one on this finger."

"You made the right choice," Mary Sue said. "Those long nails are so elegant. Wish mine would grow like that." To illustrate her point, she held up her hands, showing everyone her short, rounded nails.

"It helps to have a cleaning lady," Roxanne said. "Housekeeping is heck on a manicure."

I couldn't help but think back to the scratches on Nelda Dolan's neck and hands. Could Roxanne's tapered nails have caused those scratches? Had Roxanne's fingernail been broken in an attack on Nelda? "How'd you break your nail?"

Roxanne took a long sip of her drink before setting her glass down and answering my question. "Trying on shoes. I found this great pair of zebra-striped pumps on sale at the Opry Mills mall last Saturday morning. They didn't have my size, though. I was trying to cram my size eights into a seven and a half. Didn't have any luck, and ripped my nail in the process. Lucky for me, my nail girl could get me right in."

It seemed coincidental that Roxanne had to get her nail fixed the very day Nelda was found dead.

As Becky dealt the third hand, Mary Sue turned my way. "It was awfully kind of you not to press charges against Dakota for trespassing. I'm assuming the detective has spoken with him, too. Was he any help?"

I figured my best bet was to continue to feign no knowledge regarding the current investigation. I could only hope I'd do a better job of it this time. "The detective talked with Dakota last Saturday morning, of course, but I don't know whether they've been back in touch since."

Becky finished dealing and, after we exchanged our cards, took another sip of her punch. "Maybe it's the Jack Daniel's talking, but I find it difficult to believe Dakota didn't hear Mom go into the house and fall. The detective asked Dad and me if we'd heard anything going on over there, but the only thing I heard from outside from the time I went to bed until he came to our door Saturday morning was a couple barks from Mosey around three A.M. and Mary Sue's house alarm going off at six."

Mary Sue hunched her shoulders and cringed in contrition. "Sorry about that. I forgot to disarm the system when I went out to get the newspaper." She sighed. "Seems I'm getting more forgetful these days."

"Sorry about Mosey, too," Gayle said. "That dog is in and out all night. Can't control his bladder like he used to."

"Don't worry," Becky told Mary Sue and Gayle. "I went right back to sleep." She leaned forward over the table, as if to share some juicy tidbit. "Get this. The detective found out that Dakota pawned Mom's peacock necklace."

Roxanne gasped, her heavily made-up eyes going wide. "The one she said she lost at Lillian's?"

Becky nodded dramatically. "Detective Flynn said he's going to talk to Dakota about it, find out where he got it from and whether he knew it belonged to my mother."

Roxanne frowned. "That's probably why the detective's been asking everyone about things missing from Lillian's house. He's trying to figure out if Dakota stole something from his grandmother or Nelda."

"Oh, my!" Mary Sue put her fingers to her lips. "This doesn't look good for him, does it?" She removed her hand. "But we'd be wrong to jump to conclusions. It could just be a misunderstanding. He might have some growing up to do, but that doesn't mean he's a thief or . . ."

Becky filled in the blank with a knowing look and a single word. *"Worse?"*

Gayle fumbled with her hand and two cards slid out of her grip, falling to her lap. "If it talks like a duck and it walks like a duck . . ." She trailed off as she looked down and retrieved the fallen cards. When she looked back up and saw the rest of us watching her, she said, "Wait. Why are we talking about ducks?"

Mary Sue gave her friend a sympathetic look. "Maybe you should sit the rest the games out, Gayle. Your pain pill seems to have gotten the better of you."

"Shoot," Gayle said. "I suppose you're right, but I don't want to miss the fun."

Mary Sue stood. "I'll make a pot of coffee. Maybe that will help."

It didn't. Gayle drank three cups, and though the caffeine managed to keep her awake, it did nothing to clear the fog from her mind. While she might have been a card shark before, tonight she was more of a card cocktail shrimp, her mind cold, limp, and shriveled. Not wanting to embarrass her, the other ladies didn't point out that she hadn't actually won the pot when she laid down a jack, a queen, a king, and two threes and announced that she had a "Full flush!"

By the end of the night, I'd lost eight dollars and fifty-three cents but gained four new friends. The fact that they could be suspects in a murder investigation probably meant I should seek different pals, but I'd had a good time nonetheless. I hadn't even had to defend myself with the wrench in my pocket.

# CHAPTER 18

# SUSPECTS AND DUST SPECKS

### WHITNEY

Becky and I took Gayle's arms and helped her hobble home through the cold, dark night. With her pain meds impairing her motor skills and relaxing her muscles, it was like escorting a human-sized noodle.

Bert met us at the door, thanking us for seeing his wife home safely. "We're going to have to get back to that doctor. Those new pills are too strong. It's no good if she can't go about her life as usual."

We returned to Mary Sue's for our dishes and Roxanne.

"Don't forget to set your alarm," I told Mary Sue as we exited her front door. Whoever had come for Nelda could be targeting older women living alone. It would be wise for everyone to take safety precautions.

It was half past eleven and the three of us were heading down Mary Sue's front walk when Carl Dolan's Impala turned into his drive and parked alongside the new

Miata and Mustang. He emerged wearing dress slacks, a striped shirt, a sport coat, and a satisfied smile.

Roxanne, having polished off three glasses of spiked punch, stuck her manicured fingers in her mouth and issued a loud wolf whistle. "Look at you, handsome fella!"

Carl chuckled and turned side to side, his arms outstretched. "I clean up pretty good, don't I?"

"That you do," Roxanne agreed. "Where you been all dressed up like that?"

His smile wavering, Carl stiffened and hesitated a moment before saying, "Down at the VFW. Had a few drinks with the guys."

Becky seemed taken aback. "Since when do you dress up for beers with the boys?"

Her father's face clouded. "It didn't seem right to wear my usual jeans and sweatshirt with my wife having just passed."

It also didn't seem right that he carried leftovers in a bag bearing a steakhouse logo if he'd been having drinks at the VFW, but I didn't point it out. If Carl had killed his wife, he just might kill me, too, if he thought I was onto him. I didn't want to follow in Nelda's footsteps and take a fall down the stairs myself. I'd pass the information on to Detective Flynn, let him sort it out.

A sideways glance at Becky told me the bag hadn't gone unnoticed by her, either. Her face was pinched in confusion and concern. Like me, she remained mum about it, but the worried wiggle of her mouth said it bothered her. *Does she realize he's not being forthright? Is she wondering if her father might have killed her mother?*

Becky split off and Roxanne and I bade her goodbye.

"Poor guy," Roxanne murmured as she watched Becky and Carl enter their house. "Nelda tricked him into marrying her, you know. Carl told my husband all about it years ago. Nelda was nice to him, at first. Laid the charm on thick. After they'd been dating awhile, she claimed she was pregnant. She knew Carl would do the right thing and marry her. They rushed down the aisle and then Becky was born." She pursed her lips and cast me a look. *"Eleven months later."*

I'd heard of babies arriving a couple of weeks late, but an eleven-month pregnancy? Nope. There was no conceivable way Nelda could have been pregnant with Becky for that long.

Roxanne turned her eyes back to the Dolans' closed door. "Once they were married, Nelda showed her true colors. She was a controlling, conniving, jealous shrew. Carl tried to leave Nelda once when Becky was little, but Nelda said she'd keep him from seeing their daughter. Back then, judges always awarded the mother primary custody. Carl couldn't bear the thought of Becky having to face Nelda alone and him only getting a few days' visitation a month. He decided to stick it out and make the best of it. After a certain point, he seemed to become numb to her. He could've left Nelda once Becky grew up, but I suppose there wasn't much to be gained from splitting up after all that time."

Maybe not. Or maybe he'd had nothing to gain until he met Dulce. Maybe Nelda had threatened him again, said she'd put him through the same type of nasty divorce their daughter was going through if he tried to leave her. Maybe he'd finally had enough and snapped. *Who knows?*

I said goodbye to Roxanne, packed the cookie sheet and trifle bowl in the cargo bay of my vehicle, and climbed into the driver's seat, heading for home. On the way, I mulled things over.

Given that Gayle was impaired by medication, it was impossible to compare tonight's pathetic performance at poker to her earlier reputation as a stellar player. She could be a cheat, as Nelda had claimed, and she could have traded out the playing cards that had been in the box earlier for ones that weren't marked. Nothing that had occurred tonight had led me to any conclusions regarding Gayle's guilt or innocence where Nelda's murder was concerned.

As for Becky, I was torn between considering her a more likely suspect and a less likely one. The fact that the life insurance policy on Nelda was soon to expire could mean Becky had decided to do away with her mother while her mom's life could still result in a windfall. Becky might have been only pretending not to know that the policy would expire on her mother's upcoming seventy-fifth birthday. Of course, this same expiration date further implicated Carl as well. The fact that Becky seemed startled and anxious by her father's obvious lie about his whereabouts tonight made her seem innocent and made him seem guilty. And, of course, there was the matter of Dulce . . .

Roxanne seemed to have a valid excuse for not contacting the detective: that she'd been helping with sick grandchildren down in Shelbyville. And while the hopeless gossip had found fault with Wayne, Lillian, and Dakota, she'd refrained from making critical remarks about Nelda at the poker game, probably because Becky was present. Even if Becky and her mother had a less-than-ideal relationship, surely no daughter would want to hear a neighbor put down her mother, even if the daughter did so herself. Roxanne probably realized this and had exercised restraint, at least until Becky headed back into her house with her father.

Still, I couldn't forget the things Roxanne had said afterward, and the things she'd said at the memorial, too. How Nelda was a horrible wife and not a real friend. But would someone kill another person for these reasons? It seemed extreme. But maybe there was more to it, some deeper motive that had yet to come to light. Something much more personal. I remembered Becky saying how angry her mother would get when Carl fawned over Lillian and her pie. Had he fawned over Roxanne, too? Was Carl Dolan the neighborhood flirt? Could that have earned him some wrath with his wife, and could that wrath have turned into a feud between the women? Had Nelda made some baseless accusation against Roxanne that had enraged Roxanne enough to push her down the stairs? Or had Nelda made an accusation against Lillian, found something in the house to indicate that Lillian and Carl had been having an affair? A gift, maybe? A framed photo of Lillian and Carl together? Maybe Roxanne had come to Lillian's defense and shoved Nelda down the stairs, later returning to remove the evidence that had been trapped under Nelda's body.

Dakota was definitely up high on the list of potential killers, not only because he'd pawned Nelda's necklace but because he was nowhere to be found. Such behavior might be typical for him, but it was also typical of criminals on the run. I wondered if, when, and where he'd surface. Before, I'd been wondering if Roxanne had taken off for Canada or Mexico. Now, I was wondering the same thing about Dakota.

The driver from Hitch-a-Ride was possibly still in play, too. Though there was nothing directly implicating Bautista in any crime, Collin had said something there didn't add up. I looked forward to hearing more from the detective.

I went to bed with suspects on my mind and my cat curled up on my belly. Sawdust purred softly, the sound reminding me of Dulce rolling her *r* when she said Carl's name. *Carrrl.* Was he the one? Had he killed his wife? Was he a *murrrderrrerr*?

After a lousy night's sleep, during which the residents of Songbird Circle traipsed back and forth across my mind, I woke up to my cat traipsing back and forth across my bladder. He definitely knew how to get me out of bed when he wanted his breakfast.

As promised, I spent Saturday morning on the sofa with Sawdust, cuddling and watching professional fishermen on television. Colette had worked a late night at the restaurant and still snoozed away behind her closed door. Emmalee emerged from her room, her red hair again sticking up in all directions. Her slippers gave off a *shush-shush-shush* as she shuffled along, seemingly unable to lift her feet. *Definitely not a morning person.*

She glanced my way. "'Mornin'," she croaked.

"Coffee's ready," I called.

She put her palms together and dipped her head as if in worship. She disappeared into the kitchen, emerging a minute later with a steaming mug. She plunked herself down in her bowl-like Papasan chair, pulling her legs up and crossing them. She glanced at the television. "Fishing? Ugh."

"Sawdust enjoys this show." As if to prove my point, he twitched his whiskers and chirped at the screen.

Emmalee smiled at him before returning her attention to me. "I called the animal shelter. They said kitten season starts in February. I can hardly wait to adopt one."

I ruffled Sawdust's ears. "Hear that, boy? You'll have an itty-bitty buddy soon." It would be nice for him to have some company. I felt guilty leaving him home alone so much. At least he'd be able to come with me to the flip house today. I could only hope he wouldn't find another dead body to poke with his paw.

A few minutes and one close call with a rogue wave later, Emmalee took her eyes off the television, finished her coffee, and stood. "I better hop in the shower. I'm working the lunch shift today."

Thinking back to my last conversation with the detective, I decided to log into Instagram on my phone and see if I could find Luis Bautista's account. It didn't take long. His handle was bulldoggiedaddie. Collin was right. Nearly every post was a pic of his dog. There was one of his dog sitting on a dining-room chair at Thanksgiving, a plate of turkey and mashed potatoes on the table in front of him. Another showed his dog wearing antlers, looking like a chubby, short-legged reindeer. In another, Luis and his dog wore matching striped sweaters. Luis knelt down next to him on a patch of grass in front of their apartment building. I recognized the place by its dark blue exterior paint, the white ironwork on the balconies, and the evergreen juniper bushes. Home & Hearth managed a unit in the condominium complex next door. I'd been there recently to replace a broken garbage disposal.

*Hmm.* Maybe I was giving Luis Bautista too much credit, but I had a hard time believing that anyone who adored his dog that much could be a cold-blooded killer. But maybe I was simply finding him relatable. I had similar photos of Sawdust in my phone and posted on all of my social media platforms. He was my sweetie, my fur baby, my pride and joy.

When the fishing shows wrapped up and Emmalee left for work, I used my phone to snap pics of the antique tins I'd rescued from Lillian's kitchen. I logged into my computer, set up an account on eBay, and listed the tins for sale, pricing each of them at twenty dollars. I was curious to see how quickly I'd get a response.

My task complete, I grabbed a quick shower, pulled my hair back into an easy ponytail, and climbed into a pair of boots and coveralls. I opened the door to Sawdust's plastic carrier and he sauntered right in, eager to join me on whatever adventure I might have planned. "Good boy!" After loading my cat and my tools into my car, I headed to the flip house.

As I turned onto Songbird Circle, I saw a man walking slowly down the sidewalk. He wore tennis shoes, jeans, and a heavy blue nylon coat. With the coat's hood cinched tight around his face and a pair of mirrored sunglasses over his eyes, it was impossible to discern his age or hair color, and his face was largely obscured. Picking him out of a lineup would be next to impossible. *Maybe that's exactly what he's going for.*

A lightweight canvas bag hung over his shoulder. His head rotated slightly as his gaze traveled over the front of each house, moving up into the trees. As I watched, he pulled a green flyer from the bag and proceeded to roll it up into a small scroll. He walked up the Garners' front walk and tucked the scroll between their doorknob and the jamb.

My mind went back to what Collin had told me earlier: that burglars sometimes leave flyers at homes to see if they stack up. Flyers that aren't removed by a resident in a timely manner can clue them in that the occupants are away from home for a prolonged period, maybe on a vacation or business trip. Could this man be leaving flyers for that very reason? To find another house to target? Could he be the one who'd come into the flip house and killed Nelda? Was he looking up into the trees to see if any of them might provide access to a second-story or attic window he could use to slip inside?

I slowly rounded the circle and pulled to the curb at the exit, cutting my engine. As the man made his way around the cul-de-sac, I watched him in my side and rearview mirrors. He skipped Mary Sue's house and the flip house, but left a flyer at both the Dolans' home and Roxanne's. Clearly, he was choosing only certain homes to target rather than leaving flyers at every house. Had he skipped Mary Sue's house and the flip house because there were vehicles in the driveway, telling him someone was home? The Garners' car and Roxanne's were parked out of sight in their garages, leaving one to wonder whether anyone might be inside. The new Mustang and Miata sat in front of the Dolans' house, the paper license plates evidencing the fact that the vehicles were fresh off the lot. The man might have figured that anyone who could afford two new cars at once to park in their driveway would have some nice things inside their house, too. Maybe he'd gone up onto the porch to leave the flyer in the hopes that he could get a peek through their front window.

As he came up the sidewalk alongside my SUV, I pretended to be looking down at my phone. I didn't want to clue the guy in that I was spying on him.

He passed me and turned the corner. I gave him a thirty-second head start before starting my engine and driving around the corner after him. Again, I parked and watched as he made his way down the sidewalk, looking over each house and selecting only a few at which to leave his rolled-up flyers.

When he rounded another corner to head down a side street, I drove forward and parked at that corner where I could continue to keep an eye on him. With any luck, he'd soon return to a vehicle so I could snag his license plate and turn the number over to Detective Flynn.

The man stopped three houses down and glanced in my direction. I averted my gaze, looking down at my phone again. When I looked up, he had crossed the street halfway down. *Odd.* Wouldn't a real solicitor stick to a pattern so he'd be sure to cover the entire area? In addition to the fact that the guy seemed to be picking and choosing where he left his flyers, the fact that he'd crossed the street midblock clued me in that he might be up to no good.

Sawdust stood up in his carrier on the backseat and mewed, seeming to ask why I was engaged in this unusual behavior, driving short distances and stopping repeatedly.

"We're spying, buddy," I told him. "Trying to catch a killer."

When the man had made it down the block, I started my engine again and crept forward a few houses, where I could see his route from here. He glanced back at my car again. That he seemed to be looking out for potential witnesses raised my suspicions even higher. He stopped in front of a house and turned his back to me. He was too far away for me to tell exactly what he was doing, but after a few seconds he took off jogging down the street.

"If you think you're going to get away," I said aloud, "you are sorely mistaken."

I started my motor and headed after him. He ran to the end of the street and hooked a left, sprinting now.

*Woo-woo!*

I glanced up at my rearview mirror to see the flashing lights of a police cruiser behind me. What luck! I could send the officer after the guy.

I pulled over to the curb, rolled my window down, and stuck my head out. A male officer slid out and strolled up to my window. "We had a report of suspicious behavior."

"I'm so glad you came!" I pointed down the street. "The guy just ran that way. He's in a blue jacket with the hood up and mirrored sunglasses."

The officer cocked his head. "The report I got was a suspicious person in a red Honda SUV."

"Me? Suspicious?"

"You've been following a guy. He called it in."

"I have been following him, but he's the one who's suspicious, not me!" I explained the situation, that a woman had died in questionable circumstances in a house I owned just a few blocks away. "Detective Flynn is working the case." I pointed down the street. "That man looked like he might be casing the houses. He only left flyers at some of them."

"Hold tight," the cop said. "Let's see if we can clear this up."

He returned to his cruiser, where I saw him speak into his mic. A minute later, the officer climbed back out of his car and my eyes spotted the man I'd been following jogging back up the street toward us.

The man stopped near my car, removed his sunglasses,

and addressed the officer. "I'm the one who called her in."

"What're you doing out here?" the officer asked him.

The man reached into his bag, pulled out one of the flyers, and handed it to the officer. "I trim trees. I've been leaving flyers at houses where I notice dead trees or limbs that need cutting back."

His explanation made perfect sense.

I cringed. "Sorry! The fact that you had your hood up and sunglasses on caught my attention is all. It looked like you were trying to disguise yourself."

The man issued a derisive snort. "I'm trying to keep warm. It's only twenty-eight degrees out here. Guess you didn't notice since you were sitting in your heated car."

The officer looked up, squinting at the sky before cutting me a look. "It's sunny, too." I raised my hands in surrender. "You're right. I was being paranoid. I apologize."

Of course, the man had been the one to call the cops on me. Quickly, too. Maybe he was just as paranoid as I was, and he wasn't offering me any apologies. At any rate, we agreed to chalk the incident up to a mutual misunderstanding and go about our business.

As I drove off, Sawdust issued a *meow?*

I glanced back at my cat. "False alarm."

Minutes later, I closed the front door of the flip house behind us and released Sawdust from his carrier. "Have fun, boy. Stay out of trouble." *And please don't find another body!* I stashed his cage in the hall closet, out of the way.

Country-western tunes lured me upstairs to the kitchen. Buck's bottom half stuck out of a lower cabinet.

I bent down and peeked in at him. In addition to his usual work boots and coveralls, he'd also donned safety goggles and a disposable dust mask today. He was removing the screws holding the old kitchen countertops in place.

"What's my assignment, boss?" I asked.

He used his screwdriver to point to his right. "Get started in the next cabinet."

After donning goggles and a dust mask myself, I grabbed a screwdriver from my toolbox, opened the adjoining cabinet, and backed in to get to work. While I set about my task, I filled Buck in on the latest developments, including Carl Dolan's sweetie and the fact that he had so obviously lied about his whereabouts the night before.

"Whoa," Buck said from inside his cabinet, his voice echoing in the small space. "Carl Dolan has a side piece?"

"I suppose she's not a side piece if there's no longer a main piece." I removed the last screw, tucked it into my breast pocket, and backed out of the cabinet. "I have no idea whether Carl and Dulce were having an affair while Nelda was still alive. It could be a new relationship."

Buck sat up and poked his head out, his lip quirking in disgust. "What kind of man starts dating less than a week after his wife passes away?"

"One who's been trapped for decades in an unhappy marriage?" Carl Dolan could certainly have killed his wife. But innocent until proven guilty, right? Could be he was simply trying to move on as quickly as possible, make up for lost time, and eke as much joy as he could out of his golden years. Maybe he couldn't handle being alone and was trying to fill the void Nelda had left.

Maybe he needed a distraction from his grief. Maybe we should give him the benefit of the doubt. Or maybe he was guilty as heck.

A few minutes later, we'd removed all the screws and sliced through the line of caulk underneath the countertop. Buck grabbed one end and I grabbed the other. Together, we lifted the countertop off the cabinets and, with Buck easing backward down the steps, carried it carefully down to the landing. We had a little difficulty negotiating the turn at the front doorway, but eventually managed to carry the countertop down the lower flight and into the garage where we'd store it until we could haul it off to the dump. We did the same for the bathroom countertops before moving on to the tub in the master bath.

With all of the large structures removed, it was time to pull out the flooring. We started with the ugly shag carpet. Fortunately, this would be an easier task. Buck worked downstairs while I worked upstairs. Going room by room, I used a sharp blade to cut the carpet and padding into smaller, manageable sizes. I rolled them up together against the walls, exposing the plywood subflooring. Sawdust repeatedly settled onto the carpet where I worked and dug his claws in, refusing to budge as I pushed the roll toward him. *I should've trimmed his nails.*

I wrestled him free once again. "You're not helping, buddy." As I set him aside, the cat emitted an irritated yowl that said I was interfering with his plan for total carpet domination. He'd only just begun to shred the stuff. Why was I putting an end to his fun?

When I finished removing the carpet on the upper floor, I went downstairs in search of Buck. I found him in the sewing room, performing what appeared to be a fox-trot with a long roll of carpet he'd stood on end. "Fred Astaire's got nothing on you, cuz."

"Grab an end," he demanded.

I pointed out an obvious flaw in his technique. "Smaller rolls are more manageable. You could cut it down the middle."

He, in turn, pointed out an obvious flaw in my personality. "And you could keep your mouth shut."

"I don't think that's possible."

I took one end of the long, heavy roll and the two of us carried it out to the garage. Half an hour later, all the old carpet and padding had been taken out to the garage and a cubic ton of dust and debris had settled in our hair and on the floors. Sawdust lay on his back in a particularly dirty spot and wriggled back and forth, collecting as much dirt and lint on his fur as he could.

"Keep that up," I warned him, shaking my finger, "and I won't bring you with me on a job again."

He stopped and eyed me for a brief moment before he set to wriggling again. The cat knew my words were mere bluster. Thanks to all the dust the cat was stirring up, and despite the mask I was wearing, I sneezed three times in quick succession. *Achoo-choo-choo.*

While Buck used a claw hammer to remove the extraneous carpet nails from the plywood base, I swept up the dirt and debris. Sawdust followed me around the house, batting around a small tuft of carpet I'd missed. I ruffled my cat with my gloved hands to get the dirt out of his fur. He sent up a cloud of dust that would rival that of Pig-Pen from the Peanuts comic strip. As he scurried off, I grabbed the broom once again to sweep the dirt he'd left behind.

The shag carpeting now history, my cousin and I turned our attention to the linoleum flooring on the landing and in the kitchen and baths. We scored the flooring with a utility knife, peeled the linoleum back, and used a scraper to remove the hardened glue. *Talk about a workout for your forearms. Sheesh!* After opening the windows a few inches to ensure fresh, if frigid, airflow, Buck applied a propane torch to the stubborn spots of glue that remained, melting them and scraping them away. The air filled with the acrid smells of smoke and hot adhesive.

By late afternoon, we'd removed all countertops, bath fixtures, and flooring, and I'd dealt with so much dust I felt like a character in *The Grapes of Wrath*. In return for our efforts, Buck and I were rewarded with sore backs and aching muscles. With the demolition completed, though, we could look forward to the more interesting phase of house flipping, the renovation stage. In fact, the materials were due to be delivered any moment. I'd overheard Buck on the phone with someone from the home-improvement store a few minutes ago, verifying our address.

Seemed like a good time to take a quick break and update the detective.

# CHAPTER 19

# UPDATING THE DETECTIVE

## WHITNEY

While Buck cleaned his tools, I grabbed my water bottle and sat down on the top step of the lower staircase. I pulled my cell phone out of my pocket and lowered my dust mask.

As I scrolled though my contacts list looking for Detective Flynn's number, Sawdust rubbed himself in circles around my hips. Deciding I was too soft to provide the deep tissue massage he seemed to seek, he moved down a step, rubbing himself along the overhang. He arched his back to make full contact before moving down another step and rubbing himself in the other direction.

I found the contact, tapped the screen, and placed a call to Detective Flynn. He sounded out of breath when he answered. "You okay?" I asked.

"In the middle of a run," he replied. "Catch me up while I catch my breath."

While Sawdust continued to zigzag down the steps, I

gave the detective a rundown of last night's poker game, including the big reveal about Nelda's life insurance policy and how it was set to expire in a short time. "If Nelda had reached seventy-five, neither Carl nor Becky would have seen a single dime." I also filled him in on Becky and Roxanne's disregard for Wayne and Dakota Walsh.

"Seems Becky not only had a motivation to kill her mother," Collin said, "but she also has reason to implicate Dakota."

As much as I hated to admit that I made a terrible mole, I knew I needed to be honest with him. "The ladies seem to know that something more is going on than a routine investigation. I have a horrible poker face."

"I'm not surprised," he said. "You're an honest person. Lying doesn't come naturally to you."

*Aw, shucks.* "This may be nothing," I said, "but Roxanne was wearing an artificial fingernail last night. It came off when she was scooping up her winnings. She said she doesn't normally wear fake nails, but that she'd had her nail technician glue one on her index finger after she'd broken a nail recently."

"Did she say how she broke the nail?"

"She claimed it happened when she was trying on shoes at the mall the morning Nelda was found dead."

"But you're thinking she could have broken it during a confrontation with Nelda Dolan."

"Exactly."

"We didn't find any physical evidence like that on the staircase."

"Maybe it got lost in the shag carpeting." Of course, that shag carpeting was now all rolled up and stacked in the garage. *Ugh.* I mentioned this fact to Collin.

"Can you keep the carpet around for a while, just in case?"

"Sure. We've stashed it in the garage. It's not in our way."

"What about Gayle?" he asked. "Was she on a roll last night?"

"Not at all. She only won three hands, one of which she didn't really win but we let her think she did. She's been having knee problems and is on a new pain medication. It really messes with her head."

"So you couldn't tell whether she's a card cheat?"

"No, but we might have another cheat on our hands."

"Oh, yeah?" He cocked his head. "Who?"

"Carl Dolan." I told him how Carl claimed to have spent the night drinking beers with his buddies down at the VFW. "I didn't buy it. He was dressed for a date and holding a takeout bag from a steakhouse." If he were on trial for cheating on his wife, that bag would be Exhibit A. *Or should I say A.1., as in the steak sauce?* "Something else crossed my mind, too. Another theory. Becky mentioned that her father loved Lillian's pie, and that her mother would get irritated when he'd mention it. Do you think there could have been more to it? Do you think Carl and Lillian might have been involved while Lillian was still alive, and that Nelda just used Dakota as an excuse to come to the house and look for proof?"

"With Lillian gone, any affair they might have had would be over."

"True, but from what I gather Nelda wouldn't be the type to let something like that go. Maybe she wanted evidence of his infidelity so she could hold it over him, or use it as leverage in a divorce."

"You've given me a lot to think about," Collin said.

"I'll get in touch with Andy Walsh, find out more about the insurance policy. While I'm at it, I'll ask him about his mother's relationship with both of the Dolans, see if he offers anything of use."

In other words, Carl and Becky were back in the hot seat.

"By the way," he said, "archives finally coughed up the file on Bertram Garner. The arrest related to events that took place at a civil-rights march in support of the Voting Rights Act. Some bigot started a shoving match with those who were marching. Garner's so-called assault was determined to be self-defense. A dozen eyewitnesses provided statements on his behalf. The man who started the ruckus was convicted and served three months in jail. The charges against Bertram Garner were dropped."

*Phew.* "I'm relieved to hear that." Maybe he really was the nice guy he seemed to be.

"It still doesn't explain why Gayle lied to me about when she'd gone into your flip house."

"No," I agreed, "but her meds might explain it. She was all sorts of confused last night. She invented poker hands that don't even exist."

"So she did cheat, after all."

"Not intentionally."

With the detective now updated, we wrapped up our call. By that point, Sawdust had zigzagged his way down to the final, creaky step, which I'd planned to fix when we returned tomorrow. Two or three nails would hold it in place and stop the creaking. The cat rubbed along the step, arching his back again. This time, though, the wood on the step lifted an inch or two, falling back into place with a *slap. Looks like the stair needs more work than I'd thought.*

Sawdust turned and retraced his steps, this time rubbing his forehead along the stair. The wood lifted again and landed back in place with another *slap*. He turned to sniff along the edge of the step and set out again, pushing his head against the step. *Slap.*

Lest Sawdust accidentally pinch his ear between the riser and tread boards, I decided to go ahead and fix the creaky step right away. I rounded up a hammer and three small nails, donned my kneepads, and knelt down in front of the stair. Curious about how loose the top seemed to be, I put my fingers under the tread and pulled upward, surprised by how easily the wood lifted. *Wait. Is this step hinged?*

# CHAPTER 20

# UPS AND DOWNS

### SAWDUST

While Sawdust loved it when Whitney stroked him and scratched behind his ears, he was a resourceful cat. When she was too busy to attend to his needs, he tried his best to be self-sufficient. He'd seek out a nice corner or surface to rub against. It wasn't the same as being attended to by the woman he adored, but he realized sometimes he had to settle for second best.

He'd been doing just that, rubbing himself along the step, when the stair had surprised him by moving upward an inch or two and then falling back into place. *That's strange.* He'd rubbed on plenty of stairs before, but none had ever moved. *Why did this one move?*

When he'd sniffed the step, he noticed that the edge smelled faintly of the same floral scent he'd smelled before on the sheets in the bedroom upstairs and on the appliances on the kitchen counter and on the box of playing cards on the coffee table. Dogs might be known for their sense of smell, but cats had darn good noses, too. Whoever had slept in that bed and used those gadgets and touched the box of cards had also touched the edge of this step, though the faintness of the smell said it had been awhile. *Who was that person?*

Before he could think too much about it, Whitney had scooped him up and set him down in the hallway behind her. "Out of the way, buddy. I need to take a look at that stair."

He stretched his neck to get a better look, watching and wondering. *What is Whitney doing?*

# CHAPTER 21

# A STEP IN THE RIGHT DIRECTION

**WHITNEY**

The tread swung up and back. The flat board was indeed hinged on the backside, revealing a secret storage compartment underneath the stair. Inside the hidden space was a large manila envelope resting at an angle. *Intriguing.*

Secret closets or rooms were rare, but not unheard-of. In fact, not long ago, I'd helped my uncle Roger install a large hinged bookcase at the front of an unused alcove in a home office, giving the homeowner more usable wall space and turning the space behind the shelves into a hidden closet. Cabinets and closets sometimes had false backs or bottoms to hide plumbing or wiring. Back in the day, many pieces of furniture contained secret compartments to prevent servants or thieves from making off with jewelry or other small valuables. The tiny house fad required maximization of space, with windowsills sometimes doubling as shallow drawers, and movable flooring panels allowing access to storage underneath. Every inch counted. Still, finding this secret stash was a surprise.

I made my way up the staircase, trying the other steps. None of the others was hinged. Satisfied I'd found the only secret compartment on the stairs, I returned to the bottom and peered again into the space.

Curious, I retrieved the manila envelope. Underneath was a wooden box identical in size and shape to the recipe box that had been in Lillian's kitchen. My pulse quickened. *Could I have just discovered her secret stash of blue-ribbon recipes?*

I flipped open the lid. *Bingo!* Inside were recipe cards for her prize-winning peach crumble, the raspberry-peach tart, the blackberry-peach coffee cake, and, most importantly, the beloved peach pie for which she'd always be fondly remembered. *Hooray!*

My first instinct was to run next door and tell Mary Sue the good news, that I'd found her best friend's long-lost recipes. I'd tour the block after, let the others know, too, that the missing peach pie recipe had been discovered. *But it would be much more fun to surprise the ladies at next Friday's poker game, wouldn't it?* I wasn't much of a cook, but Colette would bake Lillian's peach pie for me if I asked. She'd been curious about the recipe herself. Maybe I could even convince her to bake several of the pies so I could surprise everyone on the circle. I couldn't resurrect their friend, but I could bring Lillian's beloved pie back to life.

Setting the recipe box aside, I turned my attention to the manila envelope.

Buck trod down the stairs, his boots loud on the wood. He stopped one step above me and stared down at the open compartment. "Well, lookie there. A hidey-hole."

"Sawdust discovered it."

Buck scoffed. "You give that cat too much credit."

"You don't give him *enough*." After all, the cat had once saved me from an intruder intent on killing me. "If Sawdust hadn't rubbed up against the step, I wouldn't have realized the tread was hinged. I would've just hammered a few nails into it from the top to stop the creaking and been done. Lillian's recipes would never have been found." They'd have been sealed away forever in their secret hiding place, like pirate treasure buried on a deserted island or ancient Egyptian mummies tucked away in their hidden tombs.

Buck gestured to the envelope in my hand. "Whatcha got there?"

Nothing was written on the front of the envelope. I turned it over. The back was blank, too, and fully sealed by both a clasp and the adhesive strip. "I have no idea."

"Gonna open it?"

"It doesn't seem right to go poking around in Lillian's business. I should give it to Andy."

Buck's eyes narrowed. "What if that's something Lillian didn't want anyone to see? That could be why she hid it under the stair. What if it's Andy's real birth certificate? What if he's the secret love child of Lillian and Willie Nelson?"

"What if you've lost your ever-loving mind?"

Buck reached down and eased the envelope out of my hand. I probably should have held on tighter to both the envelope and my principles, but to be honest, I was curious, too. What could be so secret that she'd hide it under the stairs where nobody would accidentally come across it? Obviously she hadn't told her friends or sons about this hidden compartment or they would have looked for her recipes here.

After opening the clasp, Buck eased his index finger under the flap and ran it across, breaking the seal. He opened the flap, reached inside, and pulled out a stapled document that looked to be about three or four pages in length. His gaze ran across the first page.

"Well?" I asked. "What is it?"

"Lillian Walsh's will."

I stood and he handed it to me. The first page did little more than identify Lillian Walsh as the testator and state that the document was her last will and testament, intended to replace all previous wills. The second page identified Wayne and Andy Walsh as her only children. Apparently, Lillian and Willie Nelson had not, in fact, conceived a love child. On page two, Lillian also appointed Andy as the executor of her estate. No surprise there. Though he was the younger of her two sons, he was clearly the more responsible one.

Page three was where things got interesting. This will left one hundred percent of Lillian's property to Andy. In fact, Lillian expressly noted in the will that she'd made multiple monetary gifts to Wayne during her lifetime and, as such, she considered Wayne's share of her estate already paid to him.

Given what the ladies had told me at poker last night—that Lillian had been on a fixed income and had little in the way of funds after helping to support Wayne—I'd gathered that Lillian's house represented the bulk of her estate. Per the terms of this will, the money I'd paid to purchase the house should have gone entirely to Andy. Contrary to the will, the closing documents for the house sale had indicated the net proceeds would be split equally between Andy and Wayne. The closing documents were directly at odds with the will.

While the page regarding the bequest had definitely

caught my attention, the final page caused my heart to leap into my throat and my blood to freeze in my veins. There were two witnesses to the will. One of the names was unfamiliar to me. The name of the other witness had become all too familiar by this point. The second witness was none other than Nelda Dolan.

"What's wrong?" Buck asked. "You look like you've seen a ghost."

I felt like I'd seen one, too, or at least felt one, her hand reaching out from the grave with a ballpoint pen clutched in its cold fingers. I held up the page and pointed to Nelda's signature. "Nelda Dolan signed this will. It leaves everything to Andy."

"I thought you said her sons inherited everything fifty-fifty."

"That's how the money we paid for the house was divided." I looked down at the page again. Next to each signature, including Lillian's and the notary's, was a date around a year prior. Because this will had been executed fairly recently, it was likely intended to replace a previous will. I could only wonder if Nelda Dolan's signature on the will was the reason she, too, was executed. I shared my theory with Buck. "Do you think Nelda might have questioned Wayne about his inheritance? Maybe Nelda told Wayne she'd witnessed Lillian's most recent will and that he'd been left nothing. Maybe Wayne hoped that by getting rid of Nelda, nobody would find out about this will and he'd get to keep his inheritance."

Was Wayne the one who'd pushed Nelda down the stairs? Or was I making wild accusations? Was *I* the one who was out of my ever-loving mind?

Buck looked thoughtful. "Wouldn't Lillian have given a copy of the will to Andy? After all, she appointed him executor."

"That would have been the logical thing to do," I agreed. "But she hadn't yet given anyone her blue-ribbon recipes, even though she'd promised she would. She might have planned to share the recipes and the new will at some point, but then suffered her stroke before she got around to it. Or she might not have wanted to let her sons know she'd cut Wayne out of the will. She could have told her sons to get a copy of her will from her lawyer after she passed." Thinking out loud, I argued with myself. "But if that was the case, Andy would have gone to the lawyer, obtained a copy of the will, and found out he was the sole heir. Obviously, that didn't happen."

Buck gestured to the will. "Is there an attorney's name on there? Maybe a law firm? They might could clear things up."

I looked the pages over. No law firm or attorney's name appeared anywhere. In fact, the footer that appeared in tiny type on each page indicated Lillian had obtained the will form online, from one of those do-it-yourself websites. No attorney had been involved in preparing it. Given that Lillian purportedly had only a meager income in her later years, it wasn't surprising that she'd gone the frugal route and prepared the will herself. I pointed at the footer and showed it to Buck. "This will in my hand might be the only copy."

"That would explain things," Buck said. "Andy might have divided things up according to an older will. Guess all you can do at this point is turn that document over to Flynn and let him follow up."

Though putting things in the detective's hands was likely the smart choice, once again I found myself wanting to take the bull by the horns and do some sleuthing myself. "Aren't court filings public record? That would include probate court, too, right?"

Buck raised his palms. "Don't know about that. What I do know is that you and I have a house to renovate and put on the market." He gave me a pointed look. "Your time would be better spent here, fixing up the house, than chasing down clues. Investigating is the detective's job."

Ironically, the more Buck tried to dissuade me, the more determined I was to hunt down the information. *No man's going to tell Whitney Whitaker what to do!* "A visit to the courthouse won't take long."

Buck raised his palms again, this time in surrender. "I give up. When you get that fire in your eyes there's no stopping you. It's best to stay out of your way."

Yep. My cousin knew me well.

From outside came a squeal of brakes followed by the hiss of the brakes being released. The delivery truck had arrived.

"There's our materials," Buck said.

As he turned and headed up the stairs to let the deliverymen in, I settled the stair tread back in place and tucked the will and recipe box in my purse. Buck stepped outside with the men to make sure everything we'd ordered was on the truck, while I took up a post on the front porch where I could make sure Sawdust didn't attempt an escape.

Over the next fifteen minutes or so, the men carried materials into the house. Wood flooring. Black-and-white tile. Black granite countertops. The jetted garden tub. A shower door and floor pan, along with a shower-head and faucets. Before long, this outdated interior would begin its transformation. I could hardly wait to get started!

As the deliverymen drove off, Sawdust peeked out the open door. I scooped him up in my arms and planted a kiss on his furry cheek, his whiskers tickling my face as he twitched them. As I slid my cat back into his carrier, my phone pinged with an incoming text. I pulled the device from my pocket to find a message from Detective Flynn. *Keep kissing that cat and you'll come down with kitty cooties.*

My cheeks burst into flame as my eyes locked on the security camera we'd installed on the front porch. I'd forgotten we'd given the detective the login information to watch the feeds. I wondered what else he might have seen through the camera. I raised my hand and gave him a quick wave.

Things were moving along. In a few short weeks, the house would be ready to sell. But for now, I'd better run home and clean myself up for tonight's babysitting gig.

## CHAPTER 22

# PLAYING HOUSE

### WHITNEY

Sawdust came with me to Owen's house that evening. It would give him a chance to reconnect with his brother, who had been adopted by Owen and his wife, Melissa. Their oldest daughter had named the cat Fuzzy Britches, though his moniker was often shortened to just Britches. Unlike Sawdust, who'd been the runt of the litter, Britches had a wide backside when he sat and a flabby belly that swung side to side when he trotted across the room. The cat had definitely not been working on his core.

"Hey, Whitney!" Melissa let me in the door, and I set Sawdust down on the floor and released him from his harness.

"Hey, yourself." I gave my pretty cousin-in-law a hug. I took a step back and admired her cute sweaterdress. "You look great. Where are you and Owen headed?"

"Dinner and a movie," she replied. "It'll be nice to see something that's not rated G for a change."

After Sawdust and Britches sniffed each other to

get reacquainted, Sawdust scampered down the hall to see what new territories he could conquer. His presence alerted my second cousins to mine, and they came stampeding out of their bedrooms, running my way for hugs and kisses. "Hi, girls!"

Owen emerged a moment later and came to the living room, helping Melissa into her coat and addressing his daughters over his shoulder. "You girls behave for Whitney, okay? Mommy and I want a good report when we get home."

"Whitney always gives us a good report!" cried their oldest, who was four and a half. Heaven help you if you forgot that half year. "Even when we're bad!"

I chuckled and shot her a wink. The worst thing these girls had ever done while I'd been babysitting was hide their uneaten broccoli in their pockets.

Lest we have a repeat of the broccoli incident, I ordered a pizza for dinner. The girls, the cats, and I spent the evening lounging about watching cartoons and playing with the elaborate dollhouses I'd made for each of them after they were born. The dollhouses were custom designs I'd come up with myself, three stories tall with gingerbread accents, wraparound porches, and six hundred tiny wooden shingles I'd painstakingly glued to each of the roofs. *The things we do for love.* Maybe I should've put a secret compartment in the dollhouse staircases. The girls would've loved that.

I'd filled the houses with miniature antique furniture and bought each of the girls a set of dolls, extended Victorian families that included a pair of grandparents, parents, an adolescent son and daughter, and a baby in a white gown. Not to be left out of our playtime, Sawdust and Britches each claimed a dollhouse attic for themselves, climbing up and squishing their bodies into the too-small spaces, their furry feet hanging out of the dormer windows as if monsters resided there.

The youngest, who was barely past infancy, was more interested in teething on a plastic ring than in playing with dolls. Meanwhile, the two-year-old marched her grandmother up the stairs. With her fine motor skills still in development, she had trouble easing the doll through the second-floor doorway. The doll fell from her chubby fingers and tumbled down the staircase, landing at the bottom much as Nelda Dolan had at the flip house.

"Hey!" cried her older sister. "That grammy belongs in my house, not yours!" She reached over, grabbed the doll from the floor of her sister's dollhouse, and returned it to her own, putting the elderly woman to work at the miniature wood-burning stove in the kitchen.

When my younger cousin's eyes brimmed with tears and her lip began to quiver, her sister handed her the doll that belonged to her set. "This grammy's yours."

Appeased, thankfully, the younger one blinked back her tears and attempted a second ascent up the stairs with her own doll.

The girls' exchange got me wondering. The doll had easily been moved from the floor of one dollhouse to the other. Could a similar situation have occurred with Nelda Dolan? Might she have been killed at another location, fallen on top of something there, then been moved to the flip house hours later, after she'd become stiff and her blood had settled? The scenario would explain why Dakota hadn't heard Nelda fall. It could also explain why the item under Nelda could not be readily identified. Maybe it had never been in the flip house to begin with. The killer or killers could have moved Nelda's body to the flip house to throw suspicions off themselves, or to try to frame Dakota Walsh or even me and Buck.

Gayle, Roxanne, and Mary Sue had keys to Lillian's house and could have used their keys to open the front door and dump Nelda's body. Still, Nelda wasn't a small woman, and any of them would have had trouble moving her alone. Bertram could have helped Gayle, or maybe two or three of the ladies could have worked together to move Nelda. Gayle had joked at the poker party about being rolled home in Mary Sue's wheelbarrow. Maybe that wheelbarrow had been used not long before to roll Nelda Dolan to the flip house. Or maybe Becky or Carl had killed Nelda at their home, and then moved her to the flip house hours later. Either of them might be able to manage Nelda's body on their own. Of course it would be even easier if they worked together. If Becky had been telling the truth at the poker game, they wouldn't have had their own key to Lillian's house. But maybe one of them had seen Dakota put his key in the frog's mouth, either on the night Nelda was killed or on an earlier occasion. Maybe they knew Dakota's key would be easily accessible.

At bedtime, I helped the girls change into their pajamas and brush their teeth. I read them three bedtime stories, allowing each to pick their favorite book. After tucking them in, I settled on the sofa and sent a text to Detective Flynn to find out whether my new theory could have any validity. *Could Nelda have been killed somewhere else and then moved to the flip house early Saturday morning?*

I'd expected Collin to text me in return, and anticipated that his response might not come until much later. It was Saturday night, after all, and he was an attractive, single man. He should be out on a date, or at least doing something fun with friends. To my surprise, he called my cell phone.

"It's Saturday night," he said. "Why aren't you out having fun instead of thinking about Nelda Dolan's murder?"

"I promised my cousin Owen I'd babysit tonight in return for his help at the flip house. What's your excuse?"

"I *am* out having fun."

"You are?"

"I'm at Bell's Bend Park. It's the best place for stargazing near the city. Venus and Neptune are both making a close approach tonight. I'm out here with my telescope."

*And who else?* I was tempted to ask. Instead, I told Collin how my young cousins and their dolls had provided me with a new theory about the investigation: that Nelda could have been killed elsewhere and later moved to the flip house.

"It's something to consider," he agreed. "If Nelda's body was moved Saturday morning, it would point to someone in the circle as the killer. I can't imagine she'd have been transported far."

I told him that Lillian had given all of the ladies on Songbird Circle keys to her house, except Nelda.

"The fact that Dakota's key was wiped clean tells me the killer used it," he said.

"So Carl and Becky are looking guiltier than ever, aren't they?" After all, they were the only ones on the cul-de-sac who'd have to borrow Dakota's key to get inside. Anyone else could have used the key Lillian had given them.

"They are," he said, "but don't put too much trust in anyone just yet."

Sawdust hopped up onto the couch and settled on my lap. I ran my hand down his back. "Becky mentioned hearing the Garners' dog barking during the night and Mary Sue's alarm going off early in the morning. Mary Sue said she'd forgotten to disarm her security system before going outside to get her newspaper. But maybe Mosey got riled up when Gayle and Bertram were handling Nelda's body. Or maybe he heard something going on in the circle, or smelled a stranger, and that's why he raised a ruckus."

"Could be," Collin said. "Then again, Becky might have been trying to implicate her neighbors."

It seemed every new theory led to multiple interpretations. Solving a murder wasn't easy, that's for sure.

We ended our call and I tuckered out on the couch. I was awakened by the sound of Owen and Melissa returning at a quarter to midnight.

I stood to meet them as they came in the door. "How was the movie?"

"Who knows?" Owen slipped out of his coat. "We fell asleep before the previews were over."

His wife turned to him. "Remember when we used to go dancing until all hours of the night? What happened to us?"

They shared a knowing smile. I suspected that even though they'd slept through the movie, they'd enjoyed having some time together as a couple, without the kids.

"The girls were perfect," I said. "The cats, on the other hand, discovered that they could climb the dining room curtains and play with the tassel tiebacks."

Owen turned to Britches and pointed a finger at him. "That's it, cat. You're grounded for two weeks."

After farewells hugs were exchanged, I bid my cousin and his wife good night, and Sawdust and I headed home.

After a long night's sleep, I woke Sunday morning feeling refreshed and re-energized. I rolled out of bed and aimed for the kitchen. My nose told me one or both of my roommates were already up, and someone had made coffee.

I traipsed into the kitchen. "Buck?"

To my surprise, my cousin sat on one of the barstools. Colette sat on another. The two were angled toward each other, talking.

Buck looked over at me. "You are a downright scary sight, nitwit."

While Colette had already cleaned herself up, my hair looked like a tumbleweed, and no doubt my face was splotchy from sleep. But I wasn't about to make any apologies for my appearance. "You come by before I've had my coffee, this is what you get." I shuffled over to the pot, grabbed the biggest mug I could find from the shelf, and filled it to the brim. Turning around and leaning back against the counter, I said, "What are you doing here, anyway?"

"I brought some wood to build a raised-bed garden out back." Buck went on to say he'd come up with the plan while he and Colette had waited for me in his van at the flip house on Tuesday evening. "Colette mentioned a new farm-to-table restaurant that opened up in town."

While I had no objections to a vegetable garden, I reminded Buck that he'd chastised me for my plans to run by the probate court. "I thought you wanted to get the flip house done as soon as possible."

"I do," he shot back. "But even the Big Man Upstairs rested on the seventh day."

Was it my imagination, or did he look a little sheepish? Besides, what he said wasn't logical. Here he was debating rest when he planned to spend the day building a garden.

Before I could call my cousin out on his inconsistency, Colette chimed in. "It's a great idea. We can grow vegetables right in our yard. They always taste best when they've just been picked."

Fresh, free produce sounded great. The only question now was whose domain a vegetable garden fell under. "Would I be responsible for tending to the garden as part of my lawn-care duties, or would it be your job since it would replace grocery shopping?"

Buck solved the riddle for us. "Whitney, you would water and weed it. Colette would do the harvesting."

"Works for me." I walked to the back window and looked outside. A number of four-by-fours and three tall stacks of boards lay on the lawn, enough to enclose nearly the entire backyard. "Just how big is this garden going to be?"

Buck raised a noncommittal shoulder. "As big as y'all want it."

Colette took a sip of her coffee. "We might want to think of planting some fruit trees, too. They're not just for food. They're also pretty when they flower."

"Speaking of fruit," I said to my roommate, "I found Lillian Walsh's peach-pie recipe yesterday. She had a whole 'nother box with all of her blue-ribbon recipes in it hidden under a stair." I raised a finger to let her and Buck know I'd return in just a moment. I ambled to my room, retrieved the recipe box, and moseyed back to the kitchen, setting it down on the counter in front of Colette. "Any chance you'd be willing to bake some peach pies for me on Friday? I'd love to surprise the ladies at poker."

"Sure." My roommate opened the lid and flipped through the cards. She pulled out the one for peach pie and read it over. "Lillian got creative with this recipe. This calls for fresh ginger, Mexican vanilla, lemon extract, and six tablespoons of maple syrup. Dark brown sugar inside the pie, with coarse white sugar crystals sprinkled across the top. She used nectarines rather than regular peaches."

"Sneaky."

"Nectarines are technically a type of peach," Colette clarified, "so she wasn't a liar."

Buck raised his mug in salute. "Leave it to a chef to know the ins and outs of fruit."

"Speaking of nectarines," Colette said, "they're not in season here yet. Won't be for months. I could substitute canned peaches, but it would change the flavor. Want me to check with the restaurant suppliers? Surely one of them can find me some imported nectarines by Friday. It'll cost you, though."

I didn't mind paying a premium for the peaches if it meant I could surprise the gang. "Thanks, Colette. You're the best."

The three of us spent the late morning and early afternoon building a twelve-foot-by-six-foot enclosed bed in the backyard. Fortunately, Old Man Winter seemed to be taking a coffee break, and the outdoor temperature was in the midfifties, perfect for working on a project outside. We could work without either working up a sweat or risking frostbite. It was fun to have some time with

Colette, too. With both of us being so busy with work, we didn't get nearly enough time together these days.

While my roommate was a wiz with kitchen tools, her skills with power tools were another matter entirely. After she botched her third attempt to use an electronic screwdriver, Buck stepped into place behind her, wrapping his hand around hers to guide it. "Like this," he said, speaking over her shoulder. "Don't force it. Let the tool do the work for you."

She cried out in glee when the screw hit its mark this time. "I did it!"

By two o'clock, the enclosure was complete. As Buck packed up his tools and gathered the unused wood, he promised to fill the bed for us once the home improvement stores put out their spring gardening supplies in another month or two. "They make a type of soil specifically for raised beds. It's got a lot of compost and fiber mixed in, retains moisture well."

I picked up the final four-by-four to carry back to his van. "How do you know all that?"

"Looked into it online."

"You sure put a lot of effort into this project." I slid him some side-eye. "You got an ulterior motive?"

His gaze cut to Colette for an instant, so quickly I might not have noticed if I hadn't been watching so closely.

"Now I get it." I stood the four-by-four on its end and held it with one hand while I put the other on my hip. "You're hoping if you build this garden for Colette, she'll let you drop in for free meals."

A mischievous grin tugged at his mouth. "You got me. It's all about the food."

When his focus went Colette again, I had to wonder if there just might be more to it.

# CHAPTER 23

# WHERE THERE'S A
# WILL, THERE'S A WAY

### WHITNEY

Monday morning, I performed a walk-through at one of Home & Hearth's rental houses. Fortunately, the two men who'd rented the place had been model tenants. Always paid their rent on time. Maintained the place well. Never made unreasonable demands. *If only every tenant could be so easy to work with.* "You'll be getting your full deposit back, guys."

They were glad to hear it. They'd bought a townhouse and planned to use the deposit for a new big-screen TV.

After I'd wrapped things up at the rental house, I swung by the county tax office to drop off a check for property taxes on one of Home & Hearth's listings that was scheduled to close in a few days. The bank and the buyer wanted proof the taxes had been paid, which required the assessment to be paid in person given the short time frame that remained before closing.

As I waited for the receipt to print, my eyes spotted a pamphlet in a display on the counter. Bright red letters across the top read TAX SALES. I finagled one of the brochures out of the display and looked it over. The pamphlet detailed the process for bidding on properties that had been foreclosed on by the government for delinquent taxes. Although I felt sorry for anyone who lost their property to foreclosure, I also realized a tax sale could pose an opportunity for me and Buck to buy a property at a discounted price. Once we sold the house on Songbird Circle, we'd be in the market for another house to flip. Perhaps we should give a tax sale a try.

I tucked the pamphlet into my purse and took the receipt from the woman working the payment window. "Thanks."

She didn't even wait for me to step away before calling out, "Next!"

My property-management duties done for the time being, I hopped back into my car and headed downtown to the Davidson County Courthouse. Lawyers in business suits and their nervous clients walked the halls, some of them waiting on benches. I meandered the main foyer for a few seconds before spotting a directory posted on the far wall between two elevators. After consulting the board, I headed to the office for the probate-court clerk.

Working the counter was a middle-aged man with a slight paunch under his cable-knit sweater. He was the epitome of efficiency, answering questions quickly and sorting and stamping paperwork like a robotic machine on an assembly line.

I had to wait in line for a few minutes before it was my turn. As a woman walked away, I stepped up to the counter and exchanged a cordial greeting. "Are wills public record?"

"If they've been filed for probate, they are. Got the name of the testator?"

"Lillian Walsh. She died a few weeks ago."

"You can run a search there." He motioned with his arm, directing my gaze to a trio of computers at a table on the side of the room. Two were already in use. "The screen will tell you what to do. It's pretty self-explanatory, but if you have any questions, let me know. It's twenty-five cents per page for copies, an extra dollar if you want the copy certified."

I thanked the man and walked over to the table, taking a seat at the available computer in the center. As promised, the system was easy to use. I typed Lillian's first and last names when prompted, and up came a list of the documents in her file. A petition. An inventory. Something called Letters Testamentary. I had no idea what the latter was, but because it had a word akin to *testament* in its title, I tried it first. The document popped up on the screen and I read through it. Turned out to be the order appointing Andy Walsh as the executor of his mother's estate. *Not what I'm looking for.*

I backed out of the document and clicked on the petition. *Here we go.* The will was attached to the petition for probate. My pulse throbbing in my ears, I leaned in to take a look and scrolled through it. *It's a different will!* Sure enough, unlike the will I'd discovered under the stair, this will bequeathed equal shares of Lillian's estate to Wayne and Andy. *Could the revised will have given Wayne Walsh a motive for killing Nelda Dolan?*

I scrolled down to the final page. Nelda had witnessed this will as well. But this time I recognized the name of the second witness. Roxanne Donnelly. This will was dated a dozen years ago. The fact that it didn't mention

Lillian's husband told me Lillian had drafted this particular will after he'd already passed.

I clicked on the button to print the document, exited the computer file, and returned to the counter to pay for the printout, splurging on a certified copy so the detective would know it was legitimate. After thanking the clerk, I tucked the document into the manila envelope with the other will, slid the envelope into my purse, and returned to my car.

Whipping out my phone, I googled the name of the second witness on the more recent will I'd found under the stairs. Although various links popped up, none of them related to the recent death of a person with that name in the Nashville area. Ditto for the notary. *Good. Looks like they haven't been targeted.* Not yet, at least. If the newer will did indeed have something to do with Nelda's death, could the other witness and the notary be next on the killer's list?

It was straight-up noon when I closed the web search and placed a call to Detective Flynn. "I found something interesting I want to show you."

"I've got some things to discuss with you, too. I'm on my way out to lunch. Why don't you meet me?"

We arranged to join up at a quiet café in twenty minutes. I drove over and found him already seated in a booth in a back corner, perusing the menu.

I slipped into the other side of the booth. I reached into my purse, retrieved the manila envelope, and slid it across the table. "The certified copy is the will Andy Walsh filed with the probate court. It was drafted over a decade ago and splits the property equally between him and his brother. The other will is more recent. It leaves everything to Andy. It was in a secret compartment under a stair in Lillian's house."

"A secret compartment?" He arched a brow. "Where was it and how'd you find it?"

"I didn't. Sawdust did. He was rubbing himself along the steps and the bottom one moved. I'd noticed the stair creaked and had planned to fix it, but I had no idea there was a storage area underneath."

"Maybe your cat should become a detective. He's got a knack for digging up evidence."

It was true. The first piece of evidence he'd ever dug up was a dead body, though. I wish he had a knack for finding buried treasure instead.

The server came by to take our drink orders. While I drank iced tea in the warmer months, today was a hot tea kind of day.

"Coffee for me," Collin told the server before turning back to me. "I've been surviving on caffeine and Chinese takeout for the last month. With that new DNA technology, the chief's assigned each of us some cold cases to follow up on. Got a lot on my plate right now."

"It's nice to know we taxpayers are getting our money's worth."

"With all the hours I've put in, I'd have made more money flipping burgers." He pulled the documents from the envelope and looked them over, his head bobbing as he confirmed the information I'd told him. When he finished reading the wills, he set them back on the table and met my gaze. "Assuming the will you found under the stair is the only copy, Wayne Walsh would have a motive for killing Nelda Dolan. Whether he had the opportunity is another question."

"What do you mean?"

"For him to be the killer, he would have had to be in the house the night Nelda was killed. It's possible he was, but I'll have to talk with him, see if he has an alibi for that night. It's also possible that his son took care of this problem for him."

"Dakota?"

Collin nodded. "Maybe Nelda mentioned the will to Dakota, and Dakota realized she could cause his father to lose his inheritance. Dakota clearly had an opportunity to kill Mrs. Dolan, and now he's got a potential motive, too." He ran a frustrated hand over his head. "I'd just crossed him off my list of suspects, too. Guess I'll have to put him back on it."

"You crossed him off? Why?"

"He surfaced yesterday evening at his parents' place. I went by and talked to him. He said he'd lost his old cell phone and bought a new one. He didn't port his old number over. That's why we couldn't reach him at the number we had. He's been crashing at various friends' places the past few days. He told me he found the peacock necklace when he was scrounging around in the sofa for loose change. My guess is that it fell off Mrs. Dolan's neck when the clasp broke, and slipped between the cushions. Dakota said he had no idea it had belonged to Mrs. Dolan."

"What about the other jewelry he pawned?"

"I thought he might have stolen it from his grandmother, but he said she asked him to pawn pieces for her a few times when money was especially tight. She told him that because she didn't have a daughter or granddaughter to leave her jewelry to, she might as well sell it off. She told him she'd pawned a few pieces herself before, but that she was afraid the neighbors would see her going into the pawnshop and gossip about it. She swore Dakota to secrecy. She didn't want Wayne and Andy to know, either. She didn't want them to worry, and she didn't want Andy to bail her out or Wayne to feel guilty for borrowing from her."

"Did Dakota's story check out?"

"It did. I contacted the pawnshop this morning. Their records show Lillian pawned three pieces of jewelry herself prior to the first time Dakota pawned anything there."

"He told the truth, then."

"About the jewelry, anyway," Collin said. "That doesn't mean he's been honest about everything. This will gives me pause. Any chance it was in some kind of box when you found it?"

"No. It was in that envelope." In other words, it wasn't the thing that was taken from underneath Nelda. I supposed if the will had been under Nelda and was the reason she'd been killed, the killer would have destroyed the document and I never would have found it in the first place. It seemed far more likely she'd merely referenced the will in conversation with her killer.

Flynn drummed anxious fingers on the table. "I wonder if Wayne and Dakota were aware of the secret compartment. If they were, it seems they would have realized Lillian might have stashed a copy of her will there, and they would have removed it. Any chance I can interview them at the house? I'd like to mention it, see where their eyes go when I ask. Their body language might clue me in as to what they know."

"Of course," I said. "We found a box of Wayne's inventory in the attic. Silver polish. I can return it to him at the same time."

Collin said he'd get in touch with the two and let me know when they'd be coming by. The server swung by our table to deliver our drinks and take our food orders.

As I looked through the selection of hot teas the
server had left, I asked Collin whether he'd spoken with
Andy about the life-insurance policy Carl Dolan had
taken out on his wife.

"Spoke to him this morning," Collin said. "He confirmed that the policy had been taken out decades ago,
when he first opened his insurance agency. He said all
the couples on the circle bought policies that expired
when the insured reached seventy-five, though the policy Carl purchased on Nelda was worth double what the
others bought and he was the only one who'd added a
child as a beneficiary. That said, the value remained the
same over all that time. He never raised it."

I dunked the teabag in the hot water, the brew steep-
ing as I mulled over what he'd just told me. "So there's no
smoking gun, like Carl recently increasing the amount
he and Becky would be paid if Nelda passed away."

"Right. But the policy could still be a motive for
killing her. The fact that her birthday was approaching might have reminded him, or Becky, that the policy
would soon be worthless and that they better make a
move quick if they wanted to collect on it."

"What about Roxanne?" I asked. "Have you talked
to her?"

"She finally returned my call this morning, but she
had nothing to offer."

"You sure about that? She could have Nelda Dolan's
DNA under her fingernails." I held up my hands, curling
my fingers like claws.

"Could be," he acknowledged, "but there's not
enough evidence to support the search warrant I'd need
to find out. Besides, it's been over a week now. Any skin
cells she might have had under her fingernails would
have long since been washed away."

"What about Luis Bautista?"

"My gut is still squirming a little," he admitted, "but my brain keeps telling me he's the least likely suspect and not to waste my time running down a rabbit trail." With nothing left to say about the investigation, Collin inquired about the remodel. "Things moving along?"

"It's picking up. The materials have been delivered. Buck and I will install the new kitchen appliances and tile this week, start on the painting. A plumber's coming to install pipe for the new shower stall in the master bath."

"Y'all don't waste any time, do you?"

"Don't have any extra time to waste," I said. "I got a credit card for the home-improvement store and we'd like to get it paid off as soon as possible." I gave him a pointed look. "Once word gets out that Nelda Dolan's death wasn't an accident, we may have trouble selling the house."

"I'll keep things as quiet as I can," Collin promised. "For what it's worth, the media doesn't seem to pay much attention when an everyday person dies, unless it's particularly gruesome."

I realized the detective was trying to make me feel better, but in an odd way it made me feel worse. The only person who seemed to care much about Nelda Dolan was her killer, and the killer had wanted her out of the picture. But I suppose there was nobody to blame for that but Nelda herself. After all, you reap what you sow.

# CHAPTER 24

# TAKING STOCK

## WHITNEY

I woke Tuesday morning, pleased to discover upon checking my computer that the tins I'd listed on eBay had sold. I decided the fair thing to do was split the proceeds three ways, with Buck, Colette, and me each getting an equal share. Though Buck and I technically owned the tins, we wouldn't have realized they had any value if not for my roommate mentioning it. I retrieved some cash from my wallet and left it with a note on the kitchen counter where I knew Colette would find it later. It wasn't a lot of money, but she could apply it toward that air fryer she'd been thinking about.

On my drive to the flip house that morning, I was overcome by both hunger and curiosity and I found myself turning into the parking lot at the grocery store where I'd seen Carl Dolan speaking with the bakery clerk, Dulce, last week. I wasn't sure if Dulce was working today, but either way it wouldn't be a total waste of my time. Colette was working on locating nectarines for the peach pies she planned to bake on Friday, but I needed to shop for the other ingredients.

Mother Nature had taken pity on Nashville today. While the temperature remained frigid, she'd at least turned on the sun, the early rays providing little in the way of warmth but promising better days just around the corner. *Mother Nature can be such a tease.*

I rounded up a cart at the front of the store and rolled it inside, aiming for the bakery department. Country music played softly over the store's sound system, and I found myself improvising a two-step as I made my way. One glance behind the counter told me that Dulce was indeed working today. Working hard, as a matter of fact. A line of no less than seven customers waited at the bakery counter while she and a tall, thin young man scurried about, boxing up donuts, bear claws, and éclairs. Rather than spend unnecessary time waiting in line, I decided to go in search of the ingredients for the peach pie first. Maybe the rush would be over by the time I returned.

Looking up at the signs posted over the aisles, I scanned them until I spotted the one that read BAKING SUPPLIES. Off I went.

Lillian had been precise in her recipes, not only with her measurements but with her preferred brands of ingredients. She'd specified which brands of sugar to use, as well as which brands of extract, flour, cinnamon, and maple syrup. She hadn't made it easy to find her award-winning peach-pie recipe, but she'd made it easy as pie to follow.

Once I'd filled my cart with the ingredients, I ventured back to the bakery department. The scent of yeast and cinnamon enveloped me. *Someone must be baking in the back.*

Only one person stood in line now, a young mother with a fussy, toothless baby on her hip. She ordered a blueberry scone. When Dulce handed it to her, the woman opened the bag, broke a piece off the scone, and handed it to the baby. The fussing ceased immediately and the drooling began as the baby gummed the treat.

Dulce smiled at me over the glass display case. "Can I help you?"

I gestured back to the baby. "I'll have what she's having. Make it a half dozen." Buck would happily devour a couple of the scones, and I'd save at least one for Detective Flynn. He'd texted me late yesterday evening. He, Wayne, and Dakota were scheduled to come by the house at half past ten this morning.

Dulce grabbed a piece of waxed paper and a bag, and bent over to round up the scones.

I did my best to sound and appear casual. "You're a friend of Carl Dolan's, aren't you?"

She glanced up at me through the glass of the case, her expression surprised and wary. "He comes in here quite a bit," she said after a moment's hesitation. "He's got a donut addiction."

"Is that all?" I said. "I was hoping it was more than that."

She tucked the scones into the bag and stood up, confronting me straight on. "What do you mean?"

"He's a very nice man. I just hoped he wasn't lonely, is all." I extended my hand over the counter. "I'm Whitney, by the way. I bought the house next door to Carl. My cousin and I are fixing it up to sell."

Looking more relaxed now, she took my hand and gave it a friendly shake.

I laid it on as thick as the cream-cheese frosting on the carrot cake on the bottom shelf below. "Carl's planning some updates to his place, too. He asked for our input on paint."

"He mentioned that he was thinking of painting his house."

I took a chance. "Was that over steaks last Friday night?" I tempered my question with a knowing but non-accusatory smile and a coy tilt of my head, hoping not to alarm her.

She blushed and curled her fingers over the top of the case, leaning toward me. "You know about us?" she whispered.

*A-ha!* I knew Carl had been lying about going to the VFW Friday night. "He didn't say anything to me," I replied, "but he didn't have to. He came home with a grin on his face and lots of giddy-up in his gait." I shot her a wink.

She blushed even redder, but smiled. "I had a good time, too. We're going back this Friday."

I wondered how long Carl and Dulce had been dating, whether Dulce knew Nelda had passed less than two weeks prior. I was trying to come up with a way to ask her without being obvious when the customer behind me cleared his throat. "I hate to butt in, but I need four dozen donuts for a meeting that's starting in half an hour, and if I'm late my boss will chew me out."

I took my bag of scones, raised my hands, and backed away from the counter. "Sorry! Don't want you getting chewed out on my account." I offered Dulce a smile in the way of goodbye, grabbed my cart, and headed to the checkout.

Buck was already at the house when I arrived. I found him in the kitchen, preparing the tools and equipment we'd need to install the black-and-white tile flooring.

Along with the stacks of tile, he'd amassed a tub of grout, a mason's trowel, a tape measure, a bubble level, and a wet saw, as well as a bucket of water and a sponge. He scowled. "You're late."

"You're ornery."

I tossed the bag his way and he snatched it out of the air, opening it to glance inside. "You're forgiven."

"You're still ornery."

As he bit into his scone, I gave him a heads-up about the detective coming here to question Wayne and Dakota about the will. "Don't say anything about where we found it," I told him. "The detective wants to see how they react when they learn there's a secret hiding place in the house."

"I'll play dumb," Buck said.

"Luckily for you," I joked, "you don't even have to pretend."

Our ribbing finished for the time being, I donned my kneepads and grabbed the measuring tape. When installing tile, the process should start in the center of the room to ensure the best look. I measured from several directions to determine exactly where the center of the room was, and marked it with a piece of chalk.

Buck finished his scone, and the two of us got down to business. We'd just finished installing the first line of tile, alternating the black and white tiles in what would be a checkerboard pattern, when a knock sounded at the front door.

I stood and brushed my hands on my coveralls before heading down the unfinished steps to let Detective Flynn inside.

"'Mornin'."

I repeated the greeting. "Got an extra scone if you're interested."

"Heck, yeah. I got called in early and had to skip breakfast this morning. We got a hit in one of those cold cases. Officer Hogarty and her partner are on their way to make an arrest as we speak."

"Glad to hear it." I went up to the kitchen, careful to avoid the newly installed tiles, and retrieved the bakery bag from the counter.

Collin waited in the doorway, eyeing the tile. "I always liked the checkerboard look. The black and white reminds me of a police cruiser."

I handed him the bag. "That's the look we were going for. Classic cop car with early American influences."

He opened the bag and looked down into it before turning his green eyes on me. "Thanks."

"A man can't survive on coffee and Chinese takeout alone." As he devoured his scone, I gave him the scoop on Dulce and Carl. "I bought the scones at the grocery store where I saw Carl speaking with the bakery clerk. I was able to slip into conversation that I bought the house next door to Carl. Dulce admitted that they went out to dinner last Friday."

Collin swallowed the big bite he'd taken. "The VFW was a lie, then."

"Mm-hmm. I don't know how long they've been dating, though, or whether she's aware that Nelda just passed."

"I'll talk to her," Collin said. "Get the details."

*Ding-dong!*

The detective glanced at his watch. "They're early." He crumpled up the bag and tossed it into a plastic trash bin Buck had put out to collect our refuse. As Collin headed down the stairs, I followed after him. I'd been the one to come across Nelda Dolan's body. If Collin was about to nail her killer, I wanted to see it happen.

Two shapes were visible through the frosted-glass oval on the front door. The detective opened it to reveal Roxanne and Gayle standing side by side on the porch. A silvery head popped up between them as Mary Sue stood on tiptoe to look over their shoulders.

Gayle pointed over her shoulder. "We saw your car out here again."

Roxanne poked her fake fingernail into the detective's chest. "What's really going on here, mister?" She jabbed a second time. "We have a right to know!"

"Actually," Collin replied, the epitome of calm as he stepped back out of finger range. "You don't."

Roxanne crossed her arms over her chest and huffed, her breath creating a cloud in the air in front of her, as if she were a fire-breathing dragon.

Gayle tried a different tack, opening her eyes wide and sticking her neck out in hope. "Would you be willing to tell us anyway? Please? We're worried."

"All right," he acquiesced. "I have reason to suspect that Nelda Dolan might not have tripped and fallen down the stairs."

Not strong enough to remain on tiptoe, Mary Sue disappeared again behind her taller friends. But while she could no longer be seen, her voice could be heard. "You mean she might have died some other way? Broke her hip and lost her balance, or suffered a heart attack or stroke?"

Roxanne tossed an irritated look over her shoulder. "The medical examiner would have been able to tell if Nelda had a broken hip or died from a stroke or heart trouble. If the detective's here, that means he thinks she was killed on purpose." She turned her narrow eyes back on the detective. "Doesn't it, Detective Flynn?"

Seeming to realize there was nothing to be gained by arguing, he gave a single, definitive nod.

The women immediately crowded forward, like hens around someone tossing chicken feed, their quick questions like the clucks of an anxious brood.

Roxanne demanded to know, "Why would someone kill Nelda?"

Gayle wanted to know *how.* "How do you know it wasn't an accident?"

Given that the *where* and *when* were already established, Mary Sue went for *who.* "Who do you think it could be?"

Collin raised his hands. "Sorry, ladies. I've said all I'm going to about Nelda Dolan. But I will suggest that you be sure to keep your home-security systems activated at all times, if you've got them, and be extra careful coming and going from your homes."

Mary Sue's mouth fell open. "You think the killer could come for us, too? That he's targeting elderly women?"

"It's possible," the detective replied. "Older people are seen as easier targets. You can't ever be too careful."

Wayne Walsh's green minivan pulled to the curb behind them. Dakota sat in the passenger seat. Both of them looked over at the women on the porch and turned to each other, exchanging words.

As Wayne and Dakota climbed out of the car, the detective cued the ladies to disperse. "Y'all will have to leave the premises now." Probably realizing he'd have more luck if he promised to follow up with them, he added, "As soon as I learn anything, I'll make sure to let you know."

Roxanne harrumphed and turned to her friends. "I

don't know about the rest of you, but I'm going to the sporting goods store right now to buy me a gun."

Mary Sue worried her lip. "You know how to shoot a gun?"

"Not at all," Roxanne said. "That's why I'm going to get a shotgun. You hardly have to aim those suckers. You just pull the trigger and anything in its path is blown to kingdom come."

*There's a happy thought.*

The women turned en masse to go, Mary Sue now in the lead as they descended the porch steps.

As the women passed him, Wayne ignored them. Dakota, on the other hand, remembered his manners, greeting each of them by name and giving them a warm smile and nod. "Good morning, Mrs. Mecklenberg. Mrs. Garner. Mrs. Donnelly."

Wayne barged right into the house without being invited, acting as if he still had a right to be here. Dakota was more tentative, stopping at the threshold and waiting for an invitation. Apparently, he'd learned his lesson about trespassing.

Collin motioned the man-boy inside with his hand. "Come on in, Dakota."

The landing was crowded and I eased back, climbing a couple of steps up the upper staircase to give the three men more room and myself some personal space.

Wayne didn't even wait for the door to close before he hooted. "What a gaggle of hens, am I right?"

Though I, too, had noticed a similarity between the women and birds, I knew that the correct term was brood. A gaggle referred to geese, not chickens. I'd also had the good sense not to say something so insulting out loud. Once, on a field trip to the zoo in fifth grade, a classmate had pointed out that, with my long limbs, I resembled a giraffe. When I'd blushed in embarrassment, he decided I looked more like a flamingo. I'd attempted to even the score by saying, "At least I don't smell like the back end of an elephant!" The comment had only made him and his friends laugh. I got my revenge years later, in high school, when I'd taken the WD-40 I'd bought for shop class and squirted it through the vents in his locker. I never got caught, either. But I supposed the statute of limitations for my petty act of vandalism had long since passed.

Though Detective Flynn had essentially told the women only a minute before that this investigation was none of their business, he came to their defense now that Wayne had poked fun at them. "It's only natural for neighbors to be curious why a police detective is on their street."

Wayne wasn't having it. "Bunch of busybodies, if you ask me. All they do is gossip, gossip, gossip."

Though Roxanne certainly wasn't shy about sharing juicy tidbits, Wayne's assessment wasn't entirely fair. Nelda Dolan aside, much of the ladies' talk about their neighbors' business seemed to arise not from any malicious intent, but from a genuine concern about each other's welfare and an interest in their lives. *Nothing wrong with people looking out for each other.*

"So?" Wayne leaned toward the detective in his usual too-familiar way. "What're we here about?"

Flynn focused on their faces. "The secret compartment in this house."

Wayne and Dakota exchanged a look, but it wasn't a knowing look. Rather, it was an *un*knowing look. *Were they not aware of the compartment?*

Wayne shook his head once, as if he thought he'd

heard wrong and was attempting to rearrange the detective's words in his mind so they'd make sense. "Say what now?"

"This house has a hidden storage compartment," the detective said evenly. "Your mother must have told you two about it."

Wayne merely shook his head again, more emphatically this time. "Nope. She didn't say anything to me."

Dakota's face darkened, as if he felt hurt that his grandmother hadn't trusted him with this secret. "Granny never told me about it, neither. Where is it?"

Flynn held his cards close to his vest. "That's classified."

"Well?" Wayne circled a finger in the air as if to speed things up. "I assume you found something in it. If it was empty, you wouldn't have called us here. What did you discover?" He barked a laugh. "Please tell me it was a dozen gold bars."

"No. No gold bars." The detective reached into the inside pocket of his jacket, removed a folded copy of the will I'd found under the stair, and handed it to Wayne. "Your mother had hidden this."

As Wayne ran his gaze over the first page, Dakota sidled closer to his father and glanced down at it. "Is that Granny's will?"

"One of them," Collin said.

Wayne looked up from the page. "You mean she made more than one copy?"

"No," Collin said. "I mean it's a different will than the one that was filed for probate." He gestured to the will in Wayne's hand. "The one you're looking at leaves everything to your brother Andy."

Wayne's demeanor hardly changed as he flipped through the pages and looked them over. "This says everything goes to Andy, all right." He looked up from the document a second time. "I guess Mom must've changed her mind later and decided to split things evenly between us."

"No. That will in your hand is more recent than the one that was filed for probate."

Wayne's face screwed up as he tried to process the information. "Wait. Are you saying this is the right will? That the one that split everything fifty-fifty is the wrong one?"

"Yes," Flynn said. "That's exactly what I'm saying. Andy should have received all of your mother's property."

Wayne scoffed and threw up his hands. "Well, heck! I done already spent most of my share paying off bills. Ever' one of my boys had an overbite. You got any idea how much an orthodontist charges to put braces on a kid's teeth?"

*Did Wayne have any idea that he was digging himself in deeper by pointing out his financial woes?* The detective eyed him, assessing, as Wayne lowered his hands.

Wayne's demeanor mellowed, his tone now wistful. "I wouldn't even have all those boys if my wife and I hadn't been trying to give my mother a granddaughter."

*Ick.* I didn't want to think about Wayne and his wife "trying." Maybe if I stuck a screwdriver in a socket it would zap the thought from my brain.

"Mom only had me and my brother," he said. "Once she had Andy, I think she was disappointed when I came out a boy, too. She never said as much, but I could read between the lines. She was always talking about how much she'd love to have a granddaughter to dress up and dote on, do her hair and play tea party with. She said it wasn't fair Nelda got twin grandgirls when she was too much of sourpuss to enjoy them the way she should."

Well, heck. A minute ago I was sure this guy was a murderer, and now he had me feeling sorry for him. Maybe Lillian realized Wayne was trying to give her the little girl she'd always wanted, and that's why she'd helped him support all the boys who'd come along instead. Of course, one of those boys was Dakota. I shifted my gaze to his face. He had a hangdog look about him, his shoulders slumped and his gaze directed downward.

As if realizing he'd hurt his son's feelings, Wayne put a hand on his Dakota's back. "I didn't mean nothing by that, Dakota. You know your grandmother thought the world of you and your brothers." He leaned in and whispered. "You were her favorite, though. You know that, right?"

On hearing this last bit, Dakota perked up, his back straightening.

Having placated his son, Wayne turned back to the detective. "What do I do now? Do I have to pay Andy back?"

"I suppose that's up to him." Flynn redirected the conversation. "Are you surprised your mother cut you out of her will?"

"Truthfully? Can't say I blame her one bit." Wayne finally had the sense to look at least a little ashamed. He glanced over at his son, his voice softer when he returned his gaze to the detective. "She bailed me out a few times over the years when I got in over my head. More than a few times, if I'm being honest. It's only fair she'd leave her estate to Andy. I'm not mad about it, but I have no idea how I'm going to make things square with him." As he pondered his predicament, his face tightened with befuddlement. "Why didn't Andy file this will? Mom would've given him a copy."

Collin said, "I'm wondering the same thing." He turned to Dakota. "What about you? Did you know about this will?"

"No." Dakota shook his head. "Granny never said nothing about it."

The detective turned back to Wayne, staring him down.

Realizing the stare was a challenge, Wayne flexed his jaw and a jagged blue vein pulsed in his neck, like liquid lighting under his skin. "What's it to you, anyway, Detective? What's it matter who my mother left her property to?" His eyes cut to me as if to determine whether I was in on the secret.

"Look at the last page of the will," Collin told him, "where the signatures are."

Wayne shifted his focus from me to the will, flipped to the final page, and eyed it. "Yeah? So?"

Collin said, "Nelda Dolan witnessed that will."

"Like I said, *so*?" Wayne still didn't seem to get it, hadn't made a connection. But was he merely pretending? Had he known that Nelda had witnessed his mother's recent will? Again, his gaze darted between me and the detective.

"*So*." Collin said, "The fact that Nelda Dolan witnessed the will means she knew you weren't supposed to inherit anything. That could put you at odds with her."

Wayne chuckled mirthlessly. "Everyone was at odds with that woman at one point or another. She wasn't exactly what you'd call a nice person."

Seeming to realize he'd have to be blunt, the detective said, "That will could have given you a reason to want her gone. It could implicate you in Nelda's death."

Dakota sucked in air and Wayne jerked his head back as if slapped. "I thought she fell down the stairs."

Now that my cat had found the hidden will, Flynn had no choice but to let the cat out of the bag in regards to the investigation. "She did fall down the stairs. But she was helped."

"Helped?" Dakota's eyes popped wide. "Are you saying someone pushed Mrs. Dolan down the stairs?"

Collin nodded.

"Oh jeez, oh jeez, oh jeez!" Dakota's breaths came fast and he wrapped his arms around his torso in a subconscious and instinctive act of self-protection. "That means a killer came in this house while I was sleeping! I could have been killed, too!"

The way Dakota was freaking out made one thing clear. *He didn't do it.* Even Meryl Streep couldn't pull off such a convincing act.

# CHAPTER 25

# COVERALLS AND COVER-UPS

### WHITNEY

Wayne gripped his son's shoulder. "Calm down, boy! You're still with us." Releasing his son, Wayne turned to the detective and crossed his arms over his chest, much like Dakota. In this case, though, Wayne's body language was defensive. "I didn't kill Nelda Dolan, but I can tell you who might've. Roxanne Donnelly. Those two women butted heads for years over some nonsense or other."

My mind filled with an image of Nelda and Roxanne going beehive to bouffant in bell-bottom pantsuits. Not a pleasant image, but much better than the one of Wayne trying to conceive a baby girl with his wife.

Wayne rambled off a list of Nelda's and Roxanne's grievances. "Those two got in a dither about Roxanne's redbud tree dropping leaves on the Dolans' side of their shared fence. Where visitors should park in the cul-de-sac. Outdoor Christmas decorations. The smoke from the Donnellys' backyard grill. Nelda was always the

one to start things, but Roxanne didn't back down. *Ever.*
Mary Sue Mecklenberg always had to intervene. Mom
tried to stay out of it. She didn't have much of a stomach
for that type of unpleasantness."

The detective stared at Wayne for a long moment,
as if attempting to bore into the man's mind and access his memory banks, see if an image of Nelda Dolan
tumbling down the staircase was tucked away in some
deep, dark recess. "That's all I need," he said finally.
"You two are free to go. But not a word about this to
Andy until I've had a chance to speak to him. Understood?"

Wayne dipped his head. "Understood."

Dakota nodded in agreement.

As Wayne grabbed the door handle, I remembered
the silver polish. "Wait!" I pointed up the stairs, into the
kitchen. "Don't forget your inventory."

I turned around to head up and reflexively reached for
the loose banister to steady myself. I cried out and stum-
bled as the railing pulled free from the wall, the metal
wall plate and screws clanking and tinkling to the steps.
One of the screws bounced down the stairs—*clink,
clink, clink*—until it landed at Wayne's feet, rolling in
a circle until the sharp end pointed at him accusingly.
I was left holding an eight-foot pole in my hand like a
Shaolin stick fighter in a martial arts movie. Despite
what the song says, not everybody was kung fu fighting.
Some of us were just trying to make a living. Unfortunately, some of us had just produced sizable holes in the
drywall that would need to be patched.

Hearing the noise, Buck looked down from the
kitchen doorway. "It was only a matter of time until that
thing came loose."

*Guess we should've made the banister a higher*

*priority.* I climbed the steps and leaned the rail against the wall in the upstairs hallway.

Wayne turned to Dakota again and gestured up the stairs. "Scoot on up there and get the polish for me, son."

Dakota came upstairs and followed me to the kitchen, where Buck had already returned to working on the second row of tile. "Cool. The floor looks like the racing flag from Super Mario."

Buck sat back on his heels and cut Dakota a look. "Dude. All racing flags look like this. Lay off the video games and watch some NASCAR like a real man."

I'd been afraid Buck's words would hurt Dakota's feelings, but instead Dakota laughed. *Men interact differently than women, that's for sure.* I retrieved the box of Starlight Silver Polish from the pantry and handed it to Dakota. "Here you go."

"Any chance y'all might need some help?" Dakota's hopeful gaze moved from me to Buck. "I'm looking for work."

"Laying tile takes practice," Buck said, "and it's backbreaking work."

"I'm willing to learn," Dakota said, "and I'm stronger than I look."

My cousin and I exchanged looks. My look said, *This kid hasn't been able to hold a job. Hiring him could be asking for trouble.* Buck's look said, *We need to get this house done and sold. I've got no qualms firing the punk if he messes up.* I raised my brows and pursed my lips, my look now saying, *If this goes south, it's on you.*

Our telepathic conversation completed, Buck eyed the young man and conversed audibly. "Tell you what, Dakota. We'll give you ten dollars an hour to paint. Think you can handle that?"

Painting was tedious work. Ten dollars an hour was a bargain. Dakota could save us time and effort, as long as he did a decent job.

The boy shifted the box of silver cleaner into his left arm and stretched out his hand to shake mine, then Buck's. "You've got yourself a deal."

"One screwup," Buck said, leaning down to look into Dakota's face, "and we're done."

"I understand, sir."

*Sir.* I had to snicker at that.

Buck, on the other hand, smiled smugly and released Dakota's hand. "When can you start?"

Dakota shrugged. "Now?"

Buck turned to address me. "Show him the ropes. Start him on the downstairs bedrooms."

"Okeydoke."

Dakota carried the box down to the landing. I followed him.

He looked up at his father. "They've hired me to paint." He angled his head to indicate me. "She's gonna show me what to do."

"Don't that beat all," Wayne remarked. "One minute you're calling me a killer, and the next minute you're hiring my son to work for you." He snorted. "What time should I pick him up?"

Knowing that Buck and I planned to put in a long day, but that it could also be difficult to pinpoint exactly when we'd be at a convenient stopping point, I said, "Six o'clock. Ish."

"He's all yours, then." With that, Wayne reached out to take the box of silver polish from his son.

"Leave it for now." Collin motioned for Dakota to set the box down on the landing. "I'll need to take a quick look before any property is released from this house."

Wayne raised his hands and brows. "Whatever you say, officer." With that, he headed out the door.

Collin jerked his head toward the door. "Wait outside, too, Dakota. I'll let you back inside in a minute or two."

Dakota stepped out onto the porch and the detective locked the door behind him. He gestured at the frosted glass pane in the door and whispered, "Stand in front of the glass so he can't see in. I don't want him to see where the secret compartment is located."

I stood with my back to the door, raising my arms over my shoulders as if I were going through an airport scanner so that I'd block as much of the glass as possible. Collin eased himself down the steps until he reached the bottom, the telltale step giving off its signature creak. He pulled a pair of disposable latex gloves from his jacket pocket, donned them, and pointed at the bottom step. *This one?* he mouthed.

I nodded.

He lifted the step and peered into the now-empty compartment. Bending forward, he examined the hinges. When he finished, he carefully lowered the step and returned to the landing, still whispering so Dakota couldn't overhear. "It's still possible Wayne killed Nelda, but it's clear he didn't know about the hidden will or he would have taken it with him to eliminate the evidence. Dakota's reaction tells me he didn't kill Nelda."

"I reached the same conclusion."

Collin returned to the landing and opened the box of silver polish. "These bottles are rectangular, and one is missing."

"You think that's what could have been under Nelda? You think she snagged a bottle of this stuff while she was here? Or that whoever pushed her dropped the bottle and it ended up under her?"

"One way to find out."

He opened the front door to address Wayne. "There's a bottle of polish missing from your box. Where is it?"

"Mom bought a bottle from me to polish her silver a few months ago, before she passed. Only bottle I ever sold. Nobody else seemed to be interested. I left the box here thinking maybe she could sell some to her friends, but she must've had Andy put it in the attic. I forgot all about it until she mentioned it." He pointed to me.

"Where's that bottle now?" Collin asked.

"Heck if I know. If the bottle wasn't with Mom's other cleaning supplies, she must've used it up."

Collin turned to me and I shrugged to let him know I hadn't seen the bottle anywhere.

The detective handed the box to Wayne and told him he was free to go before closing the door again. Collin tugged the gloves off his hands and tucked them under his arm, digging in his pants pocket for his car keys. "I'm off to speak with Andy and Dulce. I want to know if Andy was aware of the newer will. I also want to know more about Carl and Dulce's relationship. I'll talk to Carl, too, see if his story and Dulce's jibe. I'm going to speak with Roxanne again, also. I want to know just how deep a feud she had with Nelda Dolan."

I wanted to know, too.

With that, he headed off. I could only hope that the next time we spoke, he'd have some answers.

Leaving Dakota on the porch, I went to my SUV and retrieved the same paint-spattered pair of coveralls he had used to keep warm the morning we'd discovered Nelda Dolan in the doorway. He could have them. They

were about ready for the trash can anyway. I returned to
the house and held them out. "Come in and put these on.
They'll protect your clothes."

We stepped back inside, where he slid into the garment. I had several inches on the kid. While the coveralls fit me just fine, the legs puddled around his ankles
and the sleeves swallowed his hands, much like the ill-
fitting suit he'd worn to Nelda's memorial service. To
rectify the problem, I grabbed my staple gun from my
toolbox and proceeded to improvise a hem at the bottom of each leg. "Roll the sleeves back," I instructed.
Once he had, I slid the gun under the edge, squeezed
the handle, and stapled the rolls into place. *Kachunk.*
*Kachunk. Kachunk.* "That ought to do ya." I returned
the staple gun to the toolbox.

I led him out to the garage, where we bypassed the
rolls of old carpet to round up canvas tarps, painter's
tape, rollers, brushes, stirrers, trays, and cans of paint.
We carried it back to the bedroom where he used to
sleep and spent the next twenty minutes engaged in a
detailed lesson on the ins and outs of painting. How to
apply the tape to protect the trim. When to use regular
brushes, when to use foam brushes, and when to use a
roller. How to avoid leaving brushstrokes in the paint.
The importance of thoroughly stirring the paint before
applying it.

"The most important thing to remember," I told him,
"is not to get into a hurry. If you rush, you'll end up
splashing and dripping. You've got to take your time
and do it right so it doesn't look sloppy. Got it?"

"Got it."

He'd seemed to be paying attention, and had even
asked a couple of perceptive questions. Maybe he wasn't
the total screwup the ladies of Songbird Circle seemed

to think he was. At least he couldn't do any permanent damage here. If he did a poor job, we could always paint over it. And if he did a good job, Buck and I could focus on the bigger tasks.

I handed Dakota a brush. "Here you go, Michelangelo."

He smiled, and I was pleased he'd gotten the reference. But then he spoiled it by saying, "You like the Teenage Mutant Ninja Turtles, too?"

*What have Buck and I gotten ourselves into?*

# CHAPTER 26

# HITCHING AND SNITCHING

**WHITNEY**

I checked Dakota's progress repeatedly throughout the day, putting more and more time between my visits downstairs as I became more comfortable that he was doing a competent job. He'd been exceedingly careful at the points where the wall met the trim, his lines razor straight, not a single smudge in sight. I spotted only a couple fresh drips on the coveralls and canvas tarps. Thanks to me and Buck, this kid might have just found his forte.

After Wayne picked Dakota up Tuesday evening, and despite the fact that we had plenty of home-improvement projects to complete, I proposed another project to Buck—Operation Hitch-and-Snitch. The detective might not be sure whether to listen to his gut or his brain, but as long as there was any chance Luis Bautista could be Nelda's killer, I thought the matter was worth pursuing. If her killer was safely confined behind bars, we'd have a much better chance of selling the house for a decent price. The sooner the better, too. The more time we could put between the killer's arrest and listing the house, the greater the chance that the local news cycle would have moved on to another story and Nelda's murder would no longer be on everyone's news feed and minds.

Buck was all in. "Is Colette free tonight?" he asked. "It could be helpful to have her along."

"She's got the night off," I said. "Which means she's probably cooked something at our place. Come over and we'll see if we can convince her to join us again." We were hardly Seal Team Six, but we'd successfully run surveillance together in the earlier investigation, followed a potential suspect, and interrogated her at her apartment. The suspect had thrown a glass of iced tea in my face, but I'd learned from the experience. If the driver from Hitch-a-Ride tried to throw anything at me, I now knew to duck.

As we headed out to our cars, my eyes spotted a large red sign posted in the flowerbed next to Roxanne's front porch. It featured an image of a gun and read THIS PROPERTY PROTECTED BY SMITH AND WESSON SECURITY. A glance around the circle told me that most of the others had taken a similar but slightly different tack. Gayle's wooden fence now bore a posted placard that read BEWARE OF DOG. *Is she referring to Mosey?* That dog was anything but dangerous. Then again, there was a risk someone could trip over him. Mary Sue had placed a preprinted sign in her front window that read THESE PREMISES UNDER 24-HOUR VIDEO SURVEILLANCE. A camera that I suspected was a fake was mounted over her front door. Carl and Becky Dolan were the only ones on the block who hadn't posted some type of warning. Did that mean anything?

While I certainly couldn't blame the neighbors for feeling anxious, I wasn't sure how effective the measures would be. I also had no idea how Roxanne thought she'd be able to fire a gun with those long fingernails getting in the way. She'd have a hard time getting her index finger on the trigger. Anyone who got a glimpse of Mosey would be able to tell he was no real threat. The camera over Mary Sue's door looked cheap and flimsy, a dead giveaway that it was merely a decoy.

Buck followed me home. As we stepped inside the stone cottage, we were met by the enticing scents of garlic and pesto. Looked like Colette had made Italian tonight.

"I'm home!" I called out to her.

"I'm making pizzas!" she called back.

"Hope you got enough for me!" Buck added.

She poked her head around the doorway of the kitchen. "Buck's here? Darn," she teased. "There go our leftovers."

After cleaning ourselves up, Buck and I joined her in the kitchen. She'd prepared a caprese salad and margherita pizzas with pesto sauce.

I filled my plate with three slices of pizza and enough salad to feed a dozen bunny rabbits. Physical labor sure makes a girl work up an appetite.

Buck followed suit. "Guess I'll have to save that frozen TV dinner for another night."

Sitting on stools at the breakfast bar, I explained my plan to Colette and Buck while we ate. "I'll download the Hitch-a-Ride app to my phone. I know where Luis Bautista lives from the photos he posted on social media. He told Detective Flynn that he only drives at night. We'll park somewhere near his apartment and I'll request a ride. If I don't get him on the first request, I'll cancel and try again until I get him as my driver. You two can each follow his car, make sure he doesn't drive off into the boonies somewhere to kill me. I'll request a ride to Tootsie's on SoBro."

Tootsie's or, more formally, Tootsie's Orchid Lounge, was a Nashville landmark, having been in business since the 1960s. It sat right around the corner from the Ryman Auditorium, the original home of the Grand Ole Opry. Among Tootsie's early customers were Patsy Cline, Kris Kristofferson, and Waylon Jennings. Several movies had been filmed on site, too. It would be a safe, public place for Bautista to drop me off.

Buck raised a slice of the delicious pizza from his plate. "It might make more sense for Colette and me to follow you together in one vehicle. That way, the driver can keep an eye on traffic and the passenger can keep an eye on you."

One car, two cars, it really didn't matter. "However y'all want to do it is fine with me. Just make sure you don't lose him."

Colette bit her lip. "This is crazy, Whitney. If Luis Bautista murdered Nelda and he figures out you're spying on him, he could kill you, too."

"I'll have these in my purse." I held up the pepper spray she'd given me and the large wrench that had become my defensive weapon of choice.

Buck didn't seem to share Colette's concern about my safety. He finished chewing his pizza and said, "She'll be fine. Bautista can't kill Whitney while he's driving, and if he pulls over somewhere, we'll be right there to make sure it doesn't happen." Buck pulled a heavy-duty metal hammer from his own toolbox and held it up, flexing his well-developed bicep. "I'll keep this in reach. If he tries to hurt my cousin, he'll be sorry. This thing could smash a skull."

It was nice to know he had my back. "Thanks, Buck."

He reached into his toolbox and pulled out a long screwdriver, holding it out to Colette. "Here. You can stab him with this."

She looked down at the screwdriver and crinkled up her nose. "I've got something much better." She stood and stepped over to one of the kitchen drawers, opening it to retrieve what appeared to be a medieval torture device. The steel tool had a straight handle attached to a flat plate sporting a mass of sharp, pointed nails. She brandished it. "How about I take this instead? It's my best meat tenderizer. Twenty-eight ultra-sharp prongs." She faked a couple of swings in Buck's direction.

"Yikes," I said. "That tenderizer could turn a person into a pegboard. I wouldn't want to be on the receiving end of that thing."

Buck tossed the screwdriver back into his toolbox. "Whatever suits your fancy."

When we finished our meal, I downloaded the Hitch-a-Ride app. Armed with pepper spray, a wrench, a hammer, and a meat mallet, we climbed into Colette's car and drove to the apartment complex where Luis Bautista lived. I didn't know which particular unit he resided in, but I figured we could identify his car by the glow-in-the-dark stickers all Hitch-a-Ride drivers sported in their front and back windows. Since it was dark outside already, I didn't have to worry that he might spot me performing surveillance from the backseat of Colette's Chevy.

We were circling slowly through the lot when I saw a thumbs-up sticker glowing in the back window of a silver Honda Accord. I pointed. "That must be his car. Looks like he hasn't headed out yet."

Colette drove to a nearby shopping center, and I climbed out to wait in front of a florist's shop. The place was closed for the night, but maybe Bautista would assume I worked here and had been making floral arrangements after business hours to be delivered tomorrow. After dropping me off, Colette and Buck waited in front of a barbershop at the far end of the parking lot while I logged into the app.

The first time I requested a ride to Tootsie's, the request was accepted by a driver named Ronnie K with a bald head and broad smile. *Darn.* I hated to disappoint Ronnie K, but he wasn't the guy I was looking for. I jabbed the button to cancel the ride and waited ten minutes before trying again. I got lucky this time. Luis B picked up the request. If I survived the ride, I'd treat myself, Buck, and Colette to drinks at Tootsie's.

A couple of minutes later, when headlights approached the florist and seemed to be slowing, I glanced down at my phone's screen. The Hitch-a-Ride app indicated that Luis Bautista was only a hundred feet away and closing in. As he pulled to the curb in the Accord we'd spotted in the apartment's parking lot, the app issued a cheery *beep-beep* and flashed a message. *Your ride has arrived!*

I stepped to the curb and bent over to look in the front passenger window. The driver rolled the window down. Sure enough, the guy at the wheel wore his longish black hair pulled back in a man bun. While he resembled the person in the Instagram photos, in the parking lot's dim light and without a photo pulled up to compare I couldn't be sure he was the same guy.

"Are you Luis?" I asked.

He nodded, and I climbed into the backseat, scooting into the middle where I could keep an eye on him in the rearview mirror. "Hi," I said with forced friendliness. "I'm Whitney."

He replied with a curt "Hi," and pulled away from the curb, glancing over to consult the map on the screen of his phone, which rested in a mount affixed to the dashboard.

As he pulled out of the lot, I attempted small talk. "Sure was nice weather today. I'm glad it warmed up a bit."

He said nothing in reply. Then again, I supposed I hadn't actually asked him a question.

I posed a simple one to start. "How's your day going?"

"Okay."

*Hmm. Not one for words, is he?* "These ride services are great," I said. "I hate waiting for the bus, especially in the evenings when they don't run very often."

He responded only with a nod. Clearly, he wasn't going to make it easy for me to glean anything from him. But I was nothing if not persistent.

"How long have you been driving for Hitch-a-Ride?" I asked.

"A little while." He took the turn as directed by the voice coming from the GPS.

*A little while?* That was a vague, imprecise answer. But maybe it only seemed that way to me because my job required precise measurements. I constantly used my measuring tape and rulers—*measure twice, cut once*.

"Do you like driving people around?" I asked.

"It's all right."

*Ugh*. What could I do to get this guy to open up, show

me a glimpse of personality so I could try to determine whether or not he was Nelda Dolan's killer? Then again, what, exactly, had I expected? It was doubtful the guy would come out with a complete confession during the drive. But I'd hoped to hear or see something that would provide some evidence to either incriminate or exonerate him. I glanced around the car, looking for anything that he could have pulled out from under Nelda's body as she lay on the landing. I saw nothing.

*What can I ask him next?* Having heard of drivers going on strike, I knew their pay and working conditions weren't optimal. While some drove full-time, others held regular full-time jobs in addition to driving for the ride services. "Do you work a day job, too?"

His eyes cut to the rearview mirror, meeting mine. Lines of suspicion formed around them. He hesitated a moment before replying, "No."

The guy appeared to be in his early twenties, not much older than Dakota. My gaze traveled the front windshield before I discreetly cast a glance behind me to see if the back window bore a student parking decal. Sure enough, in the lower back corner was a sticker bearing the name of Aquinas College, a small Catholic institution in the southwest part of the city. "I noticed your parking decal. What are you studying at Aquinas?"

He shifted in his seat, seeming uncomfortable with my personal question. "Philosophy."

"Ah. *I think therefore I am.*" It was the only philosophy I knew. Well, other than the metaphysical musings of Charlie Brown as professed in the Christmas special and the Peanuts comic strips.

Again, the driver failed to respond verbally, though I thought I discerned a slight eye roll at my quote. He probably heard it from everyone who learned he studied philosophy. It was one of the most well-known philosophical statements, after all. A moment later, though, his attitude seemed to change. He still seemed suspicious, but he was no longer so quiet. Maybe his guard was up due to the fact that Detective Flynn had questioned him recently. His narrowed gaze locked on me in the rearview mirror. "The app indicated you canceled a ride request a few minutes before I accepted."

*Shouldn't his eyes be on the road, not me?* "That was an accident," I said. "I'm new to the system. Just signed up this evening. Still learning how to work it."

He glanced at the road before turning his laser-like stare on me again. "Sometimes people cancel rides if they're trying to get a specific driver."

"As long as I get where I'm going," I said with a casual lift of my shoulders, "I don't care who drives me there."

Aside from trying to figure out if this guy was a killer, I couldn't imagine why anyone would necessarily choose to ride with him. It certainly wasn't because his car smelled nice. The vehicle had a distinct scent of drive-through burritos. And I couldn't claim it was his hospitality. He hadn't offered me water, gum, or a phone charger.

Luckily, he seemed convinced by my words, and his face relaxed. A minute later, as the driver headed up the entrance ramp to the 440 loop, my phone chimed and lit up with an incoming text from Detective Flynn. It read: *What are you doing in that car?* He followed his words with an angry-face emoji. *Uh-oh.* Collin had caught me playing private investigator, going well beyond my role as mole or confidential informant. He clearly didn't appreciate it, either. But he couldn't really blame me. I had a personal stake in this case. A financial one, too. A quick resolution was in both his interest and mine.

For the detective to know I was in the car, he must have been following it, too, just like Buck and Colette. I typed a response. *Trying to see what I might find out.*

As I hit send, another incoming text note sounded, this one from the front seat. One glimpse up front told me it didn't come from the phone mounted on the dash, however. Rather, it came from a second phone stashed in the cup holder. *He's got a burner.* Only people up to no good carried burner phones, right?

The driver turned the phone so he could read the lit screen. From the space between the seats, I could read the screen, too. It displayed a text that read *Mayday! Mayday! We're out of potato chips!* The screen indicated the text had been sent by Luis Bautista. But how could the driver receive a text from himself? *He can't be Luis Bautista, can he? Who is he really? Has he killed Luis and assumed his identity?* I couldn't be sure who the guy was, but at least he seemed to be wearing his own face. There was no telltale line of torn skin along his jawline. *My imagination is running away with me, isn't it?*

I discreetly snapped a quick pic of the burner phone's screen and sent it to the detective along with another text. *This just came in on the driver's second phone.* After I sent the text, I kept pretending to type, tapping my short thumbnails on the screen, *tap-tap-tap*, buying myself some time as I waited for a response to come in. None did. Seconds later, however, the car lit up as the flashing lights of a police cruiser illuminated the road behind us and a siren sounded. *Woo-woo-woo!*

## CHAPTER 27

# END OF THE ROAD

**WHITNEY**

The driver's eyes popped wide as they went to the rearview mirror and met mine. With me blocking his view of the road behind us, he turned the other way to consult the side mirror. "I wasn't speeding. Why are the cops pulling me over?"

I didn't reply. The question seemed to be rhetorical, not addressed to me. Besides, he'd been none too responsive to the questions I'd asked him. He could figure this one out on his own. *They're pulling you over because they think you might be a killer. Duh!* This thought was followed by another that was much more worrisome. *What if he tries to outrun them?* I was trapped in this backseat. What if we wrecked, or hit a pylon, or rolled down an embankment? The car could burst into flame! I could be severely injured, or worse!

Fortunately, while I sat in the back seat panicking, the driver slowed and eased over onto the shoulder of the freeway, muttering curses under his breath. Once the car was stopped, he rolled his window down, letting in the brisk early-evening air. I took a deep breath to calm myself, regretting the action when my nose filled with automobile exhaust fumes. I glanced back to see Officer Hogarty at the wheel of the cruiser and the detective sitting in the passenger seat. As I looked back, Buck and Colette drove by on the freeway, both of their heads turned in my direction. My gaze followed Colette's car now. She signaled and took the next exit.

The sound of the cruiser's door closing cut through the night from behind us, followed by the sound of footsteps approaching. Officer Hogarty strolled up alongside the car and bent down to look inside. Her gaze went from the driver to me, her expression souring. She returned her focus to the driver and held out her hand. "License and registration, please."

Gripping the wheel so tight he appeared to be strangling it, the driver looked up at her. "Why did you pull me over? I was careful to make sure I wasn't speeding."

"We'll get to that," she said. "For now, show me your license and registration."

Exhaling sharply, the driver reached over to open the glove box. Lest he pull out a weapon, I unzipped my purse, shoved my hand inside, and gripped the wrench, ready to whack his wrist with it if he grabbed a gun. Fortunately, all he retrieved from the compartment was a slip of paper. He handed it to Officer Hogarty.

She glanced down at the page. "This car is registered to Luis Bautista." Her gaze moved to the driver's face. "That you?"

He paused a long moment before releasing a long breath. "No."

I had to fight the urge to shout, "A-ha!" Collin's gut had been right. Something was up here.

"Who are you?" Hogarty asked him.

"Caesar Santos," the driver said. "Luis is my room-mate."

So the driver was Bautista's roommate, not his killer. Less dramatic, sure, but I suppose it was a good thing the body count so far remained at one. Their relationship also explained the emergency plea for salty snacks. *Must be this guy's turn to buy.*

Hogarty waggled her fingers and Santos reached into his back pocket, pulled out his wallet, and produced his license. "Hang tight," she said. With that, she returned to her cruiser.

Although I had lots of questions for the driver— *Why was he driving under his roommate's name? Why couldn't he use his own name? Did he really think a man bun was his best look? How did he plan to make a living as a philosophy major? Had he tried salt and vinegar chips? They're delicious!*—I realized it would be best to back off and leave the investigation in the hands of the professionals in the cruiser behind me. Collin and Officer Hogarty were already irritated at me for butting in.

Officer Hogarty returned to the window a moment later with Detective Flynn on her heels. "Step out of the car, please," she directed Santos.

"Why?" he cried. "I haven't done anything wrong!"

Hogarty skewered him with her squint. "Step. Out. Of. The. Car."

He exhaled an indignant huff, but complied. She took him by the shoulder and turned him to face the vehicle. He glanced in at me and seared me with his stare, as if he knew I had something to do with his arrest. I did my best to look innocent, opening my eyes wide and batting them as if I were totally bewildered by this unexpected predicament. *Who me? A spy? Why, that's crazy talk!*

As Hogarty cuffed Santos, she said, "You're under arrest for fraud."

He remained silent as Hogarty read him his rights. *Silence was an option. Anything he said would be fair game in court. The usual stuff about lawyers. Blah, blah, blah.* Once she'd finished and marched him back to the cruiser, I grabbed my purse and climbed out of the car.

Collin leaned on the fender, his arms crossed over his chest. "You have no business being here. You could've botched our investigation."

"But I ended up giving you a reason to pull Santos over." Really, without my photo of the text from Bautista, would they have had a reason to pull the guy over and arrest him? No. They would've had to keep following him until some other incriminating evidence reared its head. Or at least until he committed a traffic infraction. As careful as he'd been behind the wheel, they might have had to follow him for weeks. "The way I see it, I saved you some time and effort."

Collin cocked his head and eyed me. "I can't decide if you're a thorn in my side, a pain in my neck, or—"

"The wind beneath your wings?"

There was no doubt about it this time. Collin definitely rolled his eyes. "I hope you had a weapon with you. This guy could be a killer."

"I know that. I'm armed." I pulled open my purse to show him the wrench.

He peeked inside and shook his head. "You've got some screws loose, Whitney. Maybe you should use that tool to tighten them."

"This is a wrench, detective. A screwdriver is for tightening screws." I zipped up my purse and gave him my best eye roll in return. "If you're going to insult me, at least do it right."

He conceded with raised palms. "Point taken. I just don't want to see you get hurt."

Our gazes locked for a moment. I felt my cheeks warm with a blush, and saw his cheeks darken as well.

He scowled. "I don't want to see *anyone* get hurt."

I repeated his palms-up gesture and echoed his phrase. "Point taken. By the way, what did Andy Walsh say when you showed him Lillian's revised will this afternoon? Was he surprised?"

"Not in the least. His mother had given him a copy shortly after she'd had it signed and notarized. He says he didn't file it because he didn't want to hurt his brother's feelings. He says Wayne isn't lazy, he's just misunderstood, that he works hard but hasn't seemed to have found his niche yet."

The theory was certainly plausible. After all, Dakota seemed to be in the same situation. He'd had trouble holding other jobs, but he'd worked diligently for us today, done a meticulous job. I hadn't thought he'd had it in him. I was glad to be proven wrong.

"Andy doesn't need the money," the detective added. "He makes a good living from his insurance business, and he doesn't have a family to take care of. He was more than happy to let his brother have half of the estate. In fact, Andy's put his half of the inheritance into college funds for his nephews."

No doubt Wayne would be happy to learn that his brother didn't expect him to pay his share back. "What happened when you spoke with Dulce and Carl?"

"Dulce admitted that she and Carl have engaged in harmless flirtation for years, but she swears nothing happened until Nelda passed. She said their date last Friday at the steakhouse was their first. Carl said the same thing. He says he wasn't honest when he ran into you and Roxanne after your poker game because Roxanne is a gossip and he didn't want everyone in the neighborhood talking about him and Dulce behind his back."

"Roxanne is definitely a gossip," I concurred. "But she wouldn't have had much to gossip about if Carl had waited a respectable time after his wife's passing to start dating."

"Carl's aware of that, too," Collin said. "But he told me, man to man, that he'd been miserable with his wife for years and that he didn't want to put off being happy any longer."

"He admitted he'd been miserable? That seems surprising. He had to know it could make him a suspect in Nelda's murder."

"True, but he was probably well aware the other ladies would have told me about him and Nelda already, how difficult she could be and how unhappy he must have been. He might have thought by putting a happy face on things, he'd look like a liar and only seem more guilty."

"In some warped kind of way, that actually makes sense."

"Roxanne was the one who surprised me."

My nerves tingled. *Had I been right about Roxanne all along? Was there something sinister about her? Or was she just a brash blabbermouth?* "How, exactly?"

"When I asked her about her relationship with Nelda, she broke down in tears. She said it was all such silly nonsense, that they'd spent years bickering over petty grievances that didn't amount to a hill of beans. That she wishes she could take back some of the things she'd said."

"Like what?"

"She once called Nelda an uptight busybody to her face."

"That's no worse than what Nelda called her." In fact, *hussy* was more insulting. The term insinuated a lack of morals. Roxanne's reaction surprised me. It seemed like overkill. Then again, maybe it did have something to do with killing. Maybe Roxanne had broken down because she felt guilty for pushing Nelda down the staircase. I posed the theory to the detective.

"I wondered the same thing," he said. "I even gave her some nudges to see if she might confess. I suggested that Nelda's constant name-calling and nosiness could lead a family member or friend to lose their cool and give Nelda a push. That if someone had pushed her, it didn't necessarily mean they were a bad person, that everyone snaps at one point or another."

"She must not have confessed or you'd have her in custody."

"She agreed with me, but she didn't confess. In fact, she said she hoped that, if someone had simply snapped, they would come forward and admit what they'd done."

*Hmm. Does Roxanne suspect someone in the circle?*

Now that he'd brought me up to date, he asked, "Do you need a ride?"

"No," I said. "Buck and Colette are nearby."

"I thought I'd spotted them following you." He glanced back at the traffic zipping by on the freeway. Most drivers hadn't bothered to slow down, though a few cut their speed and gawked as they rolled past. "At least let us get you off this road. There's a gas station at the next exit. We'll drop you there."

*HOOONK!* Hogarty lay on the horn, letting us know her patience with our chitchat had run out.

I angled my head to indicate the patrol car. "You going to let her treat you like that?"

"Heck, yeah," he said. "She's terrifying." The grin tugging at his lips negated his words. Still, it was clear he respected his former training officer even if he didn't fear her. "I'll be back in touch once we figure out what's going on." With that, we walked to the cruiser. He directed me to sit up front with Officer Hogarty while he slipped into the back with Santos. "Drop her at the gas station up there," he instructed the officer, pointing at the illuminated sign up ahead. "She can call for a ride from there."

Hogarty pulled onto the freeway, drove for a short way, and took the same exit Buck and Colette had taken. No need for me to call them. Colette's Cruze was parked at the edge of the gas station's lot.

As I hopped out of the squad car, Collin climbed out of the back and took my seat up front. Once they'd driven off, I headed to Colette's car and slid into the backseat.

Both Colette and Buck turned to look at me, bumping foreheads in the process.

"Ow!" Colette rubbed her head.

"Sorry," Buck replied. "Want me to kiss your boo-boo?"

I addressed my friend. "Want me to blast him with my pepper spray?"

A smile skittered across her face before she became serious again. "What happened back there?"

I gave them an update. The driver was not, in fact, Luis Bautista. His alter ego had texted during the ride, outing his roommate as a fraud. The driver's real name was Caesar Santos. Why he was pretending to be Luis was anyone's guess at this point but, with any luck, Detective Flynn would soon get to the bottom of things.

Colette turned around to start her engine. "It seems coincidental that Dakota would have taken a ride with a person pretending to be someone else on the night Nelda Dolan was killed. I bet Caesar Santos pushed her down the stairs."

Buck clucked his tongue. "Nah. I still say Carl Dolan killed his wife."

One of them could be right. But I still couldn't shake the sneaking suspicion that Roxanne Donnelly and her long fingernails might have had something to do with it. While I couldn't solve the case tonight, I could treat my best friend and my cousin to flavored moonshine and live music. "Aim for Tootsie's," I told Colette. "Drinks on me."

# CHAPTER 28

# SHATTERED

**WHITNEY**

The sun had just come up when I pulled into Songbird Circle at a quarter past seven Wednesday morning. A patrol car sat in front of Mary Sue's house next door. Detective Flynn's plain sedan was there, too. *Oh, my gosh! What happened? Is Mary Sue all right?* Though her curtains were closed, it was clear from the sliver of light between the panels that the lights were on in her living room. *Is she inside? And, if so, is she still alive?*

Just as I'd panicked last night when I thought the driver from Hitch-a-Ride might make a break for it, I felt myself panicking again at the thought that someone might have hurt Mary Sue. My skin throbbed with a frenetic pulse and an instant sweat slicked my skin, gluing me to my coveralls and rendering my heavy coat unnecessary. I gunned my engine, screeched to a stop in the driveway of the flip house, and jumped from my car before it had even settled in place. I ran next door as fast as my legs could move.

I jabbed the doorbell repeatedly, the *ding-dong-ding-dong-ding-dong* sounding especially loud in the quiet, still morning. I willed the cops or detective to come quickly to the door. *Hurry up! Hurry up!* My ears picked up a shuffling sound from behind the door, probably someone looking out the peephole, before I heard the sound of the deadbolt sliding back. The door opened to reveal Officer Hogarty. She wore her stiffly pressed uniform and a frown.

"Is Mary Sue okay?" I cried.

Before Hogarty could respond, my elderly neighbor's voice came from inside. "I'm not hurt!" Mary Sue called. "But I had the bejeebers scared out of me!"

Part of me wondered what, exactly, a bejeeber was, and how many a woman her size might contain. Another part of me thought I needed to get my mind back on track. "May I come in?" I asked Hogarty.

The officer turned and repeated the question to the detective. "Hey, Flynn. Can Ms. Whitaker come in the house?"

"Sure."

I stepped inside, stopping on the rug in the entryway. Mary Sue sat on her sofa, dressed in her nightclothes, a thick robe, and house slippers. She wore no makeup, only her glasses, and her hair was covered in a silky wrap.

She clutched her robe at the neck. "Someone tried to get into my house!"

I gasped and my head seemed to go hollow. What had been only conjecture a moment before was now real. *Had the killer come back? Was the killer targeting older women, like the detective had surmised earlier?* I rushed over to the couch. "What happened?"

"I was fast asleep," she said, looking up at me pie-eyed, "when a noise woke me up. It sounded like glass breaking. I thought maybe it had come from outside, but the next thing I knew my alarm kicked on. I didn't turn it off. I locked myself in my bedroom and let it keep right on blaring until the security company called. I told them to send the police right away."

Collin looked up from the couch. "Someone broke her downstairs powder room window from the outside."

I closed my eyes in a silent, grateful prayer. Whoever was preying on these vulnerable women deserved far more than a whack with a wrench. I hoped whoever it was would get their due, and soon. It was nerve-wracking enough for me merely working on the circle, but Mary Sue, Roxanne, and the Garners had to live day in and day out under the constant fear that Nelda's killer might return to claim another victim. Carl and Becky, too. That stress had to be taking a toll on them.

I opened my eyes and racked my brain. It had been another frosty night. The grass was still coated in frozen dew. If the intruder had come through the yard, he would have left a trail, right? I addressed the detective. "Are there footprints you could follow?"

"Unfortunately, no. There are concrete pavers down the side of the house all the way to the back fence. My guess is that the burglar traveled down the pavers, hopped the locked fence, and stood on the patio to break the window."

I returned my attention to Mary Sue, dropping to one knee next to her coffee table so we'd be at the same eye level. "Thank goodness the alarm scared him off and he didn't get inside."

She shuddered and pulled even tighter at the neck of her robe. "I don't even want to think about what he might have done then!"

"Tell you what," I said, "as soon as the police are done here, I'll take a look at your window. If it's a standard size, the home improvement store is likely to have a replacement in stock. If so, Buck and I can fix it for you right away. If not, I can pick up some plywood to seal off the hole until a window can be ordered."

Her eyes blinked, misty, as she offered an appreciative smile. "You'd do that for me?"

"Of course," I said. "We're neighbors. That's what neighbors do." *Or they kill each other.*

I turned to Collin. "Will you let me know when things are done here?"

He nodded.

I stood and gave Mary Sue a supportive pat on the shoulder. "I'll be back."

"Thanks, Whitney. You're a godsend."

As I exited her house, I found Gayle, Bertram, and Roxanne rushing toward me up the driveway. All three wore their nightclothes with their winter coats thrown on over them. Roxanne's pajamas bore a racy leopard print.

"Whitney! Whitney!" Roxanne raised her clawed hand, too, as if I would somehow not see or hear the group otherwise. "What's going on?"

I held up my palms. "Mary Sue's okay. Someone broke the window in her powder room, but the alarm scared them off."

Despite her limping gait, Gayle never broke her stride. "Goodness! We better get in there!"

The three rushed past me and barged right into Mary Sue's house without bothering to ring the bell.

Officer Hogarty halted the onslaught. "Hold on, folks!"

A crime scene van rolled up to the house as I made my way to the flip house next door. *Will they find prints?*

*Some other evidence that will tell us who tried to break into Mary Sue's place? And if they do, will it also tell us who killed Nelda Dolan?* It was possible that the attempted burglary was unrelated to the intruder who'd shoved Nelda down the stairs next door. But it seemed awfully coincidental that there'd be two different intruders in adjacent houses within a matter of days. *It has to be the same person, doesn't it?*

I went into the flip house, locking the door behind me. Even with armed law enforcement next door, it felt eerily dark and quiet inside. I scurried around, turning on every light in the place. Not exactly the most economical or environmentally friendly thing to do but, until either Buck arrived or the sun was fully up in the sky, I'd leave them burning.

I was working on the tile in the master bath when Buck arrived half an hour later.

"It's me!" he hollered.

"I'm in the master!" I called back.

A moment later, he appeared in the doorway. "There's cops out there again. What in the Sam Hill is going on now?"

I told him that someone had smashed Mary Sue's window. "The crime scene team is searching for clues."

He frowned, his features rigid. "It's a shame that poor old lady had go through such a fright, but maybe they'll find a clue and nail whoever's been causing all this trouble."

"Speaking of nails, I told Mary Sue we'd fix her window as soon as the police are done over there."

"It's the least we could do. I have half a mind to install a trip wire around this entire circle."

My phone chimed with an incoming text from the detective, providing both a photo of the broken window and the measurements. *23.75″ × 53.25″*. Good. The glass was a standard size. I texted him back a thumbs-up and returned my attention to my cousin. "I'm heading to the hardware store for a window. I'll be back ASAP."

"All righty. While you're gone, I'll finish up the kitchen floor."

I climbed back into my car. Luckily, the engine was still warm enough I could use the heater right away. I drove to the home-improvement store, snatched a cart, and aimed directly for the door and window department. After selecting the proper-sized window, I found myself winding my way to the aisle stocked with protective gear. I bypassed the tool belts, safety goggles, and hard hats to stop in front of the small display of basic coveralls. I selected a gray pair in men's size small and tossed them into my cart. I bought a box of disposable shoe covers, too. *In for a penny, in for a pound.* I charged the window and coveralls to my credit card, and returned to Songbird Circle.

As I approached our house, my eyes caught a glimpse of Carl heading up Mary Sue's walk with a pink bakery box. Looked like he'd gotten his hands on more of Dulce's *dulces*. Someone must have notified him about the attempted break-in.

Was Carl truly being thoughtful, taking a treat to a friend and neighbor in need of comfort? Or was he playing a role, feigning concern when he was actually trying to get the inside scoop on the investigation? And how would Officer Hogarty and Detective Flynn feel when he showed up with donuts, a typical cop cliché?

I parked in the driveway of the flip house and sat there a moment, pondering things. Carl was up relatively early today. He'd slept in quite late the night after Nelda had been killed, and hadn't ventured out to look for his wife. But maybe he'd risen early today because he'd gotten a call from Roxanne or the Garners about the incident. *If he'd been the one to end Nelda's life, is he also the one who'd smashed Mary Sue's window?* Could be. If he'd been caught outside, he'd have a ready excuse. He could claim he'd spotted a prowler and come over to investigate. No one would be the wiser. But had he broken Mary Sue's window to throw suspicion off himself? To make it appear that the murderer was someone targeting other residents or houses in the neighborhood, not just Nelda in particular?

Having left the bakery box behind, Carl emerged from Mary Sue's house and headed back to his own. It would certainly be ironic if the police were at the house on one side of our property while the killer and window-smasher wiled away his morning in the house on the other side. Buck and I would be stuck in the middle. I already felt that way, in a sense. All of the folks on the circle were suspects, but they were also neighbors who were fast becoming friends. It was growing harder and harder to remain objective.

Carl's front door closed behind him, shutting his secrets in with him. Buck and I might get the truth out of Carl if we applied thumbscrews. I had some large screws in my toolbox that would do the trick. But I supposed I'd only end up getting arrested for assault myself. Besides, I didn't have the stomach for such violence. But I did wish we could get to the truth.

I went back inside to find Dakota had already arrived, punctual and prepared to paint. Despite the fact that he wore my hand-me-down coveralls with the stapled hems, he looked more grown-up today. He carried himself more confidently, held his head higher, bore a determined glint in his eye. Discovering something he was good at seemed to have buoyed his self-esteem. It was nice that something positive had resulted from recent events.

"Heads up!" I tossed him the packaged pair of coveralls, followed by the box of booties. I gestured to the stapled and colorfully paint-splattered coveralls he currently wore. "Those old coveralls are ready for the trash heap, not to mention they're a tripping hazard. The new ones should fit you much better."

He looked down at the items before lifting his head. "Thanks. I was getting a little tired of looking like a birthday clown."

I was putting the finishing touches on the bathroom's backsplash an hour later when a knock sounded at the front door downstairs.

"Can you get that?" Buck hollered. "I'm knee-deep in grout here!"

"I got it!" I called back. I headed out of the bedroom, into the hall, and down the stairs. Even though his image was blurred by the frosted glass, I was familiar enough with the detective by now to recognize his dark hair, navy police jacket, and his self-possessed-yet-vigilant posture. I opened the door.

While his spine stood straight and strong, his face appeared weary, drooping and sallow. The investigation seemed to be taking a toll. "We can't seem to go more than a few hours without crossing paths, can we?"

"Sure seems that way. All done at Mrs. Mecklenberg's?"

"We are. Let me come in out of this cold and I'll tell you what we've found."

"Of course." I stepped back to let him in. "Just so you know, Dakota's working downstairs."

He gestured up the staircase to the second floor. We

went upstairs and into the master bedroom, where he closed the door behind us. "The pinky swear applies to what I'm about to tell you, okay?"

I raised a crooked pinky in acknowledgement.

He kept his voice low lest it travel through the vents and ducts. "The crime-scene techs found no prints on the scene. They didn't find any clothing fibers on the top of the fence, either."

"Is that unusual?"

"Not necessarily. Depends on the fabric the burglar wore. Some fabrics, like wools or knits, shed and snag more easily than others. The burglar might have been wearing something smooth, like denim, nylon, or spandex."

"Spandex. So the intruder could have been a ballerina or a yoga instructor."

"At this point, a ballerina or yoga instructor is as likely as anyone else. None of the other leads have panned out."

*Speaking of those leads . . .* "What about Caesar Santos? Did you find out why he was driving under his roommate's name?"

"Caesar has a felony conviction. He was pulled over for expired tags a couple of years ago and the patrol officer noticed a prescription bottle of Ritalin lying on the back floorboard. Ritalin is a stimulant. It's prescribed to people who suffer from narcolepsy and to kids with attention deficit hyperactivity disorder. It's also a controlled substance, so possession of Ritalin without a prescription is illegal. Based on the amount in the bottle, Santos was initially charged with a Class C felony, which is punishable by three to six years in prison and a fine of up to a hundred grand."

"Whoa." The state of Tennessee certainly didn't mess around when it came to drug offenses.

"Santos claimed then, and still claims now, that he gave some other students a ride earlier that day and that one of them must have left the pills in his car. None of those students would own up to having stolen the drug or buying it off someone with a legitimate prescription. Unfortunately, college kids with valid prescriptions sometimes sell their pills to other students who think it will help them cram for exams, have better focus and get better grades."

"Isn't that what coffee's for?" I wouldn't have made it through college without copious amounts of caffeine. But an illegal prescription drug? I never would have dreamed of taking something that hadn't been prescribed to me. What if it had unexpected side effects or a bad interaction with another medication? Those kids were taking serious chances with their health.

"Coffee's a much better option, that's for sure," Collin agreed. "At any rate, because it was his first offense and Santos was otherwise doing well, attending school and working part-time as a busboy at a barbecue joint, the defense attorney representing him was able to wrangle the prosecutor down. Santos pleaded guilty to a Class E felony, and his sentence was probated."

"So he never actually went to jail?"

"Correct. He fulfilled the terms of his probation. The conviction remains on his record, though. When he quit the barbecue place, he had trouble finding work because of his criminal history. He came up with the plan to sell his car to his roommate for a dollar so they could put the vehicle in Bautista's name. He convinced Bautista to apply to drive for Hitch-a-Ride, but Santos is the one who actually did the driving and kept the earnings. He also paid all of the expenses related to the car, and reimbursed Bautista for the income taxes he had to pay on the earnings reported to him."

Although the arrangement was a sham, it was understandable why Santos felt forced to resort to it. Tuition and living expenses weren't cheap, and with a drug-related felony on his record he might not be eligible for a federally guaranteed student loan. "Do you think he tried to burglarize this house? To steal something he could sell for money? Could he have killed Nelda during the process?"

Collin's eyes crinkled in skepticism as he gave his head a slow shake. "Santos might have been impersonating his friend to make a buck, but he gave me no reason to believe he'd come in here and killed Nelda Dolan. Gaming a system to earn a living and burglarizing a house are two very different things. My gut says he wasn't involved."

"Your gut was right before, when it said something was up with the driver."

"Let's hope it's right this time, too. I'm going to feel really stupid if I had a killer in my grips and let him go."

"Are you going to charge him with fraud?"

"No," Collin said. "At least not yet. I've told him to in no uncertain terms to stop driving for Hitch-a-Ride immediately, and to transfer the car back into his name. I also put him in touch with a group that helps offenders find work. The longer he keeps his nose clean, the less likely an employer is to consider the Ritalin offense a deal breaker. I told him as much."

"I hope things work out for him."

"Me too."

We wrapped up, and after enlisting Buck and Dakota to help me, I headed over to Mary Sue's with the window tucked under one arm, my toolbox in my hand, and my cousin and new employee on my heels. Although law enforcement and the crime-scene team were gone, Roxanne and Gayle remained, keeping their frightened friend company.

Despite the early hour, the ladies were sipping wine. Roxanne picked up the near empty bottle and tilted it to and fro. "All that shattered glass called for a bottle of shard-o-nay!" She dissolved into giggles, telling me she'd had more than her fair share of the libation. How her liver hadn't yet given out was anyone's guess.

Gayle groaned. "If you keep up with those puns, Roxy, I'm going to have to run home for one of my painkillers."

Buck, Dakota, and I donned heavy work gloves and got right down to work. We crowded into the powder room, removing the old broken window and carefully placing it in a trash bag lest a sharp edge rip a hole in the plastic. Buck and I explained the process along the way, and showed Dakota the tools we used. Might as well make it a learning experience for our new apprentice.

Oddly, the point of impact seemed to be near the bottom of the window rather than the middle. I was no expert on window-smashing, but I had done demolition work. It would have been more efficient for the intruder to aim for a spot in the middle of the glass, closer to the lock that would have to be opened for entry into the house. But I supposed people who burgled houses for a living weren't generally the sharpest tools in the shed. Besides, maybe this one was short, a kid even. I'd heard of teenagers breaking into houses, especially when they were out of school on summer break and people were gone on vacation.

I borrowed a whisk broom and swept up the broken

glass, wiping the floor with a wet paper towel afterward to ensure I'd picked up even the tiniest fragments. I turned on the flashlight I kept in my toolbox and shined it about, checking to see if we'd missed anything. Nothing reflected light back. *Looks like we've got it all cleaned up.*

Buck unboxed the new window. After using my caulk gun to apply a layer of the sealant, Dakota helped me wrangle the new framed glass into place. I handed him my electric drill. "You can do the honors." I gave him step-by-step instructions on how to install screws using the drill. When he finished, I gave him a thumbs-up with my work glove. "Good job."

He beamed. "This is fun. I'm learning all kinds of new stuff."

"There's a shortage of contractors and handymen," I told him. "If you learn how to handle tools, you could make a decent living doing this kind of work."

When we finished, I rounded up my tools and toolbox, and called Mary Sue in to inspect our handiwork. Her friends followed her, all five of us crammed into the tiny space.

Mary Sue slid the window up and down and tried the lock. "It's perfect! Thanks Buck and Whitney!"

"Dakota helped, too," I said, wanting to make sure credit was given where credit was due. These ladies had sold him short. Heck, I had, too, at first. I wanted them to know he wasn't as useless as they'd thought. "He seems to have a knack for home improvement."

Roxanne gave the boy a nod. "That's good to hear." She took another sip from her wine glass and turned to Mary Sue. "Maybe you should think about adding burglar bars. Maybe we all should."

"But they're so darn ugly," Gayle lamented.

I chimed in. "They make ornamental ones now. They're much prettier. There's some with fancy scrollwork, leaf patterns. They even come in different colors. Black. White. Gray."

Gayle wasn't budging. "Every time I see burglar bars on a house, it makes me think the neighborhood isn't safe."

Roxanne arched a brow. "One of our neighbors was pushed down the stairs and died from a broken neck. Another had a break-in. That ship has sailed." With that, she tossed back the last of her wine. "Mary Sue can stay with me for a while. Anyone tries to break into my place, I'll blast them with my shotgun. Shoot first, ask questions later. That's my motto."

I wasn't sure whether to be comforted or terrified by her words. I directed my next question to Mary Sue. "Any idea what the prowler used to smash your window?"

Mary Sue shrugged. "His fist or his foot, I suppose. Maybe a flashlight. The detective didn't find anything outside."

"Too bad," I said. "It might have provided the intruder's fingerprints."

"Speaking of prints." Mary Sue pulled the hand towel from the rack and rubbed it in a circle on the glass, cleaning off the fingerprints Dakota and I had left behind. When she finished, she rehung the towel and looked up at me. "What do I owe you for the window, Whitney?"

"Nothing." I shot her a wink. *"It's on the house."*

Gayle groaned again. "I knew I should've run home for that pain pill!"

# CHAPTER 29

# SUGAR AND SPICE AND EVERYTHING NICE

### WHITNEY

My mother called and gave me an earful. "Your aunt Nancy says the lady who died at your flip house was murdered!"

Her shriek was so shrill my eyelids fluttered of their own accord lest my eyeballs explode.

"Why didn't you tell me?" she screeched.

*To avoid exactly what's happening right now.* That darn Buck and his big mouth. If my mother knew the house next door had been targeted now, too, she'd probably try to ground me. "We've installed an extensive security system," I assured her. "I keep a big wrench in my pocket, and Buck and our new assistant are always here with me." Well, *almost* always, anyway. "I'm not here at night."

"I still don't like it," she said. "You should take that agent's exam."

"Real-estate agents show houses to virtual strangers

all the time," I said. "They hold open houses where anyone can wander in. I don't see how that's much safer."

My argument backfired on me. "Then come work in your father's practice," she insisted. "He can always use extra help in the office."

How many times would I have to tell my mother that I needed to make my own way in the world? "That doesn't interest me, Mom." Knowing I had to offer her something more, I said, "I'll make you a deal. If I get murdered in the flip house, you can say 'I told you so.' Okay?"

"That's not funny, Whitney."

"Look, Mom. There's no reason for whoever killed Nelda Dolan to come back here. The house is empty. There's nothing to steal. And if they came here intending to kill her, they accomplished their aim. It's done." Even as I said the words, I wasn't entirely sure I believed them. The case felt like an incomplete story, a novel dog-eared at one of the later chapters, waiting to be picked up and finished.

"You're so stubborn sometimes."

*Gee, I wonder where I get it?* I got lucky and she received an incoming call from my father's office, ending our standoff for the time being.

Dakota did another outstanding job on Wednesday, adding a second coat of paint to what used to be his grandmother's guest bedroom and laying down the first coat in the sewing room, laundry room, and hallway. He'd left no discernible brushstrokes, the paint smooth and even. He even helped Buck install the cut tiles around the outer edge of the kitchen floor.

"That flooring looks fantastic," I said when they finished. Potential buyers would love the timeless, classic look.

When I returned home at half past six, I was greeted

at the door by my sweet little cat and what appeared to be a full bushel of ripe nectarines that both smelled and looked delicious. My mouth watered in anticipation. I gave my cat a scratch under the chin and my roommate a bear hug. "That peach pie is going to mean so much to the ladies of Songbird Circle. Especially now."

She cocked her head. "What do you mean?"

"There was an attempted break-in this morning at the house next door."

Her mouth gaped. "The killer came back?"

"The police don't know for certain, but it sure would be a coincidence if it were someone else. What are the odds two houses that sit side-by-side would be hit by different burglars so close in time?"

She bit her lip. "I'm worried about your safety. Can't you and Buck put off the renovations for a while? Get back to work once the police solve this case?"

My roommate was sounding a lot like my mother. *Maybe I should start listening to them.* "I wish we could. But I've got payments due on the mortgage note to the Hartleys, and the longer we hang on to the house the more of this year's property taxes we'll be responsible for. It'll cut into our profits. Besides, things are always slow for Whitaker Woodworking this time of year. People tend to schedule their home improvement projects before the holidays so their houses will look good for guests. It's always quiet for a few weeks afterward." In other words, my uncle didn't need me or Buck helping in his carpentry business right now. He was doing all right with just Owen's assistance. My only source of potential income at the moment, other than my paltry pay for my part-time property management duties, was the income the sale of the flip house would generate. Buck and I had to keep forging ahead.

"At least we're not there overnight," I said. "That seems to be when it's the most dangerous in the neighborhood." I turned to the basket of nectarines and picked it up to carry it to the kitchen. The thing was darn heavy, about fifty pounds if I had to guess. Good thing my carpentry and rehab work had helped build my muscles. I inhaled deeply. "These smell so good."

"I know." She offered a contrite cringe. "I have to confess I've eaten three of them already."

"Don't blame you one bit."

She followed me into the kitchen. "How many pies do you want me to bake?"

I placed the basket on the breakfast bar and performed a quick computation on my fingers. "One for us to share at Friday night's poker game, and one each for the Garners, the Dolans, the Walshes, Mary Sue, and Roxanne."

"*Six* pies?" She scoffed. "That'll keep me busy all day Friday. You're pushing the limits of friendship."

"I know, I know. It's a lot to ask. How about if I repay you with that pasta-drying rack you've been wanting?"

"I'm not above taking a bribe."

"Good. I'll order it right away."

She picked up a nectarine and tossed it in the air, catching it before tossing it up again. "There's enough fruit here for a dozen pies. I suppose I ought to bake one for us while I'm at it. One for Buck, too. If Lillian's peach pie is as good as those ladies say, we'll be sorry we don't have our own."

"You're a peach yourself." I gave her a grateful hug. "You busy Friday night?"

"No," she said, returning the nectarine to the basket. "I've got the night off and don't have any plans."

"Why don't you come to the poker game?" I suggested. "The more, the merrier."

She cut me a dubious glance. "You said one of these women could be a killer. You've already asked me to bake them pies, and now you're inviting me to play cards with them?"

"When you put it that way, it sounds kind of crazy."

"It *is* kind of crazy, Whitney!"

"Well, they can't *all* be the killer," I said, as if that was somehow better. "Probably none of them are. Buck thinks it was Carl Dolan. It could even have been a random intruder."

Colette tilted her head in thought. "Even if one of those ladies did kill Nelda Dolan, I suppose they wouldn't try to kill the entire group at once. That would be darn near impossible, I suppose."

"They'd have no reason to want to off the others, either. They're a fun group of women. Besides, if you come to the poker game, it'll give you a chance to see how they respond to the pie." Colette liked to see how people responded to her culinary creations.

"All right," she acquiesced. "After all the trouble we've gone to, I would like to see how much they enjoy it. I haven't played poker in ages, though. I might be a little rusty."

"No worries," I said. "They don't take it too seriously. Playing cards just gives them a reason to get together."

She eyed me intently. "Think we'll still be friends when we're in our eighties?"

"I *know* we will."

She smiled. "I know it, too."

She strode over to the glass front cabinet, opened it, and retrieved the recipe box with Lillian's blue-ribbon recipes in it. She pulled out a card before returning the box to the cabinet. She glanced down at the card and turned back to me. "This recipe for the peach pie says it's best served warm." She suggested we pack the pies in the insulated carrier she'd used for catering gigs in culinary school. "That'll keep them from cooling off."

"Good idea." I could hardly wait to see the ladies' reactions, especially Mary Sue's. She'd had a tough few months, losing her best friend, a neighbor, and now suffering a break-in. She'd be tickled pink when I showed up with Lillian's prize pie!

On Thursday morning, I rolled into the circle to see everyone's recycling bins standing sentinel at the curb next to their driveways. Had it really been only a week since I'd found Dakota's pawnshop ticket in the recycling bin in the garage at our flip house?

It seemed like so long ago. So much had happened since. Dakota had gone from being a prime suspect in Nelda Dolan's murder to a solid subcontractor for me and Buck. Sawdust had discovered Lillian Walsh's revised will and award-winning recipes hidden in the secret compartment on the stairs. Carl had wasted no time sitting on his newfound freedom and had begun dating Dulce. Becky had used her share of her mother's life-insurance proceeds to buy herself a new car, and one for her twins as well. The driver from Hitch-a-Ride had been arrested, identified, and released. Roxanne had broken down in sobs, finally showing some heartfelt emotion over the feud she'd had with her murdered neighbor. Mary Sue's window had been smashed, presumably by the killer, returning to burglarize another home on this circle of senior citizens.

As I climbed out of my car and rounded up my toolbox

from the cargo bay, my gaze seemed to move of its own accord to Mary Sue's recycling bin. Mary Sue might have slept at Roxanne's last night, but she'd remembered to put out her bin. Just like last week, it overflowed with newspapers, the red brick sitting atop the stack to hold them in place lest the wind pick them up.

*Hmm.* Something niggled at the back of my brain, something my mind couldn't seem to fully grasp at the moment. *What is it about those newspapers?*

Before I could give it much thought, Wayne Walsh's minivan rolled up to the curb and Dakota hopped out, proudly sporting his new coveralls.

"Looking good!" I called.

"I'm going to be extra careful," he said. "I don't want any paint getting on 'em."

Pristine coveralls were a sure sign of a renovation rookie. But no sense telling him that. He'd learn over time, probably even in a short time, when Buck inevitably teased him about the clean, spotless garment.

After we went into the house, I armed the security system behind us and ventured downstairs to install new tile in the guest bath. As I worked, my mind wandered aimlessly about, coughing up random images and snippets of conversations that had taken place since I'd found Nelda's body. At last Friday's poker game, we'd discussed the night of Nelda's death and the questions the detective had later posed to the people he'd interviewed. Becky had noted that the only thing she'd heard between going to bed that fateful Friday night and the detective coming to their door Saturday morning was a few barks from Mosey around three and Mary Sue's house alarm going off in the early hours. Mary Sue had said she'd forgotten to disarm the alarm when she went out to get her newspaper.

*Wait.*

Hadn't I seen Mary Sue's newspaper lying under her bushes after I'd arrived at the house that morning? I'd almost swear to it. Then again, I'd been so discombobulated by finding Nelda's bent and broken body that I couldn't entirely trust my memory. Besides, even if the newspaper had still been lying under her bushes, it could mean Mary Sue had abandoned her mission when she'd inadvertently activated the alarm, forgetting why she'd gone outside in the first place. She'd said she was getting forgetful. Ironically, I remembered that part for sure. Or maybe she'd simply decided it was too chilly to go outside at that early hour and decided to round up her newspaper later in the day. She was retired, after all, not in any hurry or bound to a particular schedule.

But had Mary Sue been telling the truth about her alarm? Or could she have set it off accidentally after sneaking back into this house to pull something out from under Nelda? As the thought popped into my mind, my mouth popped open, silently gaping. *Did Mary Sue kill Nelda?*

My skin thrummed with a nervous energy. The thought was incredibly preposterous, yet at the same time it made my knees fold of their own accord. I sat down on the side of the bathtub and forced my quick breathing to slow down so I could think clearly. *Breathe in, two, three. Breathe out, two, three.*

Assuming, for the sake of argument only, that Mary Sue had pushed Nelda down the stairs, what would she have taken out from under Nelda? What would have been of such high value to either of them, or been so condemning, so clearly pointing to Mary Sue as the killer, that she would have felt the need to risk a return to the house later to remove it?

The only thing of Lillian's that seemed of any importance to Mary Sue was the peach-pie recipe. Of course, the recipe was important to the other neighbors as well. But Mary Sue had been Lillian's best friend, had been right there by Lillian's side when she'd won the blue ribbons. The pictures in the photo albums proved it. *Maybe I should have hung on to those . . .*

Could Nelda have known about the secret compartment under the stairs? Had she come into the house to get the hidden recipe box? Had Mary Sue spotted Nelda entering her friend's home and come over to chastise or question her for it? Was there any chance this seemingly wild speculation could, in fact, explain how Nelda Dolan had ended up facedown and dead in the doorway of this house?

Once I could get my knees to work again, I left the bathroom and went outside to my car where I could make a private call to Detective Flynn. He answered on the first ring.

"I've got a new theory," I said. "What if Mary Sue killed Nelda?"

He paused only a second before saying, "Go on."

"It's recycling day in our neighborhood," I said. "Mary Sue's bin is always full of newspapers. She puts a red brick on top to hold them down so they won't blow out of the bin. Anyway, when I saw them this morning, something about them jarred a memory loose." I told him about the thoughts that had crossed my mind, how I believed, but couldn't be certain, that Mary Sue's newspaper hadn't been picked up the morning Nelda's body was found. That she might have set off her security alarm when she'd been returning from removing a recipe box out from under Nelda.

"There were two recipe boxes, right?" he said. "The one Colette took, and the one you found under the step?"

"Yes. They were identical."

"Where are they now?"

"They're both at my house."

"I'll have the lab check them for prints. When can I swing by and pick them up?"

We arranged to meet at my place during his lunch hour.

I thought aloud. "Mary Sue is purportedly the peace-maker of the group, but when I think back to our conversations, she sometimes seemed to subtly goad people into saying incriminating things about themselves or others." She'd led Roxanne to tell me and Buck about all the names Nelda had called everyone, she'd gotten Becky to admit that neither she nor her mother had much respect for Dakota or Wayne, and she had nonchalantly dropped the information about Nelda's life-insurance policy being on the brink of expiring, implicitly implicating both Carl and Becky.

"It could have been unintentional," Collin said with his usual healthy share of professional skepticism. "But she might have been stirring the pot, trying to throw suspicion off herself. Hard to say."

"What about her broken window, though? Doesn't that point to her being innocent?"

"It could," he said. "But she could have broken it herself."

If she'd been the one to smash it, it would explain why the point of impact was at the lower part of the window. With her diminutive stature, she would have trouble reaching much higher. Still, the woman hardly seemed like a killer. She simply seemed like a nice neighbor who wanted everyone to get along. I felt a little ashamed of suspecting her.

Before we ended the call, I asked, "You think I might be onto something? Or do you think I'm nuts?"

"I think you're nuts, regardless," he said. "You don't know when to back down from danger."

He had a point. I'd taken some risks in the interests of getting to the truth and protecting my property value. But I couldn't just sit back and wait. It wasn't my style.

"As for Mary Sue?" he said. "Everyone who knew Nelda Dolan gave me the impression they'd wanted to shove her down a staircase at one time or another. Mary Sue knew Nelda, ergo . . ."

He didn't finish. He didn't have to. While his words weren't exactly an endorsement of my theory, he apparently thought it plausible enough to pursue. Then again, he'd run out of other leads by this point. *What would he do without help from me and my cat?*

# CHAPTER 30
# EVIDENCE COLLECTION

## WHITNEY

When lunchtime rolled around, I begged off for a couple of hours, telling Buck and Dakota that I had a property management issue to take care of for Home & Hearth. I'd tell Buck the truth later, but I didn't want to risk Dakota overhearing. Sure, I'd given him a job and he appreciated me for it. But he'd known the women on Songbird Circle since he'd been born. If he knew what I was doing, he might let it slip that I'd accused Mary Sue of murder. Heck, he might go to her and tell her outright. If she was innocent, she'd surely be upset by the slander, maybe even sue me. A jury would probably take one look at me, in my physical prime and towering over the frail and fragile Mary Sue, and award her a million-dollar verdict.

Collin was already at my house when I arrived. Sawdust perched at the top of his cat tree, watching us out the front window as we came up the walk. As always, he met me at the door when I opened it. *Mew?*

I picked him up and gave him a kiss on the cheek. "Hey, boy. Did you miss me?"

He rubbed the side of his face against mine, telling me that yes, he'd missed me very much.

Emmalee was curled up in her Papasan chair. When she saw the detective behind me, she sat up straight. "What's going on?"

Unsure what I was permitted to share with my roommate, I looked to Collin.

"Evidence collection," he said, which was both true and vague.

Still carrying my cat, I led Collin to the kitchen, where Colette was cutting nectarines into slices. "Figured I'd get a head start on tomorrow's baking." She pointed her knife at the detective. "What are you doing here?"

"Evidence collection," he repeated.

I pointed to the glass-front cabinet where we'd stored the recipe boxes. "There they are."

He donned latex gloves and pulled the cabinet open. Before removing them, he turned to me. "Who all has touched these boxes?"

"Just me and Colette," I said. "Maybe Emmalee, if she needed to get to something behind them. Colette does most of the cooking."

"It's true," Colette concurred. "All Whitney and Emmalee do is reheat leftovers in the microwave."

Emmalee leaned against the doorjamb, her arms crossed over her chest, one orange brow raised in amiable accusation. "You love cooking for us, Colette, and you know it."

"That's true, too," Colette said. She turned back to the detective. "They're my guinea pigs for new recipes. Those two will eat anything I set in front of them."

"Hey!" I said. "We burn a lot of calories renovating houses and waiting tables. We can't help it if we're hungry."

Collin carefully removed each of the recipe boxes from the cabinet and placed them in separate evidence bags.

Colette pointed her knife at the recipe card lying on the counter. The card bore bent edges, smudges of flour, and brown spots where drops of vanilla had spilled on it over the years. "Do you need the recipe card for the peach pie, too?"

"No," he said. "Just the boxes." He looked from Colette to Emmalee. "Are you two willing to give me your prints so I can identify them if they show up on the boxes?"

"No problem," Colette said.

"Happy to," Emmalee added.

Collin eyed Colette and cocked his head. "Am I pushing my luck if I ask you to bake me a pie, too?"

"How can I say no to a man with a gun and a nightstick on his belt?" Colette tossed him a smile and a chuckle to let him know she was only teasing. She'd be more than happy to bake him a pie, too. Feeding people was her purpose in life. Mine was housing them. Collin's was to keep them from killing each other, or at least to bring them to justice when they did.

The detective directed my roommates to wash and dry their hands. Once they'd cleaned up, he rolled their fingers in ink and transferred the prints to fingerprint cards. He already had my fingerprints on file, so there was no need for me to repeat the process. He thanked them and I bade them goodbye. I gave Sawdust a smooch on the head, and Collin and I went back out front to our vehicles.

As he opened his trunk, I noticed something else inside, also enclosed in a clear plastic evidence bag. A red brick, just like the one Mary Sue always placed on top of the newspapers in her recycle bin so they wouldn't blow away.

I gestured to the bag. "Is that the brick from Mary Sue's recycling bin?"

He raised a finger to his lips to let me know it was a secret before leaning toward me and whispering. "I snagged it after you and I spoke earlier. I'm going to have the lab take a look at it, too."

"Why?"

"It might have been used to smash her window."

"But she keeps the bin and the brick out of sight somewhere," I said. "Her garage, probably. She only brings them out on recycling day. How would someone else have gotten to it?"

His lip curled up in a sly smile. "Who says it was someone else?"

*A-ha!* Maybe I wasn't so crazy to suspect Mary Sue, after all. "You really think it could have been her?"

His sly smile slipped away, replaced by a frustrated frown. "Honestly? I'm just trying to eliminate the possibility that it was an inside job. The crime-scene techs examined the glass and found tiny bits of red dust on the edges of the shards. The dust could have been from this brick, or one like it."

"Did you have to get a search warrant?" I asked. "Does Mary Sue know you seized the brick?"

"No," he said. "I was discreet. Posed as a jogger, stopped to tie my shoe when I reached her bin, and grabbed the brick."

"Clever ruse."

"Eh." He lifted a shoulder. "I needed a workout. Killed two birds with one stone. No warrant was needed. Law enforcement has the right to search trash and recycling that's been put out for pickup. It's considered discarded at that point."

"I guess criminals have to be careful what they throw away."

"True. Lots of DNA evidence has been collected from disposable cups that have been tossed in the trash. Envelopes, too, if the suspect licked the seal." The detective slid his toolbox back into the trunk of his car and slammed the trunk closed. "I'll let you know once I hear from the lab about the recipe boxes."

With that, we both returned to work.

As I turned into the cul-de-sac, I spotted Mary Sue's newspapers strewn about her yard. Without the brick holding them down, the wind had picked them up and tossed them about willy-nilly. After retrieving a heavy piece of scrap tile from inside the flip house, I gathered up the loose newspapers and returned them to Mary Sue's bin, topping them with the tile to weight them down.

I went back inside and returned to the guest bath. While my hands might have been installing tile in my flip house, my mind was on Mary Sue next door. I'd been suspicious of her earlier, especially after learning the detective had seized the brick, but my suspicions gave way to increasing skepticism as the day wore on. Mary Sue was the pacifist of the group, smoothing things over between the others. She was also small and lightweight. Nelda had been a stout, sturdy woman, even into her later years. Would Mary Sue even be strong enough to push Nelda down the stairs? I supposed it was possible, especially if Nelda wasn't expecting to be shoved and wasn't hanging on to a railing.

On the flipside, someone had broken Mary Sue's window. Had Buck, Dakota, and I not fixed it for free, she would've been out several hundred dollars to have it replaced. Mary Sue didn't seem to be struggling, but she didn't seem excessively wealthy, either. She'd certainly realize, too, that breaking her own window could backfire. The investigators might realize she'd faked the break-in. If she had used the brick to smash her own window, she would have gotten rid of it, wouldn't she? These facts pointed to another person being the killer, didn't it? The newspaper was a flimsy clue, at best. I might have merely sent the detective down a rabbit trail.

Unfortunately, at this point, rabbit trails seemed to be the only trails we had.

# CHAPTER 31

# HOUSE CALL

**WHITNEY**

I was on my way to the flip house Friday morning when the detective called with the lab results. I pulled into the parking lot of a fast-food restaurant to take his call.

"The only prints on the recipe boxes are yours and Colette's. There's no other prints on the boxes."

My heart pounded triple time in my chest. "That means they were wiped clean, just like the key and the front doorknob. That means whoever killed Nelda was after the recipe, right?"

"Not so fast," he said. "Just because they were wiped clean doesn't mean the same person who cleaned the knob and key cleaned the boxes. Cooking is messy. Lillian might have gotten flour or sugar or some other ingredient on the boxes when she was preparing the recipes. She might have wiped them down herself before she passed away."

"But her family and friends were actively searching for her peach-pie recipe," I insisted. "They might not have known about the recipe box hidden under the stair, but they would have noticed the one in the kitchen and looked inside."

"They might have also noticed it was dirty and wiped it down with a kitchen towel."

*Argh!* "You're infuriating."

"You're not the first person to call me that."

"Who else called you infuriating?"

"My mother. Officer Hogarty. My ex-girlfriend."

Everyone infuriated their mother and coworkers on occasion, but I had to admit I was curious about his relationship with his ex. I knew what Collin was like professionally. Determined. Smart. Perceptive. But I'd only gotten glimpses into who he was on a personal level. I'd like to know more. "What did your ex-girlfriend find so infuriating about you?"

"That's not really any of your business, is it?"

Of course it wasn't. But that wasn't about to stop me. "Aw, c'mon," I cajoled him. "I've been doing free investigative work for you. The least you could do is share something with me."

He heaved a dramatic sigh. "All right. My ex got tired of my erratic work schedule, of me having to break dates, of my mind being on my cases when we were together."

My schedule was erratic, too. I never knew when a tenant would call with a problem at a rental property, and home renovation could be unpredictable. Unforeseen snags or delays were common. "You can't control your work schedule," I said, finding myself coming to his defense. "It's not like criminals work only nine to five Monday through Friday."

"That's what I told her, in so many words."

I flipped, coming to the defense of his ex now. "As for your mind being on other things when you were together, I can see how that would be hurtful to her."

"I couldn't help it," he said. "I'm not good at compartmentalizing. My mind is constantly working my cases."

"I can relate," I told him. "My mind is constantly rehabbing houses. It's the curse of having a job that means something to you, that you love."

"Finally! Somebody gets it."

Flip-flopping once again, I thought that maybe Collin wouldn't have been so distracted by his work when he was with his girlfriend if he'd been more interested in her. Turning the conversation back to the matter at hand, I said, "Tell me about Mary Sue's brick."

"The lab found tiny remnants of glass in a couple of the holes. Basically glass dust."

"That means the brick was used to smash the powder room window, doesn't it?"

"It certainly looks that way."

My heart shook like a gallon can of latex paint in an electronic shaker. "Are you going to arrest her?"

"I'm going to talk to her," he said. "Unfortunately, there were a lot of prints on the brick. Some were Mary Sue's. We were able to match them to prints on a small bottle of juice I also snatched from the bin. We don't know who the others belong to. It could be sanitation workers, family members, even the landscapers who installed her flower bed. But some of them could have belonged to whoever broke her window. There's also a possibility that she'd had some glass in her recycle bin that broke, and that small fragments ended up on the brick."

"So you can't be certain the brick was used to break the window?"

"No, but we saw no glass fragments in the bottom

of the bin like we'd expect if a glass bottle or jar had broken inside it."

"Maybe she cleaned the bin out."

"It's possible. But Mary Sue is going to have to come up with a good explanation as to how someone could have accessed her bin and obtained the brick to break her window. Otherwise, I'm going to take her down to the station and give her a grilling."

We ended our call and I continued on to the flip house. Buck was already there, starting the installation of the hardwood flooring. Once it was laid, it would need to be sanded and stained. We were in for several weeks' work on the wood floors alone. Good thing we now had Dakota to help.

Dakota arrived not long after me. After I opened the door to let him in, he stood on the porch and motioned next door, worry lines creasing his forehead. "The police are at Mrs. Mecklenberg's house again. You think somebody tried to bust into her house again? Should we go see if she's okay?"

I poked my head out and glanced over. Both Detective Flynn's unmarked sedan and a police cruiser were parked at the curb. Knowing the reason for their visit, I dismissed Dakota's worries. "If she wasn't okay, they'd have called an ambulance. They're probably just following up on the break-in."

His face relaxed. "Oh. Okay." He came inside and I closed the door behind him.

Buck appeared at the top of the stairs. "There's my right-hand man." He waved Dakota up the stairs. "Come on up. I'm laying hardwoods in the master. I'll teach you how. It'll give you strong arms and shoulders. The girls will like that."

On hearing that last bit, Dakota couldn't get up the stairs fast enough.

Though I had some finishing work to do in the guest bath downstairs, I was far more interested in knowing what was happening at Mary Sue's house. I decided to start on the living-room floors, where I could keep an eye on things out the front window. If she was going to be hauled off in handcuffs, I wanted to see it.

While I normally wore noise-canceling headphones to drown out the banging and electric saw noise when I installed flooring, I decided to forego the headphones today. The last thing I wanted was someone, especially a killer, sneaking up on me. I needed all my senses at full power.

Twenty minutes later, Mary Sue's front door opened. I stepped to the corner of the window to get the best view. Officer Hogarty and Detective Flynn emerged, but they didn't have Mary Sue in handcuffs. Rather, she gave them a friendly smile and a wave goodbye as they departed, as if they'd stopped by for a cup of tea. *What the heck had happened in there?*

The instant the detective closed to the door to his car, I dialed his phone. "What did she say?"

Glancing up through his windshield, he met my gaze. He put me on speaker and sat the phone down in his cup holder. "Let me get out of here and I'll fill you in."

He started his engine and drove off, following Hogarty's squad card. A minute later, the engine noise quieted as he apparently pulled over somewhere. "Her garage is full of junk," he said. "Pretty normal for someone who's lived in one place for a long time. She's barely got room for her car in there. She keeps her garbage can and recycle bin on her covered patio out back."

In other words, the recycle bin and brick were within

easy reach of a prowler looking for something to use to smash Mary Sue's powder room window.

"The recycle bin was pushed under a potting table. When we came by after the break-in, she'd said nothing on the table appeared disturbed, so we didn't pay it much mind. We assumed the intruder had used his elbow or a tool he'd brought with him."

Hindsight was twenty-twenty, of course. Knowing now that the brick had probably been taken from the bin to smash the window, it seemed that the potting table and bin should have been inspected more thoroughly. Then again, maybe Mary Sue hadn't wanted them to spend too much time looking around there, discover the brick she herself had used to smash her window. Maybe she had intentionally misled them when she said nothing looked disturbed. Then again, maybe the glass fragments on the brick were from a broken jar of applesauce she'd dropped in her recycling. Who knew? *Only Mary Sue. That's who.*

"She said she was wondering what happened to her brick," Collin added. "She noticed it was missing when she retrieved her bin late yesterday afternoon."

"You told her you took it?"

"I had to. Otherwise I couldn't explain how we knew the brick had glass dust in the holes. But I made it seem casual, like the department was just keeping an eye on the neighborhood for safety's sake and happened to notice the brick in her bin, thought maybe it was something a prowler would pick up to smash a window. I told her the same thing I told you, that things in the trash and recycling can be picked up by law enforcement without a warrant. I told her I hadn't come to her door because I didn't want to disturb her or get her hopes up that we might catch the prowler if it didn't pan out."

"It seems unlikely a prowler would have smashed the window with the brick, then returned it to the bin." It seemed far more likely a prowler would have dropped the brick when the alarm went off, or maybe run off with it.

"I'm not saying you're necessarily wrong, but we can't jump to conclusions. My job is to build a case I can take to the district attorney. I can't build a case on suppositions and guesses alone. I need cold, hard proof."

*Cold, hard proof.* Where could we get some?

"Even if Mary Sue faked the break-in," he added, "it wouldn't prove she killed Nelda Dolan. She's a widow who also lost her best friend in recent months. Maybe she just wanted some attention."

The thought hadn't crossed my mind, but it made sense. Mary Sue was relatively plain and reserved, easy to overlook when compared to the vivacious and verbose Roxanne. Gayle still had Bertram to keep her company. Maybe Mary Sue was lonely, looking for sympathy and companionship.

"Be careful tonight," he warned. "Every woman at that poker game is still a potential suspect."

"Don't worry," I told him. "Roxanne's hosting. She's got her shotgun at the ready."

"That's exactly what I'm worried about."

Leaving the hardwood floors for later, I returned to finish the tile work, no longer buoyed by the hope of resolving the case, but feeling as mired down in muck as the tiles I coated with grout and stuck to the wall. Maybe we'd never figure out who killed Nelda Dolan and why. Maybe the identity of her murderer was destined to forever remain a mystery. Although a short blurb had appeared on the evening news and in the newspaper about the investigation, nobody had contacted the Nashville police department with any clues.

I pushed another tile up against the wall. *If only these walls could talk. They could tell us what they witnessed the night Nelda took her tumble down the staircase.*

## CHAPTER 32

# HEARTS, SPADES, DIAMONDS, AND CLUBS

**WHITNEY**

My mood improved when I went home at the end of the workday and smelled the enticing scent of freshly baked peach pies. Buck had followed me to the house so he could pick up his pie and take it home with him. Cradling Sawdust to my chest, I ventured into the kitchen to find the pies lined up on the breakfast bar and Colette sprinkling the still-warm crusts with coarse sugar.

"They look like works of art!" I exclaimed.

Each pie had a different fancy crust. The one she'd made for tonight's poker game had followed Lillian's instructions precisely, and bore a tightly woven lattice top with a crimped edge. The crust on another was decorated with small stars Colette had cut with a cookie cutter. A third had what appeared to be a braided crust encircling it and lying across the top. In yet another she'd etched intricate flower-shaped vents in the crust.

Colette yanked a stretch of aluminum foil from a box

and tore it off with a loud *rrrrrip*. "I had some fun with the crusts. Couldn't help myself."

As she wrapped the pie for the poker game in foil, I said, "You are going to make a lot of people very happy, Colette."

"One of them is going to be me," Buck said. "Which pie is mine?"

Colette swept her hand in an arc over the uncovered pies. "Take your pick."

Buck chose one with twisted lattice ribbons. "Dibs on this one."

Colette ripped off another sheet of foil and held it out to Buck. "I bake. You wrap."

"Works for me." He took the foil from her and carefully laid it over his pie, bending it over the edges to secure it.

"I'm going to clean up," I told Colette. "I'll be ready to go in half an hour."

Sawdust lounged in the bathroom sink while I showered and shampooed. He followed me to my bedroom afterward, where I fixed my hair, applied my makeup, and dressed. Ready now, I returned to the kitchen, surprised to find Buck still hanging around, sitting on a stool with a small plate and a bottle of beer in front of him.

"It's Friday night," I told him. "Go out somewhere. Get a life."

"I'd rather eat this guacamole." He snatched another blue corn tortilla chip from the bag on the counter and scooped up a huge blob of the green stuff.

I slapped his hand. "That's for tonight's poker game!"

"Don't worry," Colette said. "We've got plenty of avocados. I can make some more." She reached over to the big red bowl where she kept fresh fruit and vegetables, fished out an avocado, and held it to her ear.

Buck stopped before taking his bite and snorted. "What's that all about?"

"She's the avocado whisperer," I said.

Colette returned the avocado to the bowl. "That one won't be ready for seventeen more hours." She fished out another and held it to her ear. "Almost." She raised three fingers, then two, then one as she counted down. "Three. Two. One. Now it's ready."

Buck continued to hold his loaded chip aloft. "That's the most ridiculous thing I've ever heard. It's right up there with 'Mary Sue Mecklenberg killed Nelda Dolan.'"

I scowled at my cousin. "How do you know she didn't do it?"

"Because she weighs all of ninety pounds soaking wet and is about as ornery as a butterfly."

"You only spoke to her once, at the wake. What do you know?" I pushed his hand toward his mouth and shoved the chip inside. *That'll shut him up for a bit.* Of course, Buck could be right. I could be way off base. In fact, after speaking with the detective earlier in the day, I was fairly certain I was so far off base that I wasn't even on the field anymore. Mary Sue had needed help lifting her cast iron skillet the last time we'd played poker. She wasn't strong enough to push someone down a flight of stairs, was she?

I glanced at the clock on the stove. "We better get going or we'll be late."

Colette carefully slid the pies onto the shelves of her insulated warming box, while I snapped a lid onto the plastic bowl of guacamole and rounded up a fresh bag of chips. Colette had also prepared a colorful stacked salad in the trifle bowl this time, layering shredded lettuce, cucumbers, purple cabbage, cherry tomatoes, and chopped carrots like an edible rainbow. She'd also prepared a warm baguette topped with olive tapenade. The ladies were sure to love these offerings almost as much as Lillian's pie.

Buck carried the catering equipment out to my SUV and loaded it in the back. We placed the other food items next to it, and climbed into the front. I started the engine and blew a kiss to Sawdust, who'd resumed his usual spot at the top of his cat tree and was watching us depart. He raised a paw and touched it to the glass, as if catching my kiss. My heart became as warm and gooey as the pie filling. *I love that furry little guy.*

As we drove, the delicious scent of warm peach pie filled my car. Somebody could make a fortune manufacturing an air freshener with the fruity scent. Before long, we were in the driveway of the flip house, rounding up the appetizers and salad. Mary Sue wandered out of her house next door with her cast-iron skillet cradled in both arms. She really is frail, isn't she?

"Let me carry that for you." I scurried over to relieve her of her heavy burden.

"Thanks, Whitney." She raised her nose to the air and sniffed, her brows drawing in to form a befuddled V. I motioned to Colette to close the door to my cargo bay before Mary Sue could figure out it was full of peach pie. No sense ruining the surprise. Luckily, a brisk breeze blew in from behind the woman, whisking the pie aroma away with it.

After I introduced my roommate and my neighbor, Mary Sue said, "That fruit salad you put together last week was so pretty we almost couldn't bear to eat it."

Colette held up the colorful trifle bowl. "I tried something different tonight."

"Oh, my!" Mary Sue exclaimed. "That's almost too pretty to eat, too!"

Colette grinned proudly. "My philosophy about food is that presentation enhances taste. People enjoy food more when it looks good, too."

"Shucks." Mary Sue gestured to the skillet I carried. "I bake my cornbread in a boring old cast-iron fry pan."

"Cast iron has personality," Colette reassured her. "It's homey and comforting."

Not to mention heavy. My wrist was being put to the test.

We headed up to Roxanne's door, Colette cutting her eyes to mine when she spotted the Smith and Wesson warning sign posted in the flower bed. When Roxanne opened the door, we could see the shotgun in plain sight in her front hallway, the stock sticking up out of an umbrella stand. I hoped she wouldn't reach for it on accident the next rainy day. She might blow a hole in her ceiling.

Gayle was already in the kitchen, cutting a casserole into squares. She looked up as we came into the room, spotting the pretty salad. "You're putting us all to shame," she told Colette with a smile.

"That's not what I hear," Colette said congenially. "Whitney raved about the wonderful food you ladies prepared for the last poker game."

The others smiled, clearly pleased by the compliment. As usual, Colette had made fast friends out of virtual strangers. Becky came in the door bearing a tray of mini spring rolls and sweet-and-sour dip. I introduced my roommate all around and each of us fixed a plate, moving to the dining room to eat and chat.

Colette took one bite of Mary Sue's cornbread and moaned. "It's so moist and flavorful. It doesn't even need butter."

"That's special praise," Mary Sue replied, "coming from a professional chef."

Becky asked me about the status of the renovations on Lillian's house. "Are you on schedule?"

We were on the revised schedule we'd come up with after being delayed by her mother's death on the property, but I saw no reason to mention the tragic incident and bring down the party mood. "So far, so good," I said. "Dakota's picked up a lot of the slack. He's nearly done painting the downstairs and hasn't made a single mistake yet. He's helped with the flooring, too. We've been impressed with his attention to detail. He seems to have a real knack for renovation."

Becky arched an astounded brow. "What do you know. Maybe Dad should hire him to paint our house."

"I think he'd do a good job," I told her, "especially since he seems eager to impress Daisy."

"Speaking of my girls," Becky said, "they took the bus home from school this weekend. Got home about an hour ago. They took one look at that Mustang in the driveway and hugged me like they haven't since they were kids. You'd think I was mother of the year. Of course, it didn't last long. Once I handed over the keys, they jumped inside and took off to show their friends. I'll be lucky if they spend any time at home this weekend."

Roxanne drizzled vinaigrette dressing over her salad. "You can't blame them for wanting to spread their wings. My twenties were some of the best years of my life. Of course, so were my thirties, and forties, and fifties. My eighties aren't turning out so bad, either!" She put down the dressing and raised her glass of wine in salute before tossing back a sip. I was beginning to wonder if, rather than pickling her liver, the alcohol was actually preserving her instead.

Gayle fished another olive-topped slice of bread off the platter on the table and placed it on her plate. "My granddaughter won her school's spelling bee. She's moving on to the district-wide competition."

"Congratulations!" I raised my glass in a toast, clinking it against Gayle's. The other ladies did likewise.

"As long as we're sharing news," Mary Sue said, "I've looked into the ornamental burglar bars Whitney mentioned and ordered some for all of my downstairs windows." She issued a mirthless chuckle. "There goes my social-security checks for the next three months. But it'll buy me peace of mind. I'll be able to sleep in my own house again." She turned to Roxanne. "As soon as they're installed, I'll be out of your hair."

Roxanne reached across the table and patted her friend's hand. "*Mi casa es su casa*, Mary Sue. You're welcome to sleep in my guest room as long as you like." She lifted her shoulders and looked around the table. "It's kind of fun, actually. Like a girls' slumber party." She picked up the bottle of wine and topped off Mary Sue's glass. "*Mi vino es su vino*, too. Drink up!"

Mary Sue took one look at the full glass and said, "If I drink all that, I won't be able to find my way to your guest room."

"That's okay," Roxanne replied. "I can drag you by your ankles."

When we'd finished our meal, Becky put a hand on her belly. "I'm so full I couldn't eat another bite right now." She suggested we play a few hands of poker before dessert.

The others agreed.

"One more bite," Roxanne said, "and I just might burst out of my Spanx!"

Although I was eager to see their reaction to the pie, I, too, had eaten so much I couldn't force down another bite at the moment. Colette and I gathered up the dishes and silverware and carried them to the kitchen sink, giving them a quick rinse before loading them into the dishwasher.

The dishes dealt with, we returned to the dining room and dug through our purses for change. Given that I'd lost nearly every hand the week before and had only used my debit and credit cards since, I had limited spare change and had been forced to run by the bank for rolls of coins during my lunch break. Colette had traded with Emmalee, who had an old pickle jar of coins in her bedroom. When you worked for tips like Emmalee did, you ended up with a lot of spare change.

We tossed our ante into the pile in the center of the table, and Gayle dealt the first hand. Again, she was the most difficult player to read, having no tell that I could see. As I'd learned last time, she was also a good actor, giving subtle cues that may or may not be faked. With her performance skills, the woman could have had a career on Broadway.

We'd played a dozen hands, Gayle winning seven of them, when Roxanne said, "My dinner's finally settled. Anybody else thinking about dessert yet?"

"I am," Gayle said.

I looked around the table, unable to fight a grin. "Colette made something extra special for y'all tonight. I think you'll really enjoy it."

While Roxanne rounded up dessert plates and forks from the kitchen, my roommate and I went out to my car and grabbed the peach pie from the warmer, keeping a close eye on our surroundings lest the prowler approach us. We went back inside and I ceremoniously placed the pie in the center of the table. "Ta-da!"

"What is it?" Roxanne reached out and removed the foil. When she saw the pie underneath, her mouth fell open. "Is that what I think it is?"

Gayle's mouth fell open, too. "Lattice top. Big sugar crystals. That looks just like Lillian's peach pie!"

"But it can't be!" Mary Sue insisted, staring at the pie and shaking her head. "The recipe was never found."

Rather than tell them myself that I'd found the hidden recipe, I decided to let their taste buds do the talking. I cut equal slivers of pie and put them on plates, admonishing nobody to take a bite until everyone had their piece. Once they did, I said, "Okay. On your mark. Get set. Go!"

We all forked our first bite into our mouths. The fresh, fruity flavor was like sunshine on my tongue, the little kick of lemon and ginger teasing and tantalizing my taste buds. There was no question in my mind why the pie had won blue ribbons, why the neighbors had enjoyed it so much, why they'd missed it so badly once Lillian had passed on.

Eyes bright with glee, Gayle put her hand to her mouth, incredulous. "This doesn't just look like Lillian's peach pie, it *is* Lillian's peach pie!"

"Glory hallelujah!" Roxanne raised her hands toward the heavens, waggling her red-tipped fingers. "I can't believe it! I never thought we'd taste this pie again!"

Becky closed her eyes and went limp, as if experiencing rapture, offering an elongated moan as well. "Mmmmm. I've died and gone to heaven."

Laughing, I turned to Mary Sue. With the other ladies

having such excited reactions, I could only imagine how Mary Sue must be feeling. Lillian had been her best friend for decades. She'd be thrilled that Lillian's pie wasn't lost to history.

Except she wasn't.

Her silvery eyes, once pussy-willow soft, now flashed dark and angry, as if a thunderstorm were raging in her head. Her gnarled hands fisted on the tabletop and her chest expanded and contracted like a bellows as she processed huge huffs of air.

*Whoa.* I felt my grin slide down my chin as my mouth fell open. This wasn't the reaction I'd expected at all. "Are you okay, Mary Sue?"

"I'm fine," she squeaked. "I just need some water. Excuse me."

She rose from the table and stalked stiffly into the kitchen.

I glanced around the table, but none of the other women seemed to have noticed. They were all caught up in the excitement, chattering on, euphoric that Lillian's long-lost peach pie was lost no longer. I pushed back from the table and followed Mary Sue into the kitchen. She stood at the sink, looking down into the basin, the window behind it reflecting the top of her head. Her cast-iron skillet sat on the counter next to her, a single piece of cornbread remaining in it.

I stopped a couple of feet behind her. "Are you sure you're all right?"

She raised her head and her gaze met mine in the window. Never before had I witnessed a look of such feral ferocity, heard such an inhuman growl come from a person. "You have no right to that recipe!"

Before I realized what was happening, she'd grabbed the skillet by the handle and whirled on me, wielding it like a paddle. Her blazing gaze was locked on my head, as if she hoped to smash my skull. Luckily for me, she wasn't strong enough to lift the pan that high or my life might have ended right there in Roxanne's kitchen, my death certificate noting I'd died of blunt force trauma, the undertaker having to pick cornbread crumbs from my hair. All I could do was turn away and bear the brute brunt of her cast-iron skillet on my right hip and buttock. *BAM!*

*Had I actually heard a clang, too, as the skillet hit bone or was just in my imagination?* The agony took me down to my knees. *Yowza!* Fearing she'd take the skillet to my head now that it was within range, I did the only thing I could: roll over onto my uninjured side and raise a leg in self defense. She swung the skillet at me again, but I fended it off with my foot.

Collin had said he needed cold, hard evidence. The skillet might have been room temperature, but it was as hard as it comes.

"Mary Sue!" Becky cried as she rushed into the kitchen. "What has gotten into you?"

Becky grabbed the edges of the pan and wrestled with Mary Sue, who had an astoundingly strong grip on the handle. There was no doubt in my mind now. My seemingly dubious suspicions had been confirmed. Mary Sue had snapped and pushed Nelda Dolan down the stairs. I didn't know the exact circumstances, but I knew with absolute certainty that Mary Sue had killed Nelda.

I reached up to the counter and pulled myself to a stand, hobbling toward the wrangling women. Colette appeared in the doorway next, followed by Roxanne and Gayle. All of their mouths gaped as Becky and Mary Sue both held tight to the pan, Becky using it to steer Mary Sue back against the wall.

As Becky pressed the pan against the elderly woman's chest, pinning her to the outdated floral wallpaper, realization seemed to dawn on her, too. "You killed my mother, didn't you? You killed her over that peach-pie recipe!"

Three gasps came from the doorway.

Mary Sue snarled like a rabid possum. "Lillian was my best friend, and she hadn't even shared her recipe with me! I wasn't about to let your mother have it!" She turned her head to address Gayle and Roxanne. "Nelda had no right to that recipe!" she roared. "No right to be in Lillian's house!" She looked at me. "You had no right to that recipe, either!" Her roar abated and she burst into sobs, releasing her grip on the skillet and sliding down the wall until she was a mere heap on the floor, much like Nelda Dolan had been when I found her. "I didn't mean to kill Nelda!" she managed between sobs. "I only meant to stop her!"

When she'd swung that cast-iron skillet at me only seconds before, it was pretty clear she'd wanted to kill me, at least in that moment. No doubt she'd snapped when she'd confronted Nelda in Lillian's house, too.

Now that she'd learned the truth, Becky seemed to lose her strength. She dropped the skillet and it clattered to the floor. Colette rushed over and grabbed it before Mary Sue could do any more damage to anyone else. Gayle entered the kitchen and eased a crying Becky back into one of the padded dinette chairs.

Roxanne shook her head. "I spent three hundred dollars on that shotgun to protect myself from a killer, and she was under my roof the entire time." Her eyes met mine. "Don't that beat all."

Speaking of beatings, my bum throbbed like the bass line in a nightclub. I looked over at Colette, in so much

pain I couldn't speak, hoping my eyes would make a
plea for me. They did. She ran to the freezer, yanked the
ice tray out, and asked where Roxanne kept her plastic
bags. After filling one with ice, she handed it to me and
I held it to my rear. Hobbling back into the dining room,
I pulled my cell phone from my purse and dialed Detective Flynn. "I've got a bruised behind," I told him, "but
I've also got your killer. Get over to Roxanne Donnelly's
house right away."

# CHAPTER 33

# QUEEN OF CLUBS

**WHITNEY**

To thank me for my role in resolving Nelda Dolan's murder, Collin took me to a show at the science center's planetarium Saturday night, followed by dinner at Merchant's, an upscale bistro on south Broadway, not far from Tootsie's. After a delicious dinner, we lingered over coffee and dessert. He'd ordered the blondie, while I'd opted for the butterscotch pie, but we'd ended up sharing both of them. As for the peach pie Colette had made for him, he'd picked it up the night before, after seeing me to a twenty-four-hour medical clinic and driving me home afterward. Luckily, an X-ray confirmed that no bones had been broken when Mary Sue took her cast-iron frying pan to my backside.

Collin leaned back in his seat and eyed me while sipping the last of his coffee. When he set his cup down on the table, he said, "I just realized something."

"What is it?"

"I haven't had a single thought about any of my cases since I picked you up four hours ago."

I raised my coffee mug to my lips so he wouldn't see my smile.

He cocked his head and arched a brow, his green eyes alight with a roguish gleam. "What about you? Has your mind been performing renovations this entire time?"

I wouldn't lie to him. I'd had a wonderful time tonight and enjoyed both the star show and his company. I liked that while he respected my capabilities as a carpenter and a house rehabber, he nonetheless treated me like a lady once I'd changed out of my coveralls and was off the clock. But there was no sense in letting the guy get too cocky, right? "I did have a fleeting thought about tin ceiling tiles."

"One fleeting thought." His lips curved in a sly grin. "I'll consider that a success."

When he drove me home, he walked me to my door and left me with a single, soft kiss that left my nerves buzzing as if I were operating a silent, invisible band saw. Would tonight lead to something more? I supposed that would be the next mystery Collin and I would solve together.

The next few weeks were a flurry of activity, and a resolution of outstanding questions.

With numerous witnesses to her confession, Mary Sue had no choice but to plead guilty to voluntary manslaughter. We learned that she'd been taking a bill payment out to her mailbox that fateful Friday night when she'd spotted Nelda fishing the key from the frog's mouth and using it to enter the flip house. Realizing Nelda was likely going inside to search for Lillian's treasured recipe, Mary Sue became enraged. She marched over and used the key herself to gain entry to the house.

Nelda had been standing on the landing, about to exit

the house, when Mary Sue swung the front door open. Mary Sue saw the recipe box in Nelda's hand and told Nelda that the peach-pie recipe wasn't in the box. Mary Sue hadn't known that Lillian kept her award-winning recipes in a box that was identical to the one on her kitchen counter, and that Lillian had hidden the second box under the last step on the lower staircase. Mary Sue thought Nelda was holding the recipe box from the kitchen.

Knowing she indeed had the prized recipe in her hands, Nelda turned and ran upstairs into the kitchen. Mary Sue followed her, shocked to see the recipe box still on the kitchen counter. She looked inside to confirm its contents. It held only Lillian's everyday recipes.

Mary Sue asked about the box in Nelda's hand and demanded to know where she'd found it. Nelda admitted she'd spotted Lillian stashing her will in the secret compartment under the bottom step after she'd gone to the print shop with Lillian to serve as a witness to her will. Lillian had invited Nelda over for a slice of pie afterward to thank her for serving as a witness. Nelda had used the guest bath downstairs and, as she opened the bathroom door to exit, caught a glimpse of Lillian slipping the will into the secret compartment under the stair.

After Lillian's death, Nelda had wondered if Lillian might have stashed her special recipes in the same place. When neither Wayne nor Andy came up with the recipe, she realized they weren't aware of the secret compartment. She didn't want to bring the matter up to either of them because she knew they'd share the peach-pie recipe with the other ladies. Like Lillian, Nelda had wanted the pie recipe for herself and only for herself, so that she could be the only one to bake it for Carl.

Though Nelda hadn't come right out and said so to Mary Sue, it was clear she'd been looking for an opportunity to get into the house and check under the stair. When she was closing the bedroom curtains late that evening and saw Dakota go into the house and leave the key in the frog's mouth, she seized the opportunity. Unfortunately, Mary Sue spotted her and followed her into the house.

After a heated argument in the kitchen, during which Mary Sue repeatedly tried to grab the box away from Nelda—no doubt causing the scratches on the woman's hands—Nelda made a mad dash for the stairs. Mary Sue said she first reached out to pull Nelda back. But when Nelda easily wrenched free from Mary Sue's grasp, Mary Sue snapped, going berserk just as she had in Roxanne's kitchen the night she paddled me with her frying pan. I was lucky I'd lived to tell my tale. Nelda, unfortunately, had not been so lucky. Mary Sue said she hadn't intended to kill Nelda when she pushed her, only to make her drop the box. She didn't realize Nelda would hang on to it so tightly, at her own peril. Lillian had fled the scene, but later realized the recipe box could implicate her. She returned to fish the box out from under Nelda. Though she'd been tempted to remove the recipe card for the peach pie, she knew if she was found with Lillian's recipe card in her possession, she'd become the prime suspect. She'd settled for copying the recipe by hand before she'd returned it to the box, so she could at least bake the pie for herself now and again. After copying the recipe, she'd wiped the box clean and returned it to the hiding place under the stairs.

When Mary Sue felt that Detective Flynn was closing in on her, she'd panicked and faked the break-in at her house, hoping it would throw him off. Later, when she

found the piece of tile I'd put in her recycling bin to replace the brick he'd seized, she'd suspected I'd been the
one feeding him information, fueling his suspicion of
her. Just another reason for her fury toward me the night
of the second poker game.

It was a dark, sad story. But at least the truth was
out now, allowing everyone to begin the long process
of healing and moving on. Because her crime had not
been premeditated, because she hadn't intended to kill
Nelda, and because of her advanced age, Mary Sue was
sentenced to three years in prison, the shortest term for
the offense. I wondered if she'd arrange a poker group in
prison, or if Roxanne or Gayle would try to smuggle her
one of Lillian's delicious peach pies. While the women
certainly abhorred Mary Sue's recent actions, they
had many memories of her as a caring and thoughtful
friend and neighbor, and had no plans to totally give up
on her.

We learned that Gayle had indeed been under the in-
fluence of the pain medication when she'd misled Detective Flynn about the time of day she'd gone to the flip
house to retrieve the playing cards the day Nelda had
died. She'd wrongly remembered it as being the morning, because she'd eaten pancakes when she returned
home. Turned out Bert was a lousy cook. Pancakes were
one of the few things he could make. He'd cooked pancakes for dinner that night because Gayle's knee had
been acting up and, as loopy as her pain pills made her,
she couldn't prepare their meal.

Wayne Walsh finally found a get-rich-quick scheme
that actually worked. He compiled his mother's recipes
into a cookbook called *Pie to Die For.* A tacky title to
be sure, but when he offered to split the proceeds with
Becky so she could use the funds to pay Dahlia's and

Daisy's remaining tuition, the Dolans and the ladies of Songbird Circle silenced their protests. The case came to be called the Peach Pie Murder by the media. The notoriety of the case helped sell the cookbooks, and they flew off the shelves as fast as the bookstores and local gift shops could stock them. A few weeks later, Wayne followed up with a sequel of his mother's recipes, *Casseroles to Live For*. It, too, was a great success.

The grocery chain Dulce worked for bought exclusive rights to produce the pie under the *Pie to Die For* trademark. The deal earned the families even more funds and landed Dulce a promotion for bringing the opportunity to the attention of her regional manager.

On recommendation from Buck and me, Dakota was hired full-time by a painting company we'd worked with on several occasions. He was making a decent living, enjoyed the work and camaraderie, and had recently moved into his own apartment and bought a used car. Things were definitely looking up for the young man.

Daisy's singing career had taken off, too. While she still yearned to be invited to sing at the Grand Ole Opry someday, she'd landed a coveted Saturday-afternoon slot at one of the honky-tonks on south Broadway, the perfect time to milk tourists for tips and grab the attention of a music producer on the search for new talent. She remained enrolled at the University of Tennessee, but drove home in the new orange Mustang to perform on the weekends.

My derriere bore a big purple bruise for weeks. I had to sit on a soft pillow like some type of fragile princess or show dog until it healed, but my injuries could have been much worse.

Fortunately, because Nelda Dolan's death was ruled manslaughter rather than murder, the incident had only a minor effect on the market value of the flip house. While some lookie-loos came to our open house to see where she had fallen, many were quickly distracted by the beautiful new flooring and updated kitchen and baths. The house was on the market only two weeks before we had a solid offer for full asking price. Buck and I would enjoy a nice profit. Before handing over the keys, I retrieved the smiling ceramic frog from the porch and turned him over to Dakota, who wiped a tear from his eye.

He swallowed hard as he took the frog from me. "I miss my granny."

I gave his shoulder an affectionate, supportive squeeze. "She'd be proud of you. You're really making something of yourself."

He blinked back his tears and gave me a grateful smile.

# CHAPTER 34

# SALE-A-BRATION

**WHITNEY**

We gave the Hartleys the first grand tour of our finished flip house and closed the sale on the place in late April, just as the climbing roses along the side of the house had begun to bud and bloom. Immediately afterward, I made out a check to Mr. and Mrs. Hartley to repay them the remaining balance on the promissory note. It might not have been entirely professional to write *XOXOXO!* in the memo section, but they deserved hugs and kisses for everything they'd done for me. Buck and I took them out to dinner at Mrs. Hartley's favorite Italian restaurant to celebrate. I handed them the check over an appetizer of roasted eggplant and garlic bruschetta, and a nice bottle of Montepulciano d'Abruzzo that Colette had suggested we order.

"We can't thank you two enough." I reached out to take the Hartleys' hands in mine and gave them an appreciative squeeze. "Buck and I couldn't have done this flip without you."

When I released her hand, Mrs. Hartley waved my

words away. "That loan to you was the safest investment we ever made."

I raised my glass to propose a toast. "To our first successful house flip!"

"Hear, hear!" the others called out in unison, clinking their glasses to mine. We all took a healthy sip of our wine.

Buck set his glass back down on the table and addressed the Hartleys. "We're planning to invest our profits in another property. Know of any current listings that might make a good flip house?"

"Not at the moment," Mrs. Hartley said. "But I'll keep an eye out."

Mr. Hartley had another suggestion. "Have you considered the county tax auctions? Sometimes a buyer can snag a property for the taxes due plus a small markup. Of course, there'd be more competition for some of the properties than others. They post the listings online in advance. It's something to consider."

It certainly was. I'd been pondering the idea myself since reading over the brochure in the county tax office. I turned to my cousin. "What do you think, Buck?"

"Can't hurt to take a look."

My cousin and I reviewed the listings for the upcoming tax auction, and decided a few of them warranted a look-see. We drove to the first property and climbed out.

Buck stared at the wood-frame single-story house that leaned precariously to one side while its chimney leaned to the other. Not a single window remained intact. "I was wrong. It *can* hurt to take a look."

I had to agree. The place was too far gone, too long neglected. Besides, many of the other houses along the street had been razed for entirely new construction.

"Whoever bids on this house will have to tear it down
and start from scratch."

"Building from the ground up? That's more than
we're prepared to handle."

I had to agree again. It was one thing to fix up a house
with good bones, to make minor repairs and cosmetic
updates, but it was another thing entirely to design and
build a house from scratch.

We climbed back into Buck's van and drove to the
next house. This second property was no more enticing. So many additions had been added to the front,
back, and sides of the original modest brick home that it
looked like a mismatched, mishmashed maze or a Hollywood celebrity who'd had far too much plastic surgery.

Buck groaned. "They couldn't pay me to take this
property off their hands."

There was only one more property on the tax foreclosure list that was in our price range. All we had was an
address on north 1st Street, directly east of downtown
on the other side of the Cumberland River, not far from
the stadium where the Tennessee Titans played football.

Buck's lip quirked. "Isn't than an industrial area?"

"Far as I know," I said. "But I suppose a few houses
could be tucked away in there somewhere."

We arrived a few minutes later. Rather than a single-
family residence, the place turned out to be a commercial property. The 1960s-era motel was single story and
L-shaped, featuring scratched pink doors and seafoam-
green stucco that was horribly pockmarked, as if someone had used it for target practice. What parts hadn't
been riddled by holes had been decorated in colorful
graffiti using just as colorful language. Plastic tarps or
plywood had replaced the glass in many of the windows.

The windows that remained looked out from the

twelve units onto the parking lot, where a small rectangular pool sat inside a crumbling brick wall. The entire thing was surrounded by light-duty chain-link fencing that was bent in several places. On the back left side, the fencing had been pulled back at the bottom, leaving a space big enough for a person to crawl through. We know it was big enough, because we crawled through it. After all, the NO TRESPASSING sign no longer read as such. It now featured a crude, spray-painted drawing of what was either a male member or a member of the squash family. Butternut, perhaps?

We meandered across the lot to the cockeyed gate leading into the pool area. The swimming pool was cracked and empty, save for a puddle of green muck surrounding the clogged drain at the bottom. *Ew! Something's wiggling in the sludge!* In fact, a lot of somethings were wiggling and wriggling about. *I hope it's tadpoles!*

The broken neon sign out front was in the shape of an acoustic guitar and identified the place as the Music City Motor Court. When the last visitors had checked out of the hotel was anyone's guess, but from the abandoned look of the place it appeared no one had stayed here in years.

Buck took a long look around the place. While I'd expected him to say no, instead he said, "Huh."

I'd had the same thought. *Huh.* "It's not at all what we were looking for."

"No, it's not," he acknowledged.

"But this is a prime location."

"Yes, it is."

The hotel was within easy walking distance of the pedestrian bridge that led to downtown Nashville and the restaurants, shops, and honky-tonks. The Country

Music Hall of Fame, the Ryman Auditorium, and the Nashville Predators' hockey rink were right there, too. The Gulch neighborhood on the other side of downtown had been the most recent area to pop, but with that territory nearly fully developed now, it was inevitable that things would start to move this way, right? If we were one of the first to build here, we could make a fortune.

I shared my prediction with Buck. "This seedy motel could be a gold mine."

His head bobbed slowly, indicating he was interested but retained a healthy skepticism. "A little motel like this wouldn't bring in much money, though. It would make more sense to tear it down and build something taller. 'Course, we're not in a position to take on a major project like that."

I stared at the rundown property, trying to look past the rusty rooftop HVAC units, the faded curtains hanging askew behind the windows, and the cracked asphalt parking lot to its possibilities and potential. "What if we redesigned the place so that it wasn't a motel anymore?"

"What are you proposing? Something like the Loveless Cafe?"

The famous local restaurant, known for its delicious biscuits, was surrounded by a motel-turned-retail marketplace. But given the demise of so many brick-and-mortar stores, shopping wasn't what I had in mind here. I shared my vision with my cousin. "What if we reconfigured each unit into a studio apartment? Better yet, we could turn each pair of adjoining rooms into one-bedroom apartments or condominiums. One of the rooms would remain a large bedroom with a bath, and we'd turned the other into a combination kitchen and living space."

His index finger bounced as he counted the doors. "Six units in all, you mean."

"Exactly. The motel office could be remodeled into a laundry room and fitness center. All we'd have to do is add a few washers and dryers, along with a treadmill, an exercise bike, and a universal weight machine. Or we could put in some furniture and make it a clubhouse in case the residents wanted to entertain. We could clean and resurface the pool, add some potted plants and a picnic table, maybe a grill and a pergola. It would make a nice outdoor space with a great view of the river and downtown. People would pay a premium for the view and location."

His head bobbed again, though faster and more enthusiastically as he seemed to visualize my concept. "Rich folks who work downtown would fall over each other to buy 'em, I'd bet. But that'll entail a whole lot of refurbishing. We made some nice bank on the Walsh house, but it's not enough profit to cover six bathroom renovations and six brand-new kitchens."

"True." And with both of us obligated to pay the mortgage on the house I lived in, we wouldn't qualify for a loan large enough to pay for all the work. My parents would loan us the funds if we asked, but I refused to take money from them as a matter of principle. I wanted to succeed on my own. Borrowing from the Hartleys had been different. Though they sometimes felt like a second set of parents to me, they were technically my bosses and business associates. Still, I didn't want to borrow from them again, either. It would be taking advantage. Luckily, a clever idea came to me. "We could start by fixing up one unit for show, and finish the outdoor space. Then we could presale the other units, let the buyers pick their flooring, fixtures, cabinets, and countertops. Interior paint, too. We'd require a down payment of forty or fifty grand, enough to cover the costs of renovating the unit."

"What do you know?" Buck said. "You did learn a thing or two in business school."

My mind had taken off like an Olympian out of the starting block, and was running a mile a minute with ideas for the motel. But I was getting ahead of myself, wasn't I? There was a good chance we wouldn't be the highest bidder at the tax sale. Maybe one of the nearby businesses would want the property for expansion, or maybe the property had already been spotted by another real-estate investor with deeper pockets than me and Buck. Even so, I wasn't ready to give up all hope. The small size of the property limited what could be built there. Maybe we'd get lucky.

"It has promise," Buck said, "but I'm still not sold. A multi-family property would come with a lot more headaches than a single-family home. I need some kind of sign that this is the right place."

We wandered to the closest window to get a look inside. When we still couldn't see much inside the unlit space, Buck pulled a bandana from his pocket and ran it in circles over the glass, removing the caked-on dust. We stepped up side by side, shielding our eyes with our hands as we peered through the glass. A dresser missing most of its drawer pulls was pushed up against the left wall. A king-size bed with a thin floral spread and a concave mattress sat cockeyed atop a box spring. A small metal device with a coin slot stood on the bedside table.

"What do you know." Buck tapped his index finger on the glass. "There's my sign right there."

"What is?"

"The vibrating bed."

"How is that a sign?" I asked.

"It means good vibes."

I shrugged. "That's good enough for me."

# CHAPTER 35

# KITTEN SMITTEN

### SAWDUST

He watched from the top perch of his cat tree as Whitney climbed out of Emmalee's car. Emmalee got out too, then reached for something in the backseat. *Is that a pet carrier? Is there something inside?*

He was certainly curious now. He hopped down to the lower perches and then to the floor, waltzing over to wait at the door. A moment later, he heard the jingle-jangle of keys, and the sound of the lock releasing.

"Hi, boy!" Whitney strode inside, picked him up, and cuddled him to her chest, resting her chin on his head.

While he normally lived for her affection, right now what he wanted most was to find out what was in that carrier Emmalee had just set on the floor. He planted a flat paw on Whitney's chest and pushed back, giving her the stiff-arm treatment.

"Okay, Sawdust. I can take a hint." Whitney set him down on the floor.

Twitching his whiskers and tail, he took a couple of tentative steps toward the carrier, which faced the other direction. He stopped and lifted his nose higher, flaring his nostrils. *Is that another cat I scent?*

As he circled around to the side, which had vents cut into the top half, he saw the tip of a tiny ear sticking up. His cat's heart rate was normally 180 beats per minute, but now it seemed to be ten times that, *boom-boom-booming* in his furry chest. Had Emmalee brought another cat home? Into *his* territory? *How could Whitney have let this happen?*

He circled around to the front of the carrier and got his first full look at the itty-bitty kitten cowering in the back corner. He could tell from her scent that she was female. He could tell from her big eyes that she was scared. And he could tell from that warm, fuzzy feeling spreading through him that he'd just met his new best friend.

Read on for an excerpt from


# MURDER WITH A VIEW—


the next engaging title in Diane Kelly's
House Flipper series, available soon from
St. Martin's Paperbacks!

# CHAPTER I
# AUCTION ACTION

## WHITNEY WHITAKER

On a sunny day in mid-May, my cousin Buck and I walked into the Davidson County Courthouse with a spring in our steps, big ideas in our heads, and a certified check for ninety-five grand in my purse. We'd earned a nice profit on the recent sale of a Colonial we'd purchased and remodeled, and planned to plunk that profit down on another property and see if we could double or maybe even triple it. Flipping houses was a risky venture, real estate roulette. But we had nothing to lose unless you counted our money, our solid credit ratings, and our confidence in ourselves.

The property we'd set our sights on was, ironically, not much to look at. The abandoned one-story motel dated back to the 1960s, when men with mutton-chop sideburns and women with bouffant hairdos pulled into the place in their Chevy Chevelles, Plymouth Barracudas, or Ford Fairlanes. Currently, the place sported sea-foam green stucco and scratched pink doors, along with plastic tarps and plywood. Years had passed since anyone had paid taxes on the place, slept in its beds, or swum in its now-cracked pool. But with my mental crystal ball, I could envision the twelve motel rooms turned into six one-bedroom condominiums with contemporary conveniences and a charming retro façade that incorporated the guitar-shaped neon sign in the parking lot. With the property's prime location just across the Cumberland River from downtown Nashville, we could earn a huge gain—assuming we were the highest bidders at today's tax auction.

We checked in with the female clerk at a table outside the room where the auction would be held.

"Name?" she asked, looking up at me and my cousin.

"Whitney and Buck Whitaker."

She wrote our names down on a sheet of paper and held out a numbered paddle. "Here you go."

I eyed the paddle. Number 13. Call me superstitious, but I got a bad vibe. "Any chance we could get a paddle with a different number?"

The woman eyed the line forming behind us and sent me a sour look. "No. Sorry."

Buck pushed me forward into the courtroom and muttered, "You get what you get and you don't throw a fit."

"I wasn't throwing a fit," I said. "I just don't want to be jinxed."

But jinxed we appeared to be. There, in the front row, sat Thaddeus Gentry III. Even from behind, I recognized his stocky physique and thick, wolf-like salt-and-pepper hair. Thad Gentry owned Gentry Real Estate Development, Inc., also known as GREED Incorporated. Gentry was a ruthless real estate developer who swooped down on older, unsuspecting neighborhoods and rebuilt them, running off long-term residents in the process. Rather than rehabbing rundown areas in modest and affordable ways that would allow residents to remain, he strategically purchased plots, razing old homes and building new, bigger, upscale houses in their stead. Older homes would end up sandwiched between his expensive new structures, which caused lot values to soar. The neighbors would find themselves unable to pay the increased property taxes on homes they'd lived in for decades. Gentry would buy them out when they were forced to put the homes they could no longer afford on the market.

Not long ago, Gentry and I had butted heads when he'd purchased the house next door to the one in which I now lived. He'd attempted to have the adjacent property rezoned from residential to commercial, which would have caused the value of my house to plummet. He'd been suspected of bribing a member of the zoning commission, but had settled the matter to prevent the truth from coming to light. I'd somehow managed to beat him then, but could I beat him now? It was doubtful. Our funds were limited. Gentry's, on the other hand, were limitless.

I elbowed Buck in the ribs to get his attention and jerked my head to indicate Gentry. Rubbing his side, Buck followed my gaze and frowned. He knew why Gentry was here. For the same reason we were. To put in a bid on the Music City Motor Court. Although the land on which the motel sat was a mere half acre in size, its prime location made it a potential gold mine.

Buck and I slipped into the back row and put our heads together.

"We can't let Thad Gentry steal this chance from us!" I whispered.

"How can we stop him?" Buck asked.

I bit my lip and raised my palms.

Buck's eyes narrowed as he thought. "You think the Hartleys would make you another loan?"

Marv and Wanda Hartley owned Home & Hearth Realty, the real estate company where I worked part-time as a property manager. They'd generously loaned me the funds to buy the Colonial that Buck and I had flipped. They'd give me another loan if I asked, but I'd really hoped the arrangement would be a one-time thing, that Buck and I would be able to buy another property on our own this time, without help. My parents would gladly loan me some money, too, as would Buck's. But with me having reached the big 3-0 and Buck being on the backside of thirty, we were getting a little too old to run to mom and dad for help. We earned decent livings and could support ourselves, even save a little, but maybe we were trying to bite off more than we could chew here.

Before I could respond, the courtroom doors opened and in walked Presley Pearson on a pair of four-inch heels. Designer, no doubt, though I'd be hard-pressed to identify any footwear brand not sold at Tractor Supply, where I purchased the steel-toed work boots I wore when making repairs at rental properties or helping out in the family carpentry business. Presley was smart and chic, with a short angular haircut that framed her dark-skinned face. Presley could be the solution to our problem—if she didn't still hold a grudge against me. She and I had a checkered past. I'd bought my current home from her former boss, and she'd been rightfully upset that he hadn't offered the house to her first. But by the time I'd learned she was interested in the property, the deal was done. Her boss was later found dead in the front flowerbed, so she'd dodged a proverbial bullet. Buck and I were stuck with the now unmarketable house.

I stood and raised a hand to stop her. "Presley. Hi."

She turned my way and her face tightened. A reflexive reaction, I supposed. "Hello, Whitney," she said in a tepid tone.

"We'd like to talk to you."

Buck stood. "We would?"

"Trust me," I whispered to him. I held out a hand to invite Presley to sit next to me and Buck on the bench. After she'd taken a seat, I asked, "Which property are you planning to bid on?"

She kept her cards close to her vest and turned the tables on me. "Why don't *you* tell *me* first?"

Unlike her, I exposed my hand. "The Music City Motor Court."

Her face sank as she realized she had competition for the property she'd hoped to purchase.

I angled my head to indicate the front row. "See Thad Gentry up there? I have a hunch he's here to bid on the motel, too."

She sighed. "There's no way I could beat his bid."

"Neither can we," I said. "Not alone anyway. But what if we pooled our resources?"

She stared at me for a long moment, evidently engaged in a mental debate with herself, before arching a brow. "How much were you going to bid?"

"Ninety-five thousand. You?"

"Sixty-eight," she said. "It's all my savings."

$163,000 would be chump change to Gentry, and we all knew it. I gave Presley a quick overview of our plans for the property, assuming we were lucky enough to land it.

"Condos?" she said. "That's a fantastic idea. They'd go fast and for a high price, too."

*She's in. Good.* I looked from Presley to Buck. "Are you two above pulling a fast one?"

Presley scoffed. "On Thad Gentry? Heck, no. He's a pompous you-know-what."

"So you've dealt with him, too?" It wasn't surprising that Presley and Gentry would have interacted at some point. After all, Gentry and Presley's former boss were two major players in the Nashville real estate scene.

"He came to the office once," Presley said, "but he didn't even glance in my direction. I've only spoken with him on the phone. He was always rude and pushy."

*Good.* The fact that she hadn't dealt with him in person meant he wouldn't recognize her. He wasn't likely to recognize Buck, either. As for myself, that was another matter. Thad Gentry and I had a run-in at our properties a while back, and there was no love lost between us. He'd recognize me and he certainly wouldn't trust me.

We put our heads together and came up with a plan. Even after a property had been auctioned off in a tax sale, the county would not issue the winning bidder a valid deed until the expiration of the applicable redemption period. During the redemption period, the delinquent owner could redeem the property by reimbursing the purchase price paid by the bidder, as well as the delinquent taxes, penalties, interest, and court costs. Purchasing a property that was likely to be redeemed was a waste of time and would tie up funds that could be better invested elsewhere. If we could convince Gentry the motel was at risk of being redeemed, maybe he'd decide not to take a chance on it.

Buck took our #13 paddle, and he and Presley headed to the second row, taking seats behind Gentry. I, on the other hand, slid down to the end of the back row, doing my best to make myself invisible.

As the room continued to fill with people interested in placing bids in the tax auction, Buck and Presley made what appeared to be idle conversation, but what was actually full of fibs about the property. Though I was too far away to actually hear their discussion, I knew it went something like this:

Buck: *"No point in bidding on the Music City Motor Court. I met the owners when I was checking out the property yesterday. They're pulling funds together to redeem it."*

Presley: *"Are you sure?"*

Buck: *"Yep. Their new investors were with them. Couple of wealthy guys from Chicago. Flew down on their own private jet. Anyone who bids on that property is a chump. I've set my sights on that parcel off Lebanon Pike. There's an old farmhouse and barn on it now, but apartments are sprouting up all around that area. It's just a matter of time until a developer comes a-calling."*

Gentry turned his head slightly, clearly listening in on Buck and Presley's conversation. But if he overheard something they said and took it to heart, that was his problem, not ours. He shouldn't be eavesdropping on a private discussion.

A few minutes later, the room was full and the auction began. Several smaller houses sold before the auctioneer announced that the next property up for bid would be the one along Lebanon Pike. Several bidders raised their paddles, including both Gentry and Buck, who was toying with the tycoon. Others dropped out as the price went up. The auctioneer continued to raise the price by five-thousand-dollar increments until Buck bailed out at $80,000.

Gentry raised his paddle one last time and the auctioneer brought his gavel down. "Sold for $85,000 to bidder number eight."

Gentry cut a smug look back at Buck, who shook his head in pretend disappointment. I fought the urge to laugh out loud. Gentry was a smart man, but he was also a fiercely competitive one and didn't like to lose. He shouldn't have been so hasty. He'd just bought a worthless piece of land in the Mill Creek flood plain. Before it could be developed, expensive grading and flood-control improvements would have to be made. *Sucker!*

His business concluded, Gentry stood and left the room to finalize the paperwork in the clerk's office down the hall.

The auctioneer announced the legal description of the next parcel of land and said, "Otherwise known as the Music City Motor Court." When he started the bidding, a dozen paddles shot into the air. *Darn!* Looked like we weren't the only ones who realized the property's potential.

Buck raised his paddle over and over as the price went from $100,000 to $110,00 to $120,000. About half of the bidders dropped out at that price, but several remained. The bid went up to $130,000, $140,000, and $150,000. By then, only Buck and one other man were still in the game. My intestines tied themselves in knots. We wanted this property, *bad*, and it looked like we might lose it!

The auctioneer raised by only $5,000 this time around. "Do I hear $155,000?"

We had only $8,000 more to go before we'd have to drop out. *Argh!* I crossed my fingers. For good measure, I crossed my toes, too. Not easy to do in steel-toed boots.

Buck hesitated a moment before raising his paddle, a strategy to make the other bidder think twice about further raising his bid.

Seeing the hesitation of the remaining bidders, the auctioneer increased by a smaller amount. "Do I hear $158,000?"

Both Buck and the other bidder waited a moment, before Buck slowly raised his paddle. The other man did likewise. I fought the urge to scream. I'd already visualized exactly what we could do to the property, had jotted down notes and doodled sketches. This man was screwing around with my plans, and I didn't like it one bit!

"Do I hear $160,000?" The auctioneer's head swiveled as he looked from Buck to the other bidder.

The other bidder raised his paddle and sent a scathing look in Buck's direction. Buck raised his paddle as well.

"Can I get $162,500?" the auctioneer called, his eyes wide with anticipation.

The other man exhaled sharply, frowned in defeat, and shook his head. He'd reached his limit. Buck raised both his paddle and a victorious fist as the auctioneer brought his gavel down. "Sold to bidder number thirteen!"

Maybe 13 wasn't such an unlucky number after all. We even had $500 left over.

Buck and Presley stood and made their way down the aisle, both of them beaming.

I met them at the door. "We did it!" I only hoped we could all work well together. Buck and I had developed a system. Adding another person to the mix could complicate things. But we'd cross that bridge if and when we came to it.

We headed down the hall to the clerk's office and stepped up to the counter beside Thad Gentry. He did a double take when he recognized me. I gave him my best smile.

The matronly clerk took the approved bid from Buck and said, "You bought the Music City Motor Court? I stayed there once back in the day. Got sunburned out by the pool. Had a fun time, though."

Gentry's head had snapped in our direction when he overheard the woman mention the motel. His eyes narrowed as he looked from me to Buck and back again, seeming to notice the family resemblance.

I looked at him and shrugged. "Didn't your mama tell you not to trust in rumors?"

The man skewered me with his gaze and chuckled mirthlessly. "Well played, Miss Whitaker."

*Well played, indeed.* Thad Gentry might not like me, but at least now he respected me.

# CHAPTER 2
# SITE VISIT

## WHITNEY

Buck, Presley, and I decided to celebrate over an early lunch. We toasted our good fortune with sparkling wine, and worked out the particulars of our arrangement over our meal.

Fortunately, Presley agreed to leave the details of the renovation up to me and my cousin. "I don't like to get my hands dirty. I'll come by to check on my things now and then, but for the most part I'll be a silent partner." Recognizing that, in addition to our monetary investment, Buck and I would invest sweat equity by performing much of the construction work ourselves, she agreed to accept 30% of the net profit as full payment for her share in the venture, with payment due upon sale of the last condominium unit. We jotted the details on a napkin, signed our names to it, and sealed the deal with a handshake. Attorneys around the state would cringe at our lackadaisical approach but, if Presley was going to trust me and Buck to do a good job on the remodel, I'd trust her to keep up her end of the bargain, too.

After lunch, Presley headed off to her job, while Buck and I swung by the motel to prioritize our "to do" list. The property sat on North 1st Street, not far from the football stadium where the Tennessee Titans played. The dilapidated inn was also within walking distance of the pedestrian bridge that spanned the Cumberland River. The bridge connected the east side of the river to downtown Nashville and the South Broadway tourist area. "SoBro," as locals called it, encompassed a variety of restaurants, shops, and honky-tonks, as well as the Predators' hockey rink, the Country Music Hall of Fame, and the Ryman Auditorium where the Grand Ole Opry had been launched decades ago. The location would appeal to well-heeled singles or couples who enjoyed the downtown scene.

We parked on the street beside the L-shaped motel and stood side by side on the sidewalk, looking through the flimsy wire fencing that had been erected to keep people off the property. The asphalt parking lot was cracked, the rooftop HVAC units were rusty, and many of the windows had been patched with plywood or plastic tarps. The seedy motel was a far cry from the Ritz-Carlton, but with some hard work we'd transform this derelict lodge into a place anyone would be proud to call home.

"First thing we do," Buck said, "is get that sign fixed." He pointed to the guitar-shaped neon sign. "We light that up and people will be curious about what's going on over here, start talking about it."

"Can't hurt to generate some buzz," I agreed. "Maybe we should string up a banner, too, one that says 'Coming Soon - Music City Motor Court Condominiums.'"

"Good idea."

We circled around the parking lot and Buck reached down to lift up a loose edge of the flimsy wire fencing.

We bent down and ducked under the flap to access the property.

As he let the fencing fall back into place, he said, "We'll have to find a better way to secure this place. That lightweight chain link isn't gonna cut it."

The bent fencing, the graffiti on the building, and the broken windows evidenced vandals having come onto the property. We'd have to do something to keep trespassers out. We couldn't afford to have our building materials stolen or someone getting hurt on the premises and filing a lawsuit.

I made a suggestion. "What if we install decorative iron fencing around the place? It'll be useful now, and prospective buyers will like the added security, too." Not that we were going for snob appeal, but the gate would add an air of exclusivity.

Buck cocked his head. "You got a guy who will install a fence at a reasonable rate?"

"Of course I got a guy," I said. "I always got a guy." Working as a property manager, I knew more than my share of people in the construction and repair trades. Plumbers. Electricians. Flooring installers. Fencing specialists. Painters and landscapers, too. My contacts came in handy in our house-flipping business. Many of the contractors would cut me a good deal in return for sending business their way.

As we proceeded along the walkway in front of the rooms, Buck stopped in front of the door to Room 9, which sported plywood over its window. Buck pointed to the door. The metal was bent around the lock. "Someone took a crowbar to this door." He reached out a hand and pushed the door open.

Sunlight streamed into the room, dirt specks sparkling within the bright beam like magical fairy dust. We peeked into the space to see a red Kawasaki motorcycle with studded faux-leather saddlebags parked on the far side of the bed, a book lying open and facedown on the nearest nightstand, and a sizeable lump under the worn covers of the king-sized bed. An instant later, the lump sat up, becoming a fortyish man with shaggy brown hair, a burly beard, and a smile as bright as the sunlight. "Good morning, folks!"